"[Robards] brings all of her expertise with sensual romances to the pages of this deliciously romantic romp that shows her extraordinary talent for combining passion, engaging characters, and an intriguing plot."

—*Rendezvous*

"The story line is fast-paced, but it is the characters who make it so much fun to read. . . . A cleverly designed tale that will please historical-romance fans."

—*Midwest Book Review*

"Truly an entertaining, enjoyable read."

—*Old Book Barn Gazette*

If you love page-turning historical fiction from bestselling author Karen Robards, you'll love her spellbinding novels of contemporary romantic suspense!

## *TO TRUST A STRANGER*

"Robards is turning into a top-notch romantic-suspense writer. . . . Readers should be advised to start reading when they have a large block of time available because no one will want to stop reading Robards' steamy novel until the last page is turned."

—*Booklist*

"[A] tough, sensual romantic mystery from the prolific and popular Robards."

—*Kirkus Reviews*

## PARADISE COUNTY

"Robards maintains the suspense with carefully plotted details that build to an exciting and emotional resolution."
—*Houston Chronicle*

"[A] racy read."

—*Cosmopolitan*

"Along with exceptional heroes and heroines, Robards has delivered wonderfully drawn secondary characters. This makes her tales of romantic suspense feel all the more satisfying."
—*Romantic Times*

"Suspenseful and atmospheric, another winner by [Robards]. . . . Readers will cheer and care for her protagonists."
—*Publishers Weekly*

"A high-caliber romantic-suspense novel featuring realistic characters struggling with a rainbow of feelings. . . . A strong tale that will excite readers."
—Harriet Klausner, BookReview.com

"Steamy. . . ."

—*Kirkus Reviews*

"You'll find this thriller hard to put down. Don't miss it!"
—*Old Book Barn Gazette*

# Irresistible

Karen Robards

**POCKET STAR BOOKS**
New York   London   Toronto   Sydney   Singapore

This book is a work of fiction. Names, characters, places and incidents are products of the author's imagination or are used fictitiously. Any resemblance to actual events or locales or persons, living or dead, is entirely coincidental.

An *Original* Publication of POCKET BOOKS

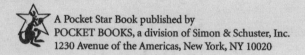

A Pocket Star Book published by
POCKET BOOKS, a division of Simon & Schuster, Inc.
1230 Avenue of the Americas, New York, NY 10020

ISBN: 0-7434-1060-2

First Pocket Books printing September 2002

10  9  8  7  6  5  4  3  2  1

POCKET STAR BOOKS and colophon are registered trademarks of Simon & Schuster, Inc.

For information regarding special discounts for bulk purchases, please contact Simon & Schuster Special Sales at 1-800-456-6798 or business@simonandschuster.com

Front cover illustration by Brian Bailey

Printed in the U.S.A.

This book is dedicated, as always, to my husband, Doug, and my three sons, Peter, Christopher, and Jack, with love. I also want to send special love to Peter, my technical support, who's off to his freshman year of college.

# Irresistible

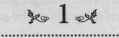

## 1

*January 1813*

If they caught her, she would die.

"Damn ye, where are ye?"

The disembodied voice sounded eerily close. That it reached her ears at all over the roaring of the surf terrified her. They were near. The knowledge goaded her to greater speed despite the treacherous nature of the path underfoot. She had to keep moving. . . .

" 'Twill be the worse for ye, ye little besom, once I get me hands on ye again."

The voice came from almost directly overhead. Daring a quick glance upward, Claire saw that the chilly white saucer of a moon had risen just high enough in the sky to be visible over the lip of the cliff. By its wintry light, she could barely make out the speaker's dark shape through the thick gray fog that had rolled in from the sea sometime in the long hours after sunset. Her heart pounding, she shivered and fought to keep her breathing from degenerating into terrified, and possibly audible, panting. Dangerous as the trail she crept along was, it was her only possible escape route. The spit of land her pursuers searched was narrow, and it ended in a straight drop of more than ninety feet to the tumultuous Atlantic just a few hundred yards past where she clung to the cliff. Had she still been on that marshy outcropping and been forced by its geography to turn back, she would have run straight into the arms of those who meant to kill her.

"Ye'll rue the day you tried to make a fool of me, missy, I promise ye that."

He knew, or at least suspected, that she was near, Claire realized with a clutch of horror. Otherwise, such threats would be meaningless. Forcing herself to forgo the dubious comfort of another glance up for fear that he might see the pale flash of her face against the blackness of the rock, she fought to keep panic at bay as she crept onward. Without warning, her foot slipped. Barely suppressing a cry, she grabbed at the wall for support. Her outflung hand scrabbled desperately over the rock and closed around a jagged jut of stone that saved her. For a moment after she regained her balance she stood perfectly still, her heaving chest pressed tightly against the unforgiving granite, heart pounding, eyes closed, as she willed her breathing to return to something approximating normal.

If she fell, she thought seconds later with a flash of bleak humor, glancing down at the whitecaps pounding the rocky beach as she negotiated the tricky spot, at least she wouldn't have to worry about being killed by her pursuers. She would have done the job quite thoroughly herself.

The thought of falling, of her body hurtling helplessly down to be broken on the sharp rocks below, was almost enough to cause her to freeze in place. But then she had a hideous mental vision of the fate her pursuers intended for her. Tied to a filthy bedstead in a room off the kitchen of the farmhouse where her captors had taken her, she had overheard their plans: In the small hours of the morning, when all honest folk were asleep and all of the other sort knew to look the other way, they meant to take her out to sea and drop her, bound hand and foot, into the frigid depths. Drown 'er like a mewling kitten, was how their leader had put it, his voice spine-chilling in its careless joviality. Claire shivered again, violently, as the callous words replayed in her head.

This band of brutal strangers meant to kill her. But why? *Why?* She had racked her brain but found no answer that made sense. Ever since she had tricked the man above her into releasing her from her bonds by claiming she had to make urgent use of the chamber pot, then clouted him over the head with said chamber pot when he grudgingly handed it to her and turned his back, she had quit asking herself why. She'd been too busy running for her life. She could figure out the why behind this nightmare later. If she survived.

"Eh, Briggs, what're you doing? Ye're afrighting the poor lassie."

This second voice sounded as close as the first. Claire recognized it as belonging to the group's leader. This time, despite the best will in the world not to do so, she was unable to prevent a terrified glance up. There were two dark forms standing close together near the very edge of the cliff, which was now some forty feet above her head. From their stance, they were, presumably, looking toward where the others still searched for her along the spit. Another quick, reflexive glance down revealed little save the frothing breakers and the inky infinity of the night beyond the fog. But she knew that another fifty feet or so of treacherous cliff still stretched between her and the relative safety of the beach.

Did they know of this path? Did they know that she had taken it and was directly below them even as they spoke? Were they toying with her, like cruel cats with a terrified mouse? This possibility, which had just popped into her mind, terrified her.

Please God, she prayed with a quick glance up into the ether, she did not want to die. Not tonight, not like this. She was only twenty-one years old.

To her horror, she felt her knees begin to shake.

This would never do. Take a damper, Claire, she ordered herself sternly. She was *not* going to die. She had already lived through so much: the far too early death of her mother; a childhood made dark and frightening by the cruelty of her father; a promising marriage turned bleak and empty; and the crime that had given her over to her pursuers. She had survived too much to die now.

Fiercely telling herself that, Claire stiffened her knees and inched onward. Pebbles underfoot made her slide precariously a second time, and again she nearly cried out. But she managed to choke back the sound even as she recovered her footing, and then, gritting her teeth, she forced herself to go on. With luck, they would believe her hidden somewhere in the prickly gorse above. With luck, they would never even think of looking down.

Once she reached the beach, she reminded herself in between sliding footsteps and deep, calming breaths, the safety of Hayleigh Castle, her husband's family seat, was less than an hour's walk away. Although she had hated the vast turreted pile from her first sight of it, her heart yearned for it now. How ironic was it that her husband was there, all unknowing of the danger that threatened her, while she fought for her life practically in the castle's shadow? Strain though she might, she could see nothing of it through the fog-shrouded darkness. But she knew it was there, perched like a great stone falcon on the rocky promontory overlooking the sea that was this one's twin. The high granite cliff on which the castle was built and the one she was presently descending, known as Hayleigh's Point, served as end posts to a half-circle of cliffs surrounding a bay that looked as if a hungry giant had taken a bite out of the coastline. From the castle to this spot was a distance of perhaps six miles. To the east was desolate marshland dotted with beacon fires ready to be lit at a moment's notice should Boney, now fortunately occupied in Russia, at last decide to invade. To the west the land fell away in a sheer vertiginous drop straight down to the turbulent waters of the Atlantic. The only way up, or down, was via perhaps half a dozen narrow paths winding precariously through the rocks. The locals called them smugglers' paths because, once the province of goats, they were now used almost exclusively by the "gentlemen," as the smugglers were known in these parts, who over the course of the war had turned the running of the French blockade into a fine art.

Tonight this particular path had saved her life, so whatever quarrel anyone else might have with those who traded clandestinely with the hated French, she herself was grateful to them.

"Come, milady, stop your foolishness now and ye'll see we'll not harm ye." The leader's accent was pure Sussex. His voice turned wheedling as he raised it to be heard over the pounding of the surf. Clearly he too knew—suspected—that she was near. "We'll carry ye back home, all right and tight, just like we intended all along, see if we don't. 'Twas merely the matter of a small ransom, which has since been paid."

Milady . . . a ransom . . . paid? Did they know, then, that she was Lady Claire Lynes, wife of the heir of the Duke of Richmond, one of the richest peers in the realm? But David, her feckless husband, had little money of his own, and could get his hands on no very substantial sum until he inherited, if indeed he ever did. As the present Duke, who had lived abroad for many years, was both unwed and childless, David cherished some hopes in that direction. But still, hopes would not pay a ransom. In any case, her abduction was only hours old. There had been precious little time. . . .

But no. It was a lie, a trick meant to cozen her into revealing herself. She was not such a fool as to fall for that, no matter how much she might wish to believe that it was true. She had heard their plan with her own ears, and there was no reason to suppose that it had changed with her escape.

You'll not catch me that easily, Claire vowed silently to the men above her. Continuing to move, she willed herself to think no more about the plot against her until she was once again on solid ground. Situated as she was, a single misstep could prove fatal. Instead, she concentrated on the rhythmic slap of the waves against the rocks below in an effort to calm herself. Sweaty palms, shaky knees, and a racing pulse were a recipe for disaster, she knew. Wetting her lips, she was surprised to taste salt in her mouth. Only then did she realize that the great plumes of freezing spray from the sea that had intermittently blown up to splatter the cliff had left her wet through. She was beyond cold; her hands were as icy and lacking in feeling as those of a corpse. Though her high-necked, long-sleeved traveling dress was made of wool, it was a fine kerseymere variety that provided little warmth, and certainly it had not been designed to withstand exposure to the elements. And her boots, her cunning little half-boots that were so fashionable this season, had equally not been designed for a death-defying climb down a near-vertical cliff. Their smooth leather soles slipped and slid like skates over the slippery ground. She did not have even a cloak to ward off the elements. Like everything else she had brought with her on the journey from her sister's home in Yorkshire to Hayleigh Castle, it had been left behind in her carriage when she'd been dragged out.

"If ye put me to the trouble of fetching the dogs to sniff ye out, milady, it'll be the worse for ye." The leader's coaxing tone had deteriorated into pure threat. Claire dared another scared glance up and saw that the men had not moved. But they held a lantern now; its warm yellow glow swayed gently in the leader's hand as, back turned to her and the sea, he held it aloft to illuminate the night.

The light, she realized, her breath catching on what was almost a sob, was bright enough to allow her to see a bleeding scratch on her hand where it clung to an outcropping of rock. If the men turned and looked over the edge of the cliff, it was also bright enough to give her away.

She was more than halfway down now, she reckoned, as, unnerved by the light, she stopped, holding tight to the rocks with both hands. Closing her eyes and pressing her forehead against the spray-slick granite, she sent another prayer winging skyward and took another calming breath. If she could just reach the beach, she would run as if her heels had sprouted wings. Somewhere at its far end lay another path that led to the castle and safety. But first she had to reach the beach, and to reach the beach she had to move.

Gritting her teeth, she did.

"Very well, milady, ye've brought it on yourself." The leader's raised voice was harsh with frustration. Claire listened with a sick feeling in the pit of her stomach as he called out, presumably to the rest of the band who still searched the spit: "There'll be bloody hell to pay if she's not found, ye understand? Bloody hell. Briggs, go fetch Marley's hounds."

"Aye."

A glance up confirmed that only one dark shape was now visible above her. Briggs had vanished into the night, presumably gone to fetch dogs to hunt her down as if she were vermin. Claire's heart leaped and her breathing quickened as panic threatened once again to overtake her.

Why would anyone want to do this to her? Try though she might—and despite her determination to do so, she hadn't been able to dismiss the question from her mind—she couldn't make sense of it. Was it some unlucky happenstance of time and place, as she had first supposed, or, as was seeming increasingly possible, was it a carefully executed plan directed specifically at her? She had spent Christmas in Yorkshire, in the bosom of her own family, choosing to go to Morningtide, her sister Gabby's home, over a celebration with her husband and his mother. Her excuse had been an urgent desire to be with Gabby, who was all but bedridden by a most difficult first pregnancy. With both her parents dead—her abusive, unloving father, the Earl of Wickham, three years before, and his third wife, her beautiful but modestly born mother, when Claire was a mere infant—her two sisters, and now Gabby's husband as well, were her family, as well as being the people she loved most in the world. The holiday had been the merriest she had known since wedding David, and she had enjoyed every minute of it. Then, a week after Boxing Day, she had reluctantly bowed to David's wish that she join him and a party of guests at the enormous, drafty anachronism that was Hayleigh Castle, her husband's family seat since the days of William the Conqueror, and set out. That had been two days ago.

Shortly before dark her traveling carriage had neared its destination. She had been aware of a not-unfamiliar lowering of her spirits as the reunion with her husband drew ever closer. The day was gray, cheerless, threatening rain, its bleakness a perfect match for how she was feeling. Then, in a dense wood not many miles from the castle, her carriage had been attacked. Without warning a band of masked riders had appeared out of nowhere, surrounding them, forcing the vehicle to halt. The coachman, fumbling for his blunderbuss, had been shot from his seat forthwith. The horror of that had scarcely sunk in when the carriage door was wrenched open and two burly men peered in. With the best will in the world to show courage, she had screamed as hysterically as her maid, Alice, a sweet country girl from Gabby's household recruited to take the place of her own beloved Twindle, whom she had left behind to care for Gabby. Shrinking back into the plushly upholstered corner of the seat, she had tried to fight off the rough hands that reached for her. Her efforts availed her nothing. In an instant she was dragged from the carriage. She fuzzily recalled Alice being pulled out behind her; the maid's screams had abruptly stopped just seconds before a foul-smelling rag had been pressed over Claire's nose and mouth. After that, she remembered no more until she had awakened upon that bed in the room behind the farmhouse kitchen, quite alone.

" 'Tis your last chance to behave like a sensible lassie, milady," the leader called, bringing her back to the present with a jolt. Glancing up, Claire realized that she could no longer see him. He must have moved away from the edge of the cliff. Only his voice and the lantern's glow that limned the cliff edge in gold told her that he was still near. Obviously he did not know of the path's existence, or had forgotten it if he did. It was her good fortune that the crime had occurred in country she knew. She had spent the first months of her marriage at Hayleigh Castle, and David himself, in one of his even then increasingly rare charming moods, had shown her this path down to the windblown gray shale crescent of a beach.

The sea was roaring in her ears now as, inch by perilous inch, she crept closer to it. Through the fog she could see the curvy white lines of foam where the waves broke against the shore. Beyond that, the black vastness of the ocean blended with the black vastness of the sky so well that one was all but indistinguishable from the other.

She had only twenty or so feet to go, she calculated with a fresh surge of hope. Once on the beach, she would run as if all the hounds of hell were after her—which, by then, they might well be.

A tiny pinprick of light, warm and yellow amid all the cold blackness, shone briefly on the surface of the sea. Her eyes widened and her step faltered. The light was there, and then gone even as she strained to see. So fast did it appear and disappear that she was not quite sure her eyes were not playing tricks on her—until it flashed again.

Still staring in some perplexity out to sea, she at last arrived at the uppermost reaches of the beach, stumbling a little as she made the transition from slippery path to uneven ground. Frowning, she continued to probe the blackness for another glimpse of light. Then she gathered her sodden skirts in one hand to clear her feet and started to scramble over the rocks toward the beach proper. Had she imagined it? No, there it was again. There was no mistake.

Were her pursuers coming after her by boat now? she wondered, panicking anew. But no. A glance up confirmed that they were still above her, presumably searching the cliff. The yellowish glow of the lantern light through the fog was unmistakable.

But she had seen something. Perhaps it was no more than a fairy light, she thought, shivering as she clambered over another rock and at last reached the relative flatness of the beach itself. The moors thereabouts were legendary for elusive beacons sighted briefly in the dead of night, and fairy lights were the name the local folk gave them. Or perhaps it was a fisherman, late getting in. Or, more likely, smugglers . . .

A muffled crunch on the shale behind her was her only warning. At the sound, Claire's heart lurched. She whirled, but it was too late: A man loomed behind her, a tall dark shadow just separating from the legion of shadows that were rocks and cliff and sea, close enough to touch. She was caught! She would be killed. . . .

She never had time to let loose the scream that tore into her throat before something slammed hard into the back of her head and she crumpled without a sound into blackness.

## 2

*"*hat were simple enough." James Harris's voice was hushed but cheerful as he lowered his pistol.

Hugh Battancourt, who instinctively caught the collapsing female around the waist to keep her from measuring her length on the shiny-wet shale, cast his henchman a sardonic look, which of course, thanks to the fog-shrouded darkness, James didn't see.

"Simple indeed."

"We'd best be loping off, then, before them that are with her come nosin' around. Seein' as how we're not exactly the party they're expecting."

Hugh, having come to that conclusion on his own, already had the woman hoisted over his shoulder and was heading back toward the sea. As James had said, this particular part of the job, which in theory had seemed rife with possibilities for error, had so far been problem-free. Under the circumstances, he preferred not to tempt the gods of disaster any further than he had to.

A successful mission, after all, was one carried out in secrecy, with the enemy not finding out they had been bested until it was far too late.

"Wait to give them the signal until we're well away from shore," he said over his shoulder as, with a great deal of relief, he lowered his limp burden into the long-boat that awaited.

"Aye, with any luck they'll be thinkin' the Frenchies have her safe." James chuckled, clearly relishing the notion of pulling off so neat a scam. "At least, until they meet up with the Frenchies."

For the past two days, Hugh had been suffering from a premonition that this, his latest mission, was destined to end badly. The premonition had arrived the week previous in the form of a toss from his horse, which embarrassing mischance had happened to him only a handful of times in his adult life, all just before some far more dire mischance had overtaken him. This particular spill had been spectacular, in full view of a courtyard full of snickering French lords and ladies, and had left him with, among other less tangible injuries, several badly bruised ribs. Despite the resultant stabbing pain in his midsection whenever he made an unwary move, and the corollary catastrophe he had learned such a fall invariably seemed to portend, he had nevertheless answered the call of duty when it had sounded upon his door.

That call had come in Paris, where, in his role as the mincing *cher ami* to the fabulously rich Louise, Marquise de Alençon, he had been observing with keen interest the return to Paris of Napoleon Bonaparte, along with the straggling remnants of the French Army. The little general, apoplectic at finding his troops defeated by the harsh Russian winter, had already turned his rapacious gaze once again to England as he plotted fresh and, as he undoubtedly hoped, redemptive atrocities. As yet Hugh had not been able to ascertain just what form those atrocities were to take, although he did not doubt that he soon would.

It was his job, after all, and he was good at it.

Then an urgent message had arrived via the usual channels: Through a disastrous breach in security at the War Office, his identity, along with the identities of several other British operatives working clandestinely in France, had been uncovered. The acquisition of such information would be a major coup for the beleaguered French and a disaster of equal proportion for the British. According to Hugh's source, the possessor of that information had not yet had a chance to reveal any details to the enemy other than the fact that he possessed it. The would-be informant was now in hiding in England, waiting to be plucked under cover of darkness from a certain Sussex beach and conveyed to France, where he would turn over the information to the interested parties for a fat fee. If the informant was not silenced in time, Hugh's usefulness as a British spy would be over; his life would be over too, should the French catch him before he could get out of their country. There were roughly a dozen like himself whose lives and jobs were imperiled by the leak.

His mission: to intercept the traitor at the point of rendezvous, recover the information, then interrogate and subsequently rid the world of his prisoner.

In the forty-eight hours since the matter had been laid before him, he had ridden *ventre à terre* from Paris to Dieppe, boarded a leaky three-masted schooner under the command of a loyal privateer, crossed the storm-tossed English Channel, and gotten to the rendezvous point in time.

Only to find himself in the heroic position of abetting in the brutal bludgeoning of a woman.

He should have turned down the job. The tumble from his horse should have warned him. Indeed, it had, but he had thick-headedly refused to heed that warning. He could blame no one but himself, then, for subsequent events. From the outset, one thing after another had gone wrong. First, of course, there were his damned ribs. They ached like a sore tooth when they weren't outright stabbing him, rendering him as ill tempered as Prinny when his corset pinched or, as a nice alternative when he rebelled against their rule, doubling him over with pain. Then there was the fact that it had rained from the moment he had left Paris. A cold, pouring rain, driven by high winds, that had turned the roads to quagmires and the fields to impassable swamps. On horseback as he'd been, there had been no respite from it. Raindrops had found their way beneath the turned-up collar of his greatcoat in a steady stream and wilted the once-curly brim of his beaver until it drooped soddenly around his ears. His disapproving companion, plain James Harris before they had gone to France and now (because of an excruciating French accent) known to all and sundry as his mute manservant Etienne, was another source of annoyance, and one moreover whose presence was almost as unwelcome as the rain. But, as James had opened the door to the bearer of the ill tidings and, by dint of sly listening at a closed portal, been privy to the lot, there had been no dissuading him from coming, short of murder, which Hugh, sneakily fond of the annoying fellow as he was, was loath to do. Finally, the privateer's crew had been alarmingly undisciplined, the sea had been rough, and—the coup de grâce—a message had been waiting for him on board identifying the traitor as a woman. To whit, one Sophy Towbridge, a

London high-flyer who had apparently purloined a packet of letters containing the information, which she hoped to sell, from her benefactor, Lord Archer, an elderly peer who still tottered around the War Office.

The revelation of his quarry's gender had knocked Hugh back on his heels. He was supposed to interrogate and kill a *woman*? Hildebrand hadn't told him that. But then, Hildebrand was a master at keeping certain select facts to himself when it suited him. He certainly knew that Hugh would have balked at doing violence to a woman, war or no war.

But, having acted in the teeth of the cosmos's repeated attempts to dissuade him, here he was, saddled with the mission. Now, in the interests of his country's security, to say nothing of his own, he had no choice. Hildebrand would have known that, too.

Damn Hildebrand. And Boney. And all the bloody Frogs. And the woman before him, unconscious and curled childlike into a ball in the bottom of the gig that was even now taking them back to the ship, where his job would be to relieve her of the incriminating letters she had stolen, discover what had prompted her to steal them and other details surrounding the crime, and then, when he knew enough to plug the leak at both ends, dispose of her like so much garbage.

Hugh hadn't realized that he was cursing aloud until James, seated tailor-style on the woman's other side as he shuttered the lantern he had just used to signal that all was well to the woman's erstwhile companions, met his gaze and nodded agreement.

"Aye, and damn this bloody weather, too. We're like to be frozen through before we get back to the ship—*if* we get back to the ship, that is."

This dark afterthought was in apparent reference to the swelling waves that pitched the longboat up and down. Spray showered them like rain; the bottom of the craft was awash.

"We'll not be lettin' ye drown, Colonel, don't fash yerself about that." The nearest of the men working the oars addressed this remark to Hugh, shouting to be heard over the roar of the sea.

The fact that the sailor knew his military rank did not really surprise him. In another ringing endorsement of War Office security, all aboard the *Nadine* seemed to know that he was a British intelligence officer on a *very important mission,* as had been made clear to him from the moment he had set foot on the ship. Fortunately, the French vessel that had been scheduled to make this pickup had, thanks no doubt to the good offices of Hildebrand, not yet put in an appearance at the rendezvous point, and the escort that had accompanied Miss Towbridge to her destiny was now well out of earshot, which made discretion a little less imperative than it otherwise would have been. Still, he had lived in the shadows for so long that the fact that the sailors, seasoned smugglers all, seemed to a man cheerily cognizant of every detail of his mission made the hair rise on the back of his neck.

"Blimey!" James said as the little boat slid down the back of a wave into a trough as deep as a canyon.

With the plunge, Hugh's thoughts were diverted to concerns of a more immediate nature. Glancing up, he saw the ship that was their destination rearing high above them like a spirited horse. Seconds later, the longboat shot up the back of another rolling wave. The sea was worsening, no doubt about that. He was glad that they would be back aboard the *Nadine* before the storm he feared was in the offing struck in earnest.

"Mmm."

With his hand on the woman's head, he felt rather than heard the soft sound she made. Glancing down, he watched her stir as more icy water sloshed over the side of the boat, soaking her anew. She was already lying in an inches-deep puddle. Hugh knew just how cold and deep it was, because he was sitting in it himself, cross-legged, one hand exploring her scalp to determine the extent of her injury, while with the other he held on to the side of the boat for dear life.

"Is she dead then?" James asked without noticeable regret, apparently having just then noticed Hugh's digital exploration of their prisoner's skull.

It was James who had clouted her over the head with his pistol when Hugh had walked up behind her on the beach.

"Not dead." If Hugh's tone was wry, James appeared not to notice.

The woman's hair beneath Hugh's fingers was wet, cold, and fine textured. It had fallen from its pins to straggle over her face like long tangles of silk thread, and in the darkness looked as black as the sea. She was both nicely shaped and easy to carry. He knew that too, almost strictly from touch, because after catching her as she collapsed he'd reflexively put his shoulder to her stomach and lifted her over it—only to have his ribs exact a teeth-gritting price by the time he reached the gig.

He'd had to steel himself to ignore the knifelike sensation in his midsection as he had bundled her into the rowboat that, as the extraction had been accomplished

so quickly, the sailors had still been in the process of se-
curing. If the distance had been much farther he was
very much afraid he would have been forced to let his
pride go hang and pass the wench off to James, who'd
been clucking like an old hen beside him for fear he'd do
himself an injury all the way. He would have hated like
the devil to pass the wench off to James.

The *traitorous* wench.

Hugh reminded himself of that deliberately,
dwelling on the word with grim determination in an
effort to steel himself for what he had to do. The slight
body curled with helpless vulnerability before him belonged to one who was a danger to them all, a danger to
England.

He would not even think of her as a traitorous
wench. Just a traitor, gender immaterial.

The thought performed the necessary function of
hardening his heart. Nevertheless, he could not help but
be aware that her skull felt unmistakably feminine beneath his hand, her skin was soft, and her hair had a dis-
concerting tendency to curl around his probing fingers.
Dammit to bloody hell, she felt like a woman.

Ignoring that as best he could, he continued the
search. His efforts were rewarded when he encountered
a warm stickiness just behind her left ear: blood.

"She's bleeding." His tone held no inflection. That it
cost him some degree of effort to keep the label "traitor"
rather than "woman" at the forefront of his mind was
something that only he needed to know. Having determined that the injury did not appear to be life-
threatening, he disentangled his hand from the clinging
tresses. A glancing blow to the head would be the least of
what would befall her now that she'd been apprehended,

he reminded himself grimly. If the notion made him secretly queasy, then it was time to remember that he was, first and foremost, a soldier in time of war. No one had ever promised him that the things he would be required to do for his country would be pleasant, or easy.

"Aye, well, I'm not surprised. I hit the beldame bloody hard."

James, who seemed to suffer none of his own qualms about the gender of their prisoner, was twisted around, looking over his shoulder at the *Nadine*, which was so close now that when they reached the crest of the wave her starboard side loomed above them like a giant black wall. Faces illuminated by the flickering glow of lanterns could be seen on her deck as half a dozen or so men massed at the rail, making ready to bring them up. The schooner's sails were down, leaving her bare masts to thrust through the darkness like skeletal fingers reaching toward the storm-heavy sky.

"Pull hard to port!" someone yelled. The men complied, and the longboat's stern swung around.

Braced against the pitching waves, one hand now pressed flat against the woman's back to keep her secure, Hugh watched as a rope ladder unfurled down the *Nadine*'s side. The first part of his task was complete: He had the traitor in his possession. In a few minutes they would be safe—from the sea at least—on deck. Then the second part of his task would begin.

Thinking about what that might entail, he set his jaw in a grim expression.

"Come about!" a sailor cried.

The sailors pulled hard at the oars once again, bringing the longboat alongside and parallel to the *Nadine*. And just in time, too. The storm was coming on fast.

The waves were taller now, closer together, frothing white at the tops with mounting anger. Even as Hugh registered that, another powerful swell caught the longboat up, carrying them high and away from their goal as it sprayed its freezing spittle over them.

He grasped a handful of frock—it was fine cloth, expensive—between the woman's shoulder blades to keep her safe as the longboat slid down from the peak and inconveniently away from the *Nadine*. She stirred a little, moaning. Again he felt rather than heard the small sound she made. There was a helpless quality to it, and to her as she lay curled now against his bent legs, that made him want to ram his fist through something— preferably Hildebrand's face.

He was many things, most of them thoroughly dissolute, as he would be the first to admit, but he had never in his life physically harmed a woman.

Now, for his country, he would have to possibly torture and certainly kill this one.

Christ.

Her back arched up against the flat of his hand as she inhaled. That he was touching a feminine form was unmistakable. Flexing his fingers in silent protest, Hugh thought again, grimly, that Hildebrand had made a bad choice: He was not the man for this job.

Although in the end he would do what he had to do, as he always did.

Hildebrand would have known that, too, Hugh reflected bitterly. Damn him.

*F*loating around just on the edges of consciousness, Claire felt the shock of an icy shower
pelting her and opened her eyes. They immediately
stung. Blinking rapidly, she realized that the reason they
stung was because they were awash with salt water, and
the salt water came from the sea. The sea was, of course,
the bucking, heaving beast upon whose back she now
seemed to be riding. Instinct warned her not to reveal
that she was once again aware; she curled her fingers
into fists to resist the impulse to rub her burning eyes,
and continued, discreetly, to blink until the worst of the
pain went away. Wet to the skin and so cold that she felt
rather like a fish laid out for sale on a slab of ice, she was,
she realized, huddled in the bottom of a heaving small
boat that was being rowed, in the teeth of foaming black
waves and a blowing wind, on a steady course that
doggedly kept putting more distance between them and
shore.

Soon, when they were far enough out, she would be
tossed overboard.

They had caught her.

The thought made her forget all about her physical misery: her stinging eyes, her aching head, her frozen fingers and toes. Her heart raced. Her stomach churned. Her throat went dry. Fear instantly tightened her muscles, sharpened her senses, brought her to hair-trigger alertness where only seconds before she had been struggling with the last remnants of grogginess.

*Drown her like a mewling kitten*—she could almost hear the cruel nonchalance in the leader's voice. It was her kidnappers' plan—the plan they were at that very moment in the process of carrying out. Quickly, convulsively, she moved her hands, her feet. They were not bound. After knocking her out, had they decided not to bother tying her up? Or had they merely forgotten—and if so, would they remember before they threw her overboard? Of course they would. She dared not gamble that they would not. Her life was the stakes in this desperate game, after all.

A hurried, slightly blurry glance around told her that there were six men: four at the oars, two seated in the bottom of the boat trapping her between them, guarding her. Six men whose goal was her murder.

How could she get away?

A hard knot formed in the pit of her stomach as she faced the truth: This time, escape looked all but impossible. Rather than face one oaf, as she had in the farmhouse, she now had to outwit six, with no hefty chamber pot at hand. And instead of a window opening onto the firmness of earth, the only place she had to go if she should manage to break free of her captors was the sea.

On the other hand, however bleak the prospect for success, she had to do something. If she did not, and pretty quickly too, she was going to die.

A whimper crept into her throat. She swallowed it with difficulty before it could make itself heard. Every instinct she possessed urged her to jump to her feet, to fight, to flee. But her instincts were worse than useless under the circumstances, she realized. She resisted them, forcing herself to lie perfectly still while she took stock of the situation.

She could swim, after a fashion. Her monster of a father and his equally debauched friends had, one summer, passed several afternoons of sport in which they had tossed her and her younger sister, Beth, from a sailboat into a lake near their Yorkshire home, betting on which girl would make it to shore first and never mind the fact that both children were terrified and screaming as they were thrown from the deck. She and Beth had survived then against the odds and their own expectations, and now, amazingly, Claire thought that those hellish swimming lessons might stand her in good stead.

Another surreptitious glance around dashed even that faint hope. She could not swim in this—this seething caldron of wind-whipped waves. Her skills were no match for the sea's savagery.

But she feared that it was swim—or die.

Fighting against the rising terror that threatened to render her immobile, Claire carefully took stock one more time. The boat was long, narrow, and open to the elements, rolling and sliding as it attacked the waves. Crowded closely in that confined space, the men were little more than shadowy shapes against the shiny blackness of the water and the more amorphous darkness of the foggy night. The rumbling sky was nearly as black as the sea; the moon was now completely obscured by clouds. The hiss of the sea was punctuated by the rhythmic sound of dipping oars.

A man's knuckles pressed uncomfortably between her shoulder blades. Claire frowned over that, considering. Her back was curled against his hard shins; he was, she realized, holding on to a handful of her frock as insurance against losing her prematurely to the heaving sea. She could feel the shape of his fist like a large rock digging into her flesh, its only positive attribute being that it faintly warmed the point of contact. Not that his grip on her was reassuring; not when she thought about it. With terrible clarity, she foresaw that as soon as they reached whatever spot they were making for—presumably somewhere well beyond the breaking waves, so her body would not immediately be carried back to shore—he would use that grip against her. It would serve to prevent her escape while they bound her hand and foot and threw her over the side.

Better to go overboard by herself, unbound, under her own power than to wait for them to bind her and toss her out.

The dreadful realization made her eyes squeeze shut and her heart lurch. Better to drown herself than let them drown her? How so? Dead, she thought with an inward shudder, was dead.

She *so* did not want to die. Not tonight. Not until she was an old, old lady, and then, pray God, peacefully in her bed.

In the interests of survival, she forced herself to open her eyes again, this time just slits. There, directly in her line of vision, were several items tucked beneath one of the seats: a coil of rope, an unlit, battered lantern, and a jug. A large jug with a handle and a cork, made of some sort of light-colored crockery. She could just discern its squat shape through the darkness. Even as her desperate gaze assessed it, the surging puddle of water in the bottom of the boat caught it up, turned it on its side, and swept it toward her. Whatever it had once held—spirits maybe, or water—it was obviously empty now. It floated.

It floated.

In a flash Claire knew what she had to do. She was afraid to move—the men were paying her no attention, and she didn't want that to change—but the jug bumped against her knee as the boat heeled, and she knew that it would be swept out of reach again as soon as the boat dipped the other way. She knew, too, that the jug represented her best chance—maybe her only chance—for survival.

Sending another quick, fervent prayer skyward, she made a stealthy grab and succeeded in closing her hand around the slippery handle.

"Awake, are you?"

The man with his fist in her back must have either seen or felt her movement, because he bent nearer, leaning over to speak almost in her ear. The warmth of his breath feathered across her cheek. His accent was that of the British upper classes, and it surprised her, given the speech patterns of his cohorts. Involuntarily, before she could debate the wisdom of doing so, she glanced up, registering the glint of his eyes, the darkness of his hair and skin, the intimidating breadth of his shoulders against the backdrop of the peaking waves. Then all coherent thought left her as she realized that she might very well be looking into the face of her murderer.

Stark terror froze her in place. Her breathing

stopped. Even sitting cross-legged in the bottom of the boat as he was, he was a large man, she could tell. A large, strong man, muscular and fit. He could kill her himself, with his bare hands, with ease, if he chose to do so—and there were five more like him.

The knot in her stomach twisted tighter. Fighting panic, she willed herself to breathe again and drew in a shaky, quavery draft of salt-and-fish-tainted air.

It was now or never.

Grasping the jug as if it were her only hope of salvation—which, indeed, it was—Claire drew on every ounce of strength and determination she still possessed and surged to her knees. Her gown jerked free of his hold. He looked at her in surprise as his hand fell away. On her knees as she was, with him sitting cross-legged before her, they were practically nose to nose. Their gazes met, locked, for the briefest of moments. He was opening his mouth as if to say something as she swung her improvised weapon at him in a desperate arc. The heavy jug crashed into the side of his face with a sound that was clearly audible over the rushing sea.

"Dammit to bloody hell!"

Clapping a hand to his face, he fell back even as shock waves from the impact shuddered up her arm, nearly making her drop the jug. Hanging on to it for dear life, her pulse racing, she scrambled clumsily for the side.

"Master Hugh!"

The other previously cross-legged man, on his knees now too, snatched a handful of her skirt, pulling her back when she would have dived into the sea. Yanking free, she was undone by the rocking of the boat and toppled against the man she had hit. For a stunned instant

Claire felt the hard strength of his body against her back. Then he grabbed her arm, hurting her, and with a strength born of utter desperation she turned on him, beating at him with the jug and screeching like a bedlamite.

"Christ Almighty! Grab her, James!"

"Aye, I've got her!"

She was still swinging as the second man snaked an arm around her waist and pulled her off. He felt softer than the first; the spongy resilience of his stomach cushioned her back. In the background the oarsmen shouted, moving so unwarily as they hastened to come to their companions' aid that they nearly overturned the already wildly pitching boat.

Frantic, Claire jammed her elbow into that spongy stomach. He groaned, his grip loosening. She managed to wrest herself free only to have her wrist grabbed by the first man. Heart thumping, throat so dry that her screams now emerged more as harsh croaks, she slewed around.

"Enough, vixen!"

The words were a snarl. He was breathing heavily, but his hold on her wrist was as unbreakable as a vise. For an instant, as she drew in much-needed air, she stared into eyes that were, in that gray light, as black and pitiless as twin voids. She could see the gleam of his teeth as his lips drew back from them. Her left hand, with his right one wrapped around her wrist, was upraised between them. Her right hand still kept its death-defying grip on the jug. Behind her, the second man was already reaching for her again.

The battle was done.

But no. This battle was for her life, and she would

not, could not, be bested while she yet breathed. Terror stoked by the cold breath of looming oblivion gave her a last burst of strength. Quick as a cat she lunged forward, sinking her teeth into that imprisoning hand.

"Eeow!"

He howled, snatching his hand away, and suddenly she was free. Still hanging on to the jug for dear life, she leaped for the side. The boat pitched, fortuitously this time, and through no further effort of her own she was suddenly overboard, tumbling headfirst into the icy depths of the frothing sea.

# ❧ 4 ❧

The water was so cold that for an instant after the sea swallowed her it seemed that every system of Claire's body was suspended. Then her heart gave a great reviving leap. Warm blood began to race through her veins. Her eyes popped open and she could move again. A surge of exhilaration gave her renewed energy. She had done it! She had escaped.

Her joy was, unfortunately, of extremely brief duration. Struggling against a sucking current that seemed determined to drag her down, hampered by the weight of her soaked skirts as they wrapped about her legs, she found herself at the mercy of the sea. Air became an increasingly urgent necessity; she clawed and kicked for the surface. Though her eyes were open, she could see nothing; in the impenetrable darkness, up and down were, horribly, one and the same to her.

But the jug, filled with air, was bent on rising. It was, as she had known it would be, her salvation. Clinging to it with desperate strength, she rose with it. Her head broke the surface, and she was weak with relief. She gulped air like a starving man might food—and then a wave rolled over her and sent her choking and tumbling to the depths again.

Once again the jug sought the surface, taking her along. Then, without warning, her frozen fingers betrayed her: They could not maintain their grip on the slippery surface. One minute her fingers were curled around the handle. The next, the jug shot from her grasp like a greased pig.

Terrified, Claire snatched after it, but it was gone as quick as a blink, disappearing into the swirling darkness above her head. Panic-stricken, floundering, she tried desperately to swim, and her limbs valiantly reconstructed the motions from memory. But she was fighting without substance, and to her despair she realized that her struggles were puny useless things against the might of the sea.

I'm going to die, she thought, still not really grasping the truth of it although now, as if to prepare her, the words formed crystal clear in her mind. Without the buoyancy of the jug to counteract it, the current, like some giant sucking mouth, pulled her down. Her heart pounded. Her lungs began to ache and burn. She needed to breathe, but there was no air. Water was all there was. Water everywhere, surrounding her, in her eyes, her ears, trying to push into her mouth and nose, freezing her, suffocating her . . .

She had to have air. Where was the surface? In that chaotic liquid darkness she became totally disoriented, unable to tell up from down. Not that it mattered. Try though she might, she could not swim in such a sea. Her efforts to defy its force were pitiable. It would do with her as it would, chewing her up and spitting her out at its whim. She was as helpless against it as a babe.

The funny thing was that she was not even really afraid any longer, she mused as her frozen limbs grew heavy and clumsy and her struggles grew weak. She was light-headed, woozy. Her still desperately beating heart felt heavy and swollen, as though it might burst at any second. Her lungs throbbed. It was all she could do not to respond to their urgent need by inhaling and having done with it. Inhaling water . . . that was to drown. Vaguely she wondered, Does drowning hurt?

With a fresh burst of terror, Claire realized that she was close to losing consciousness, to succumbing to the cold, the lack of oxygen, the darkness, the despair.

Images of her sisters appeared in her mind's eye: Gabby and Beth—the one slender, chestnut-haired, pregnant with her first child; the other a plumply pretty redhead, eagerly looking forward to her first Season. They would be grief-stricken if she died. Beth's debut would have to be postponed; with Gabby indisposed, Claire had undertaken to bring her younger sister out this very spring. Plans to have Beth join her in London in March were already well under way. Now Beth would have to wait another year. And Twindle would grieve. So would Aunt Augusta, in her own gruff fashion. Nick, Gabby's husband, would grieve too, although the bulk of his concern would rightly focus on Gabby, already in such distress from her pregnancy. David, her own husband, would not grieve. Oh, he would put on a great show of sadness, he and his mother, but in their secret heart of hearts they would not mourn.

The bitter truth of that startled Claire into awareness once more. Rebelling against it, she gave a mighty kick for the surface; her numbed arms flailed. . . .

Her hand brushed something—something solid—

something covered in cloth. Abruptly her hair was snagged. The sudden, sharp pain in her scalp almost made her gasp, which would certainly have ended the struggle right then and there. Her head whipped around, but this watery hell in which she was trapped was too dark: She could see nothing of what had caught her. It yanked her in the direction she thought was upward. Because of that she did not struggle as it towed her in its wake. She went with it, using her hands and feet to push against the black water. Her lungs were now aching, burning instruments of torture in her chest. Her heart beat against her ribs like the wings of a caged wild bird. Blood pounded feverishly in her temples. Suddenly she realized that she had the answer to her question: Yes, it hurts to drown.

With that thought, miraculously, her head popped through the surface. Her staring, stinging eyes recorded blurry images of surging waves topped with white foam swelling against a starless sky. Her mouth opened instinctively, like a hungry baby bird's. She sucked in air, blessed air, in a greedy gasp. But the crashing sea broke over her even as she filled her lungs, forcing her under once again.

This time, though, as she choked on salt water and fought against the freezing depths, she was not alone. She felt a solid presence behind her, kicking and fighting with her. Something wrapped around her waist—an arm, she thought. From the size and iron strength of it, a man's arm. Whoever had dragged her from the abyss by her hair was with her still. One of her would-be murderers, bent on saving her from the depths so that he could drown her in a fashion more to his liking? The absurdity of it boggled her mind.

Not that, at the moment, she even cared about his reasons, she realized as her lungs began to burn again. All she cared about at the moment was having air to breathe. . . .

As unexpectedly as she'd gone under, she surfaced again. Or, rather, they surfaced. Her rescuer was right behind her. She heard his harsh gasps for air underlining her own. His arm was wrapped around her rib cage now just beneath her breasts. As unyielding as a manacle, it locked her, with her back to his front, against a large, strong body in constant motion as it fought to keep them afloat. Even with his best efforts, and her own, her chin just barely cleared the surging water.

Still, she could breathe.

"Master Hugh!"

Claire instinctively glanced in the direction of the shout. So intent on drawing in air had she been that she only just now noticed the longboat riding the waves some little distance away. The lantern had been lit; held high, its yellow glow illuminated the boat itself and the roiling black water. She and her rescuer, however, were well beyond its range.

"Here!"

The answering shout boomed nearly in her ear, its timbre hoarse but its volume startlingly loud. Claire started, and felt the arm tighten beneath her breasts. The chest against which her back rested heaved. She felt the movements of strong legs kicking beneath hers, saw a brawny arm in a soaked white sleeve, twin to the one that shackled her to him, carve through the dark water in front of her, and again tried to help. But her limbs were numb, and her movements were feeble.

"Fight me, vixen, and I'll knock you unconscious."

The threat was a savage growl in her ear. She felt the rasp of a sandpapery jaw against her cheek as he spoke, and realized that his grip on her had tightened to the point where it was almost painful.

"I'm not fighting." Her voice was almost unrecognizable to her. It was husky, ragged, barely audible above the roar of the sea. She wasn't even sure if he had heard.

She was, she realized with dismal clarity, beyond struggling. Her strength was spent. Breathing took all her energy. He, and he alone, was keeping them afloat. Her arms and legs were numb and all but lifeless. She could not have fought him if she had wanted to. But she didn't want to. The prospect of drowning, which she would surely do if he let her go, terrified her more at the moment than anything else; it terrified her more than he did.

Another wave exploded in her face. Claire choked, gasping, as torrents of water cascaded over her. Forced under, she made her frozen limbs move by sheer force of will. The arm beneath her breasts tightened punishingly as he kicked with her. Seconds later her head once again broke the surface, and she sucked in air.

"Be still, damn you."

He was hungry for air, too. She could hear the harsh rasp of his breathing even as his bristly jaw once again scraped her cheek. His arm around her was so tight that her chest could barely expand to let air in. She squirmed against it in feeble protest.

"I can't breathe. Your arm . . ."

He made a harsh sound but he must have understood because his hold on her relaxed by the smallest of degrees. She inhaled thankfully. Her heart was still beating at triple time, and her limbs could have been made of lead. Her head, too, suddenly felt amazingly heavy, too heavy for her neck to support. It drooped backward of its own accord and found a resting place on her rescuer's broad shoulder. A sideways glance revealed that his lips were parted as he, like she, struggled to breathe. What she could see of his profile was limned in dull gold. His forehead, nose, and chin, she noted in passing, were well-shaped and unmistakably masculine.

"Master Hugh!"

The cry, louder than before, brought her attention around to her left. There, miraculously, was the longboat, now just a few yards away. Of course, the high-held lantern accounted for the glow that outlined her rescuer's features. They were now within its nimbus of light.

Even as she registered that, a rope, sinuous as a snake, sailed through the air and struck the rippling surface beside them before quickly starting to sink. He grabbed it before it could disappear, a strong male hand latching on ruthlessly to a lifeline, and with a series of deft twists of his wrist wrapped it several times around his palm. Then his fist closed over it, and, whether through his efforts or the efforts of the men in the boat, they were suddenly being propelled through the water with a force and speed that defied the swelling waves.

Thus, she thought bleakly, ended her effort at escape. Claire accepted that even as she realized that the safety the boat represented was nothing more than an illusion. What she was really doing was merely exchanging one horrifying death for another, later, one.

But the prospect of life, for however much longer it was granted her, was suddenly unbearably sweet.

When two of the men reached over the side, grasping her under the arms and hauling her on board, she could not be other than thankful.

"Watch her," her rescuer said as she collapsed in a soaked, shivering heap in the bottom of the boat.

Coughing in shuddering spasms as her body fought to rid itself of the water it had taken in, she lay huddled in a ball much as before, but conscious now and cured of all thoughts of escape. Her tongue felt fuzzy and swollen. Her eyes stung.

She watched blearily as he, too, was pulled from the water. Grimacing, he maneuvered himself into a sitting position close beside her huddled form. His back rested against the edge of a plank seat, and his arms stretched across his bent knees so that his hands hung free. They were strong-looking hands with long fingers from which water dripped in a steady rhythm. He was coughing too, though not as violently as she was, and then the cough turned abruptly into a wheeze. She could hear the painful-sounding whistle of air between his teeth as he inhaled.

The other man, the one with the lantern, crouched beside him, looking him over with concern. By its light she saw that this second man boasted a neatly trimmed beard and was, as she had suspected, quite pudgy. Her rescuer, on the other hand, was muscular and lean.

"For God's sake, put out the light," her rescuer said testily between wheezes.

"Oh, aye."

The lantern door was opened and the flame extinguished. Plunged into darkness once more, the boat rode the waves in near silence, save for a mutter or two among the sailors and the sounds of the dipping oars and roaring sea.

"Drink this, Master Hugh."

The pudgy man produced a jug much like the one that had seduced and betrayed her and held it to her rescuer's lips. With an irritable sound, her rescuer took the jug and chugged down a goodly portion of the contents. Lowering it at last, he wiped his arm across his lips.

"Give her some." He nodded at Claire.

The pudgy man glanced at her with dislike, but he took the jug and turned to her.

"You. Drink."

The words registered, along with the hostility that lay beneath them, but even had she wished to, movement of any sort was beyond her for the moment. When she did not respond, he made an impatient sound under his breath and reached over to lift her head so that it rested against his leg. Putting the jug to her lips, he tilted it. Claire instinctively opened her mouth to a rush of liquid.

It was ale, she discovered, so raw and unpleasant-tasting that she almost gagged. But it was wet, and it cut through the horrible salty taste coating the inside of her mouth. She swallowed, then swallowed again. As it hit her stomach she was conscious of a slight, spreading warmth that was very welcome. Finally, coughing, she could drink no more, and pushed the jug aside. Without a word, the pudgy man moved away.

Emotionally as well as physically spent, reduced to a mass of what felt like shivering jelly, she lay miserably at her rescuer's feet, awash in seawater, no longer coughing but still so cold and exhausted that she was only peripherally aware of what was happening around her.

Someone pulled her wrists behind her and bound them, and she didn't struggle. Then her ankles were bound, too, not tightly but just enough to prevent her from using her feet. Glancing down, she saw that the pudgy man was the one tying her up. Clearly he was taking precautions against another escape attempt.

Or he was trussing her up to toss her back into the sea?

Her gaze met his as the last knot was tied, but it held no rancor, no dislike. She should have felt frightened, she knew, but instead she felt—resignation. Closing her eyes, she realized that she was glad of the utter dispassion that gripped her. It made everything so much easier to bear, such as the knowledge that, sooner or later on this hellish night, she was going to die.

Some minutes later, shouts and a flurry of activity on the part of the men caused her eyes to blink open. A stab of fear penetrated the impassivity that cloaked her as she wondered if all the commotion meant her time was at hand. A great black hulk of a ship met her gaze, rising like a mountain in front of the small boat. The rowboat was, she realized, now parallel to the enormous newcomer.

Frowning, Claire tried to fit the appearance of the ship in with what she knew of her captors' plans, and couldn't. She was still puzzling over it as lines were thrown and caught and the rowboat was steadied.

"You, take her."

The voice was her rescuer's. The words were clearly a command. Claire's gaze was swinging around to find him when, with the rowboat pitching drunkenly, a brawny sailor stepped over the plank seat behind her and, with legs braced wide apart, bent over her. Without further warning, she was picked up and hoisted over a stout shoulder, then left to dangle head-down while the man carrying her ascended a rope ladder that had been thrown down from the ship.

## ❧ 5 ❧

·······························

*T*he ladder was a flimsy thing that twisted and swayed with each roll of the sea, but the sailor seemed to have no difficulty managing, even with her added weight to contend with. For her part, Claire didn't struggle. One horrified glance down into the roiling black water was enough to convince her of the suicidal folly of that, and bring on an immediate attack of nausea-inducing vertigo to boot.

For the seeming eternity of that perilous ascent, she remained limp as a sack of meal, eyes closed tightly and mind engaged in fervent prayer. With her hands bound behind her, she had no means of steadying herself. Her shivering body shifted with the sailor's every movement. If he lost his grip, she would plunge straight down into the little boat below—or, worse, the hungry waves.

Please God, don't let me die tonight, was the refrain that ran over and over through her head. She felt like she had been saying it forever. How, how had she come to this? Less than a dozen hours previous, she had been safe in her own coach.

With a heave and a jolt that almost caused her to bite her tongue, she and the sailor were over the rail.

"Eh, will you look at that? Young Corbin's done brung us a present!"

"Well done, lad!"

"I'll trade ye me rum rations for 'er."

"Ah, she be worth more than that! I'll tell ye what: I'll give ye my timepiece."

With catcalls and whistles and so many bawdy comments that Claire closed her ears to them, what seemed like the entire crew surrounded them as they moved across the deck. Claire's eyes opened wide as, without warning, she was shrugged from the sailor's shoulder to fall into the hands of a crowd of men all too eager to receive her. Perhaps six of them caught her, their grasping hands saving her from landing painfully on the deck. But, she thought seconds later, even that would have been preferable to the means they used to keep her from it. Bound as she was, she had no way to prevent them from sliding their hands over her knees, her calves, even up her thighs. Her slim pale legs were bare, she discovered to her horror as they grabbed at her; the sea had obviously claimed her half-boots and stockings without her being aware of it. More hands slid beneath her arms, where they lodged with fingers splayed uncomfortably close to her breasts. Horrified, Claire realized that the men were enjoying themselves, enjoying touching her.

She shuddered in disgust. At the thought of what they might do next, her stomach churned as stormily as the sea. A rush of adrenaline strengthened her. Her gelatinous muscles, responding to the call, stiffened. She'd thought she was spent, that there was no fight left in her.

In the face of this hideous new threat, she discovered, to her everlasting gratitude, that she was wrong.

"Let me go!"

Held by who knew how many pairs of hands in a supine position parallel to the deck, she struggled to free herself, writhing like a caterpillar fighting free of its cocoon. They ignored her efforts, of course, save for smirks, and a group chortle of what sounded like delight as she managed to kick a nearly toothless old man in the stomach with her bound feet, causing him to double over. One man dangled a lantern over her; the others, gawking, crowded closer yet.

"A fine, pretty piece she is!"

"Put me down! Get your hands off me!" Anger fueled by a lifetime of having to fend off evil-intentioned men added strength to Claire's cry.

"Aiyee, she's scarin' me!"

A round of guffaws greeted this sally; the hands holding her shifted, tightened. Furious at her helplessness, she made a hissing sound through her teeth and tried again to kick. Bound as she was, the effort was fruitless. All it did was give them more to ogle as they laughed and dodged.

"Blimey, looks like we caught us a bleedin' mermaid!"

"Aye, but if she's 'alf as cold as she feels, she'll be giving us an 'ell of an icy ride."

"Hawks, ye fool, we'll warm 'er up first."

"If ye're wantin' volunteers, I'll do the warmin'."

The last speaker's grizzled face split in a wide grin; another, younger, bearded man pressed so close she could smell the sourness of his breath. He was aiming to kiss her, she realized with revulsion, and sharply turned her face to one side. His moist warm lips just grazed her neck. Her skin crawled. His mates roared approval.

"Stop it! Leave me alone!"

Struggling was useless, but still she struggled. A hand stroked caressingly along the bare underside of her calf. Sour Breath came back for another try at claiming a kiss. Claire's chest tightened and her mouth went dry with fear as she eluded him a second time. It took no very great intellect for her to realize what was about to happen. She couldn't bear it. . . .

"All right, leave off. You there, and you: Take her to my cabin."

Just a little while before, that gravelly voice had sent icy fingers of fear trailing down Claire's spine. Now she welcomed it as she might welcome the sun in the morning. It belonged to her rescuer—Master Hugh, the pudgy man had called him—who was now on deck too, and it had an immediate quelling effect on the men holding her. Sour Breath straightened. The hand that was sliding up her thigh was withdrawn. Hugh never stopped, but walked on past her and the gathered men with scarcely more than a passing glance. It was clear that having given the order, he expected it to be obeyed. The glimpse she caught of him confirmed her earlier impression that he was tall and lean, broad-shouldered, with an athlete's easy grace. He was as wet as she was: His hair, shoulder-length and dripping, was plastered tightly against his skull and gleamed as shiny black as a seal's in the lantern light. His clothes—a white shirt and black breeches—were soaked through, clinging wetly everywhere they touched. Like her, he had lost his shoes and stockings to the sea. His bare feet were pale against the dark planks, and he left a trail of water in his wake.

"Ah, sir, what 'arm would it do if we was to 'ave a wee bit o' sport with 'er?" It was a wheedling question, called after Hugh as he passed.

"You heard me. Take her to my cabin."

This man was her enemy and intended her harm. Yet, he had jumped into the sea to save her life, and now was calling off the sailors. He was no friend to her, she knew. But suddenly he seemed far more of an ally than any of the others. Just why he had saved her, and precisely how this whole scenario fit into her captors' plans to ultimately do away with her, she had no idea.

Was it possible, came a tantalizing hope, that the leader had been telling the truth after all about a ransom having been paid? Perhaps, instead of still being intent on her murder, they were transporting her somewhere where she would be released?

Yes, and perhaps she would wake up one morning as the Queen of England, too, Claire thought tartly.

The little niggle of hope just born in her mind wilted like a water-starved plant. Still, she didn't try to resist as, with one pair of hands still lodged far too familiarly under her armpits and another now gripping her bare ankles just above the rope that bound them, she was borne off toward the companionway amid much grumbling and many dark looks cast after Hugh.

As the stiff night wind hit her, Claire shivered uncontrollably. Only then did she realize that she had been shivering all along. From fear, she realized, almost as much as from the cold.

What would come to her now?

"You got your business tidied away all right and tight then, I'm thinking?"

Hugh had stopped walking and now stood with a

slightly built, bewigged man of average height and sumptuous dress just a short distance away, Claire saw. She supposed it was he who had spoken.

Behind them rose the captain's cabin, which was dark, and the quarterdeck, which was a hive of activity. Ropes snapped in the wind, and the white sails, ghostly pale in the darkness and billowing wildly as the wind caught them, were being run up the poles. In the distance, loud enough to be audible over the rushing sea, came a cranking, grinding, metallic sound that Claire decided was the anchor being raised.

"I did, Captain, and I thank you for your assistance and the loan of your ship," Hugh said, his tone courteous.

"Oh, 'twas our pleasure, you may be sure. We're all loyal subjects of His Majesty, after all."

Being carried clumsily below, down a steep companionway and along a narrow creaking hallway past innumerable bolts of cloth and stacks of lashed barrels, Claire missed the rest of the exchange. But she did hear the captain, minutes later, bellow, "Release those lines! Look lively, mates, we're away!"

Hard on the heels of that, the ship gave a great surge forward and the motion increased markedly. She was ever a poor traveler and greeted the rocking with alarm. Fortunately, her stomach was nearly empty; she had last eaten when the coach had stopped at an inn along the way to rest the horses, and she had partaken of a cup of tea and some buttered bread. With Alice—but it would not do to think of her poor maid or her possible fate. There was nothing she could do for her, or for John Coachman, or anyone else. She must just try, if she could, to save herself, and put the others from her mind.

That small meal had been more than twelve hours before, as the time, unless her calculations were far off, was well past midnight. Still, Claire was all too aware of the increased rolling as she was borne into a low-pitched stateroom so small that a grown man might stretch out his arms and almost touch both walls for the width of it, and as for the length—well, the men carrying her seemed to be practically stepping on each other's toes once they crossed the threshold. Warmth seemed to embrace her, and she realized that, down here out of the wind, the temperature was actually quite bearable. Their entry was met by a sharp heeling of the ship and the crash of a wave breaking against the hull. The boom was as loud as a cannon, and Claire was forcefully reminded of the sea's continued unease.

"Not on the bunk, ye bloody imbeciles! Can ye not see she's soaked to the skin?"

The speaker was the pudgy man, who was engaged in lighting a lantern that hung by a chain from a thick beam overhead. As the wick caught, and he closed the glass door and turned to look at them, he released the lantern and it began to swing, pendulumlike, back and forth on its chain.

Hastily Claire turned her attention to the man. He had, she observed, in addition to his beard, short grizzled hair and a long beaked nose as the most prominent among unremarkable features. He was dressed in a plain black coat and breeches suitable for a servant, with white shirt and stockings and sturdy black shoes.

"What are we to do with 'er then?"

The two men carrying her, who had indeed been making for the narrow bunk that took up almost the whole of one wall, stopped walking. For a moment

Claire hung between them, sagging in the middle like a rolled-up carpet.

"Put her on the floor."

No sooner were the words out of the pudgy man's mouth than the sailors let go, dumping her without ceremony on the hard boards. Claire couldn't control the small pained cry that escaped her as she landed abruptly on her bottom, then fell back on her bound hands. Even as cold as those extremities were, that hurt, so Claire rolled onto her side. Her cry had drawn the attention of all three men, who stared down at her. Alarmed, Claire curled up once again in a tight ball, drawing her knees up to her chest, tucking her chin on top of them, and tossing her head so that much of her hair lay across her face, serving as a wet, tangled veil over her features. Instinctively she sought to allow them to see as little of her person as possible. She was still shivering, increasingly nauseated and suffering from a headache, but those were the least of her problems, she realized, as she peered through the sheltering strands. The sailors were eyeing her avidly, and glancing down at herself she saw why. Her wet skirts were rucked up around her knees, leaving her lower limbs totally exposed to their view.

With her hands bound, there was nothing to be done about it. Exhausted and frightened, gritting her teeth in an effort to silence their chattering, she lay still and closed her eyes. Weakness washed over her in waves; her head swam. She was too tired to worry anymore about what might happen to her. Whether she lived or died was in God's hands.

"A change of clothes, James, and a towel."

With that, Hugh arrived, and despite her attempt to resign herself to whatever came, Claire discovered that she was not quite as indifferent to her fate as she had supposed. Her eyes popped open to fix on him. The small chamber suddenly felt grossly overcrowded as he stepped inside it. His large frame seemed to take up every remaining inch of space.

"Aye, you need them." The pudgy man—James— nodded, and turned to a cupboard built into the bulk-head, which he opened, reaching inside to search through what looked like a pair of saddlebags. Hugh, meanwhile, stood in a rapidly growing puddle of his own making, Claire saw, as her gaze, which she tried to veil behind lowered lashes and her curtain of wet hair, ran over him. Water ran down his bare, muscular calves in rivulets and dripped from his shirt and his black hair. He was somewhat blue about the gills, as, indeed, she suspected she was herself. A fresh-looking abrasion just above his left temple marked the spot where she had hit him with the jug. His head seemed near to brushing the beams overhead, and she judged him to be several inches above six feet. His soaked shirt was almost translucent in places where it clung to his broad shoul-ders and wide chest, and revealed a dark shadow that she suspected was abundant chest hair beneath. His breeches, while made of a sturdier material, were only slightly less revealing of an athlete's lithe hips and the hard muscles of his thighs. He appeared to be some-where in his early to midthirties, with creases around his mouth and eyes. His face, though not what she would have termed handsome, was instead striking, with boldly carved lines that added up to a whole that was somewhat harsh: His nose was masterful, his mouth long and thin-lipped, his eyes heavy-lidded. In the flick-ering lantern light their color was uncertain, although they appeared dark. They were set beneath straight, bold slashes of crow-black brows. His cheeks were lean and darkened by what appeared to be at least a day's growth of beard, his brow was high and slightly furrowed, and his jaw gave evidence of an obstinate disposition. He was as dark of complexion and hair as a Gypsy, and as forbidding in aspect as the most murderous of brigands.

Which he almost certainly was, she thought with a lurch of her heart. He had saved her from the sea, true, and from the sailors above, but that was no reason not to fear him. It was likely that his motive, if she knew it, would be enough to strike terror into her heart.

To her dismay, as her gaze returned to his face she realized that he was eyeing her with a grim expression that boded nothing very good for her future.

The unmistakable sound of smacking lips redirected her attention in a hurry. Still huddled tightly in her protective ball and trying not to move any part of her person except her eyes, she peeped out through her carefully preserved screen of hair and lashes to discover that the sailors who had carried her into the cabin now stood shoulder to shoulder above her, their gazes fastened on her bare legs. There was something in their expressions that made her think sickeningly of hungry dogs and meat pasties. Their fervidness made her flesh creep.

The use to which they would put her was clear. Carnal intent was writ plain on their faces. Again she thought, I can't bear it.

A fresh surge of adrenaline caused her heart to pump faster, warmed her cold extremities, and stiffened her will. She would fight to the last drop of her strength and beyond, before she would submit to rape.

"You may leave us."

Hugh's voice was as hard as his eyes, which, she saw as she glanced at him again, were no longer fixed on her but on the two men. He was dismissing them—thank God, thank God. At his words, the sailors looked up, and for a second the atmosphere was charged. Hugh stared them down, his stance relaxed but ready, his gaze stony. That he was holding a businesslike-looking pistol seemed to clinch matters. There was a slight but discernible change in their demeanor: They no longer seemed quite so threatening. Claire breathed a little— just a little—easier.

"Aye, sir," the taller of the two answered with resignation.

"Ye need any 'elp with 'er, Yer 'Onor, ye jest be lettin' us know." His companion was more optimistic.

"Aye, we'll be right pleased to assist with anythin' ye need," the first sailor agreed with renewed cheerfulness, flashing a wolfish grin. "Especially where yon toothsome lass is concerned."

"I'll keep it in mind." Hugh's voice was dry.

"Get along, now. Get! Go on!" James, a motley collection of what appeared to be men's clothing clutched in one fist, turned from the cupboard to drive the sailors from the cabin with a series of shooing motions, then shut the door behind them and threw the bolt. He then turned back to Hugh, who seemed to slump a little with the sailors' exit. James watched eagle-eyed as Hugh grimaced and exhaled with a soft hiss.

"Aye, ye've done yerself an injury with yer foolishness, just like I knew ye would." James's tone was grim as he crossed to the other man's side. To Claire's surprise, Hugh, who was doing something with the pistol, seemed to take no umbrage at being spoken to like an errant child.

"Have done with your scolding, James." Placing the pistol on a small, semicircular table built into the wall opposite the bunk, Hugh took a deep, slow breath. "I'm in no mood to listen to it, I warn you."

But he sank down onto a slat-backed chair James pulled out for him without protest. Wincing, he pressed one hand flat against the left side of his rib cage, rubbed in a rather gingerly fashion and leaned carefully back, stretching his legs out before him. His bare feet, Claire noted in passing, were long, narrow, and unmistakably masculine, like his hands. She was as tense as a coiled spring now, ready to seize any chance to save herself. But all she could do for the moment was lie still as a mouse, and watch, and listen.

"I'll reckon ye're not. Going into the water for such a cause, and you in such a state. Master Hugh, I'll tell ye to yer head that a lad of ten would have had more sense."

"Would you have had me let the wench drown?" The words were spoken through clenched teeth. No doubt about it, Claire thought: The man was in pain.

"I would've had you let one of the sailors go in after her, as any man of sense would have done."

"Very likely, but I didn't think of it at the time."

Claire was alarmed to find Hugh's gaze shifting to her as James dropped the clothes on the table, which, given the close quarters of the cabin, was right at Hugh's elbow. James then stepped in front of Hugh, reaching for the fastenings on his shirt and effectively distracting his attention.

Hugh swatted his hands away. "I can undress myself, old man. Contrary to your apparent opinion, I'm neither helpless nor a child. Give me that towel and have done."

With a slightly aggrieved expression, James did as he was told. To Claire's dismay, even as Hugh rubbed his head with the towel his gaze fastened once more on her.

"As for you, vixen, I'll not perjure myself by saying that it's a pleasure to make your acquaintance. I will point out that I am perfectly aware that you are present, so you may cease trying to make yourself inconspicuous by curling up into a ball."

## ❧ 6 ❧

........................................

_W_ithout warning, Hugh found himself looking into a pair of eyes that gleamed unexpectedly gold as the lamplight caught them through the black tangle of her hair. Siren's eyes . . . To his dismay, the thought registered in his brain before he could cut it off.

His expression turned grim. Those eyes were not going to be allowed to sway him. They were, first and foremost, traitor's eyes. His gaze flicked once more to James, who was crouched beside him now, attempting to dry his feet and legs. Impatiently he shifted out of reach. James gave an annoyed *tsk* and frowned up at him.

"If I hadn't witnessed it with me own eyes, I never would've believed you'd have jumped in the sea without first thinkin' to remove your boots," James said, his tone part scolding and part mournful. "And them brand-new, too, with them fine chamois tops and tassels like the tails of gold horses. Now what's to do? They're lost, and you've no more footwear with you. A pretty figure you'll cut, riding about France in your stocking feet. Not but what you didn't lose a fine pair of clocked stockings, too."

"I'll just have to wear your shoes then, won't I?"

Though he'd be hanged if he'd admit as much to James, he did slightly regret the loss of his boots. He'd taken delivery of them just the week before. "And your stockings, too."

"And what about your coat, eh? The sea has that too, and the other one we brought is still damp, and all but ruined from the rain we rode through getting here."

"You scold worse than a wife, you know that?" Hugh narrowed his eyes at his faithful retainer. "Take your sorry self off, and see what the captain has aboard in the way of spirits. I thirst."

"Aye, you'd like me to think that, wouldn't you? You're looking to the bottle to ease your hurts, I don't doubt, which ye wouldn't be needin' to do had ye not been so bloody foolish."

The trouble with servants who had been with a man from birth was that over the years they could be counted on to stop showing proper deference to him, Hugh reflected sourly, shooting James a quelling look. Having been the recipient of such a look on countless occasions in the past, James had no trouble interpreting it—or disregarding it. Giving an ostentatious sniff that expressed his feelings as clearly as any diatribe might have done, he abandoned what he would doubtless describe as his unappreciated efforts to make his master more comfortable and stood up, towel in hand.

"Very well, then, I'm going. Have a care what you're about."

Hugh didn't reply to this parting evidence that his henchman for life had little faith in his ability to function satisfactorily without him, and James, with a final expressive sniff that Hugh also chose to ignore, took himself off.

As the door shut behind James, Hugh's attention shifted back to the woman. She was huddled on her side, her face shrouded by long, tangled skeins of ink-black hair through which her eyes still gleamed at him like— not a siren's, perish the thought—a wild thing's. With her knees practically tucked beneath her chin, she was curled at the center of a spreading puddle. Her soaked skirts—they would, when dry, be a shade close to tobacco brown, he judged—lay about her like the limp petals of a wilted flower. Her gown appeared both stylish and surprisingly modest, given her profession. It was of fine wool, as he had noted before, with a high, close neckline and long mameluke-style sleeves trimmed with thin bands of what looked like dark velvet; he supposed the inclement weather must have played a factor in her choice of apparel because, under ordinary conditions, it would have been quite modest. These conditions, however, were far from ordinary, and her soaked bodice clung to firm round breasts sized to fill teacups very nicely, and revealed pert nipples, hardened by the cold, thrusting lewdly against the fabric; in addition, her skirts were in considerable disarray, rucked up and twisted so that they exposed slender, shapely calves as well as ankles so delicate and finely turned that they made the rope binding them look far thicker than he knew it was.

Had he encountered those ankles on the street, displayed by, say, a mischievous gust of wind, his reaction would have been head-turningly swift. Indeed, even knowing what he knew of her, his body displayed a disturbing tendency to react as any normal man's would to such enticements, and curbing that tendency required a considerable effort of will on his part.

If nothing else, he reflected caustically, he had to commend old Archer on his taste in ladybirds. Unless her hair concealed a face like a gargoyle's, this was a high-flyer indeed.

Having gotten himself well under control again, he completed the rest of his inspection swiftly, and in a detached, almost clinical manner for which he silently congratulated himself. Her feet were as fine-boned as the rest of her, with small toes curved like shells. What he could see of her skin was so pale it was almost translucent, with a blue cast that could, he knew, be attributed to the fact that she was as wet as seaweed and doubtless freezing. Her figure, just as he had earlier guessed from the feel of it, was that of a girl, slim and supple, with hips that were more slender than womanly and a tiny waist beneath those succulent breasts.

He found himself hoping that she was older than the girl she appeared, that the face that was still largely hidden from him was—oh, happy thought!—heavy-jowled and riddled with wrinkles or other marks of a lengthy life given over to dissipation.

Not that her age, whatever it might be, mattered a whit under the circumstances.

Standing abruptly—his ribs repaid him for the carelessness of his movement with a quick stab—he took the three strides necessary to reach the door. He had no real reason to distrust the *Nadine*'s crew, but it never hurt to be careful, so he bolted the door. Then he retraced his steps, unbuttoning his sodden shirt on the way. As he reached the table, he became aware that his prisoner was watching him as carefully as a cat at a mouse hole. The bright gleam widened as he abandoned the slippery buttons to pull the garment over his head, then was extinguished altogether seconds later as he dropped the sodden shirt onto the floor. Clearly she had closed her eyes. A modest doxy? The notion piqued his interest.

He could not afford to have his interest piqued by her.

"You're in a deal of trouble, you know."

Shucking his clammy breeches, he addressed the huddled form in a grim voice that was a pretty faithful echo of the way he felt.

"If this is about money, I'll pay you well to let me go."

Her voice was low, husky, well-coached in the cadences of a lady. It was the first time he had heard it properly, and it surprised as well as disturbed him. Like the rest of her, her voice was too attractive, too feminine, too well-bred, for his liking, considering how their acquaintance was destined to end. Her eyes opened as she spoke and then widened. For the space of perhaps a couple of seconds she watched as, naked, he toweled himself off. Then her eyes had snapped shut again.

His lips compressed. He cast the towel aside and reached for the dry shirt that James had left for him on the table.

"Will you indeed? And have you money on you?"

If she was carrying money, it stood to reason that the letters would be in the same place. Perhaps concealed beneath her skirts, safe in an oilskin bag?

Her eyes flicked open again just as he reached for his drawers. "Not on me. But—I can get it."

Of course he had not expected the accomplishment of his mission to be that simple. In this business, nothing ever was.

"Pie in the sky," he said pulling on his breeches, ser-

viceable ones of black stockinette that suited the station
of the impecunious Frenchman who, while in Paris, he
professed to be.

"It is not! I can get it! I can!"

Her eyes widened. As if in agitation, she raised her
head a few inches off the puddled floor. She shook her
head, flinging back the obscuring curtain of hair like a
wet dog indulging in a shake, and incidentally shower-
ing the immediate area with water droplets. As his last
pair of dry breeches got spattered, he glanced down with
a grimace. Then his gaze lifted, and suddenly, to his horror, Hugh found himself looking into the face of one of
the most ravishing beauties he had beheld in many a
year.

Gargoyle, indeed. Even calling her a high-flyer failed
to do her justice. What he was looking at was nothing less
than a diamond of the first water. And to make matters
worse, she looked to be scarcely older than a debutante.

Taken aback, he took his opponent's full measure
and was suddenly transported to a grim area far beyond
dismay. He'd been in the right of it when he'd termed
the golden eyes that had been peeping at him siren's
eyes, he thought. They were the color of candlelit honey,
fringed by thick black lashes and set aslant below delicate black eyebrows that seemed to take wing toward her
temples. Her face was a classic oval, with high cheekbones, a smooth, unlined brow, and a delicately molded
jaw and chin. Her nose was small and straight and elegant; her lips had been carved by a master, the upper finished with an exquisite bow in the center, the lower with
a lush curve. Even tinted faintly blue, as they were now,
they were imminently kissable lips.

At the thought Hugh pulled himself up sharply.

Beauty or no, it made no difference in the job he had to do.

"What if I told you that I have a price, but it isn't any amount of money?" he asked as he retrieved the knife he always kept concealed on his person from the table where he had placed it as he stripped. He slid it from its sheath and moved toward her, deliberately handling it so that its sharp-honed blade flashed silver in the light.

Wide-eyed, she focused on the knife, as he had intended. Fear clouded her eyes. Good, he told himself. He might well have need of her fear.

His bare feet encountered the outer edges of the cold water in which she lay, and he glanced down. Left as she was much longer, she just might succumb to exposure, in which case he would not have to involve himself any further in the process of ridding the world of a traitor.

Ah, but letting nature take its course wouldn't get him the information he needed, and was most chancy besides. She only looked fragile, he reminded himself. In his experience—and he had a large and varied experience in such matters—females of her stamp tended to be unexpectedly hardy.

"I—I would pay it." Her voice was tremulous; her eyes, wide with apprehension, were riveted on his face. Then her lashes flickered, and her lids dropped. He watched, unable to help himself, as she wetted her lips with the tip of a little pink tongue. Abruptly her lids lifted again so that those siren's eyes met his full on. "Anything."

He could not mistake her meaning. Still, that last word had a grim resolve to it that fell far short of the seductiveness such a proposal called for. Paradoxically, that she did not bill and coo at him made her offer that much more attractive.

That he found himself tempted, even momentarily, infuriated him.

"Would you indeed?" His voice had hardened along with his resolve. Still skirting the puddle, he walked behind her, the knife held purposefully in his hand.

"I— What are you doing?"

Sounding panicked now—he guessed by the knife— she tried to sit, all the while craning her neck to keep him in view. Hampered as she was by her bound limbs, her movements were clumsy flailings that, suddenly impatient, he put an end to by the simple expedient of placing a hand on her shoulder and pushing her back down against the floor. Without effort he held her there, on her side as she had been before she'd tried to sit up. After the briefest of struggles she subsided, although he could feel the tension in her muscles through the cold wet cloth that covered them.

Crouching behind her, he was treated to a view of her profile as she strained to look back over her shoulder at him: It was as perfect as a cameo. The realization had him swallowing enough curses to shock an abbess.

That his quarry had turned out to be a woman was cosmic joke enough. Making her a chit of a girl and a raving beauty to boot was overkill.

Sticking his knife into the waistband of his breeches, Hugh flipped her onto her belly without further ado.

"What are you doing?" she asked again, still watching him over her shoulder and sounding almost pitiful as he secured her by the simple measure of placing one knee in the small of her back, just below her bound hands.

"Lie still."

Careful not to let too much of his weight rest on her slight form—and thoroughly annoyed with himself for being so careful—he conducted a comprehensive search of her person, running his hands down her arms, along the insides and outsides of her thighs, around her slender waist, and over the fetching curve of her bottom. The saturated cloth kept no secrets; through it he could feel every toothsome inch. She sucked in her breath and went very still when first he touched her, but offered no resistance. When his weight shifted and his hands slid beneath her to feel their way up her rib cage, she shuddered once and seemed to shrink, but still made no protest.

Her cheek rested against the wet floor with her face turned to the wall. Her eyes were closed, and he was treated to a view of long sooty lashes curling against her cheeks, and soft parted lips trembling slightly as his hands went about their business. She looked helpless, and frightened, and about eighteen.

If Hildebrand didn't rot in hell for eternity, there was no justice in the world.

The soft roundness of her breasts under his hands and the feel of her firm little nipples thrusting into his palm were almost his undoing.

Gritting his teeth, all too aware of his quickened pulse and swelling loins despite valiant attempts to ignore both, he finally acknowledged himself outgunned even as his hands ascertained that there was nothing concealed in the near vicinity of her breasts. Silently cursing, he withdrew his hands more quickly than he would have done with any other suspect and mentally declared the search, imperfect as it was, ended.

If she was hiding the packet of letters he sought, or a

weapon, or anything else about her person, it was too well-concealed for him to find this way.

He pulled his knife from his waistband.

Her breath caught in an audible gasp. Clearly she'd been watching him from beneath her lashes.

He'd forgotten that doxy's trick of hers. Forgotten everything for a moment except the feel of her under his hands.

And that, damn it to bloody hell, was enough to dazzle any man breathing.

It would, he reflected bitterly, behoove him to be careful what he was about, just as James had suggested. Of course, James hadn't realized that the person Hugh had to be most wary of was himself.

"What are you going to do with that knife?"

"What do you imagine I'm going to do with it, I wonder?"

The harsh note in his voice was deliberate. Contrary to her obvious fears, he had already realized that using his knife on any part of her save the rope that bound her hands and feet was beyond him.

"I—don't know. Please—don't hurt me."

Her voice had dropped until it was no more than a shaky whisper. Hugh swallowed another curse. His impulse was to reassure her, but he ruthlessly suppressed it. That was the one thing he could not do.

"Don't move," he said, even more harshly than before, and shifted so that he was crouching beside her, knife in hand. She drew in a ragged breath, but lay still, watching him from the corner of her eye. She was breathing too fast; he could see that from the rapid rise and fall of her slender back.

"Your name is Hugh, isn't it?"

Uttered in that soft, throaty voice of hers, his name took on a whole new dimension. As she finished speaking, her tongue came out to moisten her lips again. Watching, Hugh felt another fierce burst of heat shoot through his loins, and steeled himself to resist her wiles and his own base impulses alike.

It was very possible, he reminded himself grimly, that she was enticing him deliberately.

"Yes."

A long shudder racked her, probably from the cold, although fear or a conscious attempt to win sympathy were other possibilities. The thought that she should be bundled in blankets and set before a roaring fire forthwith occurred to him, only to be sternly dismissed. Try though she might to seem so, she was not some small defenseless creature that required his gentle care.

She was a traitor.

"Please don't hurt me, Hugh."

There was a quaver to her voice that caused his muscles to tighten. Even knowing what he did about her, even suspecting that she was deliberately playing on his sympathies, he discovered that, though he would give much for it to be otherwise, he was not proof against her frightened-sounding entreaty.

"I'm not going to hurt you—at least, not if you behave yourself. I'm going to cut the ropes." Cursing himself for a softheaded fool, he shifted so that he was on his knees beside her. "But be warned—if you give me any trouble, any trouble at all, you'll regret it."

He felt some of the tension leave her body as he pushed aside the nearly waist-length tangle of wet hair that hung in his way and set to work. Her skin was corpse-cold, he found as he touched it, but soft and smooth, and her fingers were elegantly tapered and well cared for. There was a long scratch on her left hand, but no indication that she had ever done anything more strenuous in her life than lift a bonbon to her mouth. In short, she had the hands of a lady, he registered unwillingly. Setting his knife to the rope binding her wrists, he began to saw with some savagery at the wet hemp. He would cut her free, get her dry and warm because that was the expedient thing to do, and allow her to think that he might just let her go if she gave him what he wanted.

The letters, that is, and the full story of how and why she had obtained them and to whom she expected to give them once she reached France.

Nothing else.

"Hugh. Thank you. I would have drowned if you hadn't jumped into the water after me. You saved my life."

Clearly she was attempting to forge a bond between them. During the years he'd spent in his country's service, he'd encountered that trick more than once. It was, in fact, a classic captive-to-captor maneuver, and he was too old a hand to fall for it. Still, she was surprisingly clever for so freshly minted a spy, he thought with a welcome surge of cynicism, even as he found himself responding instinctively to the soft sweetness of her voice.

"I had a reason."

"Still. Thank you."

He didn't reply. When the rope, cut through, dropped to the floor, she pushed herself into a sitting position with a quick, fluttery-lashed glance over her shoulder at him. Drawing her bound legs up beside her, she chafed her wrists and shook her hands, presumably to get the blood flowing to them again.

Hugh started to work on the rope around her ankles without a word.

"Why are you doing this?"

"Cutting the ropes?" His question was dry. The blade continued to saw at the resistant hemp, and his attention stayed focused on his work.

"Why did you kidnap me? What do you want?"

As the last rope fell away, he glanced up at her. Her face was just inches away. With the wet, matted snarls of her hair springing out around her delicate features like a lion's mane and her eyes gleaming a feral gold in the lamplight, she looked like some untamed creature at bay. A supremely beautiful creature. Even as their gazes met, he could not help but acknowledge that. She regarded him warily but with a shade less actual fear than she had shown before. Then she essayed a little smile.

"I want the letters you stole from Lord Archer, to begin with," he said, in a tone made utterly grim by her smile. "It would make it easier on both of us if you would just hand them over and be done."

Her eyes widened into big pools of utter innocence. Her lips parted and rounded. The faux bewilderment was well done, very well done indeed. His mouth twisted as he took in every nuance of her expression. She was an actress of no little talent, without a doubt. Too bad she hadn't chosen to take to the boards rathen than betray her country.

"I don't know what you're talking about."

Her artlessness grated on him, for which he was thankful. It would be far easier to do what he had to do if he could see her as the kind of conscienceless, conniving witch she undoubtedly was instead of the ravishing young girl she appeared to be.

"Of course you don't."

Standing, he returned his knife to his waistband and looked her over sardonically. She was still giving him the big-eyed treatment when he reached down and curled a hand around her elbow, hauling her without ceremony to her feet.

Even soaking wet, she weighed surprisingly little. So little that using his strength against her bothered his conscience. Actually, it made him feel like the biggest brute alive. Manhandling helpless women was not normally his style.

She, of course, was not a helpless woman. He had to keep reminding himself of that. As he struggled mentally to replace the image of her his senses gave him with what she was in truth, she hung awkwardly in his grasp, stumbling a little as she got her feet beneath her.

"If you choose to make this difficult for yourself, then so be it." His voice was pure steel. "You will oblige me by disrobing."

A search of each garment must needs be made in case she had sewn the letters into a secret pocket in her petticoats or chemise. They were not in her bodice, he was willing to swear.

"What?"

Looking utterly taken aback, she tried to pull away then, but he held her fast. As her eyes fixed on his face they were wide with what gave every appearance of being genuine alarm. Again he gave her points for acting, although given her profession and the fact that she had already offered herself to him, she was perhaps overdoing the role of shocked innocent a bit.

"You heard me." He was deliberately brutal. "Take off your clothes."

## 7

"**Hugh**. Please. You must listen: There's been a mistake."

Claire knew she sounded desperate, which was reasonable, because she was. Her breathing came quick and shallow, and her heart pounded as she fought to keep calm, to think, to plan. Her exhaustion was forgotten. This harsh-faced man whose hand bit into her arm had a grim air about him now that frightened her anew. The decency she had thought—hoped?—she'd detected in him earlier had vanished. His eyes—they were gray, she saw now, the cold opaque gray of lead—were as wintry as the day just past. She realized that if he chose to force her to do anything, anything at all, she would be hard put to successfully resist. She was already well acquainted with his strength, and he was, in addition, far bigger than she. The top of her head fell inches short of his chin, and with his broad shoulders and wide chest he dwarfed her far smaller frame. And when he had so nonchalantly stripped off his clothes right in front of her widening eyes, she had been provided with more evidence than she had cared to see of his whipcord muscularity.

Words were her strength, practically her only strength, and she wielded them frantically.

"Indeed, truly there has been a mistake. I know nothing of any letters, and as for Lord Archer—I believe he may be a friend of my aunt's. I have never met him."

For a moment he stared down at her, his eyes narrowing. He was so close that she could see the tiny lines radiating from the corners of his eyes; so close that she could almost count each whisker that made up the shadow darkening his lean cheeks; so close that she could smell on him the faint salty aroma of the sea.

For an instant, she thought with budding hope, he almost seemed to be considering her words. Then his mouth twisted sardonically.

"I'm too old a hand to be taken in by a glib tongue and a pair of big eyes, and so I warn you. Come, we'll deal better if you'll leave off the pretense. I'll give you one chance to hand over the letters voluntarily, and one chance only. Well?"

"I don't have any letters," Claire insisted.

His lips thinned. "Not the answer I want. Try again."

Claire hesitated, nonplussed. How to convince him? Lips compressing, she searched his face. The look in his eyes was one she had never before encountered in any man: It was guarded, but beneath the wariness there was a lurking—was it disdain? She knew her own beauty, knew its power. She'd been dealing with it, for good and ill (and it had largely been ill), since she was in leading strings. To a man, every male she had ever met had regarded her with admiration. No man had ever looked at her as this one was looking at her now: as if she were the object of his—contempt.

Trying to fathom the why of it made her head swim—or maybe it was her physical state that was to blame for the increasing light-headedness she felt. She was so cold she had passed beyond shivering, so wet there wasn't so much as an inch of dry skin remaining on her body, and so exhausted her legs felt as rubbery as green twigs. It required a real effort of will to stay alert, but she knew her survival might depend on her ability to respond to the opportunity of an instant. Puzzling this nightmare through, however, was beyond her.

"I don't have any letters! I don't! I swear to you I don't!" Claire felt hysteria start to bubble up inside her. "If I had them I would give them to you, believe me. Can't you see you've made a mistake?"

"Poppycock." His face was implacable. His fingers gripping her arm hurt. When she made an involuntary movement to free herself, they tightened still more.

"You're hurting me."

Her protest was instinctive. If she'd thought about it, she wouldn't have bothered making it. She would have assumed he wouldn't care.

His lips thinned. Then, to her surprise, his grip loosened just enough that it was no longer bruising her arm, although he still did not release her.

That one small act of consideration could not be said to hold very much significance. Still, it was a hopeful sign in a bleak situation. She had been beguiling men, purposefully and otherwise, from her cradle. It was, her sisters said, a gift that came naturally to her. Already it had occurred to her that she might use her gift to save her life. Unlike her previous captors, this Hugh seemed almost the gentleman in some ways. She would try to touch any deep-buried chivalry he might possess.

"The letters, Miss Towbridge."

Just as Claire opened her mouth to assure him once again that she didn't have his letters, did not, in fact, have the least notion as to what he was talking about, the name he had called her registered. Her eyes widened as she looked at him. There, she'd known it was a mistake! The whole terrifying ordeal was the result of a gigantic error.

She felt almost giddy with relief.

"There, you see. You have it wrong. Of course I have not got your letters. I am not Miss Towbridge. I am Lady Claire Lynes."

His eyes flickered. For a moment he seemed taken aback, and his gaze moved swiftly over her face. Then his jaw hardened.

"All right, you've run your length. I've no more patience with your lies. Disrobe."

Claire met his steely gaze with dawning dismay. He didn't believe her; it was quite clear.

"I *am* Lady Claire Lynes! I am! I promise you I am!"

Again she tried to pull free of his hold. Loosened though his grip was, it was still like trying to break free of a shackle. His fingers were long enough that they almost met around her arm, and strong enough that there was no dislodging them short of hitting them with a blunt instrument, which, unfortunately, she didn't possess at the moment.

Holding her fast, he made a rude sound that most eloquently expressed his opinion of her claim. His mouth tightened to a sneer.

"This is a mistake, don't you understand? I—"

"You're wasting your breath and my time," he broke in on her impatiently, giving her arm a little shake. "I want those letters, and I mean to do whatever I have to do to get them. If you don't hand them over immediately, I'll strip you naked and search your garments and then your person until I either find them or am utterly convinced they are elsewhere. And if I am so convinced, believe me, you are going to tell me exactly where they are."

Claire was suddenly outraged. She had nearly died a dozen times tonight, and all for a mistake. A mistake that this mush-for-brains lummox did not seem to have the wit even to consider might have been made. "They *are* elsewhere! Have you no ears? Do you not hear what I'm saying? Very well, I'll say it again: I am not the person you're seeking, and I know nothing of your letters!"

"Enough." His hold tightened again, not quite hurting her this time but allowing her to feel the hard strength of his fingers. "I have no intention of bandying words with you. You have a choice: You can either undress yourself or I will do it for you."

Unable to break free of his grip although she tried once more, Claire glared up at him, rendered speechless by the sheer futility of continuing to insist on something that he patently did not believe and she could think of no way to prove. Even her wedding rings were missing, she discovered as she looked for them as proof that at least she was a married woman and no miss at all. Stolen while she had been unconscious in the farmhouse, she guessed, or lost to the sea. She almost stamped her foot in frustration, but her poor abused appendages were so cold that she feared the action would be painful, and besides, the gesture was far too childish for the gravity of the situation or, indeed, for a woman of her years.

If he could only be convinced that he had made a mistake, she would surely be allowed to go free. The problem lay in convincing him.

Taking a deep breath, Claire tried again, speaking forcefully, as she might to someone who was either hard of hearing or a trifle slow-witted, which, she considered, seemed to be the problem in this case. "You've made a mistake, I tell you: I am not 'Miss Towbridge.' I am Lady Claire Lynes."

"Of the Lynes family of Sussex, I presume?" His voice was silky. The silkiness should, perhaps, have warned her.

It didn't. Encouraged, Claire nodded eagerly. It seemed she was getting through to him at last.

"You are claiming to be a relative of the Duke of Richmond, in fact, rather than a grasping tart who has been under the protection of Lord Archer—a man old enough to be your grandfather—for nigh on a year?" His voice was satirical. "That dog won't hunt, my girl. I should inform you that I have some acquaintance with the Lynes family—and you have approximately one minute to start taking off your clothes."

He nodded significantly at a small, brass-cased clock affixed to a shelf above the table.

Claire gasped with indignation. "Are you calling me a—a lightskirt, you witless oaf?"

His eyes narrowed at her. "I'm calling you a lying jade. And by the by, you have approximately forty seconds left."

Claire opened her mouth to give voice to a heated reply, looked into his face, saw the harsh implacability there, closed her mouth, and silently seethed. She had not a prayer of convincing him, she realized. Still, she tried one more time.

"I am Lady Claire Lynes, whether you choose to believe me or not."

There was suppressed fury in her tone and in the look she gave him. Inside, she was conscious of the increased thundering of her heart as she cobbled together the rudiments of a plan.

His lips tightened purposefully.

"Very well," Claire added in some haste, as dire action on his part seemed imminent. Capitulation was her best choice, she realized. Capitulation of a sort, that is. "Since there is no help for it, I will do as you ask. Please let go of my arm."

"Wise choice." His hand dropped from her arm.

Claire was able to step away from him. Unnoticed (she hoped), she took a deep, steadying breath. She was shaky, sick to her stomach, and prey to a throbbing headache, none of which could be allowed to matter. One of those opportunities of an instant had presented itself, and she had to think how best to seize it.

Instinctively raising a hand to her head in an effort to ease its throbbing, Claire touched the seeming source and found, behind her ear, a bump the size of an egg. It was amazingly tender, she discovered as she probed it. Of course, she had been hit over the head. In light of all that had happened since, she had almost forgotten.

"Head hurt?"

There was a flicker in the gray eyes that almost looked like—compunction. Of course, he—or one of his henchmen—was doubtless responsible for the blow. It was Hugh who had surprised her on the beach, she was almost sure. His tall, well-set form was difficult to mistake. James, then, or someone she hadn't seen, must have hit her from behind.

But Hugh bore the responsibility.

"A little," she said, frowning at him.

"I'm not surprised."

This was said rather dryly, but without the slightest degree of regret that she could detect. Any compunction—if, indeed, she had not been mistaken about that—he might briefly have felt was now notorious for its absence. There was no longer even a shadow of remorse in either his voice or his expression. Which was, of course, totally in keeping with the kind of brute who would visit such violence on a lady.

As she considered just how she had been struck down from behind, her anger grew hotter. Claire welcomed the building blaze as a final antidote to her fear.

He slanted a significant glance at the clock.

"Your time is up."

It was on the tip of her tongue to once again insist that he was making a mistake. But such a protestation would not move him where the others had failed, and might, indeed, provoke him to violence. Better to take the risk of implementing her plan. She had little to lose if it failed.

She lifted her chin and looked him in the eye.

"Please turn your back." Cold dignity laced the words.

He laughed, and crossed his arms over his chest. His intention to do no such thing could not have been more clear if he'd shouted a declaration. Standing there watching her with his head cocked and his bare feet braced apart, he looked as unrepentantly villainous as a pirate.

"You would be far more believable in your role of outraged innocent had you not already offered yourself to me," he said in a drawling fashion that set Claire's teeth on edge. "You did say you would give me 'anything'—from which I presumed you were offering to share your admittedly delectable charms with me, although you may certainly correct me if I got that wrong—if I let you go, did you not?"

If he was trying to embarrass her, he would not succeed. Claire scorned to reveal or even feel the smallest degree of shame. The offer had been made in desperate fear for her life, and if such an act was the price she had to pay to stay alive, she was prepared to pay it. Since her wedding, she had become thoroughly familiar with intimate congress between a man and a woman, and it no longer held any power to terrify or even move her. Quite simply, it was unpleasant but quickly over—a small trade for one's life. One closed one's eyes and tolerated the man's beastliness for the few minutes it took until his business was done. If one was left, in the aftermath, feeling rather like a chamber pot, well, such was a woman's lot in life. In this situation in particular, she could not afford to regard the act as anything more or less than a bargaining chip—practically the only bargaining chip she possessed.

"I certainly do not deny that I am prepared to do whatever I must to survive, as any sane person would. Under the circumstances, though, I no longer feel that I have any need to make such a sacrifice: I tell you, you have mistaken me for someone else."

He grunted derisively. "You've wasted enough of my time. Come here."

He reached for her. Eluding his hands, Claire took a quick step backward.

"Keep your hands off me," she said with cold hauteur. "I'll do it."

Before he could reach for her again, she lifted her

arms, curving them behind her head to reach for the first of the two dozen tiny jet buttons that secured her frock from its neck to just below its waist. If she'd had any intention of obeying him, undressing herself would have been most difficult. The tight-bodiced, slim-skirted traveling gown she was wearing, like the majority of her raiment, had been designed to be put on and off with the help of a maid.

But then, she had no intention whatsoever of obeying him.

Defiantly she held his gaze as she wrestled the first button free. Her fingers were clumsy with cold as she set about separating the edges of the clammy fabric.

Folding his arms over his chest once more, Hugh watched with an expression that was impossible to decipher as she slowly worked her way down the row. Fortunately, he didn't seem to notice that she was also sidling backward at the same time. Or perhaps he put her backward progress down to the unceasing motion of the ship. The swaying lantern overhead and the increased creaking of the hull were ample evidence of the power of the swells; they were certainly enough to make anyone unsteady on her feet.

In any case, the scoundrel would soon discover that Claire Banning, for that was how she still thought of herself in her secret heart of hearts even so many months after her marriage, was not so easily cowed into submission. Never, until this nightmarish situation had caught her up in its toils, had she thought to be grateful for having been reared under such difficult conditions as she had experienced. But suddenly she was. If nothing else, during the course of her fearsome childhood she had learned how to survive.

Claire freed another button and felt her bodice loosen the required amount. Deliberately she shrugged, letting the neckline droop just enough to reveal the creamy tops of her shoulders and the pulsing hollow at the base of her neck. His gaze flicked down from her face to observe the distraction she had presented for him, just as she had intended. While he looked, she dropped her arms and shifted position so that she was now unbuttoning from the waist up—and she took another, slightly longer step backward.

"You might as well end this farce now, for I am not Miss Towbridge, and I have no letters. I swear it," she said, more as another distraction than because she expected the words to finally penetrate his thick skull.

"Umm." It was an absent sound, as if he was not really attending, which, clearly, he was not. His gaze was fixed on her breasts, molded to an embarrassing degree by the wet fabric as her posture caused her back to arch. There was no mistaking the gleam of very male awareness that had sprung to life in his eyes. Claire had seen that look in the eyes of enough men to have no doubt what it signified: He desired her.

In that instant, as she registered the raw sexuality in his gaze, she remembered too how what had begun as a briskly impersonal search of her person had deteriorated, by its end, into a shamefully intimate groping that he had, for whatever reason, abruptly terminated when his hands had begun to linger on her breasts. Perhaps her only bargaining chip had even more worth than she had previously realized: From the look in his eyes, his physical appetites were strong, and so was his desire for her.

A frisson of apprehension raced down her spine as

she contemplated allowing this hard-eyed stranger to slake that appetite with her body. She had only ever had intimate congress with her husband, although, she imagined, there would likely prove to be very little difference. Between the sheets men were probably much the same. Turning over in her mind the idea of lying with this man, she swallowed convulsively—and realized that what she felt wasn't only fear. It was fear mixed with—and she was ashamed to recognize it, or admit it even to herself—a kind of shivery sexual awareness of her own.

David had told her from the beginning that ladies had no liking for the marriage act, and she had never contradicted him. By about the third time he had lain with her, she had realized that he was exactly right. The first, shameful stirrings she had felt when her new husband had come to her in their marriage bed had been born of ignorance and anticipation and had been sadly dashed. Those seedling feelings remained her guilty secret, never to be revealed to anyone. Fortunately, they had quickly withered away.

But, most inexplicably and embarrassingly, she had felt them again when this criminal had run his hard hands over her body. By the time he had flattened his palms over her breasts, the secret tingling that had begun to quiver along her nerve endings in the wake of his hands had spread to her loins, where it had taken firm root. It was as if her body, long dormant, had been awakened by his touch, to yearn once more for something she couldn't quite define.

Men got some sort of bestial satisfaction from intimate congress. Women, if they were fortunate (and she had not been, and would probably not be, given the fact that David had some months since stopped coming to her bed), got babies.

Luckily, though, she wasn't going to be in this man's power long enough to have to deal with her wayward body's embarrassing quickening. At least, not if her plan worked as she hoped.

Her words seemed to register with him then, most belatedly, because suddenly he frowned and his gaze rose to meet hers. The sexual glint was gone, vanished as if it had never been. In its place was pure unyielding flint. But hide it though he might, there was no mistaking what she'd seen.

"Why don't I believe you, I wonder?" He smiled at her, but it was not a nice smile. "You are really playing your role very well, a practiced courtesan at her seductive best, aping the blushing innocent you are not quite amazingly, but unfortunately a protracted unveiling is wasted on me. It will win you no quarter. I will have those letters, and quickly, if you value your gown."

Even as this less than subtle threat to rip off her dress if she did not hurry sank in, the small of her back bumped up against the edge of the table, which had been her goal all along. Claire abandoned the buttons to stretch a stealthy hand along the smooth surface of the wood, groping for that which she sought.

"I must say, it's a great pity that you're such a fool," she said dispassionately as her fingers closed around her prize. Bringing the pistol he had very carelessly left lying on the table up behind her back, she smiled at him in turn as she positioned it in her hand. "Were you not, I wouldn't be forced to use this."

With those words she whipped the pistol into view, holding it at waist level and pointing it straight at him.

## ❧ 8 ❧

...........................................

"**W**hat the devil . . . ?"

For a moment Hugh simply stared thunderstruck at his pistol, now held steady by both her hands wrapped a little convulsively around the grip. Then, narrowing dangerously, his gaze rose to her face. Those gray eyes were cold lead no longer. Instead they shone like molten silver as the lamplight touched them. Claire's heart beat faster as she realized how angry he was.

Well, she was angry too.

"Don't move," she warned. "And get your hands up."

Growing up in a household headed by a father who had no love for his offspring and was, by nature, vicious and corrupt, and who, moreover, was frequently visited by like-minded guests, she had been forced to defend her honor on many occasions, with whatever weapon came to hand, and thus was no stranger to pistols. Those friends had considered it almost a sport to try to bed the Earl of Wickham's beauteous middle daughter. That she had managed to save her virginity for her wedding night was a testament to her resourcefulness when cornered.

It was also rather ironic, when she thought about it. Which she definitely did not, at the moment, have leisure to do.

"You hell-born vixen," he said, drawing out the words. His hands rose, palms out, until they were above his shoulders, but other than that he didn't move, and she was grateful for that.

"An intelligent man would undoubtedly realize that, under the circumstances, calling me offensive names isn't very wise," she observed pensively. "I don't particularly wish to shoot you, but I will if I must. Make no mistake about that."

"So much for your protestations of innocence, hmm? At last we get down to the truth. Since you have me at your mercy now, instead of the other way around, you might at least satisfy my curiosity and tell me where the letters are hidden."

Claire's frowned in exasperation. "I've been telling you the truth, you brainless lout: I am Lady Claire Lynes, and I know nothing of your letters. But whether you choose to believe me or not no longer matters. As you so rightly point out, I now hold the upper hand, and you will do as I say. And let me warn you: If you make any sudden moves, I will shoot you dead."

The pistol pointed unwaveringly at his chest. Claire was proud of the steadiness of her hands.

He smiled then. Claire misliked that smile.

"You may be sure that your smallest wish has become my command, my bloodthirsty beauty. But before you dispatch me, I would at least know how you discovered the letters' existence. Was it pillow talk from Lord Archer, perhaps, or did someone set you on to find them?"

Claire glared at him. "Your idiocy passes all bounds. And keep your hands up."

This sharp-voiced reminder came as his hands began to lower. She remembered the knife he had tucked into the waistband of his breeches all too clearly. No doubt he remembered it too.

"Turn your back. And keep your hands where I can see them."

His brows rose. "Are you contemplating shooting me in the back? It seems a little cowardly."

Claire scowled at him. "Turn around."

To her relief, he turned around. For the briefest moment, she looked him over without moving. His hair was drying now; it still gleamed as shiny black as a seal's pelt, but the thick strands, which reached almost to his shoulders, were beginning to wave quite disarmingly. His shoulders looked tense, as if he might indeed fear that she would pull the trigger at any moment. A picture of them unclothed leaped unbidden into her mind: They were bronzed, with satiny-looking skin covering flexing muscles. Below them his back had tapered in a vee to his waist, and then his buttocks had flared, small and round and looking as though they would be hard to the touch. But she had not meant to see him naked; indeed, she had quickly closed her eyes.

She refused to let such indecent images haunt her now. The present, and him in the present, were more than enough to deal with.

His white shirt hung loose from his breeches; it covered him to the tops of his thighs. *But she well remembered the black wedge of hair on his chest, the hard muscles of his abdomen, and the surprising size of that most private part of him.*

Oh, Lord, she had not meant to remember that. Had not meant to notice it. Had not meant to see it. Why, oh why, was it fixed in her mind?

Determinedly she banished it.

Braced apart, his legs were long and strong-looking. *The muscles of his thighs had been thick and powerful.* Below his breeches, she could see the dark hair that roughened calves sculpted of muscle. *His legs had been hairy all over, including his thighs.*

Stop it, she told herself fiercely. She would not remember how he had looked without his clothes. For a lady to carry images like that around in her mind was shameful. Worse, it was—debauched.

She would not allow herself to be interested in such things. Rather, she was *not* interested in such things.

She was not.

And, if she were to survive this encounter, she must get on with what she had started out to do.

Taking a deep breath, Claire focused on the man in front of her. The clothed and real man in front of her. His back faced her squarely, so that he was unable to see what she was doing. And thank goodness for that, she thought. At least she did not have to worry about him guessing any of her unseemly thoughts from the expression on her face.

Keeping a wary eye out for any sudden moves, Claire stepped up right behind him. At such close quarters his size was even more intimidating. She took in at a glance the daunting width of his back, the brawny strength of his forearms clearly revealed as the unfastened cuffs of his shirt fell away from his wrists, the number of inches he towered over her, and swallowed. If he whirled on her, all would be lost. Then she mentally shook her head.

No, if he whirled on her she would do just as she had threatened: shoot him dead.

Wouldn't she?

Yes, she would.

"Don't move," she warned again, hoping that he couldn't tell from her voice how suddenly dry her mouth was.

"I wouldn't dream of it."

Before her increasingly jumpy nerves could get the better of her, Claire transferred the pistol to one hand and, with the other, reached beneath his shirt, sliding her fingers around his waist until they found the cool silver hilt of his knife. There was a bruise the approximate size and shape of a large cucumber extending across the left side of his rib cage, she remembered. Dark purple with yellowing edges, it had looked painful. Her touch was instinctively gentle as her hand slid over where she knew it to be. Which was ridiculous, she told herself angrily. She was prepared to shoot the man, yet she didn't want to hurt him?

Well, she tried to reconcile the dichotomy, she would only shoot him if she must.

Despite everything, she could not help but register the warm resilience of his skin, the firmness of the muscles girding his middle, the solid jut of his hipbones, and, as her hand reached his stomach, the hard flatness of his belly and the crisp silk of the line of hair that she knew, from her earlier observation, bisected it.

To widen into an impressively luxuriant nest for that equally impressive male part.

With the best will in the world for it not to happen, that thought popped into her mind again. Dear Lord, why couldn't she get the vivid image of Hugh in all his naked glory out of her head? Was she, as she had in the past occasionally feared, totally depraved?

Thoroughly flustered now, Claire snatched the knife from its resting place and withdrew her hand from beneath his shirt. She then withdrew her entire person from his vicinity, retreating rapidly until her back was against the wall.

She was not going to think about him naked ever again.

His back was still turned to her, thank goodness. She took a moment just to breathe as she firmly closed her mind to the memory. Such a shocking image was bound to make an impression by its very nature, she reassured herself. That she remembered it so vividly did not mean that she was depraved. If her heart was racing, it was because of embarrassment at having seen so much. If she was feeling warm, it was because the cabin was stuffy.

There was no other reason.

The table was now at her left; still breathing deeply, Claire put the knife on it, then returned both hands to the pistol grip.

To her relief, she saw that her hands were steady.

"You may turn around."

Her voice was gruff. He could have no idea of the mortifying route her mind had just traveled, of course. Still, as he did as she bade him she was conscious of the hot lick of embarrassment.

"Behold me relieved to find myself still among the living."

His gaze touched on the pistol, then rose to her face. Thank goodness she was too cold to blush, was her first thought as their eyes met. Then, to her horror, Claire got the impression that he was secretly amused. Had he somehow guessed what had been going through her mind? No. It was not possible.

She would not even consider the possibility. But she felt her cheeks start to warm despite the fact that she was soaking wet and thoroughly chilled.

"I confess, you had me all atwitter: When your hand slid beneath my shirt, I was expecting to find myself, if not murdered, then at the very least ravished."

Incredibly, he seemed to be teasing her, and about the very subject that she most preferred not to allow into her mind. The infuriating thought that he could jest about such a thing had the welcome effect of steadying her nerves. She gave him a long, level look, and her embarrassment disappeared.

"If I were you, I'd keep a civil tongue in my head, sirrah. I'm still trying to decide what to do with you, and your insolence could just tip the balance."

He laughed. A sudden twinkle warmed his eyes, and the ends of his mouth turned up in a crooked smile. He looked quite engaging, she thought with some surprise, then quickly amended that to: quite engaging for a villainous, murderous rogue.

"You do find yourself on the horns of a dilemma, do you not?" he asked, sounding almost sympathetic.

She, however, was not fooled. He could try to turn her up sweet until the English Channel parted for Napoleon; she had tried much the same thing on him, after all. But it hadn't worked on him—and it certainly wasn't going to work on her. Her hands tightened around the pistol grip, and she watched him warily as he continued.

"You must be asking yourself: What do I do now? You could shoot me, of course, but if you do, what then?

You will still be in this cabin, on this ship, which is now some way out from land. For the sake of argument, though, let's suppose you shoot me and then stay in the cabin until the ship docks. You must then unbar the door, emerge, get off the ship, and somehow find your contact. But first there will be James to deal with. Even if he does not hear the gunshot with which you dispatch me—and he has ears like a lynx—he will have figured out that there is something badly amiss long before you unbar the door and will be waiting outside like an angry bear defending its cub, if he does not find some means of breaking it down beforehand. He'll be extremely wroth with you for having done away with me, I assure you, and is quite prone to violence even in the normal way of things, as you can probably tell from the bump on your head. If by some miracle you should succeed in getting by James, then you must still get past Captain Dorsey and his crew. And then, of course, you are an Englishwoman in France, which can be counted on to make you less than popular with the general run of its citizenry. And finally, if you surmount all those barriers, you must still find some way to get in touch with your contact, who has, by now, most likely thoroughly lost track of you."

Their gazes met and held. Hugh's assumption that she had some kind of contact in France aside, everything he said was true, Claire realized with growing dismay. If she killed him—which in any case she truly didn't wish to do—she would find herself no better off, and possibly in far worse case, than she was at present. Remembering the way the sailors had slobbered over her, she swallowed.

Whatever this man's faults—and they were many and varied—at least he didn't seem bent on rape.

"You make several excellent points," she said, keeping her voice cool even as she thought furiously. "All of which I will bear in mind, you may be sure. Keeping you alive does seem to be the smarter choice, at least just at present, as long as you make it easy for me to do so."

A knock sounded on the door then, startling them both and causing them to glance toward the barred portal as one. The sound was soft, almost furtive.

"That will be James," Hugh said, his gaze swinging back around to her, and smiled.

Claire felt panic rise like gorge in her throat. Her heart thumped. Her breathing quickened. Nervously she wet her lips, which still tasted faintly of ale.

"Master Hugh!"

The knock sounded again, a little more urgently this time. Hugh's eyebrows rose at her in silent question. He now looked like he was almost enjoying himself, the scoundrel.

She scowled at him.

"If you wish to remain alive, you will do precisely as I tell you," she said in a fierce whisper, cobbling together a plan even as she spoke. "We will walk to the door, you in front of me, and you will open it. Without admitting your man to the cabin, you will tell him that you have recollected an urgent circumstance that requires the ship to put back to shore. To England's shore, mind. He will then convey your order to the captain, while you and I remain here. When we dock, you will escort me off this ship. And I warn you: This pistol will be aimed at your heart the entire time. Pulling the trigger will not cost me so much as a moment's sleep."

His smile widened, and he nodded at her with apparent approval, which had the paradoxical effect of making Claire warier than before.

"A good plan. I make you my compliments. But there is one circumstance that you have failed to take into consideration: This is not my ship. I am not on such terms with the ship's company as to give an order like that and see it obeyed. Please take note of the bolted door; clearly you must see that it denotes a certain lack of trust of the crew's intentions toward me and my party on my part. We are bound for France, and to France, I very much fear, we will go."

Claire narrowed her eyes at him. It was a trick—she was almost certain.

"They will do as you say."

Her voice was coldly positive, but Claire took a sneaking glance at the door. As he'd said, it was bolted shut. Would the crew really not obey his orders? He'd given them freely enough until now, she recollected, and they'd been carried out with alacrity, as far as she could tell. Still, as he said, he was not the ship's captain. . . .

"Master Hugh!"

The call, with its accompanying knock, were both appreciably louder. An exasperated mutter followed, the tone of which was quite clear even though she couldn't decipher the words.

"Answer," she hissed, feeling rather like a cat on a hot roof: she didn't know which way to jump. No matter which way she landed, she was quite likely to end up burned.

"Keep your britches on, James. I'm coming," he called. His voice dropped confidentially as he added to Claire, "The crew will obey me only so far as it suits them, and that's the truth. Be assured that they would not mourn overmuch should you pull that trigger and thus rid the world of me. You might mourn, however, in the end. For you would then find yourself at their mercy." He shrugged with seeming nonchalance. "But then again, a woman with your—experience, for want of a better term—with men might find lying with the entire crew not beyond your powers if it will get you off the ship alive. Not that I think it will, mind."

"I'd be careful with my insults, were I facing the business end of this pistol, scoundrel," she replied sternly.

"Basically, as I see it, you have a choice: You can deal with me, or you can deal with the ship's crew," he continued, and smiled at her seraphically. "The choice is up to you."

## ❧ 9 ❧

................................

"**A**h, brandy," Hugh said, taking the bottle and glass out of James's hand with real appreciation. If his judgment of the *Nadine*'s company was on target, this would be fine French brandy reserved from a cargo recently smuggled to England.

"What's to do?" Still standing in the dark corridor, James frowned at him questioningly as Hugh continued to block the partly open doorway with his person. Slightly behind Hugh and to his right, his all-too-captivating captive held his own pistol on him just out of James's sight, her body swaying with the motion of the ship and her gaze fixed on him with the fierceness of an eagle's. The question teased at him: Would she actually pull the trigger, if pushed to it?

It would be interesting to find out.

"I'm engaged in interrogating the prisoner," he said, narrowing his eyes at James. "I don't need you right now."

"But . . ." James protested before he caught the look on Hugh's face. "Oh. You don't need me right now."

"That's right."

A slender, bare foot nudged Hugh's leg meaningfully. She was being careful, he realized, not to get too close, although her one-legged prod almost caused her to overbalance. His lip curled as he watched her sideways stagger and quick recovery out of the corner of his eye. The not-so-subtle reminder of what she had once again, in urgent whispers as she'd followed him to the door, instructed him to say was unnecessary, however. He remembered to the letter.

"I need you to convey a message for me to Captain Dorsey," he said to James. "Tell him that an unforeseen circumstance has arisen, and I require him to turn back to England. I will then be removing the prisoner from the ship."

James's eyes widened. For a moment he stared at Hugh without speaking. Then he grimaced and rolled his eyes, having clearly gotten the message that he was to do no such thing.

"Very well, Master Hugh. I'll tell the captain."

James's voice was slightly wooden. His disapproval of what he would term "such goings-on" was plain on his face. Ah, well, his response would, Hugh hoped, be convincing enough to one who could not see his expression.

"Go to it, then." Hugh closed the door, but not before James shook his head reprovingly at him.

"Very good," his captive said as Hugh glanced at her. Then, "Shoot the bolt."

"I'd be glad to, but as you see I'm slightly encumbered."

He held up the bottle of brandy with the single glass James had provided turned upside down on top of it.

"I'll hold it."

Watching him as though she expected him to jump

her at any moment, she unwrapped her left hand from its death grip on the pistol and reached toward him. Smiling faintly, he handed over the bottle and turned back to bolt the door. That done, he glanced at her.

"What now, oh powerful one?"

She chewed her lower lip, looking indecisive and also, Hugh decided unwillingly, quite delectable. Her brow was furrowed; her golden eyes were clouded with worry. Her drying hair was as black as soot and, now free of whatever pins might once have confined it, waved luxuriantly over her shoulders and down her back almost to her waist. Every delectable curve and hollow of her body was outlined faithfully by her soaked dress. Her nipples still poked pertly against the wet wool that clung to her breasts.

Just looking at them—at her—made his loins tighten. Gad, she was a beauty! And young—she could not be as young as she appeared. It was on the tip of his tongue to ask her age, but he stopped himself. He didn't really want to know—and she would probably lie anyway, just like she lied about everything else. Deliberately he thought of Lord Archer. No doubt the doddering old fool had been in alt to find such a nonpareil in his bed. How the man had allowed himself to be relieved of papers vital to his country's security by a tart was readily explained now that Hugh had taken the full measure of the tart in question. The old man almost had to be forgiven for the lapse. It would take a bloodless eunuch to resist an armful like this chit—or, he added hastily, a man with his own iron will.

He hoped.

"I want you to turn that chair to face the wall and sit down."

Her voice was coolly authoritative. It was obvious that she enjoyed having the upper hand. Fortunately, the image of poor hoodwinked Archer had cleared Hugh's mind. He himself at least had the advantage of knowing her for the treacherous vixen she was, Hugh thought, moving in the direction she indicated, and never mind what she looked like. Had he not known—and this was a thought he didn't much like, and certainly didn't mean to dwell on—he might well have made as big a fool of himself over her as Archer had done.

But forewarned was forearmed, as they said.

She stood watching him from the other side of the table as he obediently turned the chair around and took a seat facing the wall. His knife—she had placed it on the table earlier after relieving him of it in one of the more memorable moments he had experienced lately—was in her hand, obviously to keep it out of his reach. She was holding it somewhat awkwardly, as if unable to think of what to do with it. Her other hand was wrapped around the pistol grip. Held like that, the weapon looked too heavy for her. She seemed to be having trouble keeping it level. Fleetingly he hoped she would not pull the trigger by accident, then dismissed the possibility from his mind as something he couldn't control and thus couldn't worry about.

His glance shifted to the table. She had set the brandy down in the spot where his knife had rested moments before. The amber liquid sloshed invitingly against the thick glass bottle as the ship rocked back and forth like a baby's cradle. Its color as the lamplight struck it reminded him of her eyes: warmly golden and rich with the promise of all manner of sensory delights.

Vis-à-vis sensory delights, the hand that had slid

around his waist in search of his knife was small and cold; it should not have awakened in him an urgent desire to wrap his fingers around it and lead it in a more intimate direction—but it had.

"You may pour me a splash of brandy."

Her command was a welcome interruption from a sudden surge of erotic images that, try as he might, he could not banish. Registering what she had actually said took a second or two, but when he did Hugh's brows rose. Ladies did not drink brandy—but of course, she was no lady. It was an indication of how well she played the part that he was even momentarily surprised when she stepped out of her assumed role.

"Just a splash?" he asked.

If there was the slightest satirical edge to his voice, it was directed at himself because, however improbable he would previously have thought it, he was proving to be as vulnerable as the next man to the distracting effect of a beautiful woman.

"My throat is dry." There was a certain defensiveness to her tone.

"If so, it must be just about the only part of you that is." He kept his voice deliberately light as he unstoppered the bottle and poured the requested amount into the glass. Glancing up, he encountered the black hole of the pistol's mouth regarding him unblinkingly. Despite the fact that she was a young and beautiful woman, with a sweetly feminine air she seemed able to project and then drop at will, he would be a fool to doubt that she would shoot him if and when it suited her. "There are clothes you can use in the saddlebags in that cupboard. No female garments, I'm afraid, but at least the things are dry."

He indicated the bulkhead with a nod as he pushed the glass toward her. She glanced in that direction, the merest slanting away of her eyes before her gaze darted back to fix on him with suspicion. That she found the notion of getting out of her sodden garments appealing was clear from her expression.

Persuading her to remove her garments voluntarily suited his purpose much better than forcing her to strip. Wasn't there some saying about catching more flies with honey . . . ?

"There are wool stockings," he said by way of tempting her. "As well as a shirt and breeches. And, I believe, a towel."

The items mentioned all belonged to James, who had been much more careful of his clothes during their journey than Hugh had been. About all he himself had left that was clean and dry was, if he was lucky, a change of linen.

"I should think you'd want me to be uncomfortable."

As she spoke she picked up the brandy he had poured for her. For a moment she swirled it around in the glass, looking at it as if wondering if it had been doctored in some nefarious way. Then she raised it to her nose, sniffed suspiciously, and drank.

Seconds later, she coughed, grimaced, and gave a delicate little burp. Clapping a hand to her mouth, her eyes flew to his face. Her look of embarrassment was, he judged, very well done indeed.

"Not particularly," he said, refusing to admit even to himself that he'd found her reaction to the brandy charming. "What I want from you are the letters you stole from Lord Archer, along with the name of whoever set you on to do it, the name of the man you were to hand the letters over to once you reached France, and the names of anyone else who helped you along the way. Once you give them to me, I'll be pleased to speed you on your way."

If he was not being precisely truthful about that last part, at least she had no way of knowing it.

She eyed him coldly. "Clearly you're sadly lacking in either wits or the ability to hear. I repeat: I know nothing of your letters, or any of the rest of it." Then, in a warning tone, she added, "Don't get up, or make any sudden moves."

"I think we've already established that I won't."

His voice was dry. He hadn't expected her to give him what he needed just for the asking, so her reply came as no surprise. Still, that she should continue the charade even now that, to all intents and purposes, she held the whip hand pricked at him like a tiny thorn embedded deep in a thick wool stocking.

Could she be telling the truth? For the merest instant, the possibility entered his head. He considered it, and ran aground on the sheer improbability of any woman besides the one he'd been sent to intercept being found on that particular remote beach in that barely populated area of Sussex Downs in the middle of that particular night.

The chances were so slim as to be not even worth calculating. But the fact that the notion had entered his head at all—now, that was disturbing. She was dangerous indeed if even he, who absolutely knew her for what she was, was at risk of falling victim to her lies.

Lady Claire Lynes, indeed. That was overreaching by half. But to choose that particular identity as her nom de guerre, so to speak—what did that signify? It must signify something. Like her presence on the beach, there was the tiniest possibility that her choice of a false identity might be mere coincidence, but he didn't think so.

He was not a big believer in coincidence.

He looked at her thoughtfully, trying to work out the whole sorry mess in his mind. There were answers to his questions, and she had them. The key to getting what he wanted was to find out what she wanted, he mused, and dangle it as bait.

She was backing away from him toward the bulkhead, keeping her eyes—and the pistol—trained on him until she passed from his line of sight. Thoughtfully, then, Hugh surveyed the scene directly in front of his nose: the scarred paneling, softened to a surprisingly mellow hue by the shifting lamplight; three-quarters of the table, which was bare except for the brandy bottle and the glass she had drained; the round-faced clock in its shiny brass casing, bolted securely to the shelf above the table.

It was nigh on three in the morning, he registered as he looked at the clock and listened to its ticking along with the sound of the cupboard being opened behind him. A goodly number of hours remained until they reached their destination, he judged, even as a soft thump and a subsequent rustling told him she had found the saddlebags packed with gear. Then, from her, there was silence. Continuously creaking timbers and the rhythmic smack of waves against the hull joined with other background noises, making it difficult to guess what she was up to by listening alone.

"Don't look around."

This came as his head instinctively swung around to track her whereabouts.

"Why not?" Pseudo-innocent as soon as he realized that she was on the verge of changing, and totally unable to resist the impulse to tease her just a little despite everything he knew about her, he craned his neck as if to get a good view. Standing as she was just in front of the bunk now, with the cupboard door closed again and a fistful of James's clothes in hand, she met his gaze like a startled deer. Then she glared at him.

"Because I said so," she snapped, pointing the pistol at him menacingly.

"Ah, an excellent reason indeed."

A glance from the clothes to her face to the pistol, and, well satisfied, he turned back to stare at the wall.

Smiling to himself, careful not to let her see, he settled back in his uncomfortable chair, his gaze apparently fixed firmly on the wall in front of him, and did his best to ignore his ribs' retaliation for his less than judicious move. The brandy waited on the table near his elbow. He reached for the bottle and glass, congratulating himself as he did so on his cleverness in recognizing that there was more than one way to skin this particular cat.

"What are you doing?" She sounded almost panicked as he moved again.

"I thought I would pour myself some brandy. Have you any objection?"

He deliberately didn't look around at her. He didn't want to alarm her—not when things were going so nearly his way.

She made a sound that he took for permission to drink. Pouring himself a glass, he took a mouthful, savoring the brandy's spicy scent and the full-bodied strength of the liquid on his tongue with real appreciation. He felt even greater appreciation for the clock's shiny brass surface, he mused as he swallowed. It showed him her reflection as clearly as a mirror, only in miniature and tinted a warm golden hue.

A moment later, he watched with interest as, with both hands twisted up behind her back, she struggled to undo the buttons that still remained to be unfastened on her gown. She had already freed the ones that were easy to reach and was having to make quite a stretch. Looking beyond her, he located his pistol, lying a quick grab away from her on the bunk. The knife was beside it, as were James's clothes in a haphazard bundle. If he'd felt the need, he was confident he could have gotten to her before she could grab either weapon.

But then, the hand he'd been dealt was promising, and besides, if he moved he would miss the delectable prospect of watching as she stripped herself naked before his wary but still appreciative eyes.

## ❧ 10 ❧

......................................

When Claire finally got the last button undone, she sighed with relief. With a quick glance at Hugh, whose head was tilted slightly back as he tipped brandy down his throat but who still sat in the chair as she had ordered with his back stolidly turned, she freed her arms from the wet kerseymere and then, with another lightning glance at Hugh, pushed the frock down her body and stepped out of it.

The ship heeled, the movement more noticeable than anything that had gone before. Her stomach heeled with it, threatening all manner of dire consequences if the motion continued unabated. Helpless to prevent it, she tottered sideways before fetching up against the bunk and regaining her balance, then swallowed twice in quick succession in an attempt to quell her increasingly rebellious stomach. Except for the rising nausea that she was determined to ignore, she could not help but regard the sudden sharp rocking as a possibly hopeful sign. Was her ruse working? Was the ship indeed turning around?

"How will we know if your orders are being carried out?"

It occurred to her that, sealed off from the sight of the sky and the sea and all natural signs as they were, it was impossible to be sure which way the ship was heading.

"Your orders, you mean?" There was a slightly ironic note to his voice.

"All right, my orders. How will we know if the ship is turning back to England?"

"Doubtless we'll find out when we disembark."

Claire made an irritated sound under her breath. He was being deliberately unhelpful, she knew.

"Before that."

He shrugged a little. "When James returns—and he will return—you are certainly welcome to ask him."

Claire glowered at him—of course, with his back turned, he couldn't see—then gave it up. Whether they were turning around or whether they weren't, there was nothing more she could do about it at present. She might as well concentrate on getting herself warm and dry.

Ironically enough, now that she was free of her soaked dress she was suddenly freezing. Goose bumps raced up and down her bare arms and shivers once again shook her. If she had been forced to wear the drenched garments much longer, she might have found herself victim to an inflammation of the lungs or some other such serious ailment, she reflected. Which, of course, would be a problem only if she got out of this nightmare alive.

"You know, I've been thinking: Perhaps we can strike a bargain, you and I," Hugh said out of nowhere, causing her to jump. Her gaze flew to him. Thank goodness, he didn't appear to have moved. Wearing nothing but her corset and thin shift topped by a single sodden muslin petticoat, she was next door to naked. She'd been struggling with the strings of her corset, which, wet, had worked themselves into a maddening knot, and in her consternation at the unexpected interruption she had lost the end she'd been tugging at.

"What are you talking about?" she asked crossly, keeping her gaze fixed on him this time as she returned to her battle with the recalcitrant corset strings.

"I'm assuming you're being paid for the letters. Instead of betraying your country—you are aware that's what you're doing, aren't you?—why not let me buy them from you? I'm prepared to match any offer that's been made to you."

Having finally gotten the knot untangled, Claire was wriggling out of the corset when exactly what he was accusing her of struck her.

"You think I'm a traitor?" she gasped, as the corset joined her gown at her feet. "That's a horrible thing to say!"

"It's a horrible thing to do." His voice was matter-of-fact. She couldn't read his expression, but she realized from his tone that he truly believed what he was saying. Brows snapping together, she glared at the back of his head.

"You're as thick as a plank, aren't you?" she said with disgust. "Will nothing convince you that I'm not who you think I am? Let me explain the situation to you one more time: You have made a mistake. A mistake, understand? If you had the sense God granted a flea, you'd let me go and start looking for the real Miss Towbridge. She has your letters, you lummox, and I am not she!"

"Suppose I offered to double what you're being paid?"

Claire stared disbelievingly at him. The thought of

hurling something at his thick-skulled head occurred to her, but there was nothing except the pistol and the knife to hurl and she wasn't about to put either of those within his reach if she could help it. The idea of possibly knocking some sense into him held a great deal of appeal, but then, she thought as she yanked the tapes of her petticoat loose, it probably wouldn't work. Knocking sense into a block of wood was impossible. The only thing clobbering him would do was, possibly, make her feel better.

"Well?" he asked impatiently when she didn't respond.

She gave him a fulminating look, which was once again wasted as he couldn't see it—good thing, too, because she was down to her chemise, and the wet lawn was clinging to her breasts in an almost obscene fashion and was the next thing to transparent everywhere else—and took a deep breath.

"What on earth is in those letters, anyway?" she asked, exasperated. After making sure that he was showing no tendency to look around, she pulled the chemise over her head and dropped it to the floor. Naked and shivering, she cast him another wary look and reached for the towel. If she didn't get warm soon, she suddenly thought, she might freeze to death.

"Is it possible you don't know?" His voice was huskier than before, and again she glanced at him suspiciously. His gaze was still fixed on the wall, his back faced her foursquare and solid, and his right arm and hand, curled around the empty glass, rested on the table, just as it had the last time she had checked. Remembering the hot flare of desire she had seen in his eyes when he had looked at her earlier, she wondered with an unexpected little quickening of her own if the mere idea that she was disrobing behind him was enough to deepen his voice like that.

But entertaining such a thought served no purpose, and allowing herself to feel the least degree of attraction for the fellow was pure folly, and worse. In any case, a more probable explanation could be found in the bottle at his elbow, she told herself. Like the glass, it was empty. He had downed the lot. She could still taste the stuff, and, while it had wet her dry mouth and throat as she had intended, it had left an unpleasant burning sensation in its wake. He had consumed much more than she. Perhaps the searing after effect of so much brandy going down his throat in such a brief period of time accounted for his sudden gruffness.

If there should be another explanation, she was better off not knowing it.

"Those letters contain information that could severely compromise England's effort to win the war," Hugh continued, then stopped and cleared his throat. Pausing in the act of briskly rubbing life back into her frozen thighs with the towel, Claire glanced up at him again, her gaze sharp with suspicion. He hadn't moved. Nothing had moved. She was being ridiculous, of course. Doggedly she lowered her eyes again and concentrated on thoroughly drying her calves and feet.

"If the French get hold of them, many innocent lives will be lost. Innocent English lives. You don't want that, do you? Allow me to buy the letters from you, and give me truthful answers to my questions, and you can enrich yourself handsomely and yet go to sleep at night knowing that, in the end, you remained loyal to your country."

Any thoughts of him as an attracted and attractive male were swamped by a fresh tide of indignation at this new avowal that he thought her a traitor, and for that small mercy Claire was grateful. What he was, was a stubborn, stupid swine who might well murder her by mistake. That was all she needed to know of him. For a moment, as she straightened with the towel in hand, she considered repeating what had come to feel almost like her mantra: You've got the wrong person, wantwit.

But it was useless, she knew. He wasn't going to believe her no matter how many times she said it. It was bad enough that he thought her a lightskirt and a lying one at that, but now to realize that he believed her to be capable of betraying her country as well—it was too much. Blotting her hair with the towel, she eyed him thoughtfully.

As long as she had possession of the pistol, he could do her no harm, however angry she might make him. And with that thought in mind, she decided that perhaps she could make him pay, a little, for all he had put her through.

"As you say, I might very well wish to remain a loyal Englishwoman," she said, moving down to the end of the bunk and draping the damp towel over the board that served as its foot. Naked, still shivering, but deliciously dry now, she reached for the white linen shirt she had found in the saddlebags and pulled it over her head. It was truly enormous, she discovered as she freed her hair from the collar and settled the shirt into position, long enough to reach nearly to her knees and ample enough to wrap around her half a dozen times over. The sleeves were far longer than her arms, and she began rolling them up as she continued. "And, just supposing that I do, mind, you might indeed persuade me to listen to your bargain. But first you must answer my questions: What do you want with the letters? If they are so dangerous to England, who are you that I should give them to you?"

Eyeing his back, she thought she saw a barely perceptible easing in the set of his shoulders, as if his muscles, having been tensed, were now beginning to relax.

"You admit to having them, do you?" If his muscles had relaxed, his voice had not: it was decidedly grimmer than before.

She laughed, a jeering little sound, and sat down on the side of the bunk to pull on the stockings. Like the shirt, they were huge and white, of a thick weave that had her poor frozen toes wiggling in anticipation, and perfectly plain.

"I admit to nothing. But I would know what you intend to do with the letters." Poking one foot into the soft woolen well she had created, she pulled the first stocking on. It reached past her knee, and was so immediately warming that she gave a little sigh of pleasure. "Are you an agent of the British government, perhaps, sent to retrieve them and bring whoever stole them to justice? Or are you a rogue and a thief yourself, who somehow got wind of them and means to sell them to the highest bidder, should you succeed in laying your hands on them?"

"I am prepared to offer you a great deal of money for them. Say, ten thousand pounds."

Taken aback by the truly enormous amount, it took Claire a moment to realize that he hadn't told her anything at all.

"Impressive," she said, tying a clumsy knot in the stocking just below her knee to hold it in place.

"You would be wise to accept my offer, my girl." His voice had an ominous note to it now.

She raised her brows at him in exaggerated concern, then grimaced as she realized that she had forgotten once again that he couldn't see her.

"Why, if I were not the one in possession of the pistol, I might be frightened into revealing all," she said.

She was almost beginning to enjoy herself, she realized as she pulled on the second stocking. Under the circumstances, baiting him was a pleasure—certainly the most pleasure she'd had on this straight-out-of-hell day.

"Would a greater sum tempt you? Within reason, you may name your own price."

There was an undertone of contempt to that offer, faint but unmistakable. It reminded her of exactly what he thought her, and it made Claire's hackles rise.

Glaring at his back, she fumed silently for a moment. Then, in a deliberately provocative tone, she said, "Thank you, but, after all, I think I must decline."

He slewed around then, so suddenly that she jumped. The chair legs made a harsh grating noise as they scraped over the floor.

With a surprised gasp, Claire dropped the breeches she had just picked up and snatched at the pistol instead, sliding off the bed and leveling the pistol at him in a quick, if slightly less than graceful, series of motions. If, as she suspected, she looked both ridiculous and indecent in the hugely oversized shirt that covered her to her knees and the warm wool stockings knotted below, she cared not. All she cared about was that a weapon stood between them.

"Don't move," she ordered in a voice that she was chagrined to hear had turned slightly squeaky.

He was still seated, though the chair was now turned almost all the way around so that he was facing her. One hand was braced against the tabletop and his feet were planted firmly apart in front of him. He looked like he was prepared to leap across the cabin at any second and wrest the pistol from her. His expression reinforced that impression. He was glaring at her, his jaw hard and his mouth compressed into an angry line.

He looked, in a word, menacing. Was this really the man who, moments before, she had decided wouldn't actually harm her? Now he looked ready, willing, and able to wrap his hands around her neck and squeeze the life out of her, she thought, even as her pulse began to race. Though she was warm now—well, relatively warm—her hands, both of which were wrapped around the pistol grip, started to shake. She controlled the quiver just as, she hoped, she controlled the look of alarm that her face had instantly assumed: by a tremendous effort of will.

"If money was not your reason for undertaking this folly, then what was? Someone obviously put you up to it. Who? A lover? Someone besides Archer—someone you were seeing on the side? Someone younger, no doubt. An émigré, perhaps? Are you doing it for him? Who is he?"

Claire glared at him. The man's single-mindedness was maddening.

"You really cannot expect me to tell you all my secrets," she said airily.

His eyes flashed. Claire barely prevented herself from stepping back a pace. Thank goodness for the pistol, she thought, tightening her grip on it. It felt reassuringly heavy and solid in her hands.

"Whoever he is, he's using you." His voice was grim. His eyes never left her face. "Think, Sophy: If he cared anything for you, would he expose you to such danger? I tell you right now, no man would let a woman he loved risk what you are risking. But you may still save yourself: Tell me where you've hidden the letters."

It was time to have done with the whole idiotic farce, Claire realized, before she provoked him into springing at her, which he looked on the verge of doing. Despite everything, she would really prefer not to have to shoot him. Not that telling him—again!—that he had made a mistake would do any good, of course. He was clearly determined not to believe her, no matter what.

"I have not hidden your letters anywhere," she said tiredly. "I have never even set eyes on them. As I've told you more times than I can count, you've made a mistake: I am Lady Claire Lynes, not Miss Towbridge, and not Sophy."

For a moment he simply stared at her without speaking. Then his eyes turned as hard and dark as cast iron and his mouth grew thinner yet.

"Enough," he said. The chair scraped over the floor again as he got abruptly to his feet. "My patience is at an end. I'll play no more of these ridiculous games with you. If you know what's good for you, you'll tell me the truth."

"Stay where you are."

Her heart picked up speed until it was pounding in her chest like a runaway's galloping hooves. Her hands tightened on the pistol grip and her eyes went wide. He was tall and broad and dangerous-looking, his expression wouldn't have been out of place on the devil himself, and despite her best efforts not to allow him to do so, he was scaring her; harsh purpose seemed to emanate from him in waves.

He laughed, a nasty jeering sound, and came toward her.

"Stop right there," she warned, panicking, thrusting the pistol toward him as though to ward him off even as she started to back away. "I'll shoot. I swear I will."

Dear Lord, he wasn't going to stop. What was she going to do? Through her own folly, she found herself in the very situation she had most feared.

Her finger curled around the trigger, hesitated. Her breathing quickened. Her palms grew moist.

"Shoot then," he said, his gaze holding hers, and kept coming, taking slow stalking steps.

Backing up until her legs were pressed hard against the bunk's wooden frame, left with nowhere to go, Claire pulled back the hammer in a burst of dizzying fear and despair. She would have to shoot him. . . .

In the last second, as he loomed terrifyingly near, instead of aiming for his chest she pointed the pistol down, in the approximate direction of his left knee. Then she gritted her teeth and closed her eyes.

## ❧ 11 ❧

In the end, Claire couldn't do it. She just could not pull the trigger. The idea of blowing a hole through him, even through his knee, made her go all nauseated and light-headed. Or perhaps her stomach-churning reaction to the gory picture that immediately took possession of her mind was at least partly due to the heaving sea—she couldn't be sure. All she knew was that the thought of his hard male body spurting blood made her feel ill.

A hand clamped over her wrist, and the pistol was wrenched unceremoniously from her grasp.

"No!" Her eyes flew open, her fingers clenched, but her reaction was too late. The pistol was gone. She would have whirled away, out of his reach, but she could not; the bunk was behind her, its edge pressing hard into the backs of her legs, and he was in front of her, scant inches away, blocking her in, the pistol now in his possession. She had to tilt her head far back to meet his eyes. They were gray again, she saw, flinty but no longer black with anger. Still, as she stared up at him her heart raced and her throat went dry—with fear, she assured herself, refusing even to dignify any other possibility. Fear, certainly, was uppermost: The tables had turned again with a vengeance.

"What now, vixen?" he asked, far too pleasantly, echoing the question that was ricocheting through her mind. His hand left her wrist to grip her chin, warm, strong fingers holding her face up for his inspection, and he moved closer yet. He was so near now that her breasts, bare under the flimsy lawn shirt, brushed his chest, the merest butterfly contact. To her horror, she felt her nipples hardening in response. Suddenly she was as shivery inside as she had been on the outside since he had pulled her from the sea. When she moved—a compulsive reaction to such close, unwelcome contact—her bare knee brushed the smooth knit of his breeches, and she was immediately conscious of the hard-muscled leg beneath. She tried to step away, to put more distance between them, but with the bunk at her back and his hand gripping her chin, it was impossible. Frightened and embarrassed and also excruciatingly aware of her wretched body's hideously inappropriate quickening, she fought to avoid showing any of what she was feeling. To combat her weakness, she balled her suddenly weaponless hands into fists and met him stare for stony stare as he loomed over her like a conquering warrior.

"Get your hands off me." She was proud of the cool steadiness of her voice.

"You didn't pull the trigger." When Claire didn't reply but only glared at him, his mouth twisted into a sardonic smile. "Careful, if you keep on like this you'll make me think you fancy me."

Claire's eyes narrowed at that. He was making sport

of her, she knew, but that remark struck just a little too close to home for her comfort.

"Unlike you, I've no taste for violence."

"Or you've enough sense to look out for your own self-interest." The sardonic element was back in his voice now.

"That, too," she said, relieved to hear so neat an explanation for her failure to shoot him. If she hadn't been so befuddled by his nearness, she would have thought of that herself. It was, after all, perfectly true. "As you pointed out earlier, if my choice is between dealing with you and dealing with the ship's crew, I choose you."

"Very flattering of you."

His thumb moved in what felt almost like a caress over the underside of her chin. His gaze slid down to her mouth, where it lingered. Watching him stare at her lips, Claire realized that her pulse was racing again—and this time the reaction had absolutely nothing to do with fear. It struck her that his lean, harsh features were attractive in a way that had nothing to do with mere handsomeness. A way she couldn't quite describe—or didn't care to describe, other than acknowledging to herself that it had something to do with the fact that he was so very male. She was burningly aware of his closeness, of her breasts brushing his chest, of her knees brushing his legs. Suddenly she was warm all over, warmer than she had been all night, warmer than she could ever remember being.

"I wouldn't be too flattered." It required an effort, but her voice was tart in an attempt to camouflage the effect he was having on her. "That's rather like choosing between a nest of vipers and a single one. The only difference is the quantity of the poison."

His eyes rose to meet hers. "Sometimes, in just the right amount and under just the right conditions, poison can have a very beneficial effect on its recipient."

There was a gleam in the now silvery depths that caused her breathing to falter. It ignited a kind of quickening deep inside her body that both shamed and excited her. She could not, would not, let herself be attracted to him, she thought, horrified to realize that her toes were now curling in their nice warm stockings from a cause far different from cold. But her wayward body wasn't listening.

Letting her lids drop, she tried to pull her chin from his hold, suddenly panicked at the thought that he might be able to read what she was feeling in her eyes. He already thought her a doxy; she didn't want to prove it for him.

"Let me go."

"Not quite yet."

He was smiling faintly, she saw with a quick upward flicker of her lashes. Had he sensed the effect he was having on her? The thought was unbearably mortifying. Add the notion that his knowledge was responsible for his smile, and her humiliation was complete.

"You dared too much, my girl, and now there's the piper to pay." It was no longer even a smile; rather, it was just the faintest curve of his lips. As her gaze touched on that long, chiseled mouth, she found herself wondering how it would feel against her own.

Her heart pounded against her ribs.

"I said let me go!" Horrified at herself, she tried to mentally stamp out the errant images as if they were tongues of flame snaking out from a roaring meadow fire. But it was already too late. Their gazes met. He shook his head at her almost teasingly, and his thumb recommenced its gentle caress of the soft underside of her chin. Claire felt that touch all the way down to her already curling toes. Her lips parted quite unconsciously. His eyes blazed suddenly, and he bent his head.

She panicked as she realized that he meant to kiss her. She was breathing as fast as if she'd been running for miles, and both hands rose, helplessly, to curl around the strong wrist that imprisoned her chin. She tried again to free herself, but the effort was halfhearted at best and he held her fast without effort. Then, with the best will in the world to dodge or fight or scream or something, she found herself paralyzed by her own burgeoning desire. To her horror, she realized that she wanted him to kiss her. She stood perfectly still—except, if she was honest with herself, for a sudden, fierce quivering that she prayed was only internal—as he touched his lips to hers.

Her eyes closed, and she gave a little gasp. His lips were firm and warm, moving over hers with a soft intensity that made her senses go haywire. His tongue stroked her lips, then slid inside her mouth, and the quivering that had started deep in her belly raced like wildfire down her thighs and up to her breasts, causing an aching, pulsing feeling that was like nothing she had ever known. He tasted faintly of brandy, and suddenly she loved the taste. She loved the way his tongue ran over her teeth, the way it filled her mouth before being teasingly withdrawn, the way it stroked her tongue. She loved everything about what he was doing to her.

David had never kissed her like this. No one had ever

kissed her like this. She'd had no idea that there were kisses like this anywhere in the world. Suddenly realizing that she had stumbled across by merest chance what her body had been craving for years, Claire felt like the plainest of wallflowers who had suddenly been asked to dance.

Without warning he lifted his head, breaking off the kiss. Claire clutched at his wrist in protest, barely aware that her nails were digging into his flesh. Her eyes fluttered open. Her lips were still parted, still damp from his kiss. Dear God, she wanted more.

His gaze flicked over her face, touching on her mouth, her cheeks, which she knew must be flushed, and at last met her dazzled gaze.

"Sophy, my sweet dove, you could try kissing me back."

Sophy. The name brought her back to reality like a brick between the eyes. He was treating her like the veriest trollop, she realized, because a trollop was just exactly what he thought her. Ancient, doddering Lord Archer's mistress, to be precise. And there was no escaping it—she was behaving like a trollop. Humiliation washed over her in waves, nearly as burningly intense as just seconds before her desire for him had been. Realizing how he had insulted her, her humiliation turned in the space of a heartbeat to blazing anger.

"I should have shot you," Claire said, embracing the anger as the least dangerous of the myriad sensations at war inside her and using it to meet his gaze full on.

He laughed. Then he pinched her chin in an almost avuncular fashion and, to her mixed regret and relief, released it. His gaze shifted. One-handed, he brought the pistol up, pointed it almost casually at the foot of the bunk, and, even as Claire gasped in horror, pulled the trigger.

Instead of the explosion she instinctively braced for, there was a metallic click.

He pulled the trigger again, and then again.

Click. Click.

Her gaze flew to his, the kiss for the moment forgotten. There was mockery in his eyes.

"It wasn't loaded!"

"It was not," he agreed. His movements almost lazy now, he tossed the pistol onto the bunk and set both hands on either side of her waist.

Claire was trying to make sense of what had just happened. As the ramifications became clear, her eyes widened and a strong sense of ill-usage seized her.

"You knew it wasn't loaded!"

"I knew it from the time I unloaded it soon after I joined you in this cabin. I left the pistol behind in the boat when I jumped in after you, but still it managed to get wet, as I discovered when I checked it. I mean to clean it and let it dry. I hope it is not quite ruined."

"You could have taken it from me at any time."

"I could have."

"Then why—why . . . ?" Words failed her. She glared at him.

"You were having so much fun," he said with a maddening smile that made her long to hit him. "You will have to forgive me if I admit that it was somewhat entertaining, to say the least, to watch you hold the beast at bay."

"You are an utter swine."

Claire was furious, angrier than she could ever remember being in her life, so angry that she no longer cared who was holding whom prisoner. Pushing his hands away, she whisked herself sideways and away from him in a neat move fueled by rage. This time he didn't even try to stop her. Head held high, back as stiff as if she'd swallowed a poker, Claire stalked as far as the table and turned to face him, leaning back against it and grasping the narrow edge with both hands.

If anything, that maddening smile was more pronounced now as he looked her over, slowly and deliberately, from head to toe. She was suddenly uncomfortably aware of how extremely improper her attire was. The lawn of which the shirt was made was so fine as to be almost diaphanous, especially given its loose fit and the illuminating effects of the lantern. Glancing down at herself defensively, Claire realized that she could see the soft teardrop shape of her breasts moving beneath the thin cloth as she breathed. Her nipples were unmistakable: small hard pebbles that jutted against the lawn. In the face of that humiliation, the fact that the shirt ended several inches above her knees, and the stockings ended just below them, leaving her knees and a fair amount of thigh totally bare, was shorn of some of its impact. Snapping her arms across her breasts, shaking her hair forward as well, she managed to provide at least minimal coverage for her most salient parts. But the fact remained that she was just one gossamer layer of cloth away from being naked.

He was not, of course, gentlemanly enough not to look. But then, he was no gentleman, Claire reminded herself. He subjected her to a slow, thorough perusal, and by the time his gaze returned to meet hers, she was glaring at him fiercely. He made her a mocking little bow.

"Most charming," he said.

Claire's lips tightened.

"I would appreciate it if you would throw me a blanket." Her voice was stiff with dignity. She glanced significantly beyond him at the bunk.

"Would you indeed, my dove? As I said earlier, your wish is my command. Even when you are not holding me at gunpoint."

He turned, pulled the topmost cover from the bed, bundled it in his arms, and crossed the room to present it to her with a flourish.

Meeting his eyes was difficult, but she scorned not to do so. He smiled at her, so wicked a smile that she was immediately reminded of the one thing above all others in the world she preferred not to think about: that soul-shattering kiss. Lifting her chin, praying devoutly that she would not blush, she took the blanket from him with a brief nod of thanks and immediately swathed herself in yards of coarse gray wool like a corpse in a shroud.

"How old are you?" he asked abruptly, his smile vanished. He looked stern, and the lines beside his eyes and mouth seemed suddenly more sharply etched.

"I'm twenty-one." Claire smoothed her hair back from her face with one hand. Now that she was wrapped in the blanket, she felt much safer. Not that the specter of rape troubled her any longer, at least as far as he was concerned. He had let her walk away from that kiss without hindering her, and he had passed her the blanket when she had asked. Whatever else he was—and she could think of a whole list of unflattering adjectives—he was no defiler of women.

"A trifle young for this game, aren't you?" He crouched beside the wet heap of her discarded gown.

"Did your lover happen to tell you that the penalty for spying is death?"

Claire shook her head in disgust. "There is no talking to you, is there?"

"I could help you if you'd tell me the truth."

Claire's only reply was an exasperated sound. He was turning her wet gown inside out and examining, seemingly, every stitch and seam. Then he did the same to her petticoat and finally her corset and shift. After a bewildered moment, she realized that he was searching her clothes for his precious letters, and her exasperation turned to outright annoyance. Holding the blanket close, she watched without speaking. His hands looked dark against the delicate white linen of her shift; his fingers looked long and strong, as indeed she knew from experience they were, as they probed the boning of her corset. Suddenly the sight of her intimate garments in his hands was too much to be borne. Flustered, embarrassed, Claire turned her back, and found herself looking at the clock.

It was near four A.M. She should, by rights, be exhausted. As, indeed, she was, now that she thought about it. Not that acknowledging how tired she was would do her any good. She had to stay awake and alert, prepared to face whatever came. Still, she'd been without sleep for almost twenty-four hours. The previous morning she had risen before seven in order to get an early start on the road. She'd drunk tea and had a bit of a scone, and then had gotten into her coach with no inkling as to what the day would bring.

Never in her wildest imaginings could she have conjured up what would come to her. It still seemed like a nightmare from which she must soon surely awake.

Which would make Hugh what—the demon stalking her sleep?

If only it were so. If only she could just wake up, and he and this cabin and everything else would vanish in a twinkling.

Yes, and if wishes were horses then beggars might ride.

To her annoyance, Claire found that in staring at the clock, she could still see the very scene she had deliberately turned her back on. Small and golden but clear in every detail, Hugh was crouched on the floor, running his fingers along the delicate lace that edged her chemise.

It took a second or two for realization to strike, but when it did her jaw dropped under the force of it. Clearly she recalled undressing behind him along with her suspicions that he was somehow watching her.

He had been watching. Through the clock.

"You bounder!" she gasped.

He looked up then, saw what she was staring at, and came lithely to his feet.

"You cad!"

She turned as he moved toward her, leaning back against the table edge again and glaring at him. Swaddled in the blanket, her black hair, almost dry now, flowing around her face and down her back in unruly waves, her feet bare, her eyes flashing fire, she must look, she realized, like the vixen he had called her. Which was fine with her, because vixenish was just exactly how she felt.

"You were watching me the whole time!"

He stopped in front of her, hands on his hips, looking down at her with a considering expression. He was far taller and bigger than she, dark and dangerous-looking and standing not much more than a foot away, but Claire discovered that she was not the least bit afraid of him any longer.

" 'Twas quite a pretty show," he said with the merest quirk of a smile. "I make you my compliments."

Claire saw red. Her fingers curled deep into the blanket's rough wool. The fact that he had watched her as she had undressed and toweled herself dry made her want to scratch his eyes out. She'd been naked; only her maid had ever seen her in such a state of total undress. Even with David, when he had come to her bed, she'd worn a nightgown. She never would have dreamed of letting him see her naked, and he had never given any indication that he wished to. For this man, this stranger who had abducted and abused and threatened her, to see her in the altogether was so mortifying as to make her want to die—or kill. Him, to be precise.

"How dare you," she said, her voice low, almost guttural.

"Oh, come." He frowned, suddenly impatient. "This paroxysm of maidenly modesty is very well done, but totally wasted on me."

Moving, he was suddenly right in front of her, so close that her arms, folded now over her bosom inside the blanket, brushed his chest. He put his hands on her upper arms, gripping them loosely through the thick wool and looking down into her eyes.

She glared. His eyes moved over her face, and his mouth twisted wryly.

"You're a beautiful piece, a high-flyer indeed. We could deal extremely, you and I. If you are doing this for love, little dove, let me tell you that love may be found in many different places. You might even, for instance, find it with me."

His hands tightened on her arms, and he bent his head, clearly meaning to kiss her again. This time Claire was having none of it. Even as his mouth touched hers she made a furious sound—and, doubling up her fist, punched him as hard as she could in the ribs.

## 12

It hurt like be-damned. For the space of a couple of heartbeats after the blow landed, Hugh saw stars. He groaned, doubling over and staggering backward, his arms wrapped around his injured chest. Speeded by the ship's roll, he fetched up against the bunk and collapsed on it. Gritting his teeth, stretching his length out on the musty-smelling mattress, which was bare now that she was wearing all that had been provided in the way of bedclothes, he closed his eyes and waited for the spasm to ease.

When at last he opened his eyes, it was to find his nemesis standing over him, wide-eyed. Holding on to the upper bunk with one hand for balance, she was clutching the gray blanket close with the other. It concealed her curves more thoroughly than any domino ever worn by a guilty visitor to a Covent Garden masquerade. Her black hair cascaded in a waterfall of tangled waves around her shoulders. Her eyes were as big as doubloons, and almost the same color. She looked worried—and beautiful. So beautiful that Hugh groaned again, and closed his eyes.

The next time he fell off his horse, see if he didn't take heed of the celestial warning.

"Are you all right?"

Considering that she had just driven her fist into his ribs, that was almost amusing. Of course, under ordinary conditions, taking a punch to the ribs from her delicately boned hand wouldn't even have slowed him down. But just at the moment his ribs were his Achilles' heel. It was some comfort to reflect that even legendary heroes had been brought down by ill-timed blows to their weak spots. But not much.

He opened his eyes again.

"No, I damned well am not all right."

He was annoyed to hear himself wheezing between words. Fortunately, the ship was wallowing back and forth like a pig in a sty, accompanied by a medley of muted creaks and groans. With that for cover, he hoped she might miss the whistling of each slow, careful breath.

"I didn't mean to really hurt you."

Unfortunately for the success of that as an apology, there was a slight but unmistakable note of awe in her voice as her gaze slid from his face to focus on where he still clutched his ribs. She sounded most impressed with herself, rather like a green lad might if he succeeded in knocking down the great boxing champ Gentleman Jackson with a single blow.

His masculine pride was, most ridiculously, stung. Though he recognized it for the foolish vanity it was, he still could not bear to let her go on thinking that, in the ordinary way of things, a mere slip of a girl like herself could lay him low.

"I injured my ribs not long ago in a fall from a

horse." The words were forced through gritted teeth. He was disgusted with himself for feeling the need to explain—and he was still hurting.

"Everyone takes a tumble from time to time," she said, sounding sympathetic.

Hugh eyed her darkly. He was *not* going to tell her that, ordinarily, he rode like he breathed: effortlessly. It occurred to him then that he wanted to impress her, and he didn't much like the knowledge.

Until making her acquaintance, he had considered himself a consummate professional: efficient, devoid of emotion when necessary, thoroughly dedicated to getting the job done. She had him questioning everything about himself, and he wasn't any too pleased about it.

So far, he'd managed to extract about as much useful information from her as a bee trying to get honey from a rock. While she—she was chiseling away at the barrier of impersonality he always built around himself, chip by telling chip, when he was on the job.

"Shall I call someone? James?" She glanced toward the door.

Following her glance toward the barred portal made Hugh nervous. It did not require much imagination to come up with several ways in which the thrice-damned chit could take advantage of his temporary incapacitation. She could, for example, run to the door, unbolt it, and conceal herself somewhere on the ship. She could jump overboard. She could grab his knife and slit his throat. She could . . .

Oh, hell, who knew what she might take it into her head to do? The thing to do was preempt any such action on her part. Reaching up, he grabbed the hand that was holding the blanket closed and yanked. Hard.

Irresistible 129

"Oh!"

With a surprised gasp, she came tumbling down on top of him. In the interests of both protecting his still-protesting ribs and at the same time getting her exactly where he wanted her, he caught her around the waist with his free arm before she hit and rolled her across his hips so that she wound up in the space between his body and the wall. Now, to go anywhere, she had to go over him.

She landed amid a tangle of flying hair, blanket, and bare legs. Long, slim, extremely shapely bare legs, as he had observed before, that ended in enormous wool stockings that now puddled about her ankles and covered just them and her feet. James's stockings had never been so flattered by their wearer, Hugh thought with the beginnings of an inner twinkle, and vowed to tell his henchman so should the occasion ever arise. Her legs turned those homely stockings into the most beguiling of garments. He was still admiring them—and at the same time mentally berating himself for being so susceptible to her charms—when, scrabbling to rewrap herself in the blanket, she jarred his ribs with her elbow.

"Christ Almighty!" he yelped.

Clutching his side with renewed fervor, Hugh could only think himself well served. If he hadn't been so fixated on her legs, she wouldn't have been in such a scramble to cover them up.

"Don't move," he said, fixing her with a gaze that he hoped promised murder if she disobeyed. She was still wrestling with the recalcitrant blanket, trying to wriggle it down so that it covered every last inch of exposed skin. At his words, she looked up. Meeting his gaze, her eyes widened and she abruptly lay still.

Good, he thought. His message was finally getting through. When he was satisfied that she wasn't even thinking about moving again, he closed his eyes and gave himself over to recovering.

"I'm sorry if I hurt you, but you shouldn't have watched me through the clock," she said in a small but decidedly truculent voice after several minutes of silence. By then the worst of the pain had eased, and Hugh was breathing more or less normally. He opened his eyes, slanting her a jaundiced look. If this was a game they were playing, a high-stakes game, a winner-take-all game, he had to acknowledge that she was better at it than he. Outraged modesty was not an emotion normally expressed by the high-flyers of his acquaintance, which over the years had numbered quite a few.

"I apologize if I offended you," he said, very polite.

She looked at him suspiciously. "You are not the least bit sorry and you know it."

"Now, there you're wrong. Believe me, I am very sorry indeed."

"Only because I hurt your ribs."

"There's that." His voice was grave—too grave, he thought—but she didn't seem to catch the growing amusement underlying his words. Watching her scowl at him, he had suddenly, absurdly, felt that he had been transported off this worm-eaten vessel into a duchess's drawing room.

His gaze shifted so that he was staring up at the dark underpanel of the upper bunk some three feet above his head, which he absently noted was dusty and festooned with cobwebs. Frowning, he asked himself: How likely was it that a tart could give an impression like that?

If he didn't know better, he would almost have believed that her to-the-manner-born dignity was real. That her sweetness was real. That her story—too ridiculous to be even remotely possible—was real.

Did he know better?

She hadn't pulled the trigger, the letters were not anywhere on her person or among her clothes, and she didn't kiss like any tart he had ever kissed in his life. She kissed like a wet-behind-the-ears miss.

If she were acting, Mrs. Siddons had best look to her laurels.

On the other hand, she—or rather Sophy Towbridge, in case they should not be one and the same—had managed to plant some doubt in his mind. The identity scales could tip either way.

But then add the clincher: The Venus-faced girl who was even now watching him with clearly growing anxiety out of big, innocent-looking eyes had been at the rendezvous point at the appointed time. The rendezvous point arranged by the hidden web of Boney's agents in England—his own counterparts—to deliver Sophy Towbridge, and the information she possessed, into the hands of the French.

If she wasn't Sophy Towbridge, what had she been doing on that beach? And, on a corollary note, where was Sophy Towbridge? The woman could not have just disappeared into the ether.

That was the sticking point. In order to believe the charmer at his side, he had to believe that there were two women, one of whom had unaccountably gone missing while the other one had just happened to be in the wrong place at the wrong time.

Now, how likely was that?

His head told him: Not likely at all. His senses, which

were, of course, possibly clouded by the soft warmth of her pressing against his side, by the big gold eyes with the fluttery lashes that were fixed on his face and the soft pink curve of her lips, which were parted as she breathed, said: Maybe.

Careful, he warned himself. He could not afford to let a consummate actress with the face of an angel and the body of a nymph play him for a fool. There was too much at stake. And not only for himself. For the other British agents in France, and, most important, for England.

"Where did you hide the letters?" he asked almost conversationally, his gaze shifting to consider her. She lay on her side, watching him, her head resting on the bunk's only pillow, a dingy, lumpy-looking affair, her cheek nestled on one small hand, the blanket wrapped securely around her person.

As he asked the question, he felt her stiffen. The dagger-look she sent him glittered brightly gold with anger.

"Where you'll never find them," she said, too sweetly.

Now that was brilliant, he decided, shifting his attention back to the cobwebby panel and considering. That was just exactly what she would say if she was what she claimed to be—a falsely accused innocent with no idea of the gravity of the situation in which she found herself. Her snippy tone conveyed clearly that she wasn't much afraid of him. Sophy Towbridge might not know who he was, but she would be able to make a fairly accurate guess as to what he was, and she would be mortally afraid, as, indeed, she should be. On the other hand, that saucy little reply might also be what Sophy Towbridge would say if she was guilty as hell, cool as hock, clever as doxies usually weren't, and desperately trying to convince him that she was innocent.

"Actually, I don't have your stupid letters," she said in a sulky tone when he didn't reply. "For the simple reason that I am not Sophy Towbridge. My name is Claire."

Claire.

"So you keep telling me, angel eyes," he said dryly, flicking her an assessing glance. She met his gaze without flinching, and he was almost ready to swear that there was nothing of deception in her countenance.

"Because I keep hoping it will sink in. I should have remembered that very little penetrates solid rock."

He had to smile at that—being insulted by a woman prisoner as she was lying in bed with him added a whole new chapter to the annals of his career—and as she saw his smile she narrowed her eyes at him.

"I'm glad you're finding this amusing. I, unfortunately, am not."

"You should have thought of that before you took up spying."

She made an inarticulate sound of rage. Instantly mindful of the possibilities, he rolled onto his side, awkwardly because he was being careful of his ribs, and grabbed her hands—clenched into fists as he had known they would be—through the scratchy blanket.

"Ah-ah," he warned, shaking his head at her.

"Coward," she replied.

"Damn right."

She gave him a fulminating look but said nothing more. As his gaze moved over her face, he noticed how truly exhausted she appeared: Her lids drooped wearily, as if barely able to support the weight of her lashes, and there were faint bluish smudges beneath her eyes. Her skin was so pale it was almost translucent, paler even than it had been when he'd last taken note of it. Even as he registered that, she shifted slightly—the bunk was narrow, and she had very little room—and he became acutely aware that the soft warm weight of her was now pressed fully against him. Breasts, belly, thighs—he identified each point of contact automatically, and his body responded just as automatically.

Then the question occurred: Was she doing it deliberately?

He released her fists and shifted onto his back again, refocusing on the dusty wooden panel above him and frowning at it as if it could help him reason the matter through. He was, first and foremost, a soldier, and his country was in a fight to the death. For the last ten years, through campaigns fought everywhere from Africa to Spain, he had waged war against the French monster, putting country above all else. Never once had he even questioned an order. His reckless disregard for his own safety—dispatches called it bravery, but it was easy to be brave when he had entered the war not altogether certain that he wanted to make it out alive—plus his luck in always escaping disaster by the skin of his teeth, objective accomplished, had led his superiors to depend on him to carry out missions that had grown more and more dangerous over the years. His current operation in France was a high-wire act performed without a net, and vital to his country's interests.

She—Sophy Towbridge—could bring that operation down around his ears. He had been ordered to kill her.

He had never failed to carry out an order, even when he disagreed with it, which he occasionally did. And Hildebrand knew this, of course. Hugh sometimes suspected that Hildebrand knew more about him than was strictly necessary. It was Hildebrand's knowledge of him—of part of his past—that had prompted the spymaster to send Hugh after Sophy Towbridge. But Hildebrand did not know everything about him. Otherwise, he never would have charged him with killing a woman.

No, he corrected himself, he had been charged with killing a traitor. That the traitor was a woman was—or should be—immaterial.

In principle, Hugh was in full agreement with the dictum that traitors deserved to die.

But this traitor was scarcely more than a girl. She was also sweet and saucy—and heart-stoppingly beautiful. Reluctant though he was to face it, he found her more than a little enchanting.

Grimly, Hugh tried to picture himself killing her. He could not.

But the assignment was his. He had undertaken to carry it out successfully, and his orders were that Sophy Towbridge was to die.

The question then became: Was the troublesome chit lying so snugly against him Sophy Towbridge? Or was she not?

Solomon had never faced so agonizing a decision.

## 13

*S*till moving a tad cautiously, Hugh shifted so that he once again lay on his side, facing the subject of his dilemma. Propping his head on one hand, he looked down at her consideringly. Her gaze met his, a little wary but not betraying any appreciable amount of fear, and again he thought that Sophy Towbridge would have known enough to be afraid of him. As he searched her eyes for any signs of hidden fear or guilt or anything else that might persuade him one way or the other, he noticed absently that the clear gold of her irises was actually composed of shades of gold and brown and gray, rather like tortoiseshell, with a dark outer ring. Set slightly aslant beneath thick black curling lashes, they were the eyes of a female who had certainly been a heartbreaker from her cradle. Was their innocence a sham?

It would be easy to let them sway him. He'd been right in what he had first thought—they were siren's eyes.

Was he on the brink of falling for a siren's song?

"Do I have a smudge on my nose, to make you stare at me so?"

Slightly taken aback at this tart interruption to his

weighty ponderings, Hugh almost smiled. No, she didn't seem to fear him to any appreciable degree, which was telling in itself. Responding without thought, he lifted a hand to trail a questing finger down the feature in question. She wrinkled it. Adorably.

Was he being taken for a ride? It was possible. Hell, anything was possible. He very much feared that he was on the brink of losing his vaunted good judgment where she was concerned.

"Actually, you seem to be developing a spot."

"Oh, no! I am not!" Her hand immediately flew to her nose.

This time Hugh did smile. A threat to England—and she was concerned about developing a spot on her nose? His mind boggled. She dropped her hand, glared as she realized she was being teased—then broke into a roguish, dimpled grin that was utterly beguiling.

Even if she was Sophy Towbridge, he thought, teetering on the brink of total intoxication by that dazzling smile and knowing it, did she have any real idea of how deadly the consequences were in this game that was only played for keeps?

Deliberately he reminded himself that it didn't matter whether she did or not. If she was Sophy Towbridge, his orders were that she had to die.

"You should smile more," she said.

That, coming as it did out of nowhere and uttered in a vaguely disapproving tone, made him blink.

"Should I?" he asked, trying desperately to maintain some sense of balance. Her nearness—and her smile and her youth and her beauty and just about every other damned thing about her—was warping his objectivity, he feared.

"It makes you look younger."

"I'm thirty-one." His tone was defensive, as if he cared that she might think he was older than he was, and as he heard it he felt like kicking himself. In danger of losing his good judgment? Hah! Any impartial observer might be excused for concluding that he'd lost it, utterly and completely, already.

"Really? You're ten years older than I am, then."

"Hmm." If his response was less than encouraging, it was because he was struggling desperately to regroup. He just could not accept what his senses told him about her, because his senses, clouded by the look of her, the feel of her, the smell of her, were growing maddeningly unreliable. He had to remain objective, to weigh, to think.

It was difficult, though, with her resting full against him again; even through the not-inconsiderable barrier of the scratchy blanket he could feel the shape of her, the softness of her, the warmth of her. She stretched a little, catlike, and he could feel the fullness of her breasts press against his chest, and, farther down, the sweet indentation of her waist and the gentle curve of her hips and thighs. The sensation was acutely arousing. He set his teeth in an effort to combat it.

Did she know what she was doing to him? He searched her eyes again—she was watching him almost sleepily, with no apparent guard on her expression whatsoever—and he was ready to swear that she did not.

Frowning thoughtfully now, he reached out to smooth a wayward strand of her hair back behind her ear. It felt like tangled silk beneath his fingers.

She blinked at him.

"You know, you can really be very nice."

"Do you think so?" He was almost fascinated by his reaction to her. Either she was entirely guileless, or he was as susceptible to female wiles as the greenest of green lads.

"Mm-hmm. When you're not trying to frighten me."

"Is that what I'm trying to do?"

"I think so."

He worked at maintaining his skepticism, but it wasn't easy. He looked at her, hard, but she appeared utterly innocent of trying to manipulate him. Whoever she was, Sophy Towbridge or Lady Claire Lynes as she claimed, she should have been afraid of him. He was, after all, her captor, and she was his prisoner. She was totally at his mercy, and he could do anything, anything at all, anything he chose, to her with none to say him nay. But if she realized that, she didn't appear to.

"And am I succeeding?"

"Mmm. Not so much now."

This time her mouth barely curved, but her eyes smiled up at him in a way that he found, to his annoyance, made his heart beat faster. The thought of putting her innocence to the test in a decidedly nonverbal fashion occurred to him, and as he considered, it became almost irresistible. When he had kissed her earlier, she had been wide awake and more than a little on her guard. Now she was practically asleep in his arms, comfortable and far more vulnerable to letting her true self emerge.

Whoa. He pulled himself up sharply, before temptation could get the better of him. Under the circumstances, the very worst thing he could do was kiss her.

Talk about clouding his judgment . . .

"You should be afraid of me," he said on a harsher

note, his gaze moving restlessly over her face. "You're a fool not to be afraid of me."

"I must be a fool, then."

She looked up at him for a moment, her eyes heavy-lidded and slumberous, her mouth soft and sweetly curved. Quite of its own volition, his hand came up to stroke the velvety softness of her cheek. Her skin was exquisitely smooth, making him think of the petals of a rose, a white rose edged in pink, and it was warm. So warm.

He could understand that, Hugh thought. For his part, he seemed suddenly to be suffused with heat.

"You are the most beautiful thing I have ever seen in my life," he said, realizing that he was on the verge of making a mistake of quite possibly historic proportions but totally unable to stop himself. His thumb touched the corner of her mouth, feathered over it, and, still sleepy-eyed, she smiled at him.

He bent his head and kissed her. Just like that. By the time he realized just what it was he had done, it was too late. His heart was slamming against the walls of his chest and his breathing was coming harsh and fast and he was so hard and hot and hungry for her that it was all he could do not to flip her onto her backside there and then and pump out his lust between her legs with a savagery that owed more to beast than man.

What stopped him was the innocence of her mouth.

He was a grown man, a grown man who liked women and whom women found attractive. He had bedded so many members of the fairer sex that he'd long since lost count. He knew what a woman in the throes of passion looked like, what she sounded like, how she kissed.

Not like this.

Though most of the time he managed to forget it, he had been born and raised a gentleman. That distant upbringing gave him the strength he needed to pull his mouth from hers as soon as the extent of her inexperience became clear to him. He gave himself credit for that much self-control at least. But she had her hands twined in his shirt front now, which, he supposed as he lifted his head, gave him as much excuse as he needed for not peeling himself off that bunk and away from her.

The truth was, he didn't want to move off that bunk and away from her. He admitted it to himself even as she opened her eyes and looked at him as if she had just glimpsed the sun after a fortnight of rain. She was inexperienced—he knew that as well as he knew his own name. But he also knew with equal certainty that she was willing.

"Hugh?" she murmured, her hands tightening on his shirt.

That was all the invitation he needed. All the invitation he could stand.

Because the first touch of his lips to hers had set him on fire. She hadn't protested, hadn't so much as tried to turn her head away. Instead she had turned her face up to his with a little sigh, and seemed to welcome his kiss. Her lips were soft, and tremulous, and parted for him easily. By the time his eyes closed and his tongue slid inside her mouth, the blaze that consumed him had turned into a full-fledged conflagration. He had found her tongue, caressed it, probed deep inside her mouth. Her mouth had tasted, just faintly, of brandy, and was so warm, so warm and wet and sweet, that he had nearly lost himself in the taking of it. His heart had raced. His breathing had grown ragged. His body had hardened until it strained painfully against the confines of his breeches.

But she hadn't kissed him back.

This time, he was going to make sure she did.

"Put your arms around my neck," he said, smoothing her hair back from her face with a hand that he was bemused to see was slightly unsteady. She met his gaze, her eyes still faintly glazed from the kiss they had shared. He saw the minute his words registered: Her eyes flared, and she let out her breath on a long but clearly quiescent sigh.

Then she let go of his shirt, and slid her arms around his neck. The feel of those cool, silky-skinned fingers clasping the nape of his neck made his breathing stop. Fiercely he wanted them all over him; he imagined them stroking his arms, caressing his chest, clawing his back. . . .

For a moment longer he managed to remain motionless. He was leaning over her, his upper-body weight supported by his elbows, and his gaze searched her face before he said or did anything more, anything he was going to regret. The cabin, lit by a single swaying lantern, was dim. Deep in the recesses of the bunk, as they were, there was more shadow than light. But the delicate angles and elegant lines of her features were only emphasized by the shadows that danced across them, and her eyes gleamed with the soft patina of old coins. Her lips, still faintly damp from his kiss, were parted and inviting.

Looking at them, he felt his stomach clench.

"I—don't know what you want me to do," she confessed, her lashes dropping down to hide those heart-stopping eyes. She sounded very young, very shy, and he thought, again, that if she was acting she was the best, by far, he had ever seen.

But somewhere, deep in his gut, he didn't think she was acting.

"I want you to kiss me back," he said, and his hand came up to burrow beneath her long hair and mold the back of her skull. "It's not hard. Just do what I do."

He cradled her head, tilting it, angling her mouth for a better fit, and then he kissed her again, soft and sweet and slow, giving her time to get used to the feel of his lips on hers. When his tongue finally slid inside her mouth, he was gentle still, touching her teeth, the roof of her mouth, the insides of her cheeks. Patiently he coaxed her tongue into play, teasing it with his, caressing it. When she responded, hesitantly meeting caress with caress, he drew her tongue into his mouth and sucked on it, nearly killing himself with the force of his barely checked desire in the process. Sweat beaded his forehead, fierce pressure built inside his loins like steam in a boiler, and a fine tremor racked muscles tense with wanting her. Resolutely he forced himself to ignore those signs of the urgency of his need, concentrating instead on tutoring her in the fine art of kissing. He was rewarded for his patience when she shuddered and moaned and tightened her arms around his neck.

"I didn't know . . . kissing . . . could be like this."

Her words were no more than a warm breath feathering across his lips, but they stopped him cold. He lifted his head to stare down at her, wondering if his senses could actually be telling the truth, if she could really be this trustingly naive, this dizzyingly desirable, this unbelievably intoxicating, or if she was spinning the biggest web of lies since the Trojans left their gift and pretended to walk away from Troy. He was aware that he was breathing as if he'd been running for miles. He was aware that he was no longer in complete possession of his faculties, no longer objective, no longer possessing any judgment where she was concerned. Then her lashes lifted as if she would see what he was doing, and he found himself looking into eyes that were deep pools of molten fire.

"Didn't you?" he asked, knowing even as he said it that he was lost, that any further attempt at saving himself or the situation was doomed beyond redemption. Drawn by those eyes, by those lips, he kissed her again, with considerably less control this time, and she responded with a hot sweet wildness that took him by surprise. She was pressed as close against him now as ink to paper. He felt her breasts rising and falling against his chest. The blanket was no longer between them, and only two thin layers of cloth separated her flesh from his. He felt the hard little nubs of her nipples nudging his chest, and the sensation nearly sent him over the edge. He wanted her, oh, God, he wanted her. It would be easy, so easy, to take what he wanted.

But would it be wise?

Her tongue left his mouth, and he let it go as he fought to keep his mind separated from his body at least to some small degree. Then her lower body pressed against him too, pushing up against the hard hot urgency of him, rocking against him, and her tongue came back inside his mouth of its own volition and that was all it took.

All hope of keeping so much as one tiny part of his mind separate and functioning was lost in the sudden rushing blaze that caught him unaware and roared over him, consuming him in its flames. Kissing her deeply, he rolled so that she was pinned beneath him, conscious of the tiniest twinge in his ribs but not giving a damn, not giving a damn now about who she was or what she was or anything except assuaging his hot fierce need in her body. She felt so right under him, so exquisitely female, so warm, so welcoming. His tongue was in her mouth, her arms were around his neck, and he was pulling at the hem of her shirt, yanking it up toward her waist.

He was going to take her, meant to take her, had to take her, just like that, in and out, hard and fast, with no more time for pretty words or tutorials or any other damn fool thing except the hot savage ecstasy of sex. He was beyond thought, his body thick and heavy and fiercely ablaze, and the only ease for him lay in the soft yielding sweetness that quivered and quaked so excitingly beneath him.

His hand found her breast and closed over it, squeezing more roughly than he intended, but he was far gone with desire and gentleness was quickly growing beyond him. Through the thin lawn of (ridiculously, as it briefly occurred to him) James's second-best shirt, he could feel the hard little pebble of her nipple thrusting into his palm, and he gritted his teeth as his body sizzled and threatened to explode.

She, who just minutes before had been kissing him so shyly, arched up against him, moaning her pleasure into his mouth. The small sounds she made sent him out of his mind. His hand slid from her breast to fumble at the fastenings of his breeches.

He couldn't wait, not another minute, not another second. He would have her despite everything, despite anything. It was far too late and he was far too hungry to count the cost.

## ᴥ 14 ᴥ
..............................

"**N**o. Please. No. Hugh. Stop."
His hands were undoing his buttons; his knee was edging between her thighs. His body was a human torch, as taut as a bowstring, an arrow on the verge of being launched, when she pulled her mouth from his and gasped out the words.

Stop . . .

God, he didn't want to hear that. He really didn't want to hear that. He—almost—could—not—comply. Stopping hurt. Clenching his hands into fists, closing his eyes, resting his cheek against hers, he made himself go still.

Stop. She'd said stop.

He couldn't believe it. But that was what she'd said.

Whatever else he was, he was not the man to take a woman against her will. Damn it—and himself and her and the whole bloody universe in the bargain—he would not force himself on her. He'd never forced a woman yet, and he was not starting now.

But, dear Lord in heaven, it was a near-run thing.

"Stop?" he asked carefully once he could trust himself to speak. His voice was scarcely more than a croak, and that one questioning word was all he could manage for the moment. He was hurting from head to toe, and aching like be-damned at a certain crucial point in between. Even lying on top of her as he still was, feeling the naked-to-the-waist softness of her yielding to his hard weight, listening to the gentle rhythm of her still-too-fast breathing, inhaling the unmistakable fragrance of woman and sex, was torture.

The problem was, he didn't think he could move. At least, not yet.

He took a deep, steadying breath. Even breathing hurt. Good God, he hadn't experienced pain like this in years.

Not since he'd been old enough to ease it in the way nature had intended for it to be eased.

"Please stop." Her voice was low and throaty and—the death blow for his still stubbornly hoping body—entreating. She sounded like she really meant it.

"Why?"

Sweat had popped out on his brow. His teeth, in between uttering his single-word questions, were clenched tight. It occurred to him that, under the circumstances, this was a ridiculous conversation to be having. He hadn't had such a conversation in—he couldn't remember when. He'd never had such a conversation. Every woman he took to his bed was flatteringly eager to be there, from his very first at age fourteen. Women never said no to him. Never.

"B-because."

This one was saying no to him. The evidence was incontrovertible. Her hands, instead of hugging his neck as they had done up until now, were pushing at his shoulders quite unmistakably. She was—most naively—trying to wriggle out from beneath him, and doing her cause a tremendous disservice thereby.

He wanted her. He could take her. Still. She was his prisoner, after all. And she might only be pretending to object, trying to convince him that she was too sweetly virtuous to be a tart.

No.

Hugh took a deep breath and rolled off her before he could succumb to temptation. He lay on his back, panting, hurting, with one arm flung across his eyes to block out the world and one knee bent to afford himself what ease he could. Though his eyes were clenched tight—along with his teeth and every other muscle he possessed—as he fought the devil within him to a standstill, he was aware of the hasty movements she made as she put herself back together.

If she elbowed his ribs again, he thought grimly, he would almost feel like thanking her. At least it would take his mind off the fact that he was now suffering even more severe discomfort elsewhere.

Which was, again, all her fault. The whole damn fiasco, from start to finish, was her fault. No, it was his. He should have paid attention when he'd been thrown from his horse. But he hadn't, and somewhere the gods were surely laughing as he paid the price for ignoring their warning.

"Because?" he repeated on an inquiring note a few minutes later, when he had himself almost fully under control again. "Because why?"

"Because—I just can't."

Oh, enlightening. Lowering his arm, he cracked open his eyes and slanted a look at her. She was lying on her side as far away from him as she could get—which wasn't very far. The bunk was narrow, and at most, in a few places where she curved in instead of out, perhaps three inches separated them. The blanket in which she had reshrouded herself still brushed against his side, and he was perfectly—no, make that excruciatingly—aware of the feminine shape of her beneath it. Her spine was clearly pressed up flat against the wall, her arms were folded protectively over her breasts beneath the blanket, and her eyes were now wide and nervous-looking as she watched him.

Nervous. Not scared.

Which crystallized something for him: She had responded with enthusiasm, kissing him and moaning and pressing herself against him—but with a neophyte's enthusiasm. If she'd been Archer's mistress for a year, he must have scarcely laid a hand on her. This was no high-flyer, no lightskirt, no woman of experience at all. This girl didn't even have the sexual knowledge of most gently bred ladies of his acquaintance.

This woman either knew little to nothing of sex—or she was the greatest actress on earth, and he was the greatest fool.

Taking a deep breath, Hugh rolled onto his side and propped his head on his hand again, noting that her eyes widened and she tried to press herself even farther back against the wall as he moved. Her hair was swept away from her face, but the black-as-night mass of it fanned out across the lumpy pillow on which her head lay and beyond. Hugh discovered, to his annoyance, that waving strands trailed over his bent arm. The sight of the midnight silk against his brown skin and white shirt was unsettlingly intimate. It reminded him of what he was missing.

"Would you care to explain why you can't?" His voice was faintly dry. She was looking at him as if she feared he might roll on top of her again at any minute, but he was pleased to realize that he had now fully regained his self-control.

She hesitated, and her lashes dropped. Hugh found himself intrigued by the inky thickness of the curling fringe, and cursed himself for his susceptibility.

"It would be wrong," she said, and those lashes rose again and she met his gaze. Her eyes were no longer molten pools of longing, he was both glad and sorry to see. Like his, her internal temperature appeared to have cooled considerably.

"Allow me to point out that the rightness or wrongness of it didn't appear to bother you unduly when you offered yourself to me earlier."

She lowered her lashes again. Hugh found himself waiting, almost with bated breath, for them to rise. When they did, he saw that her expression was resolute, as if she had made up her mind to stand her ground with him and not let him embarrass her or make her feel shy. Again, he found himself intrigued. Or, if he was to be perfectly honest, almost—enchanted.

"Then I thought I might have to—to—you know— to save my life. Now I know you'll not harm me. At least, I don't think you will."

Hugh studied her. Was the artlessness real? God help him, he was beginning to be all but convinced it must be.

"So you would be willing to sleep with me to save your life, but not just for your own pleasure?"

She made a harsh sound that was not quite a laugh.

"It's not a pleasure," she said, and her lashes swept down to hide her eyes again.

"Now, why would you think that?" he wondered aloud, watching her as carefully as a cat at a mouse hole. "Archer is an old man, I know; was he somehow lacking in bed?"

She gave an indignant little gasp, and her eyes flew open again. "I wouldn't know. I have never had occasion to find myself in bed with Lord Archer. As I've said, I only know of him because he is a friend of my aunt's."

There was hostility in the golden eyes now.

He raised his brows at her. "Then just who was it who managed to convince you that making love is not a pleasure?"

"My husband," she said with something of a snap. "Who else would I . . . ? Never mind. This conversation is most improper."

Even under the circumstances, she managed to look haughty. Given that she was in total deshabille, next to naked, trapped in a bunk with him, and had just kissed him halfway to heaven, looking haughty was no mean feat.

"The most interesting conversations generally are," he said tranquilly. "Tell me about your husband. How long have you been married?"

"We were married a year ago last June."

"About a year and a half, then. And the bloom is already off the rose?"

"What do you mean?" She was frowning at him, from displeasure at the turn the conversation was taking, he thought, rather than from any lack of understanding.

"Well, if you no longer find any pleasure together in bed . . ."

"It was never . . ." she began. Then her lashes swooped down again, hiding her expression from him. Looking at her closely, he was fascinated to discover a faint wash of color creeping up her cheeks.

"It was never—a pleasure?" he guessed, and from the sudden opening of her eyes he knew he had hit the mark. "You never took pleasure from your husband in bed?"

"I refuse to continue this conversation," she said in a stifled-sounding voice.

"Is he an old man? Ugly?"

"David is twenty-five, and accounted very handsome," she flashed.

"David?" Suddenly he knew, or thought he knew, who her husband was. Unless, of course, she was a very clever liar indeed.

"My husband. Lord David Lynes."

"Whom you married a year and a half ago," he said slowly, still working out the probabilities in his head. If she wasn't lying . . . "Why did you marry him? For his money?"

She looked outraged. "Certainly not. He has no money."

"Then why?" he prompted, more fascinated now than she could ever begin to guess.

For a moment he thought she wasn't going to reply. Then she made a restless movement, and her mouth twisted with what he took for a touch of bitterness.

"I wanted a man who would be kind to me," she said. "And David was kind. He wasn't loud or aggressive, as some of my suitors were. He was gentle. I was quite certain that he would never beat me, or abuse me in any way. And—he was—is—handsome. He has blond hair and blue eyes, and he's slender, not so tall but taller than I am. I—I fell in love with him, and I thought he fell in love with me."

"And so you married him, only to discover that he's no fun in bed," Hugh said dryly.

"Fun?" She sounded as if the word had gotten stuck in her throat. Her expression was horrified. "I never said—I never expected . . ."

"To have fun in bed? A man and a woman in bed together should have fun, my poor deluded darling. We were having fun, you and I, until . . ."

"I absolutely refuse to continue with this conversation!"

She flounced around so that her back was turned to him. He had to dodge to save his ribs from injury. While she stared stonily at the wall, he stared at the back of her head, lost in thought. Everything she had said was spot on—if she was who she claimed to be. Could Sophy Towbridge have known so much? Perhaps. Could she have acted so convincingly? Perhaps again. Could she look like an angel, kiss like a green girl, and spin a story that, in all the particulars he was in a position to verify, rang absolutely true?

Who the hell knew?

With a hand on her shoulder, he turned her onto her back. She did not resist, but lay glaring up at him. He noted that she kept the blanket wrapped closely about her, as if it would somehow protect her from him.

If she was Sophy Towbridge, she would need far more than a scratchy gray blanket to protect her, he reflected grimly.

And if she wasn't?

"All right, my little Scheherazade, tell me your tale," he said wryly, his gaze moving over her face. "Tell me just exactly how you came to be on that beach where we—uh—first made our acquaintance."

She met his gaze, and for a moment he thought she meant not to reply. Then her little pink tongue emerged to wet her lips—a visual torture he grimly willed himself to ignore—and she sighed. Then she began to talk. By the time she had finished, a long time later, she was comfortably nestled against him again. He lay on his back with the pillow beneath his head and his arm around her. Her head rested trustingly on his shoulder, and one slender arm had emerged from the blanket to curl across his chest. Lulled by the gentle rocking of the ship, Hugh gave himself over to thought. He found himself listening to the soft rhythm of her breathing as he once again contemplated the unexpectedly intricate patterns of the cobwebs above his head.

He realized that what he had just listened to was the verbal equivalent of watching straw being spun into gold. What he had to determine now was whether the end result really was gold—or just a devilishly clever trick.

He slanted a glance at her. Her eyes were closed now, and he wasn't even completely sure she was still awake. Her face was pale, very pale, as if all color had been leeched from it. She looked young and lovely and vulnerable and trusting—the very opposite of a cast-iron-hearted harpy who could diddle one lover, rob him, set out to betray her country, and seduce the man charged with capturing her along the way.

She opened her eyes and scowled at him.

That scowl caught him by surprise. He blinked at her.

"I need to get up," she said in a small, grim voice that was like nothing he had heard from her before.

He frowned. "What . . . ? Why?"

"Let me up."

Pushing impatiently at his arm, she managed to wriggle out from beneath it and lever herself into a sitting position. Hugh, looking up at her, saw with some interest that she was even paler than she had appeared just seconds before—black hair and brows and lashes notwithstanding, she was now as white as her shirt.

"Move. Please."

His brows lifted. "Certainly. But—"

"I'm going to be ill."

As that sank in, Hugh's eyes widened in alarm. Her complete absence of color was suddenly, hideously explained.

"Good gad, are you telling me you're seasick?"

"I'm telling you I'm going to be ill. At once."

She clapped a hand over her mouth. Galvanized, Hugh rolled off the bunk, his protesting ribs ignored as the true nature of the emergency became clear. On his hands and knees, he groped desperately beneath the bunk for the chamber pot, which, fortunately, he'd had reason to locate during the previous crossing to England. Fishing it out, still on his knees, he turned and presented it to her.

Just in time.

## 15

...................................

"All right, angel eyes, up you get."

The hatefully amused voice had grown so familiar that Claire didn't even have to open her eyes to identify whom it belonged to: Hugh. He'd held the chamber pot for her while she had so ingloriously succumbed at last to the motion of the sea. Then, by dint of shouting for James, he had seen her provided with soap and water and a towel for washing her face and hands afterward, tooth powder for cleaning her teeth, and a glass of brandy to send her to sleep. Finally she had collapsed onto the bunk again, curled up into a little ball with the blanket wrapped around her, and gone to sleep. Since then, two hours could have passed, or twenty. From time to time she'd surfaced enough to be peripherally aware of what was going on around her: Hugh's deep breathing as he had slept beside her for a time, and herself, finally warm as toast, snuggled close against his side, her head on his shoulder, her arm nestled around his neck; Hugh and James conducting low-voiced conversations in the cabin, some of which had turned fairly heated; the smell of food, as Hugh had devoured a meal of bread and meat.

That last had almost been enough to send her stomach turning inside out again.

In fact, it still lingered. Sniffing the air, Claire shuddered without opening her eyes. She could smell, of all things most calculated to outrage her stomach, food.

She confidently expected never to eat again.

So when Hugh tugged at a strand of her hair and bade her get up for a second time, she groaned by way of reply, but didn't even so much as open her eyes. Her head swam, her stomach gave every indication of still taking its rebellion seriously, and she was absolutely sure that remaining prone was her best course of action.

Hugh shook her shoulder. "Up. We'll be landing soon."

Landing? As in land? That perked her up. Not a lot, but enough to make her open one eye and look at him.

"Land?" she croaked.

If possible, he looked even more maddeningly amused than he had been sounding, she discovered with some annoyance.

"That's right. Come on, sit up. Unless you wish to be left behind when James and I go ashore, of course."

At the moment, Claire was more dazzled by the prospect of going ashore than she was fearful of being left behind, but both weighed with her. She opened both eyes, closed them again as the cabin seemed to do a slow revolution around the bunk, then found her upper arms seized. Just like that, she was hauled unceremoniously into a sitting position.

"No, please," she moaned, pulling her arms free and leaning back against the wall. Resolutely she refused to open her eyes.

"You'll be better as soon as you're off the ship." He

still sounded amused. "Come on, open your eyes. You can't possibly be worried about getting sick again. There's nothing left inside you."

If there was any justice in the world, Claire thought bitterly, his tall form would be racked with nauseous spasms before he was very much older.

"James brought you some tea and bread. Get dressed, and you may have time to eat it."

Hugh said this as if he were offering her a bribe. Far from being tempted, Claire shuddered.

"Food's what you need, I promise you." He sounded amused again,

Only a monster—or an insensitive lout—would speak to her of food after having witnessed her earlier sufferings. Conclusively proving that he was, at least, the latter, Hugh chuckled, moved away, and came back bearing a tin mug full of a steaming substance that one cringing look told her was tea.

"Here," he said, and held the mug out to her.

Claire, still leaning back against the wall and feeling as limp as a soggy rag, took one look and shook her head in revulsion.

"Drink it." Hugh's eyes glinted at her purposefully, and his jaw was set in an obstinate fashion that she was beginning to recognize. His mouth—his mouth . . . Oh, dear Lord, he was watching her as she stared at his mouth. Was he remembering, as she was now because she simply couldn't help it, how he had kissed her—and how she had kissed him back?

She tore her eyes from his mouth—and found the tea mug thrust into her hand.

"Don't spill it," Hugh growled, and turned away. Claire stared at the back of his head, which nearly brushed the ceiling, at his broad shoulders and powerful back and lean hips and long legs. Had she really lain in his arms? Had she slept snuggled against the whole well-muscled length of him? Had she wrapped her arms around those wide shoulders? Had she kissed that supremely masculine mouth?

God forgive her, she had.

"The tea will be getting cold." James's voice, clearly directed at her, was something less than friendly. "You'd best drink it, miss, and have done. I have, in addition, done my best to dry your garments, though they're still a trifle damp in spots."

Until James spoke, Claire had not even realized that he was in the cabin. As her surprised gaze flew to him—he was standing in the shadows near the table, his back partially turned as he carefully placed her frock and, presumably, her other garments over the back of a chair—she became acutely aware of her state of undress. Her legs, curled beside her on the bunk, were at least covered by the blanket. But the blanket ended at her waist, and the fine lawn of the shirt provided precious little in the way of modesty. Her breasts were clearly out-lined beneath it, and the gaping neckline had slipped off one shoulder, baring it and a considerable swath of creamy skin to the view of anyone who cared to look. Shamefully enough, the idea of Hugh seeing her in such a state of deshabille was not particularly bothersome. The degree of intimacy she had shared with him in the course of their brief but eventful acquaintance had al-ready rendered such considerations as ordinary modesty almost moot. The man had, after all, seen her naked. He had kissed her till her toes curled and taught her to kiss him back in a way she would never have believed a lady would do—or would want to do. He had run his hands over her body, caressed her breasts, held a basin for her to be sick in, and spent the last few hours sleeping at her side. The conventions, as far as he and she were concerned, had long since been well and truly breached. If anyone were to discover that she had spent the night with him in this tiny cabin, just the two of them alone, she would be ruined. Even if nothing beyond that had happened.

But something beyond that had happened. Something momentous. Something life changing. The secret wantonness inside herself that she had been struggling against ever since she had discovered its existence had been most thoroughly awakened. She had loved his kisses, had loved learning to kiss him back. The feel of his body on hers had made her tremble. His hand on her breast had made her melt. She had wanted him to lie with her, to perform the most intimate of acts. . . .

"Drink your tea," Hugh said brusquely, bringing her back to the present with a start. Standing next to the bunk now, with one arm resting against the upper berth, he fixed her with a look that warned her that he meant what he said. She didn't want the tea, but she didn't feel like arguing either. Taking a sip, she made a face at the heavily sugared brew and thrust the mug back at him. Apparently taken by surprise, Hugh took it from her. With an eye on James, Claire straightened her shirt, then pulled the blanket around her shoulders again until she was decent. Hugh watched her broodingly all the while.

"I think you'll find the clothes dry enough to wear, however," James said, glancing over his shoulder at her as he arranged the last of the garments over the chair. Hugh, mug in hand, moved away from the bunk.

"She doesn't have much choice, unless she wishes to appear abroad in your clothes—or mine," Hugh put in dryly. Having taken the cup away, he set it down on the table and seated himself on the opposite side. From the supplies laid out for him, it seemed obvious that he meant to write a letter. He picked up a quill, dipped it in ink, and set the point to paper. Watching him, Claire noticed for the first time that he was clean-shaven, and that his black hair was tied neatly at his nape in the French fashion. He was wearing, in addition to his shirt and breeches, a somewhat crumpled cravat, a well-fitting black frock coat, and a pair of tall black boots. The severeness of the color, the cut of the coat, and even the slightly old-fashioned hairstyle became him admirably.

Had she ever not thought him a handsome man? She must have been mad. Tall and well-built, with that black hair and bronze skin, those cool gray eyes and lean cheeks and that long, thin, intoxicating mouth, he was breathtakingly attractive.

At least, he took her breath.

Just looking at him brought her to a state of shivery excitement that would have shamed her to the core twenty-four hours before. In the days leading up to her wedding, she had secretly fantasized about what it would be like to have David come to her bed. Her daydreams had both warmed and embarrassed her, but the upshot was that she had looked forward to her wedding night with no small degree of anticipation. Her budding interest in what went on between a husband and wife when they were private had been all but killed by the disappointing reality of the marriage act. Now, most unexpectedly, that interest had been brought to full, throbbing life again—by Hugh.

Whatever was she going to do about it? About him? To lie with a man who was not one's husband was wrong. . . .

Hugh glanced at her. Had she been staring? It seemed she had. Caught unaware, she hastily redirected her energy into clambering off the bunk and making sure the blanket was wrapped around her well enough to render her decent. Even as she recovered her composure—the man was not a mind-reader, after all, so she had no reason to feel embarrassed by her thoughts—she hoped, fervently, that he would not see and correctly interpret the color she felt creeping up her cheeks.

"James has outdone himself on our behalf. Behold my boots, and he has, it seems, even managed to acquire slippers for you."

"Thank you," Claire said politely to James, glad to find that her voice sounded almost normal. Holding on to the upper berth with one hand, clutching the blanket closed with the other, she waited to make sure her rubbery knees would support her before she took a step. In the meantime, she looked around. With a glance at the chair where a pair of black satin slippers now took pride of place on the seat, she saw that James had indeed achieved the near impossible: come up with ladies' shoes on a ship filled exclusively, saving, as far as she knew, her own presence, with men.

" 'Tis a smugglers' vessel. Most things may be had for a price."

From his tone, James was clearly less than happy, and Claire recalled that he and Hugh had engaged in some pretty sharp exchanges while she had been drifting in and out of sleep. What had been the subject of their arguments? She hadn't been awake enough to tell. But it was easy to guess that at least one topic under discussion had been herself. Whatever had been decided, James was obviously disgruntled by it.

Having laid out her garments, James moved away toward the cupboards. The stiffness of his back, to say nothing of the looks he shot at an oblivious Hugh, conveyed disapproval as clearly as if he'd shouted the sentiment aloud. Claire frowned. Only the meanest intelligence could fail to guess that his disapproval was connected with, if not completely directed at, herself.

Of course, she realized, James believed her to be Sophy Towbridge, lightskirt/spy. With her senses still so disordered, she'd almost forgotten about that. Almost forgotten most of the unpleasant circumstances that had brought her to this point, as a matter of fact.

Almost forgotten everything but what it felt like to be kissed by Hugh.

Now, suddenly, she remembered.

"When you said land, did you mean France?" she gasped, her gaze flying to Hugh.

He nodded absently without looking up.

Claire despaired. Any hopes of fetching up in England had been fragile at best, as she had known all along. Once she had realized that the pistol she held on Hugh was unloaded, she had felt quite certain that Hugh's orders that the ship be turned around had not gone any further than James. But still, to be faced with the reality of having been carried off to France—it was unbelievable. No, it was horrifying.

At home, they must all be frightened to death for her, she realized. She'd been missing now for—what? A glance at the clock made her eyes widen: it was half-past six.

"Is it morning or evening?" Her voice was little more than a croak. In truth, she couldn't tell. No outside light reached the cabin, and she could have been asleep for any length of time, short or long.

"Evening." Hugh glanced up then. The merest hint of a smile touched his mouth. "You've slept the day away."

She'd been missing, then, for well over twenty-four hours.

Gabby would have been informed by now, and Beth. They would be frantic with worry—and Gabby was already ill from her pregnancy. Claire could not bear that she should be the cause of more anxiety for Gabby. And poor Alice and the coachman—what had become of them?

"I must go home," she said. "My family will be frantic with worry by now."

Having apparently finished his missive, Hugh was now engaged in sprinkling sand over it. He nodded without looking at her.

"You shall go home. When I'm certain you are who you claim to be. Until then, you will remain my prisoner."

"We weren't sent to bring back no prisoners." James shot Hugh a speaking look, which Hugh, now folding and sealing his letter, either didn't see or ignored.

"I tell you I must and will go home." Claire's fists clenched, and she glared at Hugh. During the previous night's lengthy and increasingly sleepy conversation, he had denied any knowledge of the attack on her coach, and had even had the gall to question whether it had, in fact, really happened. The knowledge that, after all that had passed between them, he still doubted her story and questioned her identity was maddening. The notion that he considered her his prisoner was infuriating. The idea that, for whatever reason, he might be lying to her about his involvement in the attack was frightening. "You are surely intelligent enough to have figured out by now that I am not the woman you seek."

"Possibly, puss, possibly." To her annoyance, Hugh grinned indulgently at her and stood up, pocketing his letter. "I will say that of all things, your communion with the chamber pot was—um, perhaps the most convincing."

"Even traitors may get travel sick," James said sourly with another of those pointed glances at Hugh.

"I, however, am no traitor." Claire's indignant gaze swung around to James, who, turning his shoulder and busying himself with pulling saddlebags from the cupboard, seemed to close himself off from her like a turtle retreating inside its shell. Thwarted, she fixed Hugh with a fulminating look instead. "I am Claire, Lady Claire Lynes, just as I have told you and *told* you."

James made a sound that was part grunt, part snort, and all skepticism. "Aye, but what I would like to know is just how you told him, missy. Mighty convincing you were, apparently."

Claire misliked the tone of that, which, even though it was muttered under James's breath, reached her ears with perfect clarity. Her eyes shot sparks at him. The implication was insulting, and so she meant to tell him in no uncertain terms—at least until she remembered that, to some degree at least, the implication was correct. She *had* kissed Hugh, and more than kissed him. Had that influenced him to change his mind? Flustered, she felt her words of indignant protest withering in her throat.

James gave her a look that said as plainly as words, *I thought so.*

Claire stiffened with indignation, and opened her mouth to give voice to a pretty pithy reply.

"Enough, the both of you."

Hugh held up a silencing hand before Claire could get the words out. She and James exchanged mutually withering glances, but in the face of Hugh's prohibition, neither of them cared to engage in the open warfare that had been clearly imminent.

Hugh was looking at her. "If you are indeed Sophy Towbridge and are playing me for a fool—yes, James, you've made your views on that quite clear, so you have no need to repeat them—then I make you my compliments on a job masterfully done. On the whole, though, I am inclined to believe you are . . . Claire."

James shook his head in despair. "Master Hugh, I never thought to see you so gulled."

Claire glared at James.

"Whether you believe it or not, I *am* Claire." Her gaze switched to Hugh. "And I must go home, or at least send word. My sisters will be worried."

"But not your husband?" Hugh's question was soft. He was standing now, beside the table, pocketing his letter and frowning at her. She realized suddenly that she felt supremely comfortable with him—had she really first set eyes on him less than twenty-four hours before? Now he knew her in many ways better than her closest kin. He knew all about her husband and sisters and, basically, her entire life, since last night. She had told him things—about her marriage, about her childhood—that she had never before told a living soul.

Strange, until he questioned it she had not even considered how David might be reacting to word of her disappearance. Would he be upset? The truth was easier to face this time: probably not. Certainly not nearly as upset as Gabby and Beth.

She'd been so fearful of marriage, so careful to choose what she'd thought was a good, kind, gentle man who genuinely cared about her. How could she have gotten it so unbelievably wrong?

"No, not my husband," she admitted, and her eyes were filled with the pain of a hurtful truth finally realized and accepted as they met Hugh's. He said nothing, but his expression told her that he understood how difficult coming to terms with the reality of the situation was for her. Last night he had listened with every indication of sympathy when she had talked about her marriage. Smiling a little, nestled in Hugh's arms, she had described David's courtship of her, which had been distinguished by poetry dedicated to her fine eyes and the most charming of posies delivered daily and gentle kisses on the back of her hand and, finally, the culmination: his proposal, accompanied by a promise of everlasting love. Except for a single derisive snort when she had mentioned the poetry—Hugh had quickly turned the sound into a cough but Claire had known it for what it was—Hugh had been a largely silent but comforting audience as she had talked about the first few months of what she had taken for a delicate but growing friendship within marriage and then David's increasingly blatant lack of interest in her and his subsequent near abandonment. Just telling the truth about her marriage, had eased her sore heart enormously. Not wanting to burden her sisters with her unhappiness, and considering such a subject far too intimate to discuss with anyone else, she had kept everything to herself even as her marriage, begun with so much hope on her part at least, had withered away like a flower left too long without rain.

Now she had finally told someone the truth, and unlikely as her confidant was, she was glad. She felt far lighter in spirit for having unburdened herself, even to Hugh.

Or maybe, especially to Hugh.

"My husband won't be unduly worried about me. Or at least I don't think he will be. As I told you, our relationship is not—close."

"He's a bloody idiot." Hugh's tone was brusque.

Claire said nothing, but she smiled at him. To hear him express such sentiments assuaged, just a little, the once truly enormous hurt that had taken possession of her heart when, some months ago, she had begun to face the truth that she was unloved by her husband. But fortunately, that hurt, like a healing wound, had grown less painful with every passing day, and now was feeling better with every passing hour.

Because of Hugh? Of course because of Hugh.

Claire's heart began to pound as she considered the ramifications of that. Watching her, Hugh smiled, a slow and intimate smile that warmed her all over. And suddenly Claire was not so sure she wanted to go home after all.

# ❧ 16 ❧

......................................

" *G*od's teeth, Master Hugh, to see you smelling of April and May over another man's ladybird is more than a body can bear."

James was muttering to himself again, his voice pitched just loud enough to be "accidentally" overheard. Claire shot him an evil look. Hugh, roused from his warm exchange of glances with Claire, looked suddenly self-conscious, and rounded on his henchman.

"Have you nothing better to do than stand there blathering at me, old man?"

"Oh, aye, I can always busy myself with making our funeral arrangements. Because that is how this lunacy is likely to end up."

Hugh's eyes narrowed at him. "Much more of your back talk and you're liable to find yourself turned off without a character."

James snorted, clearly unimpressed. "You'll do what you like, o' course, just as you always do. If ever there was such a stubborn, reckless, care-for-nobody ..." His voice trailed off into a truly unintelligible murmur. Moving to the table, he picked up the tea mug and a saucer containing what looked like a piece of bread, and stalked toward the door.

"You might leave the lady's supper," Hugh protested, surprisingly mild as, with his arms crossed over his chest, he observed James's progress.

"I don't want it," Claire assured him with a shudder.

Hugh's glance signified acknowledgment.

"Some are the type that has to learn their lessons the hard way, no matter how much a body tries to warn them," James said as he reached the door, shooting Hugh a pointed look. Then, with another scathing glance at Claire, he let himself out of the cabin.

Instead of being angry, as Claire would have expected, Hugh looked at her, his mouth twisting into a rueful smile.

"I apologize for James. He tends to be a little overzealous in his care of me at times."

Having had considerable experience herself with fiercely devoted servants in the person of her own dear Twindle, Claire found that she was in complete sympathy with Hugh's dilemma, and was, as well, suddenly much less annoyed at James than such slanders as he had heaped on her deserved.

"My old nursemaid is exactly the same. She forever acts as if I am no more than six years old." The thought of Twindle brought thoughts of Gabby and Beth with it. She could not let them worry about her. Not for one second longer than she could help. She looked at Hugh appealingly. "I must somehow get word to them at home that I am alive and unharmed."

For a moment he looked at her inscrutably. Then he gave a curt nod.

"If you wish. Before you can get word to anyone,

however, you must first get off the ship, and to do that you must get dressed."

That was eminently reasonable, although Hugh suddenly sounded almost remote, as though he was withdrawing from her in some subtle way. But Claire had no time to try to puzzle out his sudden change of mood. The ship rolled, and her stomach rolled with it. Battling a nearly overwhelming urge to sink back down on the bunk, Claire clung to the upper berth and watched in horror as the lantern started to trace a lazy arc to the end of its tether and back. Above all else, she realized, she had to get off that ship. If she didn't, if the pitching and yawing should begin again in earnest—well, she couldn't even bring herself to think about that.

"Get dressed," Hugh said, and this time it was an order. Glancing at him even as she battled a fast-rising queasiness, Claire saw that he had suddenly changed from a man she'd thought had a care for her into a hard-eyed stranger. She was reminded that she knew almost nothing about him—except that she was totally under his control. Whatever he told her to do, if he cared to enforce it, she had no choice but to obey.

The seeming bond that had developed between them was in truth no more than an illusion wrought by an unprecedented combination of physical attraction and enforced proximity, and so she would do well to remember. It would never do to depend too much on it—or him.

"If you want me to get dressed," she said in a voice grown suddenly cool, "you must go away and leave me to it."

Hugh looked at her. For the briefest of moments he seemed to hesitate. Then he shrugged and headed for the door.

"Be as quick as you can," he said over his shoulder as he reached it. "I'll be back for you shortly. Bar the door after me."

Claire nodded. As he left she crossed to the door, feeling that there was much merit in his recommendation. Even if no threat materialized, barring the door would at least ensure her privacy.

As she dropped the bar into place, Claire could quite clearly hear James's voice on the other side of the portal. He must have been returning to the cabin just as Hugh left it.

"Yon petticoat's playin' ye for a fool, Master Hugh, can't ye see that?" James sounded both angry and anguished. "She's a looker, I grant ye, but we're talking about your life. Aye, and my life, too, if it comes to that."

"It won't come to that. I tell you, James, that chit is no more Sophy Towbridge than I am." Hugh's voice was flat.

"Aye, so she's managed to convince ye, but . . ."

They were clearly moving away from the door as they spoke, and after that Claire could no longer make sense of individual words. It didn't matter: She had gotten a very clear picture of the situation. Hugh, to a large degree, believed her; James didn't at all, and was determined to argue Hugh around.

Would he succeed?

But she had no time to worry about it now. She had no time to do anything other than get dressed. She still felt ill, light-headed, queasy, with rubbery knees. Over and above anything else, she had to get off that ship.

Just as he had when Hugh had summoned him to her aid the night before, James had set up a pitcher of water and a basin on a washstand below the cupboards, and it was to this that she went. This time a brush had been laid out beside the basin along with several of her hair pins, apparently recovered from her clothes or the floor, as Claire discovered with a spurt of pleasure as she looked down at the items provided for her toilette. There were also soap, a towel, tooth powder, and a small hand mirror. Liberal use of the soap—plain unscented lye that could have been the finest of perfumed bars for the joy she took in it—and tooth powder made her feel considerably better. Nothing she could do to her hair in the brief period of time she had available to her could render it stylish, but tangle-free she could do. Brushing it until it crackled, she twisted her hair up into a slightly precarious knot on the back of her head (she had not near enough pins to make it secure), and that made her feel better still. By the time she was struggling into her clothes—the seams of her corset were decidedly damp, as were the hem of her petticoat and the neckline and puffed sleeves of her gown, but still they fit and they were hers—she almost felt like herself again.

She was still struggling to get the blasted gown buttoned up the back when a knock sounded on the door.

"Let me in," Hugh said, and it was an order.

Padding barefoot to the door, Claire realized that she was not all that sorry to leave off struggling with her buttons. She was beginning to feel quite ill again, and was ready to leave the ship with her dress half undone if it would get firm land beneath her feet any sooner.

It was an effort to unbolt the door, and as she lifted the bar, which was heavier than she remembered, Claire felt almost ready to sink to the floor. Nervously she realized that she was growing queasier by the second. Then, as she stepped back away from the portal and Hugh entered, she saw why.

The lantern was swinging crazily on its chain again.

"I have to get off this ship," she said by way of greeting, hanging on to the door for support. Treacherous thing, it swayed just like everything else within her view.

"You do look a tad green." Hugh's gaze slid over her with immediate comprehension. He had, at least, the grace—or the sense—not to smile. "What, not finished dressing yet? The ship's docking—that's the cause of the motion you feel—and we have to be ready to move as soon as she ties up. Here, let me help you."

Wrapping a strong arm around her waist—she leaned against him gratefully, her head resting against his hard shoulder—he walked her across the cabin to where the shoes James had procured for her still waited on the chair. Picking them up, he practically pushed her down on the seat. Then he dropped to one knee in front of her, pulled one cold bare foot onto his upraised thigh—the black cloth of his breeches was smooth and snug over the hard muscles of his leg, she noted—and proceeded to fit it into a slipper. James's prowess, or knowledge of a lady's needs, had apparently not extended to the procurement of proper stockings, so her foot went into the slipper bare, and Hugh had to slip his fingers between the flimsy back of the shoe and her heel to get it on. All too aware of the lantern still moving like a pendulum overhead, Claire was content to let him do with her as he would. Feeling limp and increasingly nauseated, she sat with her hands resting on her lap and watched as he wrapped the black satin ribbons around her slender ankle as efficiently as any lady's maid. He did not, however, look like a lady's maid: far from it. The sight of his long fingers, dark and very masculine against the creamy skin of her foot, and the feel of their warm strength moving against her sensitive flesh provided a welcome distraction from the increasingly perilous state of her stomach.

If she had not stopped him, last night, she would now know for certain whether all men were the same between the sheets.

The thought popped into her head seemingly out of nowhere, and it shocked her. What shocked her more was the realization that, now that time and the cooling of passion should have brought wiser counsel, she still almost regretted calling a halt.

Looking down at his head, bent now as he tied the ribbons in a jaunty bow, all the reasons why she had stopped him—she was a lady, a married woman, and besides considerations of morals and honor she had been, quite simply, afraid—seemed suddenly far less important than the way his slightest touch made her feel. Her mouth went dry as she admitted it. She had wanted him to take her more than she had ever wanted anything in her life—and, despite everything, she still did.

"You're pale." Hugh glanced up then, caught her gaze on him, and frowned.

Claire almost fell off the chair as those gray eyes probed hers. He could not know what she was thinking, she reminded herself frantically—could he? Even as heat began to suffuse her cheeks, even as she began to suspect from his expression that perhaps, just perhaps, he could read her mind after all, her attention was captured by the lantern. For once, she blessed the thing for the distraction it provided. It was swinging more vigorously than ever. Watching it, her stomach began to churn in sympathetic rhythm. Suddenly all thoughts of lying with Hugh were banished by other, more immediate concerns.

"I need to get off this ship," she said, meeting his gaze with real desperation. Watching the lantern's peregrinations had brought her to the verge of being once again horribly ill.

"Just a little bit longer, and we'll have you firmly on dry land," he promised, his gaze dropping to his task. She watched in growing misery as he eased her second foot into its slipper. He was quick, and gentle, and if he felt anything but sympathy for her plight as he wound the ribbons around her ankle and tied them into a bow she could not tell it. All her life she had been afflicted by motion sickness, and, she had discovered, most people were impatient at best with what they considered a weakness. David, for one, was quite sure that all that was required to remain perfectly well on long journeys was strength of will, which he never hesitated to inform her she lacked. On their last journey together—from Hayleigh Castle to London four months after their wedding—he had told the coachman to spring the horses, not caring that the resulting violent rocking of the carriage, as he well knew by that time, was almost guaranteed to make her ill. When she indeed was sick, he said, *"You disgust me,"* in a tone of total loathing, and hired a horse at the first opportunity to ride the rest of the way to town. That had been the last substantive amount of time they had spent together. From that day on, it was as if he had all but forgotten her existence.

Sometimes she caught herself wondering if things would have been different between them if she had not become ill that day. Logically, she knew the answer was no, but still she had wondered. Off and on until now, actually, it occurred to her that she no longer cared.

"There."

His task finished, Hugh returned her foot to the floor and glanced up at her with a quick smile.

She tried to smile back, but it must have been a wan effort because his brow furrowed. He stood up, and before Claire realized what he meant to do he scooped her out of the chair and into his arms, holding her, legs dangling and hands frantically clutching his shoulders, high against his chest.

"What . . . ?" she questioned faintly, clinging for dear life and looking at him wide-eyed. A faint, pleasant aroma of soap clung to him. His face was very close, and as she absorbed the lean, clean-shaven cheeks, the straight nose and gray eyes and now wryly curving mouth, she felt attraction rear its troublesome head again. Despite the state of her stomach, being held in his arms made her heart beat faster. His shoulders were so broad, his arms so hard with muscle, and he seemed to carry her as if she weighed nothing at all.

Her breathing quickened as she realized how very much she liked being held in his arms.

"You look like you need to lie down." If he was aware of how his easy strength was affecting her, he gave no sign of it. He took the two quick strides necessary to reach the bunk and put her down on it. Feeling dizzier by the second, Claire sank back onto the thin mattress thankfully. As her head touched the pillow he straightened, looking down at her with a rueful half-smile and rather gingerly pressing a hand to his side.

"Aren't your ribs hurting?" she asked, feeling a little self-conscious as she remembered how she had punched him the night before.

"Nothing to signify."

His hand dropped away from his side and he turned

away from the bunk. Claire closed her eyes. She had needed to lie down, she realized. Flat on her back, she had at least some slight chance of avoiding disgracing herself again.

"Here." It couldn't have been more than a minute before he was back.

A cool wet cloth was placed on her forehead. Claire opened her eyes to discover Hugh leaning over her, pressing the towel, for that's what it was, thoroughly dampened now and folded into a neat rectangle, against her skin. It felt good, soothing. She opened her eyes and managed a faint smile as he removed his hand, leaving the cloth in place.

"Thank you. See? Didn't I say you were really very nice?"

He grunted and sat down on the edge of the bunk. "I wouldn't count on it if I were you." His gaze met hers, and she was suddenly, tinglingly conscious of his proximity. He was so close that his hip brushed her thigh. She could see a small nick in his chin where he had apparently cut himself shaving, and smell the faint aroma of soap. His gray eyes ran over her from head to toe. "Think you could turn over and let me button your frock? We need to be ready to go when James gives us the word."

"You can't button my frock for me." Despite everything that had passed between them, Claire was genuinely scandalized.

He looked amused. "Why not?"

"Because," she said firmly. Her instinct, her upbringing, her notions of propriety all shouted it: Gentlemen never buttoned ladies' frocks. It just wasn't done.

His brows rose. "Another of your becauses, hmm? Let me tell you, my girl, many more of those out of you and you're going to drive me stark, staring mad. Now turn over and stop being ridiculous. Unless you want to stay on this ship until your hair turns gray."

Thus adjured, Claire swallowed her protest and rolled over, careful to hold the revivifying damp cloth in place as she presented her back to him. He did up the remaining buttons on her frock in the same efficient manner as he had dealt with her shoes. The intimacy of what he was doing was not lost on her despite the continued distraction of her uneasy stomach. Having a man do up one's buttons was shocking, but then, so much that had happened to her since being dragged from her carriage was even more shocking that this, despite her instinctive protest, was a mere bagatelle. In any case, such an intimacy from Hugh did not feel wrong. Try as she would, she could not summon up so much as an ounce of shame.

"Feeling better?" He fastened the last button, then with a hand on her shoulder turned her gently onto her back again. He was leaning over her, close now, a hand on each side of her body, and there was something that was not quite a smile in his eyes as he looked down at her.

"No." She said it with such conviction that he laughed. She held the damp cloth to her forehead as if it were her only hope of salvation, although, warmed now to the temperature of her skin, it no longer provided much in the way of relief. But remembering the way she had felt before he had provided it for her made her loath to give it up. At that point she was prepared to embrace anything that would keep her from being sick again.

"You look better. You're a rather interesting shade of pale now, rather than being white as a snail's belly."

She eyed him darkly. "Flatterer."

He grinned, clearly finding her tartness amusing.

"I meant, of course, as white as the most precious of pearls." The smile faded from his face, and his eyes grew suddenly intent. "All right, enough nonsense. I need you to listen to me for a minute. This is important."

Eyes widening, Claire nodded. Seeing that he had her complete attention, he reached into his coat pocket and pulled a pistol from it, which he held up so that she could see it readily.

"I'm going to give you this. I want you to keep it by you, and if anything happens, if anyone should try to grab you or harm you in any way, shoot him. Don't think twice about it. You've gotten caught up in something that is more dangerous than you know, and you have to be prepared to defend yourself if necessary. And for God's sake, this time if somebody comes at you pull the trigger. The object is to make the person you're shooting unable to do you any harm, and the best way to do that is by making him dead."

Claire stared at the pistol with some distaste. It looked very much like the one she had held on him the night before. In fact, she realized, it was the one she had held on him the night before: She recognized the intricate design of the silver.

"You're lucky I didn't follow that advice with you." Recalling the preceding night's debacle, she made a face. "Of course, even if I had pulled the trigger it wouldn't have done any good: When I held it on you, it wasn't loaded."

All her remembered ire was in her voice.

His mouth turned up at one corner in a crooked smile. "Well, it's loaded now. It even fires properly. I tested it myself this morning on deck."

There was a quick knock, and then, before either of them could answer, the door opened. James stepped inside the cabin, a long black garment hanging over his arm. He closed the door, then paused as he spotted them. With a deepening frown he glanced from Claire lying supine on the bunk to Hugh sitting so close beside her. His expression made his disapproval of their posture as clear as if he'd shouted it aloud.

"Did you get it?" Hugh asked.

"I did." James nodded at the garment over his arm, his expression as sour as his voice. He moved toward the bunk, his gaze openly condemning as it touched on Claire before returning to Hugh again. "It seems the bloke with the slippers is taking home a whole trunk full of pretties for his sweetheart. This cloak here cost you half a crown."

Hugh grinned. "You've unexpected depths, James. I had no idea that purchasing ladies' garments was numbered among your many talents."

James grimaced by way of reply, then managed to look more disapproving than ever as he came to stand beside Hugh. He glanced at Claire, hostility in his eyes.

"We're getting ready to dock," James said to Hugh. "If you want to be quick off the ship, we'd best be moving."

"I do." Hugh passed the pistol to James and looked at Claire. "Just keep thinking about dry land, angel eyes."

As the endearment registered, James looked like he was choking on words he didn't quite have the nerve to say, while Hugh, ignoring his henchman entirely, reached over and removed the cloth from Claire's forehead, wadded it into a ball, and tossed it in the direction of the washstand. Then he stood, caught her hands, and pulled her into a sitting position and then to her feet.

Her head began to swim as soon as she was upright, and her stomach threatened fireworks, but she forced herself to ignore the disturbing sensations as best she could. The thought of getting off the ship at last was as potent a medicine as any tonic. If that was to be her reward, she thought, she could endure at least a little while longer.

"All right?" Hugh was holding on to her hands still, steadying her. He was standing very close, looking intently down into her face. The concern she saw in his eyes warmed her.

She nodded resolutely.

"That's my brave girl," he said, and let go of her hands. She stood there on her own two feet, trying not to so much as look at the swinging lantern, as he took the cloak from James, shook it out and dropped it over her shoulders, then tied the strings beneath her chin for her as if she were a small child in his care. Despite her worsening distress, the thought made her smile. Seeing her smile, he grinned and chucked her under the chin in an avuncular fashion that made James look outraged. Hugh then completed James's consternation by plucking the pistol from his hand and giving it to Claire.

"Keep it by you," he said, while James's eyes widened in liveliest alarm. "And try not to let anyone else see it."

"Master Hugh—she . . . what . . . ?" James sputtered, staring at the pistol, obviously aghast.

"In case she feels like shooting one of us," Hugh said, straight-faced. James looked horrified.

"He's teasing, of course," Claire said to James, giving Hugh a reproving look as she pulled the cloak more closely about herself. It was of thick, serviceable black wool with a faintly musty smell that spoke of having been kept too long in a trunk. Obviously it had been made for a far larger female than she, but under the circumstances that was all to the good. Its folds were more than ample enough to conceal the pistol if she held it in one hand and kept it close to her side, which was her intention. If Hugh thought she needed to be armed, then she meant to hang on to the weapon for dear life. Since yesterday, she'd learned all too well that the world could be a dangerous place. Now more than ever, she had no wish to die.

"I am Lady Claire Lynes, you know," she added, speaking directly to James. "And that is the truth. I swear it. You need have no fear of me."

James looked unconvinced. Hugh's eyes twinkled and he shook his head at her.

"You'll never convince him—he sees calamity behind every door." He reached out and pulled the cloak's hood over her head, adjusting it so that it all but hid her face. Claire looked a question at him. "You're too pretty by half, puss. There's no point in attracting more attention than we have to."

James looked grim.

"Thank you for the cloak," Claire said to James as Hugh moved away from the pair of them. She gave him a little smile, hoping to win him over. Being regarded as a light-skirts/traitor/potential murderess was disheartening, to say the least. "And the slippers too. It was kind of you to go to so much trouble for me."

" 'Twas not for you I did it." James nodded at Hugh, who appeared to be checking the powder of a second pistol by the light of the swaying lantern. "He told me to get what ye lacked if I could, and that's what I did." James's gaze met Claire's. There was no mistaking the hard suspicion in his eyes. "I'll tell ye straight, miss:

Without him, ye'd be dead now. Ye owe him your life. I only hope ye remember it."

Claire was taken aback, but before she could reply, Hugh rejoined them.

"All right, let's go. We want to get off the ship as quickly and quietly as possible."

"Aye." James crossed to the cupboards, extracted a pair of saddlebags, and slung them over his shoulder. Then he looked up at Hugh. "Do ye think there'll be trouble?"

Hugh shrugged. "Who's to say? Claire, you stay between James and me."

As Hugh called her so casually by her true name, Claire caught her breath. Then she smiled at him, a sweet and charming smile that made his eyes widen. James, watching, looked as if he had just swallowed a mouthful of brine. Then Hugh caught Claire's hand and headed for the door. Moments later the little party was making its way through the surprisingly busy hallway and climbing up the companionway along with sailors who by ones and twos were bearing various burdens toward the open deck.

France, at least from Claire's perspective as she followed Hugh down the gangplank to the rickety wooden dock, seemed to be composed largely of a muddy beach clawed by sloshing fingers of tide and crowds of people and pigs. Its darkness was lit by smoky torches and the air smelled of fish and burning wood. The *Nadine* was tied up next to a small armada of dilapidated-looking fishing vessels. Steep banks covered in tall clumps of marshy grass rose to shield the beach on three sides, while on the fourth, behind them, the sea hissed and growled like an angry cat. The wind was cold, but for that Claire was thankful. From the moment she had emerged onto the open deck and filled her lungs with the brisk night air, she had begun to feel better. She was still not quite herself, but she no longer felt in imminent danger of casting up her accounts.

"Stay close."

Hugh's warning, given over his shoulder in a low voice as she instinctively paused to glance around, was unnecessary. She had no intention of moving so much as an unneeded inch away from his tall form. Funny that this man whom she had mortally feared less than a day before should now be her bastion of safety, but so it was. In this strange and hostile environment—France!—she would be terrified and utterly lost without his protection.

And he would protect her to the best of his ability, she knew.

They reached the end of the gangplank, the three of them, staying close together as they turned and headed toward the darkness at the far end of the dock. They were moving rapidly, Claire thought, without seeming to give the appearance of hurrying at all. Hugh was in the lead, with Claire as close as a shadow behind him and James, a grim-faced rear guard, following. The echo of their footsteps on the wood planks was thankfully lost in all the commotion around the dock.

Claire saw that Hugh was holding his pistol close against his side as though he did not wish to call attention to it. There was a wariness about the way he moved, an alertness in the way he glanced around, a tension in his hand holding hers, which made her heart beat faster. The fact that he felt it necessary to actually have a weapon in hand told its own tale, and James was similarly armed. Her fingers tightened nervously around the grip of the pistol Hugh had given her. It was heavy and carrying it was awkward, but under the circumstances she was glad to have it. She glanced down to make sure it was still concealed by the heavy folds of her cloak. It was, as far as she could tell, and the darkness provided its own cover.

Although surely she wouldn't really need to shoot anyone; Hugh was undoubtedly just being cautious. No one seemed even to be looking their way. Everyone she could see—and there were dozens gathered around the docks—was busy with his or her own affairs.

Still, she could not help but be apprehensive, and was, as a result, keenly sensitive to her surroundings. Glancing around for the umpteenth time, she saw a village of thatched-roof cottages clustered on a ridge overlooking the beach. All the houses appeared to be dark. The village inhabitants, though, seemed to have turned out in full force to greet the arrival of the ship. Even as she watched, more newcomers flocked onto the beach to join those already there, murmuring among themselves, watching the goings-on with interest. A surprising number of pigs rooting around at the edges of the gathering drew a puzzled frown from Claire. Seeing her expression, Hugh explained that a herd of them had been driven down to the beach when the ship's signal had been spotted so that all trace of the loading and unloading of cargo would be obliterated by the next day. Indeed, the *Nadine*'s crew was hard at work, wresting iron-bound barrels down the gangplank and unloading various gunny sacks and wrapped packages and wooden chests onto the carts and drays and other assorted vehicles drawn up to the dock to receive them. Goods were being unloaded from the vehicles as well and taken aboard the *Nadine*, with locals working busily alongside the sailors. The night was dark, with no stars at all and the merest sliver of the moon, which was constantly obscured by blowing clouds. The whole business was conducted by torchlight, in near silence despite the large number of assembled people, and swiftly. It was obvious even to one as unversed in such matters as Claire that she was watching a clandestine, if familiar and well practiced, operation.

"Are they *all* smugglers?" Claire asked Hugh in a near whisper, looking out at what appeared to be an entire village of people crowding the beach. She, Hugh, and James were approaching where the walkway ended by abutting a hillock-sized dune that appeared to be composed of sand, tall grass, and shadows. So far, no one had seemed to pay them the least heed, but still Claire was growing increasingly uneasy. There was something in the air—a sense of urgency, a feeling that something could very easily go wrong.

"The locals, you mean? Yes, most of them. It's a way to make some money, and times are hard now. Practically everyone who lives along the coast here is involved in smuggling one way or another these days."

Hugh reached the end of the walkway and jumped down with a scrunch of boots upon sand. He then turned to catch Claire around the waist and swing her down beside him. For a moment, as her slippered feet hit the gritty mix of sand and rock and mud, they slid, and she kept her balance by grabbing his arm. The muscles of his upper arm bulged beneath her hand, big enough and hard enough to be felt even through the layers of coat and shirt, she registered as she glanced up at him. As her gaze met his she realized too that her head barely reached his chin, and the breadth of his shoulders was easily double the width of hers. She, who had never thought she liked big strong masculine men, suddenly discovered that she liked them very much. Or, at least, she liked this big strong masculine man very much. He made her feel—safe. And utterly feminine.

"Aye, they are, which makes it bloody hard to tell friend from foe," James chimed in, jumping down beside them. Claire, still holding on to Hugh's arm, glanced at

James even as Hugh caught her hand again and turned away, pulling her after him, towing her toward the darkness at the edge of the beach. James, however, wasn't looking at her. He was eyeing the eddying crowd with a worried expression that made Claire's heart speed up. If these two danger-hardened men were uneasy, then she was afraid.

"Ah, Colonel! Are you taking your leave of us, then?"

The *Nadine*'s captain materialized out of the crowd almost directly in front of them. His slight form was wrapped in a resplendent greatcoat with a great deal of silver lace and frogging, and the light from the flaming torch set into the ground nearby made his finery as well as his white wig appear almost orange in places. He stopped in front of them, having deliberately intercepted them, Claire suspected from his manner. Four burly sailors were at his back.

At almost precisely the same moment as she realized that the man had called Hugh "colonel," a military title if she had ever heard one, Claire felt the cold finger of fear glide down her back. A confrontation like this was what Hugh and James had been braced for, she knew with an uncanny sense of certainty. Hugh's hand squeezed hers once, in hard warning, before releasing it. Her hand, damp now with cold sweat, gripped the pistol harder. It would never do to drop it; she might need it. She might actually have to fire the thing after all—she might actually have to shoot one of these men.

Hugh's back was to her now, foursquare and solid, and she got the impression that he had deliberately placed himself between her and the sailors. Again she sensed the tension that radiated from him, and from James as well. They were on high alert, ready for anything. To her surprise, given his distrust of her, James stayed beside her, close on her right side. Following Hugh's lead, he seemed to have placed himself in a position to protect her.

Both men's pistols were at the ready, aimed at the newcomers. Unfortunately, Claire saw, the other men were also armed. Their pistols pointed back just as dangerously.

"Well met, Captain: You saved me the trouble of seeking you out to bid you farewell." Belying everything her senses told her about his state of mind—and those no-nonsense pistols—Hugh's manner was both easy and courteous. "You have been most hospitable, but we must needs be on our way."

"I think not." The captain's voice reflected mild regret, and he shook his head in a fashion that was almost commiserating. His pistol, however, never wavered in its aim, which was directly at Hugh's heart. Then he snapped his fingers. The men behind him fanned out so that the five of them formed a barrier as impenetrable as a wall. A wall armed with pistols. Claire, from her position behind Hugh's back, noticed that she did not seem to be the intended target of a single weapon, and could only thank fortune. However, she had little doubt that if shooting started she would find herself very much in harm's way. Hugh, as a primary target of all that gun power, would undoubtedly be brought down in a trice. He would die. . . .

For a moment, for Claire, time seemed to stand still. Hugh would die—at the image that conjured up, she went suddenly weak at the knees. It shook her to realize just how important he had become to her in such a short period of time.

Out in the bay, the wind blew long ruffled lines of whitecaps toward the shore. The sound of them breaking and receding on the muddy beach formed a murmuring backdrop for the low-voiced, mingled French and English conversations of the smugglers, who were still hard at labor around them and appeared largely oblivious to the scene being played out amid them. About a dozen feet to Claire's left, a wagon groaning under a heavy load of barrels got stuck in the sand. Locals converged on it, trying to push it out. The driver got down and, amid a torrent of Gallic curses, jerked the reins over his horses' heads and tried to help them pull, with no success that Claire could see. Wheels squeaked as other, apparently less heavily loaded wagons rolled past, away from the dock. From the look of things, the night's labor was almost done.

"Forgive me, Colonel, but we do much business here. Sometimes, in the name of business, we have to throw the French a bone. Tonight, you are that bone, you two and the lady here." The captain never even glanced at his henchmen as he added brusquely, "Search them. Get their weapons."

With five pistols trained on them, opening fire was clearly suicidal. Breathing fast, her knees suddenly rubbery again, Claire prayed that Hugh and James would make no move, and they did not. She stood mute, taking care to remain behind Hugh and as much out of sight as possible, as they were relieved of their pistols and subjected to a hand search for additional weapons. Hugh's knife was taken from a sheath hidden beneath the waistband of his breeches. Then the sailors stepped back, nodding at their captain as they pocketed the weapons they had taken.

Claire's blood began to drum in her ears as she realized that no one had given a thought to her. The pistol Hugh had given her suddenly seemed big as a cannon in her hand. Her fingers trembled, and she took care to press the gun close against her thigh, praying that no one would see it amid the folds of her cloak. She, alone of the three of them, was still armed. What should she do? Her mouth went dry as she considered the possibilities. She could not possibly pull a pistol on five armed men—but she could not just meekly let Hugh and James and herself be taken, either.

They would be killed, all three of them. Possibly tortured, probably, in her case, raped, but certainly killed. She was as certain of that as she was that the tide was coming in.

"No longer the loyal Englishman, Captain?" If Hugh was as frightened as she was, his voice didn't reveal it. In fact, he sounded as calm as if he and the captain were having a pleasant conversation after a chance meeting on a London street.

The other man shrugged. "When it suits me. But too many people know that you crossed to England on my vessel. If I protect you, I suffer, my men suffer, and my business suffers, and that I am not prepared to tolerate. Better to turn you over to my friend Brigadier de la Falais, and let him have the credit for capturing an English spy."

He nodded toward the far end of the quay.

Claire glanced in the direction he indicated and discovered, to her horror, a small band of French soldiers, chasseurs she believed they were called, unmistakable in their uniforms and tall hats with cockades, picking their way through the crowd on horseback. To be captured by the French—at the thought, sweat broke out on her upper lip and she had to clamp her lips together to keep her breathing under control. Would they be hanged, or shot, or imprisoned in some horrible dungeon until they died of old age? Gabby and Beth would never know what had happened to her. She would simply disappear.

But she still had the pistol. One shot. What should she do?

"Ye would turn your own countrymen over to the Frogs?" James demanded in a hoarse voice. He was betraying all the agitation that Hugh was not. His fists were balled and his beard quivered with fury. His belly seemed to swell with indignation.

Be careful, James, Claire whispered inwardly, and her hand tightened on the pistol. Should she just pull it out and try to hold five men at bay? Once the thing was fired, its value as a deterrent was spent.

"With regret," the captain said, and smiled. "Believe me, with much regret."

His gaze traveled past Hugh to find Claire, barely visible as she peeked around Hugh's shoulder. To her horror their gazes met, and she froze, terrified. The pistol seemed as obvious as a signal fire in her hand. How, she wondered, dry-mouthed, could anyone possibly miss it?

"Miss Towbridge, it would perhaps be in your best interest to walk over here to my side. You need have no fear, you know. The French will doubtless welcome you with open arms—unless, of course, you choose to cast in your lot with your unfortunate countrymen here."

Miss Towbridge. Dear Lord in heaven, he was laboring under the same misapprehension as Hugh had been at first and James still was: He thought she was a traitor to England—a spy for the French. No wonder they had not searched her for a weapon. Under the circumstances such a mistake was no very bad thing, she calculated swiftly. In fact, it might prove a godsend. A quick, frightened glance to her left, past the stuck wagon, told her that the soldiers were drawing near. There was not much time. . . .

All at once she became aware of Hugh's hand behind his back, his fingers wiggling madly. After a single startled glance, she jerked her gaze away. She knew what he wanted.

"La, no," Claire said airily, doing her best to assume the identity of Sophy Towbridge as she pressed the pistol into Hugh's hand and stepped out from behind him. Thank goodness for the torches with their flickering shadows, for the wind that sent coattails and cloaks flapping, even for the stuck wagon and the driver cursing in voluble French and those of his neighbors who were trying to help him push his load free. So many distractions could only work in their favor. She did her best to provide another one as she walked slowly toward the captain and his men, pushing her hood back from her head and smiling at them. The effect was all she could have wished for. Five pair of eyes fastened on her.

And might God help her if she should end up in their hands, she thought grimly.

"I am most grateful to you, sir, for rescuing me. I have much that they will find interesting to tell my friends in Paris. While as for these fellows—I cannot call them gentlemen—they would have seen me dead, I think."

"Perhaps we can make a deal, Captain," Hugh said abruptly.

"A deal?" The captain lifted his brows, shifting his attention to Hugh. Claire, glad of any excuse not to join the enemy, stopped where she was and turned to look at Hugh. She was only a foot or so in front of him, but his gaze just brushed her before fixing on the captain. In the torch-lit darkness, his eyes looked almost as black as his hair, and his height coupled with the breadth of his shoulders made him appear formidable indeed. The wind was blowing the tails of his coat; his hands were by his sides, the pistol lost in the shadows. To Hugh's right, James was glaring at her. Claire realized that her actions had confirmed everything he had suspected about her: He was now absolutely convinced that she was, indeed, Sophy Towbridge.

Of course, he did not know about the pistol even now in Hugh's hand.

Despite the brisk wind, she felt sweat trickling down her spine as she realized that Hugh must soon make his move. The little troop of oncoming soldiers was now almost even with the stuck wagon. It was a matter of minutes until they were upon them. Once they were in the custody of the French military, she feared, all would be lost. But Hugh faced the same problem that had plagued her: one pistol, one shot, against five armed men—and a contingent of well-armed soldiers now drawing perilously close.

"Miss Towbridge was carrying with her a letter that the French want quite desperately. I'll tell you where it is—if you let my man and me go."

The captain laughed. "What, did you take it from her? Miss Towbridge, is what he says true?"

"He is a pig," Claire sniffed, inspired by the real-life porkers, several of which were at that moment snuffling in the mud nearby. What was Hugh up to? There was no letter, nothing of the kind, as he had already discovered for himself, simply because she was not Sophy Towbridge. But she certainly hoped she was up to snuff enough to play along. "But he is telling the truth: He took the letter. I am glad he reminded me, because I would have it back."

"Well, Captain? Do we have a deal?" Hugh sounded almost bored. Claire met his gaze—her head was turned so that only he and James could see her face—and his eyes told her that, indeed, the time was at hand. She could see nothing of the pistol, but she knew it must be cocked and ready. Her muscles tensed, and she could feel the little hairs prickling to life on the back of her neck.

"Certainly, my friend. You have only to tell me where the letter is, and we will work a deal. Not for you, perhaps—I must give the French their bone after all. But for your man—freedom."

"Master Hugh . . ." James began in a hoarse voice, his gaze swinging wildly around to Hugh.

"There is no need for us both to die," Hugh said, silencing him. Then, to the captain: "The letter is in my pocket. I rely on you as one officer to another to keep your promise."

"As you may."

"Is that where you put it?" Claire, doing her best to play her part, was proud of how cool she sounded. The letter in his pocket, as she knew very well, was the one he himself had written in the cabin. Why did he draw attention to it? Was it simply a stalling tactic, or was there a reason she didn't yet comprehend? Her heart was pounding so hard now that she was surprised the sound didn't reverberate through the air. She met Hugh's gaze again, but she could read nothing in that impassive countenance.

"If you will get the letter, Miss Towbridge, and bring it to me, I would be most appreciative."

Claire nodded, and stepped toward Hugh. A more accomplished actress would doubtless have made a production of searching all his pockets, as if she didn't know where the letter might be. But she was too frightened—so frightened that her hand was trembling as it delved into the pocket where she knew very well the faux letter was. Her breathing was shallow and fast, and her heart raced. A quick sideways glance as her fingers closed on the letter told her that the soldiers on their big, glossy horses had now drawn even with the stuck wagon.

They were almost out of time. Her throat was so dry she had to swallow before she could speak.

"I have it," she said loud enough for the captain and his men to hear. Her gaze, wide and frightened, met Hugh's even as she pulled the letter from his pocket and held it up. If he was going to shoot someone, anyone, now was the moment.

"Drop it," he hissed as she was about to turn back toward the captain and his men. She must have looked incomprehendingly at him, because he said it again, in a low growl that this time she could not mistake. "Drop the bloody letter."

"Miss Towbridge, is there a difficulty?" The captain, voice raised, sounded suspicious. Had her glance, or Hugh's command given them away? He couldn't have heard the words, Claire was willing to swear. He was too far away, and there was too much noise around them.

"None at all." Holding the letter high so that he

might see it, Claire turned almost gaily to face him. "As you may see for yourself."

Then, mindful of Hugh's instructions and also of the French soldiers bearing down on them, looking tall and menacing astride their huge horses and now no more than perhaps three yards away, she opened her fingers and let the wind take the letter. "Oh! Oh, dear!"

The white rectangle fluttered, swirled in a circle, then floated to the ground. The eyes of the captain and his four men followed it down until it hit the mud and lay there, absorbing water like a sponge and threatened by a curious pig.

Claire was still staring at the letter herself when, from the corner of her eye, she saw Hugh's arm jerk up. The pistol fired, so close at hand that it was like a thunderclap next to her head. Ears ringing, she screamed; no sooner had the sound emerged from her throat than it was cut off by a tremendous weight hitting her in the back, knocking her face-first into the sand and crushing her down. As she fell she got just a glimpse of the captain's head snapping up. Then there was a tremendous boom, followed by an explosion and a rush of hot air as a fireball shot over her head, which she instinctively buried in her arms.

Screams rent the air, along with shouts and curses and the shrieks of terrified animals. Fire was everywhere, blazing brightly toward the dark sky, burning so fierce and hot that Claire felt as if her face was being singed when she dared to glance up. It was the wagon— the stuck wagon that had somehow caught fire and exploded. The captain and his men were down. One soldier was on his feet, thrown from his horse but having managed to hang on to the beast's reins, though it reared and fought as it tried to get away. She couldn't see the others, though perhaps a dozen sprawled bodies lay on the ground within her view; others were rushing to their aid. All this Claire registered as the most fleeting of impressions. Then the weight on her back lifted and she was dragged to her feet.

"Run!"

A hand locked around her wrist before the command had quite filtered past the ringing in her ears. Without any more warning than that, she was yanked into motion. Hugh was running, dragging her after him, and as his identity registered suddenly she realized that they were escaping and she began to run, too, her feet in their flimsy slippers scrabbling for purchase in the muddy sand.

"*Sacre bleu!*"

"My wagon! My so beautiful wagon!"

"Bloody English . . ."

"*Aidez-moi! Aidez-moi!*"

More explosions, fast and powerful, rocked the night. Fire, orange and yellow and red, lit up the sky as brightly as a giant's bonfire. The heat and smoke were tremendous. All was chaos, confusion; everywhere people screamed, and ran. Toward the explosion, and away.

"This way!"

Hugh pulled her behind a sand dune, into the blackness of the night beyond the reach of the worst of the fire's intensity. Claire caught just a glimpse of two more of the French soldiers, on their feet now, trying to catch their fleeing mounts, before the dunes obscured her view. Then Hugh was pounding through the tall grass toward the dark village, pulling her behind him, and she was running too, as fast as her feet would carry her. Running, she realized, for her life.

"**W**hat did you do back there?" Claire gasped out the question as Hugh lifted her bodily over a low stone wall that ran along the road in front of the village.

"The barrels in the wagon were loaded with gunpowder. I shot one of them." Placing one hand on the top, he vaulted the wall with remarkable ease.

"And they all exploded?" Claire remembered how he had knocked her to the ground a split second before the wagon blew up. "Did you know that was going to happen?"

"I hoped." He was breathless too, she noted as he grabbed her hand and pulled her after him again as he dodged behind one of the darkened houses.

"The horses—they should be in—that barn near the woods."

Claire had not realized that James was running with them until she heard his gasping voice behind her. Glancing around, she saw the heavyset man panting and lurching in their wake as he pointed toward a tumbledown barn. It was located on the far edge of the village, set back a little way from the farmhouse to which it apparently belonged and just in front of a dense copse of tall pines that swayed in the wind.

Although Claire had no idea what he was talking about, Hugh apparently did. He ran through the field in front of the barn, pulling Claire willy-nilly after him. She had a stitch in her side, pebbles in her slippers, and sand in her mouth from being facedown on the beach, but still she ran headlong over the rough ground because there was no help for it: Hugh's hand was like a vise around her wrist, and he wasn't letting go.

There was no doubt that they were being pursued. The only question was: how closely?

The barn was dark and smelled of hay and manure. Cows milled in a group at the far end of the structure, lowing as the three humans burst in to disturb their rest, their liquid eyes shining faintly at the intruders. Hugh let go of her wrist as soon as they were inside, and Claire practically doubled over in relief. Hands on her knees, she gasped for air, unable to inhale deeply because of the pain in her side. Vainly she wished her corset to perdition; the thing still continued to bind her just when she most needed her lungs to be able to expand.

"Are they here?"

James, still panting audibly, asked the question as he passed her, then followed Hugh into the depths of the barn.

"They're here. Minton's a good man. He's never let me down yet."

Still bent over just inside the door, doing her best to catch her breath and at the same time spit out sand from the beach, Claire missed the rest of the conversation. The men's voices mingled with the soft whicker of a horse, the stomping of hooves, and a leathery creaking.

After a moment, she heard them moving. Clearly they were heading in her direction. She took a deep breath and finally succeeded in filling her lungs.

"All right, then, just leave her."

At that, which she heard quite distinctly, Claire looked up. The speaker was James, his tone was urgent, and she had no doubt at all that he was referring to her. Two shapes were coming toward her, black and solid against the charcoal stripes painted by moonlight filtering through the poorly chinked walls. As the shapes drew near they resolved themselves into men and horses. Hugh and James were each astride saddled, bridled mounts.

The snippets of conversation they had previously exchanged flashed through her mind, and she concluded that someone named Minton, anticipating their arrival on the *Nadine*, had concealed a pair of tacked-up horses for Hugh's and James's use in quickly leaving the vicinity.

Realizing that there were only two horses, she had a brief flash of fear that Hugh would agree with James, and they would leave her. What would she do if they did? Her blood ran cold at the thought.

"She's coming with us." Hugh's voice was rough with impatience. Claire gave an inner sigh of relief. Of course he wouldn't leave her. She should have known he wouldn't leave her. This was a man she could trust with her life. This was a man she did trust with her life.

"Master Hugh, I'm begging you, think: We only have two horses."

"She'll ride with me."

"We're riding for our lives!"

"Damn it to hell, James, I'm not leaving her, and that's the end of the bloody discussion."

They reached her side at that moment. Claire straightened and took one more deep breath as the animals drew abreast of her. She felt the warmth of their bodies, smelled the leather of their tack mixed with the undefinable scent of horses. One snorted, shaking its head, its bridle jangling.

"Give me your hand," Hugh said. Looking up, she saw that he was reaching down to her. Like his face, his hand was a pale blur in the darkness. The rest of him was in shadow, a tall, formidable-looking shape looming high above her, mounted as he was on horseback. He kicked his foot out of the stirrup as she put her hand in his.

"Put your foot in the stirrup and swing on behind me."

She obeyed, and then he was pulling her up behind him as easily as if she weighed no more than a bit of swansdown. There was no choice but to ride astride, Claire realized instantly, although it was not a thing she had ever done. Hitching up her skirts, she gamely swung a leg over and scooted herself into position on the horse's powerful rump, her bare knees gripping the animal's warm, prickly hide for balance. Leaning forward, her breasts pressing against his hard back, she wrapped her arms around Hugh's waist.

"Hang on," he said over his shoulder. Even as she nodded, he clapped his heels to the horse's side and it leaped forward. Then they were out of the barn and away, galloping through the muddy field with its stubby remnant of a crop long since harvested. Silent as bats they flew, swift, dark figures with Claire's cloak flapping like a single great wing behind, just two more indistinct shapes among the other shadows populating the night. Looking south, Claire saw an orange glow lighting the sky: The wagon still burned. The acrid scent of smoke had drifted far enough that she could smell it distinctly. There was another smell, too, mixed with the smoke, and after a moment she identified it as gunpowder. Smuggled from England for use by Napoleon's army? It seemed so, and the perfidiousness of such an act both shocked and angered her. To think, safe at home, she had never realized that there were traitors all around her, traitors everywhere.

Suddenly she stiffened, and her hands clenched on the heavy wool of Hugh's coat. Against the blazing backdrop she could just make out the low-slung houses of the village they were rapidly leaving behind. Coming over the rise from the beach, she saw riders. Riders in tall hats . . .

The soldiers had regrouped and were coming in search of them. She had no doubt at all about their object. Could they see the galloping horses fleeing through the dark? She was able to see the soldiers only because they had been briefly outlined against the horizon by the fire, she realized. Please God, let her, Hugh, and James be securely hidden under the blanket of the night. If the soldiers should see them, she feared, they would not stand a chance. As far as she knew, neither Hugh nor James had any kind of workable weapon with them.

All they could do was flee for their lives.

"The soldiers! They're coming!"

The wind tore the words from her mouth, but Hugh must have heard because he glanced briefly over his shoulder, then nodded. He put his heels to the horse's sides again. Mud flew from the animal's hooves, which Claire could feel sliding as it pounded over the muddy ground. Without warning a stone wall appeared in front of them, a long, low, winding ghost in the darkness. Claire barely had time to tense before the horse was up and over. Holding on for dear life, she closed her eyes as they landed awkwardly in the muddy field on the other side, but though it slid a little the horse managed to keep on its feet, and she, knees clenched against its sides, managed to keep her seat. Glancing behind her, she saw James clear the wall, not gracefully but his horse stayed up and he stayed on it, which was all that mattered. Then they careened into the wood, and she hid her face against Hugh's back as branches slashed, nearly tearing them from the saddle.

They rode for a long time, at first at a dead gallop and then, with the pursuit, as they hoped, now well behind them, at a slightly slower pace. Always they stayed away from the roads, traveling cross-country because the roads, as Hugh warned in a quick exchange with James, were the first places the soldiers would look.

"What about the *Nadine*'s crew? Won't they be looking for us too?" If there was a slightly hysterical edge to Claire's voice, she forgave herself for it. It had been just a little more than twenty-four hours since she had been kidnapped from her carriage—in a crime that had seen her coachman, and possibly her other servants, murdered—had overheard plans for her own murder, hit a vicious brute over the head with a chamber pot, crept out a window, run across a boggy moor for her life, climbed down a cliff so slippery and treacherous that she had feared falling to her death with each step, been hit over the head and kidnapped yet again, nearly drowned, been terrorized and humiliated by a ship's crew and then by the very man with whom she now fled, been accused of being both a tart and a traitor to her country, held a pistol on her captor only to discover that it was unloaded, been kissed within an inch of her life and discovered that she quite liked kissing and her captor as well, gotten so horribly seasick that for a time she'd wished herself dead, come within a breath of being handed over to enemy soldiers, nearly died in an explosion—and now she was fleeing across the French countryside along with her erstwhile captor and his disapproving henchman while the French army swarmed after them like bees after a honey-stealing bear.

If her nerves were slightly frayed, she thought, hearing the shrill note in her mind, it was certainly no wonder.

"They'll leave it to the soldiers to make sure we don't get away. By now half the French army is probably looking for us. They're after James and me as spies, and you, my dove, because they think you have something they badly want. As far as they're concerned, you're Sophy Towbridge, remember, and Sophy Towbridge has information on the entire network of British intelligence operatives in France. That's what's in the letters."

"Oh, dear Lord." If that was supposed to make her feel better, it didn't. Instead it scared her to death. If they were hunting spies, the soldiers would never give up. Then it occurred to her that if Sophy Towbridge had information on British intelligence operatives in France, and Hugh, whom the *Nadine*'s captain had addressed as "colonel," had kidnapped the supposed Sophy Towbridge to somehow retrieve the information before it could reach those in France who were interested in it and was now being hunted as a spy, then he very likely was one of the British intelligence operatives in question or something very similar.

"Master Hugh! Over there!" James came up beside them before she could ask any questions, his face pale in the darkness, the dark bulk of his body awkward as he leaned over his horse's neck to point toward the west. Claire looked and gasped. There was just enough moonlight filtering through the blowing clouds to permit her to see what appeared to be an entire regiment of mounted soldiers cantering along a road that ran parallel to their own course. The soldiers were some distance away, perhaps a quarter mile or more, visible only because of the flatness of the farmland through which they rode. Obviously having seen them too, Hugh reined sharply left into the creekbed beside which they rode, and the plunging descent took them down below the level of the surrounding ground. At a word from Hugh they dismounted, and Hugh and James held their animals' muzzles so that they would not call to the soldiers' horses as they passed. Claire felt her heart drumming in rhythm to the beat of the flashing hooves, and then the soldiers turned north and rode over the horizon and out of sight.

"Were they looking for us?" Claire asked in a low, shaken voice when they were gone.

"Aye, I'd say so." James's response was grim as he clambered back into the saddle with more determination than grace.

"Don't worry, puss, they won't find us tonight. I guarantee it."

Having mounted at the same time as James, though

with considerably more ease, Hugh reached down to her as he spoke. She saw the brief gleam of his teeth through the darkness, and realized that he was smiling. Lunatic! she thought, recognizing that in some strange way he was enjoying himself. He found the danger exhilarating. While as for herself—her bottom was sore, her legs were wobbly, and her knees ached from the miles she had already ridden in such an unaccustomed position; she was scared to death, and the only thing she had enjoyed in this whole hideous saga was, if she was honest with herself, kissing Hugh. She would describe herself, if pressed, as the very opposite of exhilarated. But still as she took his hand, put her foot in the stirrup, and allowed him to pull her up behind him, she managed a smile for him in return.

Because—always providing she managed to survive it—she was beginning to feel that meeting him was probably going to be the best thing that ever happened to her in her life.

Then they were off again, and within minutes the smile had been wiped from her face. The horses were traveling like bullets, straight across the countryside as fast as they could go. Riding on the rump of a galloping horse had to be one of the most excruciating experiences of her life, she decided in very short order. Every time the animal bounded forward—that is, just about every other second—her backside was smacked sharply by a mass of bunched muscles as hard as any schoolmaster's paddle. In addition, the insides of her thighs ached like a sore tooth from gripping so tightly, and her knees felt like they were being rubbed raw by the animal's rough hide. By the time another hour had passed, Claire was in a state of real misery. She locked her arms around Hugh's waist, buried her head in his back, and set herself to endure.

Finally they came to what looked like a fishing village, spread out like a horseshoe around a glistening black bay, sleeping in the dead of night. Drooping now with fatigue, leaning heavily against Hugh's back as the only secure thing in a bouncing world, Claire glanced up bleary-eyed to see the cluster of darkened buildings on the edge of the sea, and for a moment she feared that they had somehow come full circle, ending up right where they had started. But there was no fire burning on the beach, no schooner tied up at the dock, no smell of burning. A glance up at the moon, the merest sliver of silver high overhead occasionally daring to peek through the racing clouds, told her that it was now close on midnight. She did not know where they were, but they had clearly come a long way.

A dog barked nearby, startling her into full wakefulness. They were slowing now, trotting down a muddy track close to what looked like a two-story farmhouse set a little distance from the village proper.

"Where are we?" Claire asked in a hushed voice.

"Somewhere safe. The man who lives here is a friend. He's expecting us—well, James and me."

There was a barn behind the house, more of a tumbledown shed really, and Hugh headed inside it with James close behind. A musty smell as of hay allowed to rot greeted them, and overhead a soft fluttering spoke of chickens or pigeons or some other birds roosting in the beams.

"Slide off," Hugh said, pulling the horse to a halt, and she did, then as she hit the soft turf discovered that her legs would barely support her. Leaning heavily against the horse's heaving side, hood thrown back and hair tumbling down her back, her hairpins lost somewhere on that wild ride, she watched Hugh dismount, and James.

"I'll see to the horses," James said, taking the reins of Hugh's mount as well as his own. Claire straightened away from the animal as James led it off into the depths of the barn, but as she tried to take a step back she staggered and would have fallen if Hugh had not caught her with both hands on her waist.

"Are you ill?" He was frowning as he wrapped his arms around her, pulling her close against his chest. Leaning heavily against him, grateful for his solid strength, comforted by the steady beat of his heart beneath her ear, she shook her head.

"Not ill," she said. "It is just—I am not accustomed to riding astride."

He gave a grunt of what sounded suspiciously like laughter. "Saddle sore! Egad, I never thought of that."

"Do you find the idea amusing?" Faint stirrings of indignation chilled her voice.

"No, puss, no, of course not." He said it hastily, but Claire still thought she detected the faintest hint of amusement underlying the words. "Poor little girl, you've had a bad time of it, haven't you?"

"I am not," Claire said with indignation, "a poor little girl."

Pushing away from him, she again took a step, and nearly fell as excruciating pain shot up her legs.

"Oh!" She couldn't help the little sound she made any more than she could resist the urge to rub her abused posterior.

He grunted—the sound could have been disguised

laughter, she thought darkly, then realized, with a swift glance at his face, that it probably was—and steadied her, then scooped her up in his arms before she could push away again. Claire stiffened, but didn't struggle. She was so tired, so sore, so frightened, and it felt so good to let him take care of her that she hadn't the will to fight any longer. She abandoned her irritation at him to curl close against his chest, wrapping her arms around his neck as if right where she was was the one place on earth she most wanted to be.

Which, indeed, it was.

*❝ I*'m sorry." Hugh sounded genuinely remorseful as he walked out of the barn with her and headed across the muddy lot toward the farmhouse. The moonlight struck his eyes, turning them to silver as he looked at her. With her head nestled on his shoulder, their eyes were just inches apart. "Sorry for everything. Sorry you had to get caught up in this."

"I'm not," Claire said, inhaling the musky aroma of him with every breath and feeling the warm strength of the muscles that cradled her clear down to her toes. "At least, not altogether. If I hadn't gotten caught up in this, I never would have met you."

He looked down at her sharply, and his lips parted as if he would reply. Then squelching footsteps behind them heralded James's arrival.

"I rubbed 'em down and fed 'em." His gaze swept over the two of them and he frowned, but if he had aught to say about her being carried so carefully in his master's arms he kept it to himself.

"What other animals are in there?"

"A plow horse. Some chickens, a cow, and a couple of nanny goats."

"Hildebrand's not arrived, then."

"I'd say not." James turned a frowning glance on Claire, then cleared his throat. "Master Hugh, have you given any thought as to what the general's liable to say about *her*?"

Hugh grimaced. "He can say what he likes. I intercepted the wrong woman, and there's an end to it. The only thing to do is send her home safely, and get everyone we have searching for the real Sophy Towbridge."

James coughed delicately. "Are you sure . . . ?"

"I'm sure."

They reached the back stoop then, which was no more than a couple of planks laid over a base of rocks set into the ground. Before they could knock, the door opened. A man, a farmer by the looks of him, with ill-kempt chestnut hair and a straggly beard of the same color, dressed in a loose shirt, breeches, and brogues, stood in the aperture looking at them suspiciously, a lantern in his hand.

"Well met, Tinsley."

"Colonel! Thank God! I was that afeard something had gone wrong—you're late. And General Hildebrand's not here yet." His voice with its hint of cockney revealed that Tinsley was no more French than Claire was. Was he an intelligence agent too? Her eyes widened at the thought.

"Something did go wrong," Hugh said, carefully maneuvering Claire through the narrow doorway as Tinsley, after a nod at James, stepped back for him to enter. Claire clung to Hugh's neck. If he put her down, she wasn't sure she could even stand, much less walk. "I'll tell you all about it, but first I must see the lady here taken care of. Have you a bedchamber where she can rest?"

"Aye, upstairs." Tinsley evinced no surprise at the presence of an unexpected female guest. In the spy game, Claire supposed, one learned to expect the unexpected.

"Lead the way."

James closed the door behind them, and, with Tinsley's lantern lighting the way, Hugh carried Claire up the narrow stairs and into a bedroom. It was small and very simple, its furnishings consisting of no more than a lumpy-looking bed piled high with colorful quilts, a wardrobe, a washstand, and a straight-backed chair. The walls were rough whitewashed plaster. The floor was dark scuffed wood. As Tinsley lit a candle by the bed, Hugh set Claire on her feet. Pain shot up her legs, and she immediately tottered a step and sank down in the chair, then winced as her backside made it clear that it was not in any state to welcome contact with a wooden seat.

She must have made some small sound of discomfort, because Hugh looked at her with a questioning frown. Under that weighing gaze, she managed, heroically, not to rub any afflicted parts.

"Are you all right?" Clearly he divined her trouble because, his verbal expression of concern to the contrary, his eyes twinkled. Claire eyed him narrowly.

"Just fine, thanks." She said it with a hint of a snap. The twinkle grew more pronounced.

"I would be glad to take a look. . . ."

She glared at him, and he grinned.

Tinsley, having lit the candle, left the room.

"Master Hugh . . ." As Tinsley exited, James stuck his

head through the open doorway. Hugh looked around at him. "The general's here."

"I'm coming." He glanced back at Claire, the twinkle now entirely gone from his eyes. "Stay here until I come for you."

His tone was abrupt, and there was no doubt that the words were an order.

Claire nodded. Without another word Hugh turned and left the room, closing the door behind him.

For a moment Claire simply sat, the pain in her backside engendered by sitting being less, she calculated, than the pain it would cost her to move. She could hear nothing beyond the four walls of the bedchamber. If, as she guessed, the men were conferring below, not even the faintest echo of their voices reached her ears.

She realized she was holding her breath, and slowly let it out. Hugh's sudden change of demeanor had reminded her that she was caught up in a life-and-death situation, and the thought made her shiver. It was more than certain that she was one of the chief topics under discussion downstairs, and she wondered briefly what she would do if the newly arrived general sided with James rather than Hugh about her identity. The possibility was frightening, but then she thought of Hugh and felt the worst of her tension ease. Hugh would not let any harm come to her. She was as certain of that as she was of her own name. As for the rest, there was no point in worrying about it. The only thing to do was to stay in this room and wait on events, she realized, and so set about making herself as comfortable as she could.

In this she was aided by James, who appeared not very many minutes later with a tray bearing food.

"Master Hugh thought you might be hungry," he

said in answer to Claire's questioning look as she answered the door. Claire discovered that she was, in fact, very hungry indeed. Thinking back, she remembered that her last meal had been the tea and bread and butter she had eaten in the inn just before she had been snatched from her coach. Since then her stomach had emptied itself so thoroughly that, now, the sides felt like they were touching. Eagerly she tucked into cold beef and bread and cheese, and drank the hot sweet tea.

She was just polishing off the apple that served as her final course, and feeling very much better for the meal, when another knock sounded at the door.

"Come in," she called, not wanting to put herself through the pain involved in rising and walking to the door again unless she had to. James opened the door, and when she saw what he was carrying she was ready to fall on his neck. It was a copper hip bath, old and battered but definitely serviceable, and to her, in that moment, it was the most beautiful thing in the world. Her entire being, body and soul, cried out for a bath, and she thanked him with the kind of fervency normally reserved for the turning of water into wine.

"Master Hugh's compliments," James said shortly. But despite his disapproval he filled it for her too, making several trips from downstairs with cans of hot water until there was enough for a proper bath. On his last trip, he nodded at the wardrobe. "Tinsley says you may make use of any of his wife's things as you may need. He's sent her away for the night to be safe, but he says she would bid you use them and welcome, did she know you were here. They are in that wardrobe."

Claire glanced at the wardrobe, then looked at James. His bearded face was unsmiling, and his gaze, when it chanced to meet hers, was guarded. But he had been kind to bring her food, and positively saintly to provide her with a bath even if it was at Hugh's behest, and for that she was grateful.

"Thank you, James," she said, meaning it. Their gazes met, and he nodded acknowledgment at her.

"You're welcome, miss." Then, abruptly, he added, "Master Hugh told me and—the rest of those belowstairs—that 'twas you that gave him the pistol he used to shoot that barrel of gunpowder. That means you saved our lives. However this turns out, I thank you for that."

"Is he arguing my case, then?" she asked with a small smile. "He is in the right of it, you know. I am Lady Claire Lynes. Is it so hard to believe?"

"You've convinced Master Hugh of it right enough." James hesitated. "The problem is, no one of us—not even the general—has any notion of what you—Miss Towbridge—looks like. And you were at the rendezvous point, which looks bad for you, miss, there's no denying that. Still, Master Hugh insists that a mistake has been made, and in the normal way of things he's somethin' considerably less than a flat. Though with the way you look and all . . . Still, 'tis possible I've been wrong. If so, I'm sorry for it."

"You're forgiven." Claire's smile widened and warmed. "Especially since you were kind enough to bring me that bath. It is what I wished for above all things."

James didn't exactly smile back, but the hard suspicion had left his eyes and she thought that some of the disapproving stiffness was absent from his posture as, with a nod, he turned and went out of the room.

Though she could not help but be slightly nervous about what was happening downstairs, she decided, again, that her best course of action was to trust in Hugh and not worry about it. Meanwhile, the tub beckoned. Hastily she undressed, shaking out her clothes and laying them carefully across the back of the chair for wear on the morrow. Then she stepped into the steaming water, and promptly forgot everything else. The bath was pure bliss. Sitting scrunched up with her knees beneath her chin, Claire endured the agony of sore muscles without flinching as she soaped herself from her hairline to her toes. The thought of washing her hair was tempting, but given its length and thickness it was a time-consuming process that was best tackled on a sunny afternoon. So with regret she left it alone, tying it in a knot on top of her head to keep it from getting wet. By the time she stepped from the bath, her skin was pink and glowing and the hot water had done much to ease the ache in her posterior and legs. Drying herself, she investigated the wardrobe, finding two gowns, one gray and one black, both with long sleeves, high necks, and not the smallest claim to fashion. There were undergarments of various descriptions folded on shelves, a pair of pattens, and a nightdress. Discovering the nightdress, she felt like an adventurer coming across gold. It was of white linen, coarser than she was used to, and loosely styled with a plain round neck secured by a quartet of tiny buttons, its only ornamentation a flounce edging each sleeve. Donning it, she realized that the woman it belonged to was easily twice as big around as she. But it was comfortable, and, what was more important to her at the moment, clean and dry. Pushing up the sleeves so that her hands were visible, she picked up the tortoiseshell comb that had been left on the washstand and crossed to the bed. Climbing in between the sheets, she propped the single feather pillow against the headboard and leaned back against it, luxuriating in the softness that cradled her backside and legs, more comfortable than she had been since beginning the journey to Hayleigh Castle. Then she let down her hair and, starting at the ends, began to work the tangles from it.

She was still engaged in this homely but comforting task when a soft knock sounded at the door. A nervous flutter in her stomach reminded her that she was not as calm as she might perhaps have wished. Telling herself stoutly that it was James come to remove the bath, or on another errand perhaps, she put down the comb, pulled the bedclothes high around her neck, and bade him come in.

When Hugh opened the door instead, a spontaneous smile of welcome curved her lips. He was wearing only his shirt, breeches and boots, and his hair was loose. It was slightly disordered as if he'd been running his hands through it, and hung in deep waves almost to his shoulders. Even without the added bulk of a coat his shoulders were broad enough that they almost filled the doorway, she saw as he entered, and he was tall enough that he had to duck his head to clear the jamb. His boots still had traces of mud on them, although it was obvious that some attempt at least had been made to rid them of the worst of the mire that had caked them earlier. His breeches were flecked with mud as well, but they clung to his muscular thighs and narrow hips in a fashion that made Claire quite forget that they were dirty. His shirt had been spared the worst of the mud; it looked very white in the flickering candlelight, and its loose fit emphasized the width of his shoulders and chest. Above it, his strong neck was deeply bronzed. He needed a shave; his lean cheeks were once again shadowed with stubble, and she, who had always preferred clean-shaven men, found that prickly darkness unbelievably attractive.

His eyes narrowed as they ran over her, sitting up in bed as she was with her black hair hanging around her like a silken cape and the bedclothes clutched modestly to her neck. The sudden gleam in them as they met hers told her more clearly than words could have done that he found her most attractive, too. Heat shimmered in the air between them, tangible as mist after a rain. Then the sound of a door slamming downstairs caused Claire to remember the debate he had been engaged in, and her smile disappeared.

"So have you come to deliver the verdict?" she asked, lifting her chin at him challengingly.

His mouth twisted into a wry smile as he moved to stand beside the bed and survey her from that vantage point.

"You look about sixteen, you know," he said by way of reply. "Like a schoolroom miss. Are you sure you're a married woman of twenty-one?"

She met his gaze, her own softening. "No more Sophy Towbridge?"

He shook his head. "Only Claire. Beautiful Claire."

Her smile returned, an elusive thing that just touched the corners of her mouth. "Do you really think I'm beautiful?"

"Don't flirt, puss. You know you are. So beautiful you outshine the sun."

She lowered her lashes and looked up at him

through them, her smile deepening. "Now that's the kind of flattery I like to hear. And I am *not* flirting."

He gave a grunt of laughter. "I've come to the conclusion that you flirt as naturally as you breathe." His arms crossed over his chest, and the smile faded from his eyes as he added, "I've good news: You're going home tomorrow."

He didn't look like it was such good news. Indeed, he suddenly looked almost grim.

"I am?" she asked cautiously.

He nodded. "It'll mean crossing the Channel again, but the weather's improved a great deal, so you shouldn't have too much difficulty. Tinsley will take you in his boat. He's posing as a fisherman, so the boat isn't large. But Tinsley will do his best to see that you're comfortable."

At the thought of her previous sufferings at sea, Claire shuddered inwardly. But she was in France now, and there was no help for it if she ever wanted to get home again, so, she told herself, she must endure. In an effort to give her thoughts a more cheerful direction, Claire focused on the rest of what Hugh had said, and frowned. "Tinsley is English, isn't he? If he's posing as a French fisherman, does that mean he's a spy?"

" 'Intelligence officer' is the preferred term. And yes, he is."

She looked at him consideringly. "Does that make you an intelligence officer too, Colonel?"

His smile was a touch rueful. "Caught that, did you? I thought you did. Yes, I'm an officer with British intelligence. Colonel Hugh Battancourt, at your service, milady." His hand over his heart, he made her a mock bow. "There's a network of us throughout France. And a network of them throughout England, for that matter. Though that's confidential, of course. That means, when you get home, don't go tattling about it all over England."

"As if I would." Affronted, she crossed her arms over her chest, quite forgetting about the quilts she'd been holding to her neck. When she released them, they puddled around her waist. His gaze swept her and he grinned, reaching down to tug a lock of her hair teasingly. She pulled her hair from his hold, then forgot to be huffy as she sought additional clarification. "So now you may as well admit the whole truth: Somehow one of your network mistook me for a traitor named Sophy Towbridge and snatched me out of my own carriage. Did I happen to mention, the other night when you denied knowing anything about my carriage being attacked, that my coachman was shot when I was kidnapped? And my maid too, for all I know. They may very well both be dead now, and all because of a mistake." Her tone was stern.

He shook his head. "We truly had nothing to do with that. I was sent to intercept Sophy Towbridge on the beach between Hayleigh Castle and Hayleigh's Point. Their operatives in England were to bring her to that spot and a French ship was to pick her up there and convey her to France. My job was to beat the French contingent to the rendezvous point, which I did. But in a coincidence that I find almost unbelievable, you were on the beach instead of Sophy Towbridge. I stole you away before, as I thought, the French could arrive to do so. But I—none of us, so far as I know, and I would know—had anything to do with kidnapping you from your carriage. There would be no reason for British intelligence to be interested in Lady Claire Lynes, who was on an innocent visit to her family at Hayleigh Castle, after all. Someone else was responsible for that."

"But who?" While she had thought the attack on her carriage was attributable to her being mistaken for Sophy Towbridge, it had been just barely comprehensible. But if that wasn't the reason—and Hugh said it wasn't, and she had come to a point where she believed Hugh implicitly—then who would commit such an atrocity? And why?

"I've been asking myself that ever since you told me what happened, and I don't have an answer for you. That's one reason I'm sending James with you. He'll convey you from Tinsley's boat to your home in safety and make sure everything's all right before he leaves you. And I'll be in touch with some people I know in England, who'll look into what happened. They'll find out who attacked your carriage, and why, and in the meantime you'll be protected. You need have no fear of its happening again."

One part of that speech caught Claire's attention. Everything that came after could have been in Sanskrit for all she understood of it, or cared.

"Did you say you're sending *James* with me?" Her eyes were wide and questioning. "Are you not coming as well?"

His jaw tightened, and he shook his head. "Hildebrand is already gone, and I must leave soon as well. James and Tinsley are down at the harbor now, getting Tinsley's boat ready so you can sail undetected on it when it leaves with the rest of the fishermen at dawn. I'll wait to see you safely aboard. Then I must ride for Paris. Sophy Towbridge is still at large, and the information she carries with her will put a great many lives in jeopardy if it falls into the wrong hands. I must still try to stop that if I can, and if not, then there are people who will die if they're not warned of what's happened in time to escape to England."

Claire stared at him in dawning dismay. "But—those soldiers are looking for you. Even if they don't catch you on the way to Paris, the *Nadine*'s crew knows your name; at least, the captain called you "colonel," so I assume they do. How difficult could it be to track you down? You must leave France."

Hugh's eyes darkened as they met hers. They suddenly looked almost black in the candlelight, Claire noticed. As black as the raven's-wing shade of his hair.

"Never say you're worried about me, puss." His mouth twisted almost tenderly.

If there was a deliberately light note to that, she didn't respond lightly.

"Yes," she said, and reached out and caught his hand, hoping to somehow convey the intensity of her distress. "Yes, I am. If they catch you, they'll kill you." She took a deep breath, and her eyes beseeched him. "Please, Hugh. Please come back to England with me."

His fingers tightened around hers. Then he sat down on the edge of the bed, bringing her hand to his mouth, kissing the back of her knuckles. Claire's breath caught as she looked at that head bent over her hand. As that long, hard mouth caressed her fingers, her heart began to pound. His lips were warm, and firm, and she felt his breath against her skin. She watched, mesmerized, as, lifting his head, he turned her hand over, staring down at it as if he would memorize the pale curve of her palm, the slender length of her fingers. His thumb stroked her palm, and her throat went dry. Then he looked up suddenly, meeting her gaze, catching her unaware.

Claire had the feeling that her heart shone from her eyes.

"I'm a soldier, puss, and this is a war we're fighting. I have to go. But you've no need to upset yourself over me. I'm remarkably hard to kill."

She had to deliberately take a steadying breath before she could speak.

"So you'll put me on a boat at dawn and then you'll ride away. Just like that."

His eyes narrowed, and he lifted her hand, pressing it against his cheek. She felt the warmth of his skin and the prickly abrasion of his unshaven cheeks with every fiber of her being.

"It will cause me some regret, I must admit."

He kissed her palm, warm lips moving against soft skin, then abruptly stood up. He would have released her hand, but her fingers tightened, clung.

"Hugh . . ."

"It's still some five hours till dawn. You should get what sleep you can."

"I don't want to sleep." She said it swiftly, instinctively, but even as the words left her mouth she knew they were true.

She looked up at him, looming above her now, the candlelight casting shifting shadows over the chiseled planes and angles of his face, seeking out the red highlights in his black hair, emphasizing the hard masculinity of his mouth and chin. His eyes were narrowed and dark as he looked down at her, and his thumb stroked almost unconsciously over the fingers he still held. Her gaze traveled down the whole long length of him, over the broad shoulders and wide chest, the strong arms, the narrow waist and hips, the powerful thighs. Just looking at him took her breath away. Remembering how it had felt to lie in his arms, her heart skipped a beat. The thought of how his hands had felt on her breasts caused her body to quake somewhere deep inside. When her gaze touched his mouth, curved now by a twisting smile, and she remembered how he had kissed her, her bones seemed to melt. Shaken, she tore her eyes away—and accidentally met his gaze. His eyes were black as onyx now, but in their depths she thought she saw tiny leaping flames a thousand times hotter than the candle they should have been reflecting. Her knees began to tremble. She registered the sensation with amazement.

Never in her whole life, she realized, had she felt the way she felt with Hugh.

The wantonness that had so shamed her, the wantonness that she could not quite stamp out no matter how hard she tried, the wantonness that was apparently an integral part of her nature, had reared its head again, and her heart quickened along with her body as she faced the truth.

She could not go home to England, to the sisters she loved, to her barren life with David, without ever having lain with Hugh.

Taking a deep breath, she mustered all the courage she could find, and grabbed for the one thing she had suddenly realized she wanted above all else.

"It's wrong, I know," she said steadily, her eyes holding his. "But—if we need not part till dawn, I would ask you to stay with me tonight."

## ❧ 20 ❧

......................................

*H*is fingers tightened on hers. The tiny twin flames in his eyes flared, then were as quickly hidden by his lowered lids as he looked down at their joined hands.

"If you're wanting to while the night away with pleasant conversation, I'm not able to do that, I'm afraid." His voice was courteous but distant. He looked at her again, and the flash of heat was gone. His expression was coolly remote.

She took a deep, steadying breath and willed herself to stay the course. His resistance was unexpected; she'd thought all she would have to do was give the slightest indication of willingness and he would tumble into bed with her so quickly she wouldn't have a chance to take a deep breath, much less change her mind. But here was the opportunity for second thoughts—all she had to do was follow his lead in pretending that they both didn't know very well what she'd really been asking for—and she realized that she didn't want to change her mind. This was what she wanted—he was what she wanted—and she would fight for him if she had to. He was giving her no encouragement at all—other than that brief flare of passion she was sure she had seen in his eyes. But she knew—she *knew*—he felt the connection between them as strongly as she did. Something was holding him back. What? Honor? Chivalry? The thought of the man she had not long since considered a black-hearted scoundrel being deterred by either should have been humorous, except she had since learned that the villainous rogue was, at heart, very much a gentleman. Too much a gentleman to bed her? He had shown no discernible reluctance when he had kissed and caressed her on the *Nadine*. Of course, then he had been operating under the presumption that she was very likely a trollop and a spy. Now he was accepting her for the lady of quality she was, and it might be that which was giving him pause. To her, it didn't matter. For once in her life, she knew what she wanted, and she meant to do her best to get it.

But getting what she wanted required courage of a sort that she had never before had to ascertain she possessed. The courage to state plainly what she was asking him for and thereby suffer certain embarrassment and even, possibly, rejection. Her stomach knotted. Her heart quaked. But she took her courage in both hands and looked him squarely in the eyes.

"You know very well that conversation's not what I want." If her tone was a little blunt for seduction, well, making such a statement was difficult for her. Never before in her life had she been the one to make the running after a man; always, always, men had fallen at her feet at her least glance.

His lips twisted into the slightest of wry smiles. "Angel eyes, I'm not sure *you* know what you want."

"I do. I do." She wet her suddenly dry lips and said it right out, boldly: "I want you to lie with me. I want to—to . . ."

Despite her determination, words failed her at the end, and she blushed.

He looked her over for a moment in silence. His jaw tightened, and a tiny muscle began to jump at the corner of his mouth. She saw those as signs of resistance, and felt her cheeks grow hotter. He seemed to be on the verge of saying no. Her blood drummed in her ears and her stomach sank as she watched him. He seemed to be steeling himself against her. Then suddenly the flame in his eyes returned, only now it burned so hot and so bright that there was no mistaking it for anything but what it was. Still he hesitated, making no move to come any closer, or to draw her to him. His fingers were rigid as they held hers in a grip that she suspected would be unbreakable if she tested it, but she wasn't testing it. She didn't want him to let her go. Not now. Not ever.

"You don't even know the words."

There was the slightest edge to his voice. She could feel the tension in his hand, see the rigidity in his stance. His eyes were blazing steadily at her now. Whatever was keeping him from her, it was not lack of desire, she could tell. Men had been looking at her like that for most of her life, and she knew what those leaping eyes meant.

But this was the first time in her life she had ever truly desired someone back.

"Intimate congress," she said. "I want to engage in intimate congress with you."

It was a throaty whisper, because her throat had almost closed up from the embarrassment of being so explicit, and slightly defiant in tone.

He made a sound that was part laugh and part groan. "God, you are so young and so sweet you break my heart."

The heat in his eyes scorched her face, and his fingers tightened almost painfully on hers. Yet still he looked oddly irresolute, standing there with his eyes burning her everywhere they touched and his body as still as if he'd been turned to stone.

"Claire . . ." There was a world of warning in the way he said her name. Claire's gaze met his and clung as he continued, his voice now husky and very low. "Puss, think well. I would crawl over a sea of hot coals on my hands and knees to climb into bed with you, as I suspect you're very well aware. But you—tomorrow night, you'll be safe at home in England with your husband and family. I don't want you to do something in the heat of the moment that you're going to regret, maybe for the rest of your life."

She rose to her knees, her hand clinging to his, uncaring as the modesty-giving quilts fell away. Awkward on the too soft mattress, hampered by the trailing end of her nightdress, which got caught up beneath her knees, she moved toward him. He caught her other hand to steady her, then held both her hands in a tight grip that, she thought, deliberately kept a modicum of space between them. They were still some few inches apart when she stopped. She was kneeling before him clad only in the loose white nightdress, her black hair streaming like a whisper-soft cloak over her shoulders and down her back, her eyes fixed on his with a whole world of longing in them.

"My only regret," she said softly, "would be if all we had was this one night and we didn't do this, and then I went the rest of my life without ever wanting to be with anyone as I want to be with you."

His breath caught, and his eyes as they moved over her face blazed so hot that they seemed to sear her skin. His hands flexed as if in involuntary reflex, and then his fingers twined with hers. Claire felt the warmth and strength of those hands, the slight abrasiveness at the tips of the long fingers imprisoning hers, and imagined them touching her. At the images that conjured up, she felt a shivery anticipation that at any other time would have made her hang her head in shame.

But not tonight. Not with Hugh.

"Now that," he said, his voice grown faintly unsteady, "would be a shame."

Then he gave up his unwinnable fight. Claire knew the moment he did, because his mouth twisted as if in defeat and his eyes flashed at her like black diamonds. Her heart threatened to pound out of her chest as she watched his head bend toward hers, slowly, as if he would give her one last chance to call a halt if she would. But she would not. This was what she had wanted, dreamed of, for years. To have the question answered: What was it that her body longed for? What did she yearn for instinctively without really knowing what it was? The thought that Hugh had the answers was tantalizing, tempting her beyond what she could bear. The fire that had leaped at her from his eyes had entered her blood, and now she was burning too, aflame with need. The wantonness that she had done battle with for years took up arms again, and this time she didn't even try to fight it.

Her head tilted up in heady anticipation. Her lips softened and parted before his ever touched them.

When at last they did she quivered and closed her eyes, loving the firm warmth of his lips, the way his mouth moved gently on hers, the sweet invasion of his tongue. He tasted of wine, and she guessed that the men had been drinking while she was upstairs. It was a soft kiss, a lover's kiss, and the wonder of it made her ache. But she wanted more, much more, so much that she felt almost greedy with need. He lifted his head, looking down into her eyes with an expression that combined desire and tenderness in a way that made her head spin.

"I want you more than I have ever wanted a woman in my life," he said. For all the passion that darkened his face, his expression was also faintly—was it rueful?

"So take me." She managed the tiniest of smiles. The ruefulness vanished, and he looked down at her almost gravely. Then he bent his head again as if in answer and took her mouth.

This time, the kiss was not nearly so gentle. His mouth slanted over hers, hard and demanding, and she loved the fierceness of his kiss. The rasp of his unshaven chin against her soft skin made her toes curl. Claire swayed against him, making a little sound like a moan deep in her throat as his tongue slid between her lips. His mouth was hot and wet and demanding. His tongue touched hers, stroked it, coaxed it to come out and play. She responded mindlessly as he taught her more about the fine art of kissing, and the result was all she could have wished for. She put her tongue in his mouth, and felt her loins tighten. She touched his teeth, the roof of his mouth, his tongue, just as he was doing to hers, and felt the tightening turn into a quake. She stroked his tongue with hers, and the quaking intensified until her insides were reduced to pure jelly and she had to free her mouth from his to breathe. But the temptation of his long hard mouth hovering just inches above her own was too much to be borne, and within seconds she was kissing him again, greedily, pressing her mouth to his and eagerly employing the lessons he had taught her.

During the course of that kiss, she rediscovered that his chest was firm with muscle and radiated heat, and that when she pressed close against it her breasts seemed to tingle and swell. His thighs were solid and powerful against the curving slenderness of hers. Above them, pressing into her stomach, she felt a bulging hardness. As she identified it as the tangible evidence of his desire for her, her throat went dry.

She felt almost dizzy with the sheer pleasure generated by the contact of their bodies. When he let go of her hands to wrap his arms around her waist, then pulled her closer yet so that she was plastered right up against his body from her knees to her breasts, the sensation was so intense that she almost forgot to breathe. She could feel the warmth of him, the steely strength of his muscles, the steady beat of his heart, and each, separately and together, made her head spin. Sliding her arms around his shoulders, intoxicated with the sheer sensuous pleasure of running her hands along their well-muscled width and then touching the silk of his hair and the warm satin of the back of his neck, she locked her hands behind his neck and kissed him back with abandon.

When he lifted his head at last, she opened her eyes. His face was close, so close, and he was breathing as if there were not enough air in the whole world to fill his lungs. His eyes were heavy-lidded and hot as he met her gaze.

"Your kissing has improved out of all recognition."

The huskiness of his voice did not match his crooked smile. He was trying again for a certain lightness, she thought. But the intensity of the emotion that shimmered between them would not be denied.

"My tutor is very good." She, too, replied lightly, but her eyes stayed fixed on his, and her lips, parted and tremulous, gave her tone the lie.

"Is he now?"

Still he smiled, even as his eyes scorched her. Then, moving slowly, oh, so slowly, he lifted a hand to touch her mouth. Just the faintest butterfly touch, his thumb rubbing over the soft curve of her lower lip, which was still damp from his kisses, but it was enough to make her tremble.

"Cold?" he asked.

"No."

Claire drew in a deep, shaken breath as she made the admission, knowing what it implied.

"Ah," he said, and kissed her again. This time the kiss was harder, deeper, compelling a response that she was only too ready to give. She wrapped her arms around his neck and pressed her body to his and kissed him as if she'd been dreaming of this moment all her life, which, indeed, she had been.

When he lifted his head again, they were both shaking. Claire felt the fine tremors in the arms that locked her to him, heard the harsh rasp of his breathing, saw the deep color that had risen to stain his cheekbones, and thrilled to the knowledge that he was as deeply affected by her kisses as she was by his.

"Cold?" she whispered, echoing his question to her.

His answering smile was no more than a flicker.

"No," he said.

He bent his head, but this time his target was not her lips. Instead his mouth found the sensitive skin just below her ear. Claire practically swooned as he ran his mouth down the side of her neck, pressing tingly little kisses to her soft skin. He kissed her neck, her collarbone, and finally her ear. The rasp of his beard was as arousing as the hot trail blazed by his lips.

By the time he sought her lips again, she was breathing erratically and clinging to him as if she would collapse if she let go. He kissed her, his tongue staking bold possession of her mouth, and she was happy to be possessed. Then his hand came up to cradle her neck, stroking the fragile cord he had just kissed, before sliding down over her collarbone, over the front of the thin nightdress, to close over her breast.

Claire gasped. The feel of his big hand holding her so intimately jolted through her body like an earthquake. She arched her back, pressing up against that caressing hand quite shamelessly. Her nipple was erect and so sensitive it almost ached as it thrust against his palm. He tightened his grip, and she thought she would die with the sheer wonder of it.

When he removed his hand from her breast, she felt bereft. She was breathing hard, as hard as if she'd danced for hours, and her legs were so unsteady that, when he took a step back, it was all she could do not to sink into a little heap right there in front of him.

"Let's have this off you, then." His voice was a husky murmur.

His fingers trailed around the neckline of her borrowed nightdress, just brushing her skin but making her acutely conscious of his touch nonetheless. He was watching her, waiting for her reaction, she thought, and she managed to nod. Her heart pounded so hard that it threatened to burst through her chest. Speaking was now, she feared, beyond her. He set both hands to her waist, lifting her from the bed and setting her on her feet. Claire swayed toward him instinctively, but he shook his head at her, smiling a little. Then his hands came up to cup her face, and he dropped a quick hard kiss on her lips before reaching for the buttons that fastened her gown at the neck.

He made short work of them, and then without another word he reached down and pulled the coarse linen garment up and over her head. With that single fluid movement she was naked. The slide of her hair falling back against her bare breasts startled her. Then she became aware of the cool air caressing her skin—and the hard glitter in his eyes as they moved over her.

Following his gaze, she instinctively glanced down at herself. Her breasts were perhaps a little larger than oranges, firm and full, creamy white crested in rose with small nipples, erect as soldiers at attention, that seemed to yearn toward his chest. Her waist was narrow and shapely above gently flaring hips and a flat stomach punctuated by a neat round navel. Below that, the velvety black triangle of curls that hid the delta of her sex topped legs that were long and slim and pale.

She had seen herself naked many times, in the bath and when she dressed. Ordinarily she never even thought about her body or how it looked. It was something on which to put clothes, and she liked its shape, which she knew was quite good, because she liked lovely, fashionable gowns and the way she was made helped them to look as they should on her. But she had never expected to be standing bare as the day she was born in front of a man, a man, moreover, who was to all intents and purposes a stranger, with his eyes touching her with appreciation all over and lingering with transparent pleasure on her most private places. The knowledge that he was looking at her naked made the insistent quaking in her loins grow almost urgent. Her reaction embarrassed the life out of her—and excited her as well.

But even as she acknowledged that, the precepts with which she had been raised won out over the wantonness that she considered her greatest fault. Claire blushed under his roaming gaze, and instinctively brought her hands up to cover herself in the age-old gesture of a modest woman.

As her arms covered her breasts and the black nest of curls, he looked up, meeting her suddenly shy gaze.

"You," he said, in a voice so low and scratchy that it didn't even sound like his voice at all, "are so beautiful you take my breath away. Do you have any idea how much pleasure just looking at you gives me?"

Heart pounding, Claire managed to shake her head.

"More than I can ever tell you. I love looking at you. Don't hide yourself from me."

The husky, coaxing voice and the burning eyes worked their magic. When he reached out to catch her hands, Claire let him pull them down to her sides. She was rewarded by his indrawn breath and the sudden flaring of his eyes as they moved over her, touching her everywhere, so hot they seemed almost to sear her skin.

"God in heaven." His voice was thick. "I want you more than I have ever wanted anything in my life."

Before she could even begin to formulate a reply, he reached out to grasp her hipbones. His big hands, strong and warm, held her possessively. When her hands rose to his shoulders and she would have moved into his arms, he kept her where she was, with some six inches between them, as his gaze roamed her body. She could only watch, breathless, when at last he bent his head and pressed his mouth to her left breast. As the hot wetness of his lips and tongue touched her nipple, Claire gasped. Her body tightened, wept, quaked. Looking down at his head pressed to her bosom, she thought that his mouth on her breast was the most erotic thing she had ever seen in her life.

Heart drumming, Claire watched him suckle her breast, felt the wet heat and tug and pull on her nipple with every nerve ending she possessed, and trembled as her body went up in flames.

"Hugh. Oh, Hugh," she breathed, her nails curling into the firm muscles of his shoulders. The secret place deep inside her loins was clenching and aching now, in a hot urgent rhythm that was as old as time. She wasn't even ashamed of it any longer. She was too far gone with wanting him.

When he took his mouth from her breast to straighten and look down at her, the cool air caressing the wetness at the tip of her breast was an instant reminder of what she was missing. Her breasts lifted toward him instinctively, wordlessly pleading with him for more. She felt shaken at the intensity of her need—and bereft that he had stopped.

"You like that, don't you?" His voice was thick. His hands had tightened on her hips, keeping her from closing the small distance between them. And she wanted to close it. Wanted to be in his arms. Wanted to be pressed right up against him. Wanted . . .

Claire met his gaze, helpless to hide the longing she knew must be burning in her eyes. Her innermost desires had always been a guilty secret that she had kept carefully hidden from everyone. She had always considered her sexual longings wrong. They made her, she feared, something less than a lady. Certainly she had never expected to admit to those longings to anyone, much less a man.

But Hugh was looking at her, his eyes blazing, his cheekbones stained with dark color, his mouth hard with passion—and she nodded. Shamelessly.

"Yes. I like it."

Her loins clenched, hard and tight. Just hearing herself admit to such a thing thrilled her. A blaze of satisfaction appeared in his eyes.

"I thought you would. You were made for loving."

Before she could reply—could even begin to think of a reply—his head bent again and his mouth moved to her other breast and she couldn't think at all. She closed her eyes, dazzled by the feel of what he was doing to her and by her body's shivery, quaking response. This kind of feeling, this fierce pleasure, was what she had been in search of for so many years. It was what she'd wanted, what she'd needed, what she'd dreamed of.

She'd never really believed it existed anywhere outside her deepest, darkest fantasies: the secret, shameful ones that sometimes came to her in the night. The ones she had never been able to banish, although she had most sincerely tried.

He drew the entire tip of her breast into his mouth, sucking hard. She must have made some kind of small well-pleasured sound, because he looked up, then straightened. His eyes were black and hot as they met hers. He was breathing erratically too, she saw, and the fine tremor in his arms was more pronounced.

"You sound like a little cat. A hungry little cat."

That embarrassed her. "I do not!"

"I like it."

He gave her the briefest of wicked smiles, then even as she blushed from her forehead clear down to her toes he scooped her up in his arms. Claire barely had time to take a breath before he deposited her in the middle of the bed. For a moment he leaned over her, kissing her mouth, caressing her breasts with both hands until she was gasping and arching up off the bed quite shamelessly. His fingers lingered on her nipples, rubbing them, gently squeezing the swelling nubs, until the pleasure was so exquisite she couldn't bear it. She cried out, the sound muffled by his mouth.

"Easy now. We're just getting started."

He pulled her arms from around his neck and stood up beside the bed. For a long moment he simply looked down at her, spread out like a feast before him, and this time she was content to let him look. As the heat in his eyes flamed over her she realized that emotionally and physically she was now completely defenseless with this man, whom she had hated and feared less than two days before. She was naked and quivering beneath his gaze, pliant to his every wish, his for the taking at his pleasure.

And she reveled in it. He could do with her as he would, and she had the most lowering presentiment that she was going to love every minute of it.

Then their eyes met. His were both hot—and tender. Their expression made her dizzy.

"Didn't I tell you this would be fun?"

It took a moment for that to sink in.

"Don't tease." Her voice was unsteady. Her eyes never left his face as she curled her fingers into the bedclothes to keep herself from reaching for him. How could he talk at a moment like this, when she was on fire from wanting him?

"I'm not teasing. Let me get my clothes off and I'll prove it to you."

Sitting down on the edge of the bed, he began to pull off his boots. Breathing hard, fingers clutching at the tumbled quilts, Claire watched the muscles of his broad back flex through his shirt and listened to the thump of the first boot hitting the floor with more restless anticipation that she had ever felt for anything in her life. Then she couldn't contain herself any longer. She sat up. He was close, easily close enough to touch, so she did. The linen shirt felt faintly rough beneath her palms, but it was thin enough that she could feel the heat of his skin beneath as she ran her hands along the breadth of his shoulders, over his shoulder blades, down his spine. He tensed as he first felt her touch, but after a quick glinting glance over his shoulder at her he pulled off the other boot without a word. It thumped as it hit the floor.

Then he pulled the shirt over his head. As it dropped to the floor, Claire paused, simply staring for a moment at his bare back. It was as beautiful as she remembered, all bronze skin and flexing muscle in a well-defined vee shape, with the yellowing bruise that still cut across his side as the only discordant note. She had touched his back before, fearfully, furtively, when she had slid her hand around his waist to remove his knife. This time she touched him openly, sliding her hands along the width of his shoulders and over the flexing protrusion of his shoulder blades, reveling in the warm satin-over-steel sensation beneath her fingers—and in her freedom to touch him as she would. His breath caught as her hands slid over his skin, and he stiffened.

Then, abruptly, he stood up and turned to face her, his hands moving to the buttons of his breeches. Her protest at his shift in position forgotten before it could be uttered, she watched as he made short work of his task. As she did, her mouth went dry.

She was about to get what she had long wanted. The thought reared its head in a rather cautionary fashion. A kaleidoscope of doubts, fears, and warnings swirled through her mind as she looked at the hard handsome face, the broad chest with its wedge of black hair, the bronzed, sinewy arms, the lean hips. She watched as he finished unbuttoning his breeches, then watched some more as he slid them down his legs.

The muscles of his thighs were athletic and powerful-looking, she saw, and roughened with dark hair, but it was not his legs that held her attention. It was that part of him, that enormous, jutting, swollen part, that was proof positive of his desire for her. It was far bigger than she remembered its being, far bigger than the only other one she had ever seen—David's, in shadowy glimpses once or twice as he had climbed into her bed in the dark—and far more fearsome-looking, too.

And it was about to be shoved inside her body.

Claire's heart began to thump even as she wondered, with no small degree of trepidation, whether it would actually fit.

"Hugh," she began, her fingers curling nervously into the bedclothes and her eyes wide as they focused first on that hugely inflated male part and then on his face. She had been going to say something more, warn him of her misgivings perhaps, or caution him of a possible size problem or something, but it was too late. He was coming down on the bed with her, his big body blocking the light from the candle, casting a shadow over her, then covering her, pressing his huge weight down on her, getting ready to make her his.

His knee slid between hers, nudging her thighs apart. Claire felt an icy stab of pure panic and stiffened—but she realized even as his mouth claimed hers that it was far too late to stop him now, even if that was what she wanted to do.

## 21

Hugh's kiss was slow and hot and dizzyingly sweet, and did much to reconcile her to the coming invasion of her body. He lay on top of her, warm and unbelievably heavy, his skin roughened with hair, his long, muscular body almost completely covering her smaller one. Even as her arms slid around his neck and she kissed him back, gradually surrendering to the magic only he could evoke, she was aware of myriad different sensations: the crushing of her breasts by his wide chest, the sinewy strength of his thighs nudging hers apart, the burning heat of his privates lying erect along the inside of her thigh. Despite the swooningly intense sensations he was evoking with his mouth and body, she had yet to lose herself entirely in what they were doing, and that male part was why. The truth was, she was made nervous by it. Though he had not attempted entry yet, he had parted her legs and was lying between them, and would, she knew, start wedging that thing inside her when the urge struck him, which could be at any time.

David had always put his male part into her within seconds of coming to her bed. That was the way intimate congress worked: The male part was inserted, sometimes easily, and sometimes, when it did not seem to be cooperative, with difficulty, the man rutted briefly, did his business or, if something went wrong, grew angry because he could not, and withdrew. In any case it was all over in a few minutes, and then he would lift himself away from her and leave her alone in the bed.

That was the way intimate congress had worked with David, anyway. Would Hugh be different? Already he had caused her to feel things that she had never, ever thought she would feel. When he kissed her, she grew light-headed. When he wanted her naked, she blushed with embarrassment—and got naked, letting him look his fill. When he touched or caressed or—so shocking!—kissed her breasts, she trembled with pleasure. Now that he was lying on top of her, and she was experiencing the suddenly just-right weight of him, the feeling of skin against skin, of hard male muscles against soft female curves, she was rapidly becoming curious to finally learn the truth.

Were all men the same between the sheets? Or could Hugh, who had already thrilled her with his kisses, with his touch, give her what she had only ever dreamed about?

Her heart pounded erratically as she focused with an uneasy mix of hope and trepidation on the latter. Finally, one way or another, she was going to know.

"I'm—ready," she whispered bravely in his ear. Having left her mouth to trail across her cheek to her throat, his lips were now busy tracing a line of hot, tingly kisses along her jaw.

"Are you now?" He lifted his head to look at her. One hand came up to smooth the tangled hair back from her face. Though his eyes were dark with passion, even as she met his gaze the tiniest smile curved his mouth.

She nodded, still resolute, and the smile broadened briefly before it vanished altogether as suddenly as it had appeared. He kissed her mouth, a hard possessive kiss, and even as she responded instinctively she felt his body tense, felt the hardness of him stir against her thigh, and braced herself. Here it came. He was so large—would it hurt? Or would she scarcely notice him sliding inside her, as she sometimes scarcely noticed David's entry?

She was suddenly overwhelmingly curious to find out.

Then his mouth found her breast, and all thought fled. What replaced thought was feeling, hot urgent feeling, as he suckled first one breast and then the other, laving the nipples with his tongue, drawing them into his mouth, suckling them, at first leisurely and then with increasing urgency. The quaking inside her solidified into a burning ache, a fierce hunger, a driving need. Her hands were on his head now, her fingers embedded in his hair, holding him to her. Gasping, trembling, she quite forgot about his male part as his mouth on her breasts once again worked its magic. Then his back seemed to flex, and his male part probed the delta between her legs. Breathing heavily, she moved restlessly beneath him, on fire for him, parting her legs wider, not just ready now but eager for him to come inside.

But to her surprise he shifted, sliding down her body so that his male part was no longer touching her. What was he doing? This was not what she wanted, not how it was done. Her eyes popped open as he kissed his way down the center of her rib cage to no purpose that she could see. Her fingers tightened in his hair.

"Hugh." Despite the unsteadiness of her voice, it was clearly both a protest and a question. He looked up at her, his eyes blazing, his lips parted as he breathed like a man suddenly finding himself short of air. "I said—I'm ready."

"Then you must just clothe yourself in patience, my innocent little darling, because I'm not."

As hot as they were, there was a glimmer in his eyes that was almost amusement, and then his head was at the level of her waist and he was kissing her belly button and sliding even lower. . . .

"Hugh!" This time her voice held genuine shock, and she struggled up on her elbows to see what he was about. *His face was almost at the level of the black triangle of curls between her thighs—it was there—he was nuzzling his face into the soft nest.* "Oh, dear Lord, what do you think you're doing?"

He looked up, and as Claire met his gaze she realized that the sight of him lying there between her pale spread thighs with his face just inches away from that part of her that even she was shy to look at, or touch, was so far beyond any of her tentative imaginings that she didn't know whether to scream, slap his face—or just lie back and let him do with her as he would.

"Trust me," he said, his voice so hoarse that the words were almost a growl. Even as he spoke, his hands were gently stroking the soft insides of her slender thighs, pushing her legs farther apart so that he could have more access to her most secret flesh.

Chest heaving as she fought to draw breath, trembling as if she had an ague, Claire could only watch with helpless fascination as his head dipped and he pressed his face against the velvety delta between her spread legs.

Pure fire shot through her as he kissed her in a place where she had never, ever expected to be kissed. Gasping, quivering, she sank back bonelessly to experience a delight she hadn't even known existed. Her eyes closed and her fingers curled into the bedclothes again as embarrassing little sounds of pleasure emerged from her throat. Her hips writhed under his ministrations, but she didn't care about that either. All she could focus on was the sheer ecstasy of it as he pressed his mouth against her, his tongue licking at her like a finger of liquid flame.

Tongues of fire seemed to race over her body as he concentrated on one secret point. She cried out, then cried out again, quite unable to help herself as he aroused her to fever pitch. His fingers found that moist, secret place that was her entry, and slid inside, moving boldly in and out. That made her cry out too. He kissed her and stroked her, miming the act of intimate congress with his fingers at the same time as he touched her with his tongue, using his hands and mouth together to drive her to heights of passion she had never even suspected she could reach. When the hot, fierce contractions took her, they were all she had ever dreamed of.

Then, while she was still reaching, still writhing and gasping and wanting what he was doing to her never to end, he stopped, leaving that part of her that he had been so thoroughly pleasuring throbbing and weeping with need, to slide back up her body and kiss her mouth.

Shaking with passion, Claire realized that she could taste herself on his lips. She moaned, aflame with desire and embarrassment and a blinding new knowledge. Then she locked her arms around his neck and kissed him back as if she'd die if she didn't. She felt the hot smoothness of him probe at her entry, at the place where his mouth and hands had been working black magic just seconds before. She made a tiny mewling sound deep in her throat and lifted her hips off the mattress in wordless entreaty. This time she was not merely ready: Her body ached for him, burned for him, melted for him.

He came inside her in a single slow surge, hard and hot and filling her to capacity, stretching her as she had known he must, but the sensation was wonderful, it was indescribable, it was more delicious than anything she had ever felt or imagined she could feel. She dug her nails into his shoulders and her heels into the mattress and tilted her hips to accept him fully.

Even as she squirmed beneath him, wanting more with an open, greedy hunger that would have shamed her to her core had she been in possession of even a fraction of her senses, he lifted his mouth from hers.

"Claire." It was a ragged breath.

Her lids fluttered up and their gazes met. His body was joined with hers in intimate congress and she was moving beneath him like the wanton she now knew for certain she was. Yet as she looked at him in the candlelight she was unashamed, no, bold with passion, avidly registering the hot glaze clouding his eyes, the dark color high on his cheekbones, the tautness of his mouth still damp from her kisses, the sweat shining on his brow and shoulders. It was the most transforming experience of her life.

All men were not the same between the sheets. What she had gone through with David bore no relation to this hot sweet assault on her senses.

"Wrap your legs around my waist."

Claire's eyes widened as the instruction percolated

through the steam that befogged her brain. When it did, she drew in a ragged breath. And then, trembling, she did as he bade her. Her legs lifted until her slender thighs gripped his hips and her ankles locked behind his waist. She could feel him inside her all the while, thick and hot and swollen and tantalizing, and she couldn't help herself: She moved against him again, then moved some more, then gasped at the pleasure of it.

"Now I'd say you're ready." It was a tender taunt, whispered in an unsteady voice in her ear. She felt the tremors racking him. He was tense, poised, shaking, sweating—and yet waiting for her.

"Yes. Oh, yes."

Unable to stand it any longer, Claire surged against him. The sensation made her cry out. He shuddered, tightening his arms around her so that taking a deep breath became suddenly impossible. Then he buried his face in the curve between her neck and shoulder. His mouth was open and wet and warm as he pressed it to her neck.

And he began to move.

Claire cried out again, losing every inhibition she had ever had in that moment. Wild with need, she moved with him, meeting him thrust for thrust as a firestorm built inside her. He took her hard and he took her fast and she was with him every inch of the way, going higher and higher until at last she flew higher than she had ever dreamed of going and exploded with what felt like the combined firepower of a million shooting stars and flaming pinwheels and bursting suns.

"Hugh Hugh Hugh Hugh *Hugh*."

Even as she cried out his name and was whirled away on the storm, he stiffened and groaned. Then, shaking, he held himself deep inside her as he found his own release. Still lost in her distant universe, she clung to him as he collapsed atop her. For a long time they lay together, totally spent.

Finally Claire started to be aware of little things. The weight of him atop her came first. He was a tall man, muscular and broad-shouldered, but he was also lean and it did not seem possible that he could weigh so much. But he did. In fact, now that she was not caught up in the throes of passion, he was crushing her into the mattress and suffocating her and roasting her alive to boot. She felt the sweat-slickness of his shoulders beneath her hands, heard the steady rasp of his breathing—had he fallen asleep?—and saw the back of his head as his face remained buried in her throat.

She really, really needed to breathe.

She must have moved, or made some small sound, because he lifted his head then and looked at her. For a moment she stared, mesmerized, into gray eyes that looked just as intently back. Then she remembered that she was naked and he was on top of her and all the things he had done to her with his hands and mouth and body and *how she had reacted*. Heat suffused her face, and she was suddenly, self-consciously sure she was the color of a fresh-picked, red ripe strawberry.

A long, slow smile curled his mouth as he surveyed her. She had little doubt that her heightened color had been observed and ascribed to its correct cause. Unlike herself, he looked relaxed, at ease, and totally at home in the situation in which he found himself.

"Now wasn't that fun?" The wicked glint was back in his eyes. Claire looked at him, at the lean unshaven cheeks, at the narrowed eyes and twisting mouth, and felt her heart flutter. Modesty as well as all the precepts she had ever heard about ladies and the marriage act bade that she downplay what she had experienced, that she cast down her eyes and nod shyly, or even deny that she had felt a thing. But she had always been incurably honest, even blunt at times, which, to hear her sisters tell it, could be a grave fault, and anyway he had been there with her, seen her quiver and shake, felt her squirm and writhe, heard her groan and cry out his name. He would not believe her if she tried to convince him that she hadn't had the experience of a lifetime.

So she simply told the truth.

"It was wonderful."

The smile grew more pronounced. He looked quite pleased with himself. "Was it now?"

She nodded. Then, because she really couldn't breathe, she gave a delicate little shove to his shoulder.

"Now that we're finished, would you mind getting off me? I can't breathe."

"Oh, sorry." He rolled off her, but instead of letting her go, he caught her around the waist and pulled her over on top of him. Surprised to find herself lying atop his chest, she blinked at him for a moment. But he smiled back at her with lazy charm, positioning a pillow under his head and giving every indication that he meant to stay in that position for quite a while. With the thought of what their parting would mean—she couldn't think of that now, or it would spoil what time they had left—she was in no hurry for him to get out of bed, to dress and leave her.

When he left, she might very well not ever see him again.

The thought was like a knife stabbing into her heart.

"What do you mean, 'now that we're finished'?" he asked, crossing his arms behind his head and giving her a very interesting view of two black-tufted armpits. "We're just getting started, you and I."

"Hugh." Another pang struck Claire's heart as she realized that his words, while possibly true in one sense, were the total opposite of reality in another. Completely forgetting her niggling concerns about modesty and her few remaining inhibitions and even the fact that she was nude at all as her worries solidified like a rock in her stomach, she settled down on his chest, crossing her hands under her chin and looking at him pensively. "You know, after tonight, we'll probably never see each other again."

She watched him closely, hoping to see a glimpse in his expression of the same kind of anguish that was even now ripping her heart in two. But his face remained relaxed, even faintly smiling, and his eyes bore no pain at all that she could see.

"One never knows what life may bring," he said lightly.

It was a blow, but she took it and kept her chin up. Keep it light. If she didn't want to make a fool as well as a wanton of herself, she would keep this thing between them light, which was obviously where he preferred that it stay. Had she really expected him to start spouting declarations of undying love? Not with her head. Certainly not. Only with her vulnerable heart. . . . Of course, he'd done this many times before, with many different women. It wouldn't have the same significance for him as it had for her.

The significance it held for her was mind-boggling. But she wouldn't think of that now, either. She would not think of tomorrow, or all the other tomorrows, at all. All she would think about was how much she treasured being like this with him tonight.

If one night was all she was going to have, it was still better than nothing. In fact, it was everything she had ever dreamed of, and more.

He must have seen a shadow cross her face, because he was frowning now as he looked at her. His hands came out from behind his head, and he wrapped his arms around her in a great hug, stroking her hair, her back.

"Is something wrong?" he asked. There was concern in his eyes. She looked at him, met his gaze, and shook her head. Then she smiled.

That smile, she realized, was just about the bravest thing she had ever done in her life.

"Not a thing," she said. As she sought to get her expression under control, her lashes lowered. Then she lifted them, and her smile widened. "Actually, I thank you for the lesson. It was quite instructive—and fun."

"You said wonderful." His mouth was curling at her, and his eyes were taking on a predatory gleam.

"That too."

His hands slid down her to cup her buttocks, and squeeze.

"Ouch!"

Claire yelped. As his hands lifted in surprised realization, she rolled off him with a grimace. Even with her back to the wall she was self-conscious about it, but she could not help it: She had to rub the abused muscles in an attempt to do what she could to ease the pain.

"I'm sorry. I forgot. Here, let me make it better."

He was remorseful, and persuasive, and managed to coax her onto her stomach while he massaged the aching part. His hands were gentle, and he was careful to ease rather than inflict pain, but after a little bit she quite forgot why he was caressing her bottom in the sheer pleasure she was deriving from it. When he bent over to kiss the afflicted flesh, a thrill shot through her. When he continued to press tiny kisses all over her bottom under the pretext that kisses would make it all better, she was soon melting under his ministrations. Then his hand slid beneath her to find and caress that tiny nub between her legs that had been such a revelation to her before. Before she knew it the hot, sweet clamoring that she had thought was a once-in-a-lifetime thing had taken possession of her again, and then he did too, sliding inside her from behind, taking her with a slow sureness that drove her even wilder than before and had her digging her nails into the mattress and crying out his name with every thrust.

Finally the whirlwind came for her again, and she surrendered to it with a shuddering, joyful cry that was as instinctive and primitive as anything he had done to her.

"God in heaven."

As he growled the words, she didn't know if they were a curse or a prayer. She only knew that he plunged into her at the same time as he said them, at that exact moment of her deepest pleasure, with a fierce hunger that made her cry out again too. Then he held himself inside her as his lean, strong body convulsed with long shudders. Finally he collapsed on top of her, and lay still.

After a long moment he rolled onto his side, pulling her with him. Claire was dizzy with exhaustion as she curled into his arms. She smiled at him dreamily. He kissed her mouth. She was so tired it was an effort even to kiss him back. For a few moments they held each other, exchanging whispers that made less and less sense to her. Then her lids, which had felt as if they'd had lead weights attached to them for some time, finally gave up the fight and closed for good. Just like that she was asleep, held close in his arms.

"Miss! Miss, it's time to go."

At first Claire thought the words were part of her dream. She'd been having a wonderful one—about what? She couldn't recall. The persistent voice calling to her to wake up was blotting it out. Resentful, she opened her eyes at last—to find James hovering over the bed, clearly just on the verge of nudging her arm.

She was wearing the borrowed nightdress, Claire realized with some relief as their gazes met for an instant. For the briefest of moments she was confused. Had everything been a dream, then? But no. There were too many pleasant little aches and tingles in too many extremely private places of her body for her to have dreamed what she had done with Hugh.

Hugh. Her eyes widened. A swift glance around revealed that she was not only alone in the bed, she was alone, save for James, in the room.

She opened her mouth to ask where Hugh was, then closed it again as she realized that to do so would be to reveal that she had expected him to be in the bed, or at least the bedroom, with her. Hugh was obviously gone, and had obviously put her nightgown back on before he left to spare her just that humiliation before James.

"Miss, you must get up and dress. Master Hugh is gone an hour since, and we must leave for the boat shortly."

As that registered, Claire closed her eyes and, somewhere deep inside, felt her heart break.

## 22

*April 1813*

"Imust say, drinking all that vinegar was not very
pleasant, but the results were certainly worth-
while." Turning this way and that in front of the cheval
mirror in her lavish bedroom in Richmond House in
London's posh Cavendish Square, Lady Elizabeth Banning surveyed the reflection of her newly svelte figure
with satisfaction.

"Beth, you look absolutely beautiful," Claire said with
warm sincerity to her little sister. Twindle, Claire and Beth's
lifelong nursemaid-cum-governess-cum-companion, who
had once been Claire's mother's governess and was completely devoted to all three sisters, was standing beside
Claire. Tall and spare, with a narrow, lined face and silvery
hair brushed severely back into a tight knot at her nape,
Twindle nodded at the pair sagely.

"I told you Lord Byron swore by it as a reducing
tonic, and it certainly seems to have done the job nicely
for you, Miss Beth. Any puppy fat that might once have
afflicted you has certainly disappeared."

\* \* \*

Three months had gone by since Claire had awakened to find herself alone in a farmer's bed in France. During that time, the pain of knowing that she would in all likelihood never see Hugh again had become a persistent ache that she was beginning to realize might never go away. Her fear for his life was another constant torment. Had the soldiers captured him on the way to Paris? Had someone betrayed him since? There were many fates that could befall a spy, and most of them were terrible. The worst part was realizing that he could be injured, imprisoned, or even dead, and she would not know. She would never know. But wondering and worrying paid no toll, as she kept reminding herself. All she could do was try to put her fears—and him—out of her mind.

And the only way to do that was not to give herself so much as a moment to think. As a consequence, Claire kept herself almost frenetically busy. It helped that the London Season was now in full swing, and that she, in her role as chaperon to eighteen-year-old Beth, had a full plate of activities to occupy her. Days were spent shopping, at home with callers, or paying calls, driving or walking in the park, or engaging in any of dozens of other possible amusements. Nearly every evening brought with it an entertainment of one sort or another. Tonight was Beth's very own come-out ball, and Claire had been working her fingers to the bone for weeks to prepare for it. She welcomed both the extra work and the diversion, even though Twindle, with a critical frown, had told her just that morning that she was looking worn to a bone and should rest and let the staff handle the rest of the arrangements. Claire had brushed off her concern with an affectionate word and a smile.

Twindle did not understand that Claire was hiding the kind of pain that brought strong men to their knees. All she knew of Claire's adventures—all anyone knew of Claire's adventures—was that her carriage had been attacked and she had been kidnapped and managed to escape. When her sisters had asked her about the two days she had spent as a captive, she had made up a story about being kept blindfolded in a farmhouse, assuring them, when they had grown indignant, that she had been well treated. James had suggested keeping silent about the rest—about Hugh—as a matter of national security. Claire had followed that suggestion as much for her own purposes as for any other reason: If she spoke of Hugh, even so much as mentioned his name or tried to tell the rest of the story while leaving out the most intimate and personal parts (like the part where she had ended up naked in bed with him), she feared that her sisters would immediately sense that something was being withheld and, in the way of sisters, keep at her until they had divined what it was.

Looked at in the cold, hard light of day, what she had done was called adultery. She was not proud of it, nor eager to share her guilt with anyone, and she was paying for it now with what felt like a whole lifetime's worth of pain. Lying with Hugh was a sin, and she had known it at the time and had done it anyway. Even now, when it was in the past and she was hurting so badly that just getting through each day was a struggle, she could not regret it. If that one night was all she was ever going to have of Hugh, and this dreadful grinding pain in her heart was the price she must pay for it, then so be it. If she could go back and change what had happened and thus spare herself the subsequent suffering, she would not. She would not wish away that night with Hugh even if she suffered for it the rest of her life. But she had to be careful, and she knew it. It was best that she keep her own counsel, and that meant that she must just swallow her heartbreak and go on. Because besides being a sin, what she had done with Hugh was a scandal just waiting to get out. The Banning sisters had barely survived a scandal of Gabby and her now husband Nick's making just a few years before, when Nick had posed as their brother to track a murderer, and Gabby had gone and fallen in love with him despite the fact that everyone, save Gabby, including Claire and Beth, had thought he really was their theretofore unknown brother. This drama had played out during the Season before the shocked eyes of the *ton*, and it had nearly sunk the sisters beyond hope of redemption. Fortunately their Aunt Augusta, Lady Salcombe, was a pillar of society. With her help, and aided by the fact that Nick was an extremely rich man, that scandal eventually had been papered over with just enough half-truths to satisfy the high sticklers and allow the Bannings to continue to be accepted in the best circles.

Still, if any whisper of another Banning sister flouting Society's rules should get out, Claire very much feared their reputations would be blackened forever. Beth's chances in the marriage mart would be ruined. David could sue for divorce, and that thought—the mere idea of being named an adulteress in open court—made Claire shudder. And the gossip-making details of Gabby's romance would be rehashed, along with lurid tales of their father, the wicked earl, and his four wives, three of whom had mothered one daughter each before conveniently passing on to their reward. There would be whispers of bad blood—and, worse, bad *ton*.

Those she hoped to avoid at all costs. The gossip connected with her kidnapping was bad enough, and she still got inquiries about how the search for the criminals was going. They hadn't been found, and it now seemed increasingly likely that they would not be. At both Nick's and David's insistence, the only journey she had undertaken since—from Morningtide to London— had been under the protection of armed outriders. Claire still occasionally got an uneasy feeling when she went out shopping or to visit the lending library or on other outings of that nature, but the streets of London were crowded and she was now exceedingly careful never to be alone—and anyway, what were the chances that she would be attacked again? So slim as to be practically nonexistent, she told herself firmly. If she got the impression sometimes that she was being followed, or that unseen eyes were watching her, she was ready to put it down to nerves, or even to comfort herself with the thought that if anyone was indeed watching or following her it was probably one of the men Hugh had told her would be looking out for her. In any case, she refused to live in fear, so she went on about her usual business. Fortunately the story was now well on its way to becoming yesterday's *on dit*, but at the beginning of the Season she had retold the partly fictionalized version so many times that she had almost come to believe it herself.

Except, of course, whenever she got too comfortable in the retelling, there was always her aching heart to remind her of the rest of the story.

She might have confided in Gabby—her older sister was her most trusted friend—but Gabby was abed on doctor's orders by the time Claire reached Morningtide almost two days after that bleak dawn when she had set sail from France. Stivers, the longtime family butler who had moved into Morningtide with Gabby on her marriage, had opened the door to Claire's knock, and had let out a shriek upon seeing who it was that had brought a host of servants, as well as Beth, and Gabby's husband, Nick, running.

"Miss Claire, Miss Claire, we feared you dead!" Twindle had sobbed, as first she and then Beth had fallen on her neck in floods of tears. Nick had let out a shout, and practically snatched Claire off her feet in his haste to convey her to Gabby's bedside. Not that Nick had not been out of his mind with worry over her fate for her own sake, as he had hastened to assure her later, when things had calmed down a bit. But Gabby, already weak and sick with pregnancy, had fainted upon hearing of the attack on Claire's carriage, and he had feared the effect on her should he have to tell her that her beloved little sister had suffered an even more dire fate. To have Claire turn up hale and hearty on their doorstep, when he had men searching half of England for her—and, as Nick hastily added, David had his own group of would-be rescuers hunting her as well, of course—could only be classified as a miracle.

There was a moment there when Claire had thought about confiding to Nick, not the part about sleeping with Hugh, but at least the fact that she had met him, been mistaken for a spy, and carried off to France by him by mistake. Nick was a former intelligence agent himself, although he had retired upon his marriage, and might be expected to know Hugh. But anything Nick knew, Gabby knew soon afterward. And if Gabby got hold of any part of it, she would soon have the whole shameful story out of Claire. Then would come questions about the state of Claire's marriage, and Gabby would worry herself to death if she learned how unhappy Claire was in it, and at this, the happiest moment in Gabby's life, Claire did not want to burden her with problems.

So, in the end, she did not confide in anyone. Instead she determined simply to put it all out of her mind as if it had never happened, Hugh included.

At which, so far, she was failing abysmally.

To that end, all was well that ended well, Claire told them one and all, putting on her brave, smiling face and doing her best to drive all memories of Hugh—indeed, of everything that had happened above and beyond the original kidnapping—from her mind. Actually, it was borne in on her over the next few days and weeks that forgetting the rest—forgetting Hugh—was the only rational choice, because every time she thought of him she was hit by such a wave of misery that all she wanted to do was go to bed and cry. The pain was almost more than she could stand, but she gritted her teeth and lifted her chin and bore it. The reality was that her bolt-from-the-blue love affair was over, vanished as completely as a dream when the dreamer wakes.

Even James was gone, having disappeared after he had seen her walk safely in the door at Morningtide, and without even giving her so much as a chance to charge him with a message for Hugh. Not that she would have done so. At least, not then. At that point, she had still had her pride. Now, she feared, her pride was quite gone, worn down by the constant ache in her heart. Had she the chance to do it over again, she probably would have forced James to convey her right back to Hugh and France after assuring her family that she was all right.

But that was foolishness, of course. She must just be thankful for those few hours she and Hugh had shared, for the knowledge he had given her of what was possible between a man and a woman, rather than constantly regretting that they had not had more time together. And indeed, she tried to be thankful, but it was hard—very hard.

When David—reunited with her at Morningtide some two days after her safe arrival there and exhibiting such joy at her safety that she could not help but suspect he was feigning—had tried to come to her bed for the first time in months in an apparent attempt to prove to her how truly anxious about her he had been, she had not been able to bear the thought of lying with him and had turned him away with the excuse that it was her monthly time. He had accepted that without much noticeable regret, and had not attempted to enter her bedchamber again. But someday he would. He must, if they were to have children. The thought made her shudder.

She did not love her husband. She never truly had. She had married him thinking he was what she wanted, what she needed, a kind and gentle man who would never be a threat to her in any way. But she'd been wrong about David—he was no more intrinsically kind and gentle than was a wasp. And she'd been wrong about what she needed as well. She needed a man who could make her laugh and make her furious and make her gasp with a touch or a kiss. In short, she needed Hugh.

But Hugh was gone, and she was married to David. Trapped like a fly in a web, with no way out that she could see.

So she straightened her spine, held up her head, and vowed to put a good face on the rest of her life. Her initial reward for so much bravery had been witnessing the safe arrival, just one month before, of her new niece, Anne Elizabeth Claire Devane. Gabby was over the moon with happiness at the birth of her daughter, and seeing her beloved sister both happy and speedily recovering her health was one of the two bright spots in Claire's life. The other was Beth. Without Beth, Claire didn't know what she would have done. Although Beth didn't know about Hugh either, Beth was family. Claire leaned on her, depending on her stalwart, cheerful little sister for affection and laughter and companionship more desperately than Beth would ever realize.

Bringing Beth out gave her something to focus on, Claire thought now as she surveyed her sister critically from head to toe. Something to occupy the majority of her attention until the storm assailing her heart had passed, as it would surely—please, God!—do in time.

"The pearl earrings and necklet, Alice," Claire said to the girl who was hovering around Beth, thus signaling her final approval of Beth's costume by requesting the pieces that would complete it. A pink-cheeked, bright-eyed young woman with a coronet of neat brown braids, Alice was the maid who had been in the carriage with Claire at the time of her abduction. Aside from being clouted over the head, she had not been harmed, and had returned to Morningtide in the aftermath of the kidnapping. In an effort to make up to her for some of the trauma she had suffered, Claire had offered her this chance to come with them to London as her own lady's maid, the girl who had held that post in the country having elected not to leave her family.

"Yes, Miss Claire." Alice obediently fetched the items requested from the dressing table in the other room. But upon her return with them, Beth, turning this way and that as she surveyed her gown from every possible angle, proved an elusive target.

"Stand still, Beth, do," Claire said impatiently after a minute or so of watching Alice's futile efforts.

Her sister, all of eighteen years old now, a breathtaking debutante in a white satin ballgown with a sparkling gauze overlay that made her look like a fairy princess, a new and lovely ornament on the bosom of Society, met her gaze through the mirror. Then she stuck out her tongue at Claire.

Claire barely recollected her own dignity in time to keep from pitching the spray of tiny white roses in the silver filagree holder, which she had just picked up to hand to Beth, at her saucy red head instead.

"It's a pity that the vinegar didn't have the same improving effect on her conduct as it did on her figure, isn't it?" Claire confined herself to observing.

"You're just jealous because you're an old married woman now, and I am the one who gets to have all the beaux," Beth retorted good-humoredly.

That was so true that Claire could only make a face at her sister through the mirror that was not quite as childish in effect as sticking out one's tongue, but close.

## ❧ 23 ❧

.....................................

$\mathcal{L}$ong inured to such sisterly moments, Twindle frowned impartially at the pair of them.

"That's quite enough, girls."

Claire, hearing the familiar refrain that had been a staple of her growing-up days even as she watched Alice at last manage to screw the earrings into the grown-up Beth's ears, had to smile at her own instantaneous return to the familiar patterns of childhood. If Gabby was the sister in whom she was most likely to confide, Beth was the sister whose ears she was most likely to box. With just three years separating them, they had spent their formative years bickering and battling and then turning right around and defending one another from any outsider's attacks. As dearly as she loved Gabby, Claire just as dearly loved Beth. And she was truly glad to be bringing Beth out in London. She was glad to have more time with her sister, who'd been living with Gabby at Morningtide since Gabby's marriage.

Also, if it hadn't been for Beth, Claire would by now, since Gabby's baby was born and in the interests of keeping up a good front, have returned to her own home. Strange, after almost two years of marriage, it was still hard to think of it as that. Labington, a small jewel of an estate in Dorset that David had inherited from his father, second son of the late, previous Duke of Richmond, was beautiful: beautiful house, beautiful grounds, beautiful countryside. When David had taken her to see it soon after his proposal, she had thought that she could soon grow to love the place. But what she had not then realized was that people were what made a house a home, and from the time of her honeymoon she had lived at Labington largely alone except for the servants. Not long after the wedding, Claire had realized that David despised the place, preferring to divide his time between his cousin the duke's far more elaborate properties, which David's mother, and David too until his marriage, had long occupied with the duke's permission as the duke himself, whom Claire had not as yet met, had spent the last several years abroad. Hayleigh Castle was one of those properties, and this most august of London townhouses was another.

It was ideal for holding a come-out ball, and Claire could only be grateful to her mother-in-law for permitting her to launch Beth from so peerless an address. Nick was bearing all the expenses of Beth's Season, including this ball, but, as a wealthy commoner, he could not provide the kind of cachet that was attached to Richmond House and the Lynes family. With her sister's own fiery beauty, the weight of Richmond House behind her, and no scandal to cast a spanner in the works, Beth could hardly fail to be a success.

And unlike Claire at her own debut, Beth was actually looking forward to the process. The idea of marrying held none of the terrors for her lionhearted little sister that it had held for her less courageous self. Claire had dreaded the idea of marrying, fearing that she might find herself subjected for life to the whims of an overbearing, abusive tyrant like her father. But Gabby's success at matrimony had heartened her, and the knowledge that she wanted children and a husband was the only way to get them had provided the final push. And so she had ended up with handsome David, cousin and heir to a duke, who'd written poetry to her eyes instead of kissing her and who'd sent her posies rather than sweeping her up in his arms when they danced.

Only it turned out that David wasn't what she'd wanted at all. Wasn't that the way life always worked? To learn a hard truth too late—was that better than never learning it at all? Possibly not. At least, if one never discovered what one wanted, one could never miss not having it.

But perhaps, like Gabby, Beth would have better luck with men and marriage, Claire told herself, and hoped fiercely that it would be so. Prayed that it would be so.

"Miss Claire, Miss Twindlesham, do you think a curl—so?" Haney, a tiny brunette who had been engaged in London and had been recommended as one who was a wizard at implementing the latest styles, was Beth's own maid. She coaxed one of Beth's long curls over her shoulder so that it fell in front almost to the off-the-shoulder neckline of the gown. The effect was quite riveting, Claire decided, looking at her sister with a critical eye, rather like introducing a tongue of flame into a field of pristine snow. Besides Beth's long-hated fiery hair, the only other notes of color in the picture of virginal white perfection her sister presented were her lips, touched most discreetly with crushed rose petals to enhance their color, and her sparkling blue eyes.

"That's perfect," Claire approved, and smiled at her sister through the mirror. "You look perfect."

Beth returned her smile a tad ruefully. "No, you're the one who looks perfect, of course. You always do. It's the most lowering thing, let me tell you, to have a sister who always outshines one." Then her gaze shifted to her own reflection, and her smile widened and her eyes twinkled engagingly. "But I'm used to it. Anyway, I think I look quite beautiful too. And I'm far more lively and not nearly as shy as you. So have at you, Claire."

"This is not a contest," Claire said severely, then had to grin. She and Beth had played at being pirates as little children, with sticks for swords, and never mind that they were girls. *Have at you, Claire*, was what Beth had always shouted before she went on the attack, usually to beat Claire back quite handily. "Besides, I'm married, remember? This ball—this Season—is all for you."

"It is, isn't it?" Beth turned to beam at her with undisguised delight.

"The pair of you had best be going below now. It won't do to be late to your own ball." Twindle was briskly practical as she stepped forward to shoo Beth toward the door. Reminded of the time, Claire handed Beth her flowers.

"I am so excited." Executing a few swirling dance steps, Beth stopped to give Twindle a hug and got, in return, a quick, precautionary lecture on the behavior expected of young ladies making their debut. Listening to this diatribe directed at her deserving sister with half an ear, Claire stepped up to the mirror to take a quick look at her reflection and was satisfied with what she saw. Although she had lost a little weight, perhaps, over the last three months, it was noticeable only in that her collarbone, bare along with her shoulders and the tops of her white bosom above the low neckline of her gold lace over satin ballgown, was perhaps more pronounced. With her black hair swept up à la Chinoise and Gabby's topaz set, loaned for the Season, sparkling around her neck and in her ears, she was still as beautiful as she had ever been, she decided. Though no longer in the first blush of her youth, she would do.

"Claire, come on," Beth said impatiently. Glancing around, Claire saw that her sister was already at the door.

"I'm coming." Slipping the ribbon of her chicken-skin fan with its ivory ribs and exquisite painted scenes over her wrist, Claire joined Beth, and the two of them left the room and went down the vast, curving staircase together.

Below, though the clock had just struck ten, people were already starting to come up the stairs. Lord and Lady Olive were first, Claire saw, smiling at them. Lord Olive was a nice little man, thin as a wraith and unassuming. Equally short but about as big around as she was tall, Lady Olive was quite fearsome-looking tonight dressed in puce satin with three towering plumes in her mouse-brown hair. Newcomers to the title, the couple were drinking up the joys of Society as headily as if it were ale and they were thirsty sailors. They had not yet accustomed themselves to the idea that it was fashionable to be late. Looking past them, Claire saw Graham, the impassive, elderly butler who had been with the family for decades, open the door to admit more new arrivals. Beyond him she got just a glimpse of carriages, their lights flickering like stars, lined up as far as she could see along the dark street. The sound of wheels and hooves on the cobblestones reached her ears. So did the first strains of music, from the ballroom at the back of the house. The scents of beeswax, the masses of white roses decorating the hall and the staircase and the ballroom, and the finest of wax candles that were burning by the dozens in chandeliers and sconces all over the house wafted beneath her nose, forming one unforgettable scent: the smell of a ball that was just getting started. Beth's ball.

"Hurry, or you'll be late for the receiving line," she whispered to Beth. As Beth was the debutante in whose honor the ball was being held, that would never do. Ahead of her now as they reached the marble-floored hall, Beth nodded and turned toward the ballroom. Claire stepped forward to greet the Olives as they came toward her, and suddenly noticed several dusty trunks and battered portmanteaux being borne up the stairs amid two more small groups of newly arrived guests. Her eyes widened slightly as she took in this odd circumstance, but she finished her pleasantries to the Olives without commenting on it, all the while wondering: Had an overnight guest arrived? Who? They were expecting no one as far as she knew.

She spoke to the next group, then whisked herself out of the way of the increasing numbers of new arrivals into the dining room, which, as supper would not be served until midnight or thereabouts, was empty at the moment except for servants making ready. Even as she was about to send a footman to fetch Graham so that she might ask him about the luggage, that white-maned dignitary himself came up the stairs and she was able to beckon to him.

"Do we have an overnight guest?" she asked, knowing she had to hurry to the receiving line but also know-ing that her mother-in-law, who was, hopefully, already in the ballroom greeting guests, would be upset with her if she discovered such a situation and did not bring it to her immediate notice. "Does Lady George know?"

That she did not wait for her first question to be an-swered before posing the second, more pertinent one betrayed her nervousness. As the wife of the late duke's younger brother, Lord George Lynes, her mother-in-law was known as Lady George. Although her name was Emma, Claire had certainly never presumed to call her by it, and had never been invited to do so. It was Lady George who was the undisputed mistress of the house, and Claire and Beth were merely her guests. Lady George ruled—or at least tried to rule—everyone within her orbit with a rod of iron. She would expect Claire to run to her immediately with news of an unexpected houseguest.

"Miss Claire, the duke's home." Graham sounded ex-cited, an emotion she had never expected to detect in the always stately butler. "His Grace the Duke has come *home*."

"The duke?" Claire hoped she sounded no more than politely interested. In truth, she was dismayed. After all, they were holding Beth's come-out ball in the man's house. Although Lady George was the official hostess, and had been delighted at the idea of having the ball at Richmond House, Claire suddenly felt presumptuous in the extreme. When the duke was abroad, he was no more than an abstract figure, and the house had felt like it be-longed to Lady George and, by extension, David. Now, suddenly, it felt like a stranger's house. They were using the duke's house without his permission.

"Does Lady George know?" she added hollowly.

"Yes, Lady Claire. I informed her myself."

*Thank goodness.* Claire thought it, but she just managed not to say it aloud. Leaving Graham, she slipped through the adjoining music room to a small corridor that led to a side door opening into the ballroom, thus avoiding the crowds of people already massed in the hall. A few people milled about the refreshment table, but the huge room with its red brocade walls and white moldings and floor-to-ceiling mirrors set between ornate pilasters was still very thin of company. The tall doors that led out onto the terrace were still closed, but they would be opened later, when the dancing started.

"Lady Barbara Mertz and the Honorable Mr. John Mertz."

The booming announcement was made at the main doorway to the ballroom, where the receiving line, which consisted at the moment of Lady George, David, Beth, and Aunt Augusta, stood. Claire moved a little faster. The musicians were playing, although a dance had not yet been struck up, and the three giant chandeliers overhead sparkled with hundreds of candles. Their brilliance was reflected in the tall mirrors. The heady aroma of the dozens of white flowers massed in the corners filled the room. Claire inhaled deeply, enjoying the scent, as she slipped into the receiving line between her husband and sister.

"You're late," David said in an accusatory tone out of the corner of his mouth. He seemed unusually tense, and she wondered at it. Since joining her in London the previous week—he had spent only a few days at Morningtide after her safe return before leaving to once again be about his own pursuits—he had been almost amiable, more amiable than he had been since the early days of their marriage. Of no more than average height and slender, he was looking very handsome with his blond hair combed back from his face and his pale complexion set off by the black of his evening clothes. His eyes were as blue as a summer sky, his features were finely molded and regular, and there was about him an elegant air that was one of the first things Claire had noticed. Giving him a single comprehensive look, Claire thought that she could still quite understand how she had ended up marrying him. The wrappings were extremely attractive. Who would know that the parcel actually had so little inside?

"Your cousin the duke has returned home," she offered by way of explanation.

"So my mother informs me." His voice was cold. "I fail to see how that accounts for your lateness, however."

Claire gave him a long look. His bullying tone was familiar: This was the David he had become in the months before her abduction. She had thought his recent amiability was too good to be true. He had been trying to turn her up sweet—but why? Before she could come up with an answer, or find a reply for him, more guests were announced.

"The Earl and Countess of Wickham, Lord and Lady Arthur Peale, the Honorable Charles Fawley and Mrs. Fawley."

Called to order by her sister's sharp elbow to the ribs, Claire turned to smile at her cousins. Lady George, who, with her birdlike build and once blond hair now turned stark white, looked very like David, was resplendent in palest blue crepe. She was the first to greet the guests, shaking hands with Cousin Thomas, who towered over her petite frame. Tall, thin, and balding, Cousin Thomas had taken on a new air of self-importance as he had become accustomed to wearing the title, Earl of Wickham, that had previously belonged to Claire's father and brother.

"I hear Gabby's been delivered of a girl," Cousin Thomas said in a jovial tone as he took her proffered hand.

"Yes, a beautiful little daughter," Claire agreed with a determinedly welcoming smile. The two families had never been friendly, although they were civil in public, and that didn't seem likely to change anytime soon.

"No doubt she'll produce a son next time," Cousin Maud, his wife, said as if commiserating with Gabby's misfortune while she pressed Claire's hand. "Dear Thisby has two boys now, you know."

She looked fondly in the direction of her daughter, Mrs. Fawley, who was behind her.

Cousin Maud was a wispy blond in the style of Lady George, and the two women, who were much of an age, disliked each other cordially. Of course, nearly everyone disliked Cousin Maud, so that wasn't much of a mark in Lady George's favor, in Claire's opinion. Thisby was fair like her mother, but had never been possessed of much beauty. Age—she was two years Claire's senior—had not improved either her looks or her disposition. She exchanged a few banal remarks with Claire, then eyed her husband angrily as that gentleman held Claire's hand for rather longer than was proper, the admiration in his eyes plain for everyone to see. Thankful to be released at last, Claire turned her attention to Desdemona, who was with her new husband as well, and was obviously proud as a peacock on his arm.

"Lord and Lady Jersey."

"Silence" Jersey, so called because she talked so much, was both a leader of the *ton* and a great friend of Aunt Augusta's, and she stood talking to their aunt for rather longer than was proper, holding up the line. Lady Jersey was dressed in deep green satin with ropes of pearls around her neck. Her face was square and rather plain, and her figure, if it had belonged to a less important personage, might have been described as short and dumpy. But there was a twinkle in her eye and a kindness to her smile that made up for these deficiencies. Beside her, Aunt Augusta, who was nearly six feet tall and mannish in build, looked most imposing. As blunt featured as she ordinarily was blunt spoken, she was dressed tonight in a gown of pearl gray satin that almost exactly matched the silver of the braids wound in queenly fashion atop her head. The sparkle of enormous diamonds affixed to her ears and hung around her neck completed a magnificent ensemble. Having feared her at their first meeting, Claire had grown fond of her over the ensuing years. With no children of her own, she'd been very kind to the three nieces she had taken under her wing.

"So you're Lady Elizabeth, are you?" Lady Jersey said to Beth, having wound up her conversation with Aunt Augusta at last. "Well, you're very pretty too, but why is it none of you gels look the least bit alike?" After scrutinizing her from head to toe, she stared pointedly at Beth's bright hair for a moment before glancing from Beth to Claire with a perplexed expression. Then her face cleared, and she answered herself before Beth could reply, which was probably a good thing, because Beth the fiery was starting to frown at her. "Oh yes, different mothers, weren't there? Well, that explains it all right. My lamentable memory. You must forgive me. And your sister Lady Gabriella is not here tonight?" A quick glance around, as if Gabby might pop out from behind one of the crimson velvet curtains tied back on each side of the ballroom's arched entrance, accompanied this, and then she again chattered on without waiting for an answer. "Oh, that's right, I remember you told me, Augusta, that she would stay at home this year. Well, now, Augusta, this is the last of them, isn't it? She'll do, she'll do. I shall send vouchers for Almack's just as I did for the other two. If I forget, remind me."

"I certainly will, Sally," Aunt Augusta said. Then, to Beth in a lowered tone after Lady Jersey was gone, "Well. We accomplished that handily enough. Promised vouchers already! Even though you frowned at her, which was really too bad of you. Sally Jersey may chatter, but she is the dearest thing."

"She was staring at my *hair*," Beth muttered. Claire heard that with alarm. Before she turned to greet the next person in line, she nudged Beth.

"Your hair is beautiful. It makes you stand out. It makes you unique," she whispered. "Of course people are going to stare at it."

She and Beth had been over that before. Beth hated having red hair with a passion, and had been known to thoroughly lose her temper just from having its bright hue pointed out to her, something that unfortunately tended to happen a lot.

"You've said that so much I'm sick of hearing it," Beth whispered back with a deepening scowl. "Unique or not, it's still rude to stare."

Only the fact that Claire feared Beth had not enough

countenance to keep from howling kept her from giving her little sister a sharp kick on the ankle. Frowning at Lady Jersey was not something a debutante did. Not if said debutante wanted to be a success. Frowning at other people was probably not a good idea, either.

And Claire did so want for Beth to be a success. The greater her choice of men, the more likely she was to choose well. An unhappy marriage was more of a burden than any unwed girl could even begin to imagine.

"Oh, for heaven's sake," Aunt Augusta muttered. "Don't be so quick to take a pet, child, and *smile*."

A quick glance told Claire that Beth, having apparently recollected her surroundings, was recovering from her snit in the usual quick-to-anger, quick-to-forgive way of hers. Following Aunt Augusta's advice, she smiled quite brilliantly, and now seemed determined to enjoy her debut, come what may.

By the time she was able to leave the receiving line, Claire's fingers ached. She had shaken hands with roughly five hundred guests, nearly all of whom were now squeezed into the ballroom that no longer seemed enormous at all. Others, including David and his cronies, had already disappeared into one of the small rooms set aside for cards. Still others were in the ladies' retiring room, or outside on the terrace enjoying the unseasonably warm night. Indeed, the ballroom was already growing overwarm with too many bodies too closely packed into it, and many ladies were making vigorous use of their fans. Claire had already heard several people describe the evening as a sad crush, which was a sure sign of success.

"I declare, that child has shaped up remarkably well. At Christmas she was plump as a partridge." Aunt Augusta, who was walking beside her as Claire gave her aunt an arm as far as the chaperons' chairs, had her gaze on Beth, who was at that moment skipping enthusiastically through a country dance. "Who is that boy she is dancing with? Is it one of the Rutherfords, or . . . ?"

"Claire, dear, I'd like to present my late husband's nephew, the Duke of Richmond." Lady George came up behind her, distracting her attention as she slid cool fingers around the crook of Claire's elbow just above her evening glove. "He was out of the country at the time of your wedding, but at least has had the grace to present himself now, quite two years late, the wretch."

Claire had never heard quite that same archly teasing tone from her mother-in-law before. Clearly this nephew must be someone she wished to please. Of course, he owned the houses Lady George lived in as if they were her own and, for all Claire knew, provided something in the way of an allowance for his aunt as well. David's father had not left his wife and son any too plump in the pocket, as she was well aware, and the duke was head of the family, after all. Certainly it would be in Lady George's best interests to stay on his good side.

Amused by this new and unexpected facet to her mother-in-law's personality, she turned to meet the prodigal with a slight smile on her lips—and froze in the act of holding out her hand.

She was face-to-face with Hugh.

## ❧ 24 ❧

...............................

" **M**y daughter-in-law, Lady Claire Lynes."
Claire was barely aware of Lady
George completing the introduction. She was no longer
breathing. Her heart had given a great leap in her breast
at the moment her gaze met Hugh's and was now
pounding out of control. Despite the heat of the room,
she felt suddenly icy cold. Her hand, which she had been
in the act of extending before she realized exactly whom
it was she was extending it to, was suspended in midair.
Her eyes stayed fixed on his face.

For one dreadful moment, she feared she might
faint. It required every ounce of willpower she possessed
to stay on her feet.

Was she hallucinating? That was her first confused
thought. The second was: Could this possibly be an
eerily exact look-alike? His black hair was cut short, in
the fashionable Brutus style, but nothing else had
changed. He was as swarthy as a Gypsy, his lean cheeks
clean-shaven, his long mouth smiling rather wryly at
her. She knew that smile. She knew those eyes. They

were gray as bullet lead, narrowed, watching her carefully, their cool caution belying the smile.

She was not mistaken. There was no possibility of mistake. This was Hugh. Her Hugh.

Dressed in impeccable black evening clothes that suited his tall, broad-shouldered form to perfection, he was bowing over her gloved hand, raising it to his mouth.

Watching him, Claire felt as if she were caught up in a bad dream. The man she had longed for and thought never to see again, the man whose fate had been the stuff of her nightmares, the man she had been breaking her heart over every day for the past three months, was now standing in front of her, kissing her hand as if she were a chance-met stranger and their encounter no more than everyday.

"I'm honored to make the acquaintance of so lovely a cousin."

It was his voice. Hugh's voice. There was no mistake. She would recognize it without fail, even in the darkest pit anywhere on earth. Claire exhaled slowly, willing her knees not to give way, willing her hands not to shake. She fought to keep her face impassive, but she was not sure how well she succeeded. Her gaze fixed helplessly on his face as he pressed his mouth lightly to the back of her knuckles, then released her hand and straightened to his full height, looking down at her with distant courtesy. Clearly there was something in her expression that should not have been there, because he frowned at her slightly, and there was suddenly a flicker of what could only be warning in his eyes as they met hers.

Hugh. She was looking up at Hugh. She took another deep, restorative breath, letting her lids drop to veil her eyes even as she reminded herself fiercely that whatever the rights and wrongs of this situation in which they found themselves, there was no possibility of delving into it now: They had an audience. In her initial shock, she had forgotten all about Lady George. Forgotten all about Aunt Augusta. Forgotten all about every other person in the ballroom, in the house, in the world—except the two of them.

Impossible as it seemed, Hugh had somehow walked back into her life. In the guise of the Duke of Richmond, yet. Claire frowned as she remembered that detail of his reappearance. How on earth could that be?

"You're very kind." Somehow Claire managed to speak more or less normally, to summon a hard-won smile, to utter the commonplace courtesy that was expected of her, even while a jumble of questions and thoughts and emotions tried to sort themselves out in her head.

"Lud, Duke, this is a surprise. Last report I can remember hearing of you, you were with the army in Spain. Well. It's good to have you back among us." Aunt Augusta was looking him over with approval. As well she might, Claire thought hollowly. In his new incarnation, Hugh was as devastating as he had been in his old one: He was still tall, dark, and impossibly attractive. Only now he was rigged out as befitted a duke. His evening clothes had clearly been made by a master. His coat, of severe black superfine, fit his broad-shouldered form to perfection. His breeches were black too, and hugged the powerful muscles of his long legs almost lovingly. His linen was snowy, his cravat expertly tied. A diamond glittered in its folds. There was, she saw, another diamond in the signet ring on his hand. The duke's signet ring? Of course. Near-hysterical laughter bubbled into her throat as she finally, truly realized what had happened: Her Hugh, her secret lover, her partner in an impossible adventure that she could never forget, had walked back into her life just as coolly as if they had last talked only the day before—as the Duke of Richmond.

Her mind boggled at the thought.

Those cool gray eyes were watching her carefully from beneath heavy lids, Claire saw, gauging her reaction to his new incarnation even as he responded to Aunt Augusta.

"It's good to be back—Lady Salcombe, isn't it?" Hugh's glance slid to Aunt Augusta, and Claire breathed again.

"That's right. Lady Claire—your new cousin by marriage here—is my niece."

"Ah, then I can certainly see where she gets her charm—and her looks." Hugh's flattery was charming, his smile more so. Aunt Augusta laughed, and said something about there being no need to turn her up sweet as the gel was already taken. Hugh replied—she completely missed whatever it was he said—and turned that smile on her. It was one of those curling smiles that she so well remembered, and just looking at it was enough to make the short hairs on the back of Claire's neck stand on end. Could no one but she sense the charge that heated the air between them, feel the undercurrents that ran beneath every word, every glance, they exchanged? Apparently not. A swift look around convinced her that neither her aunt nor her mother-in-law had the least idea that anything was amiss. They were both beaming at Hugh like fond parents at a prodigal son. Claire, who felt as if her face had frozen into a smile, barely managed to keep herself from lapsing into a state of pure shock. By the skin of her teeth, she kept her lips pulled back from her teeth in what she feared must surely be more grimace than smile. But still no one seemed to notice anything out of the way about her response to making the acquaintance of the head of the Lynes family. Aunt Augusta, her rather small blue eyes growing sharper by the second as she surveyed Hugh from head to toe, seemed to be busy assessing his possibilities as a husband for her niece—that would be Beth, of course—and liking what she saw. Lady George, calling a greeting to a passing acquaintance, was focused elsewhere for the moment.

Revealing that she was at all acquainted with Hugh would be fatal, Claire realized with a sick feeling in the pit of her stomach, because it would lead to inevitable questions about when and where they had met, and then, she feared, somewhere in the tangled web of attempted deception the truth would inevitably come out. The thought made her shudder. She could hardly manage to stay on her feet, much less maintain so huge a lie. Grimly Claire fought to get herself under control. Deliberately she tried to relax the tense muscles of her shoulders, her back, her arms. Her heart was slowing down on its own, its wild pounding decreasing gradually to a more regular beat. She was able to breathe again more or less normally, she discovered as she tried.

What she could not seem to do was keep her eyes from Hugh's face.

She had thought he was lost to her forever. And now, here he was, standing before her in the flesh. The question was: Was that a good thing—or a bad one?

"You did know David had married?" Lady George,

her attention restored to them, asked Hugh, and Claire forced herself to look at her mother-in-law instead. Lady George was far more keen-eyed than Aunt Augusta, and, with her loyalty firmly on the side of her son, far more of a danger to her, Claire knew. Thank goodness she had been distracted for those few moments and thus missed what Claire was certain had been a kaleidoscope of wildly shifting emotions chasing each other across her face.

The idea of her mother-in-law discovering exactly how well she knew Hugh made Claire feel ill. The scandal would be so horrible; she couldn't bear thinking about it. And Lady George would cry it from the rafters, if she somehow got wind of it. Her mother-in-law had never particularly liked her, she knew. David—what would David do? He didn't care for her anymore, if he ever had, nor she for him, but she was his wife.

Dear God in heaven, how had she ever gotten caught up in such a coil? And how was she ever going to get out of it without touching off the kind of scandal that would keep the *ton* gossiping for years?

"I found out only recently."

Hugh was no longer looking at her, Claire discovered. He was focused on Lady George, carrying on, from what she had heard of it over the pounding of her blood in her ears, a perfectly normal conversation. His expression revealed nothing but the polite level of interest the subject demanded. If she had not known better, she would have believed that he was in the most mundane of situations.

But she did know better. He had to be as shocked at their encounter as she was. He was simply more skilled at concealing it. Of course, he was a spy. Spies were good at that kind of thing. Perfectly normal females like herself were not.

Then the significance of the words *I found out only recently* sank in, and Claire realized that Hugh had in all likelihood discovered that his cousin David was married when she herself had told him of it—along with the rest of her life story while she had lain snuggled in his arms in that never-to-be-forgotten bunk on the *Nadine*. She had certainly mentioned David's name more than once, along with a number of telling details about their lives.

No wonder he had finally taken her word as to her identity. Every syllable that had fallen from her lips must have confirmed it for him.

He had known precisely who she was from that moment on. Claire began to focus on the sheer perfidy of the man, and her temper bubbled to simmering life. Her heart began to beat faster again, and her fingers curled into impotent claws at her sides. He had known who she was—and he had not said anything. Remembering how she had begged him to lie with her made her cheeks heat along with her temper. If she hadn't been so certain that she was never going to see him again, that they would have only that one night together and then he would vanish from her life forever, she would never have been so bold.

Certainly, if she had known he was her husband's cousin, the head of the family she had married into, the owner of Hayleigh Castle and Richmond House and all the other myriad properties that David and Lady George treated as their own—in other words, if she had known he was the Duke of Richmond—she would never, ever, in a thousand lifetimes, have behaved as she had done!

She had lain with him. Been naked in his arms. Permitted him to touch her, and kiss her, and perform the most intimate—she shuddered to remember just how intimate—of acts upon her person. She had allowed him to give her the ultimate joy, and had cried out his name to the heavens as she experienced it.

He had let her. He had known who she was, and he had let her.

If looks could kill, the shaft she fired at him from her eyes at that point should have slain him on the spot. His eyes widened a little as her message went home, but before he could respond, if indeed he intended to respond, they were interrupted.

"There you are, Lady Claire! I've been looking for you everywhere." The speaker was Lord Alfred Dalrymple. A tall, thin man resplendent in a magnificent purple coat and striped waistcoat that quite put the ladies' gowns to shame, he had been on the town forever and was one of the most persistent of Claire's cicisbei. In his early thirties, he was a veritable pink of the *ton* and a confirmed bachelor who tended to attach himself to married women for protection from the countless mothers of marriageable daughters who pursued him for the simple reason that Lord Alfred was said to be worth some twenty thousand pounds a year.

"Your servant, Lady Salcombe, Lady George." He executed a pair of elegant legs in the direction of those ladies before smiling at Claire. "Lady Claire, it's my dance, I believe. Never tell me you had forgotten?"

Indeed, she had. Now that he reminded her, she recalled that he had indeed asked her for the first waltz during the call he and his great friend Mr. Calvert had paid them the afternoon before. With her senses attuned to the music again, she could hear the musicians striking up. Before, she had heard little over the pounding of her heart.

"Ah, you had forgotten. I can see it on your face. Oh, faithless one, how you wound me." Placing a hand over his heart, Lord Alfred tried to look pathetic.

Ordinarily such badinage, which was his stock in trade, made Claire laugh, and reply in kind. Tonight the most she could manage was a rather forced smile. But in any case he was no longer looking at her. He was looking at Hugh, who was standing just beyond her with a lurking grin curving the corners of his mouth, and surprise was suddenly writ large on his face.

"By God, is that you, Richmond?"

"It is indeed. How are you, Alfie? And what the devil are you doing in a purple coat, of all the ghastly hues?"

"It's all the crack, I assure you." Lord Alfred looked down at himself defensively, then looked up at Hugh and laughed. "Fie on you, what would you know? You've been out of the country for—what? A dozen years?"

"Something of that nature," Hugh admitted. The two men, grinning at each other, shook hands.

"We were at Eton together, you know." Lord Alfred made this observation to the trio of women, two of whom were watching with smiling complacency and the third of whom—Claire—still felt so decidedly stunned that she was having trouble taking in anything new, then turned his attention back to Hugh. His voice took on an eager tone. "Does Dev know you're back? Or Connaught? They're married now, you know, poor fools. Set up their nurseries, the both of them. Lord, the dusts we used to kick up! Then you . . ." He broke off, looked suddenly self-conscious, and turned what he had been going to say into a cough.

"Then I ran off with a woman old enough to be my mother, killed her husband in a duel when he came after us, and had to flee to the Continent as a result," Hugh finished for him dryly. "Don't try to wrap my sordid past up in clean linen. I'm sure it'll be the talk of the town again as soon as word gets out that I've come home."

"It's been so long, I'm sure it's all forgotten," Lady George murmured in an excusing tone, while Aunt Augusta nodded agreement and Claire looked at Hugh with widening eyes. Though he seemed as familiar to her as her own face in the mirror, she realized that, in truth, she knew nothing about him. Nothing except the way he kissed, the way his hands felt on her body, the way he . . .

"I fear you've shocked my new cousin with your tales of my scandalous doings, Alfie. Perhaps I should take your dance, and try to convince her that I'm really not the monster you make me out to be." Hugh looked at Claire, and to her horror proffered his arm. "Will you accept me as a poor substitute for my loose-lipped friend, Lady Claire? I am really quite harmless, believe me."

"Oh, well, seeing as it's you, I'll stand aside. But just this once, mind."

With Lord Alfred relinquishing his claim with a bow, and Lady George and Aunt Augusta both watching indulgently, Claire could think of nothing to do but tuck her hand in the crook of Hugh's elbow.

Once again the room started to spin. Claire took a firm grip on herself. She must just hold on for a little while more, until she could get out of this thrice-cursed ballroom and away from the dozens of prying eyes. Then she could collapse. Then. Not now.

"I'm sure you are," she said, for the benefit of their

audience, and with a smile plastered so firmly on her face that it made her jaw ache, she allowed herself to be led onto the dance floor.

The waltz had already begun. Hugh clasped her hand, slid an arm around her waist, and swung her into the rhythm of the dance. She could feel the heat of his fingers through her glove, feel the brush of his knees against her own, feel the strength of his arm behind her back as he held her at the prescribed distance, which, since *he* was her partner, suddenly seemed far too close. Smiling with all the genuineness of a porcelain doll, she stared steadfastly at his neck, not daring to lift her eyes to his face until she was sure she had her expression— and her temper—firmly in hand. Her gold lace skirts brushed his black-clad legs with every movement of the dance. His wide chest in its pristine white shirt and waistcoat was only inches from the tips of her breasts, which, despite her best efforts at keeping all her erotic memories of him at bay, seemed to be swelling toward him. She was sure that, looking down, he had a most interesting view of the semibared white mounds and the deep cleavage between them. Her chest was rising and falling faster than even the exertions of the dance could account for, Claire realized with dismay. But hopefully he would not notice that—or the pulse that she could feel beating in time with her skipping heart just below the surface of the white skin of her throat. Claire was instantly, acutely aware of all these details, even as she willed herself not to be, willed herself to stay as detached from what was happening, as detached from him, as if she were in truth dancing with a man who was no more than the just-met stranger they were both pretending he was.

The music was intoxicating, a haunting, romantic invitation to lose oneself in the dance. The scent of flowers combined with the ladies' perfume to sweeten the air. The candles overhead cast a soft glow over the assembled company, and flickered like hundreds upon hundreds of fireflies as they were reflected in the mirrors that lined the sides of the room. All around them couples swayed and twirled in a vast, swirling ballet. Claire got a glimpse of Beth, looking radiant as she laughed up into the face of her partner, before a movement of the dance swept her out of sight again. Then someone stepped on the trailing hem of her gown and she stumbled a little, clutching at Hugh's shoulder for balance as she scooped her skirt higher out of harm's way. Even as Hugh's arm tightened reflexively around her, she made the mistake of looking up at him. As she met those cool gray eyes, all thoughts of her surroundings faded away.

She had forgotten how tall he was, she realized. Forgotten how broad his shoulders were. Forgotten the steely strength of his muscles, and the sensuousness of his mouth, and how easy it was to see the shadow of what would be the morning's beard darkening his lean cheeks even when he was freshly shaved, as he was tonight.

Then she realized that she had forgotten other things as well. Like how to breathe.

As she let herself acknowledge that the man holding her was Hugh, really, truly Hugh, her heart skipped a beat. Then she remembered all that he had withheld from her and how he had lied, and the anger already coursing through her veins took on a sudden searing heat.

"You cad," she said.

"Careful, your smile is slipping."

There was a teasing glint in his eyes, but she thought she saw tenderness for her there as well. Perversely, that only served to feed her anger. His tenderness, she felt, was no longer to be trusted. He was no longer to be trusted. She had told him everything about herself, given him everything she had to give, while he had taken and taken and taken and said nothing.

But this crowded ballroom was not the place to air her grievances. Her focus must be on keeping her composure, and keeping their secret. Everything else—like calling him the lying dog he was—could wait.

She stretched her lips into that ghastly-feeling smile again.

"Did you really," she asked, far too politely, "run off with a married woman and kill her husband in a duel?"

"I was nineteen and foolish," he replied with a shrug, "and her husband would have killed me if he could. I just happened to be the better shot. In any case, he deserved it. He had been beating her."

"And what became of this lady?"

"I have no idea. She ditched me for a better prospect as soon as I rid her of her husband." A smile tugged at one corner of his mouth. "Thus teaching me a valuable lesson that I find instructive to this day."

"And what lesson is that?"

"Women are the very devil." That sounded heartfelt, but there was a twinkle in his eyes as his gaze met hers.

Claire couldn't help herself. For the briefest of moments her smile slipped again and she glared at him. He laughed, seeming suddenly very carefree, far more carefree than he had any right to be under the circumstances, and swung her around in a movement of the dance with rather more vigor than was called for. To her annoyance, she was forced to cling even more tightly to his broad shoulder. Which was what he had intended, she guessed. Gritting her teeth against all she wanted to say to him, she recollected their audience and once again pinned on that blatantly false smile.

They reached the far side of the room. A welcome breath of cool air was blowing through the long windows that someone had finally opened to help cool the overheated dancers. The gauzy undercurtains that had been pulled back to lie in tandem with the heavy velvet drapes fluttered like pale moths in the breeze. Beyond the windows, there were couples strolling on the terrace. Flaming torches in ornate iron holders had been set at intervals of a few feet along the low stone parapet. Beyond the torches, in the just-beginning-to-bud gardens, all was darkness.

"I think this conversation needs to be continued in private." He looked down at her with a lurking grin. "Before your face freezes in that terrifying smile."

At that, the smile slipped dangerously before she caught herself. Even as she kept it in place, she looked daggers at him. He laughed, a low, genuinely amused sound that under any other circumstances she would have found absolutely charming. Before she quite realized what he would be about, he whirled her through the window and across the terrace. Then, grabbing her hand so that there was no possibility of escape, he pulled her after him down the shallow stone steps into the moonlit garden.

## ❧ 25 ❧

..................................

"*D*id you miss me, puss?"

The question, uttered with a sideways smile as Hugh tucked her hand securely under his arm and led her down a brick-paved path that twisted out of sight of the terrace, was absolutely the wrong thing to say. Claire had vowed that she would confine herself to polite conversation for the duration of the ball. There was no reason, after all, to even open herself up to the possibility of creating what could easily, if she gave free rein to how she really felt, be a very ugly public scene. But for him to ask if she had missed him—which of course she had, madly, a fact that was infuriating enough in itself under the circumstances and that she now never meant to admit to anyone even under pain of death—and call her puss to boot was the verbal equivalent of waving a red flag in front of an already infuriated bull.

"Why, no," she said with studied disinterest, her chin in the air. "I've been very busy since we last met, you see. Why?" And here she glanced up at him with a little trill of amused laughter. "Did you hope that I would?"

"Don't lie." His smile widened, causing his eyes to narrow and the lines bracketing his mouth to deepen charmingly. "You missed me."

He sounded so certain of it that, even as the last remnants of her smile died, Claire's eyes began to snap. She stopped walking to glare at him, luxuriating in the freedom to do so without restraint, and pulled her hand from his arm with something of a jerk. From where they were standing, in the lee of a tall, just budding lilac, she could see couples on the terrace backlit against the ballroom. It was a safe bet that more were wandering the garden's shadowy paths. But no one was near; she and Hugh were, to all intents and purposes, alone. Still, she kept her voice carefully low.

"Besides being an utter cad, a churlish lout, a mannerless oaf, and a conscienceless blackguard, you are also possessed of a truly remarkable degree of conceit, I perceive. I did not miss you." She said it almost pleasantly, with a little pitying smile of which she was pardonably proud. Then her anger got the best of her and she added with considerable heat, "In fact, I have just been reflecting on what a great pity it is that the French didn't shoot you."

"Believe me, they tried." His eyes twinkled at her. He caught her hands, holding them so that she stood directly in front of him with their linked hands between them. "I missed you, angel eyes. More than I ever would have believed possible. James is quite outdone with me over it. You've intruded on my thoughts a dozen times a day and haunted my dreams at night. No other woman has ever done as much, I assure you. Thus I left Boney to the tender mercies of another operative as soon as I conceivably could and hurried to your side."

He lifted one gloved hand to his mouth, then the other, kissing the backs of her fingers even as he watched her over them.

Their gazes met. The warmth in his eyes touched a chord deep inside her that was quite out of the control of any rational part of her mind. Despite herself, Claire could not help the sudden quickening of her pulse. That she had been in his thoughts and in his dreams was music to her ears. He had been in hers, too, almost unceasingly since they had parted. She had missed him, oh, she had! When she'd thought that she would never see him again, the pain had been almost unbearable. Had he felt the same . . . ? No, of course he hadn't, she concluded acerbically. He had known all along that they would meet again, and probably precisely where and when. He could have saved her all that misery with a word. The thought made her fury boil over.

"You, sir, are a lying dog," she said through her teeth.

He straightened, but kept his grip on her hands as he studied her face through the darkness.

"You're beautiful when you're angry." The merest hint of a teasing smile curled the corners of his mouth as he took in her rigid stance and deepening scowl. "Actually, you're beautiful any way at all. When you're soaked to the skin. When you're green with seasickness. When you're dressed in naught but my valet's second-best shirt and curled up snug in my arms. When you're not dressed in anything at all. *Especially* when you're not dressed in anything at all. Come, Claire, quit shooting dagger looks at me and cry friends. I've traveled halfway across two continents to find you again, after all."

Claire narrowed her eyes at him. "I can't tell you how flattered I am—or at least how flattered I would be if I truly believed that you had left behind a life of skull-duggery with its threat of constant death to return to a luxurious, pampered existence in your own London home solely to reunite with me. Which I don't. Why should I? All you've done is lie to me from the beginning."

"I did not lie to you."

"Indeed, *Your Grace*?" She purposefully put heavy emphasis on the honorific as she tugged at her hands, which he obstinately refused to release. "I seem to recall being held prisoner by a terrifying brigand who, when he was quite through threatening and brutalizing me, eventually introduced himself as Colonel Hugh Battancourt. Not as the Duke of Richmond, whose family name, as I happen to know from my own personal use of it, is Lynes. And I would be very much surprised if your given name is even Hugh. I've heard your given name—the duke's given name—and while I can't quite recall what it is, it isn't Hugh, I am almost certain."

"Richard." He did, at least, have the grace to sound slightly abashed. "Richard Phillip Arthur William Hugh Battancourt Lynes, to be precise about it. But I've always gone by Hugh among my friends and family."

"In other words, you lied." Despite being hushed, her voice was sharp.

"Well," he conceded without batting so much as an eyelash in shame. "Maybe a little, but no more than I had to. Be reasonable, Claire. You really could not expect me to go around introducing myself as the Duke of Richmond to all and sundry when I'm operating in a foreign country as a British intelligence officer. I thought you were working for the French as a spy, for God's sake. Why would I tell you who I am?"

On the surface, that excuse sounded almost legitimate. There was just one slight flaw in his argument. She opened her mouth to give furious voice to it, but paused to take a long, prudent look around to make certain that they were still quite alone in their dark corner of the garden before she did so.

They were.

"Because I never would have—would have—you know—if I'd known the truth," she hissed. "And you know it. Knew it."

"I couldn't tell you," he said. "What if you'd been captured by the French? They would have tortured everything you knew out of you within twenty-four hours, believe me. Once they learned my identity, my effectiveness as an intelligence officer would have been over. The operation I was engaged in would have been compromised. Besides, does the fact that I'm the Duke of Richmond rather than just plain Hugh Battancourt really make that much difference? Wasn't it Shakespeare who said something to the tune of, a rose by any other name would smell as sweet?"

"Or a skunk stink as badly?" Claire snapped back, as a prelude to a blistering indictment of his manners and morals. But she was abruptly silenced when another couple appeared around a bend in the path, walking slowly toward them, seeming so absorbed in each other that Claire doubted they were even aware that she and Hugh were present on the other side of the lilac. Still, it wouldn't do for the Duke of Richmond to be discovered in his dark garden with his cousin's supposedly newly met wife. Even as she had the thought, Hugh apparently reached the same conclusion, because his hands tightened on hers and he drew her off the path and onto the grass, pulling her behind a clump of ornamental hollies that had the felicitous property of staying in full foliage all year round.

"Rose or skunk, I'm the same man you invited into bed with you in that farmhouse in France."

With that galling whisper, Hugh pulled her into his arms. Too mindful of the approaching couple to object with anything like the vociferousness such a high-handed act called for, Claire ignored the sensations ignited by the crushing of her breasts against the warm resilience of his chest and shoved at his shoulders in a silent demand to be released.

"I did *not* invite you into bed with me." Whispering, she glared up at him in hopes that her eyes would convey all the explosive sentiments that she dared not give voice to just at the moment.

"Shh." He shot a warning look in the direction of the path, then grinned down at her teasingly. She was still glaring up at him when he bent his head and kissed her.

The feel of his warm, hard lips covering her mouth was as devastating as it was unexpected. Claire's breath caught. Her heart leaped and began to pound. For a moment, just a moment, she forgot everything except the way he made her feel. Her lids fluttered down, and she swayed against him. Her blood heated. Her pulse raced. Her knees went weak. Then, even as she started to kiss him back, she remembered—everything. Her eyes flew open, and she tore her mouth from his, shoving furiously at his shoulders at the same time. He lifted his head, looking down at her with a dark, sensuous gleam in his eyes that under different conditions would have caused her to dissolve into a steaming puddle at his feet. But tonight, under these conditions, she primmed up her lips into a thin, tight line that dared him to kiss them again. Her eyes shot bullets of pure fire at him. Her hands clenched into fists.

"How dare you?" she began furiously, doing her level best to wrench herself from his arms. Then she heard the murmuring voices of the approaching pair—Miss Bentley, she thought, and the youngest son of Lord Chester—along with the soft fall of their footsteps on the brick walk, and went both still and silent. She stood, mute but quivering with anger, trapped in the iron circle of Hugh's arms as she waited for the intruders to pass.

Like the reprobate she now knew him for, he took full advantage of their position to try to kiss her again. This time, prepared, she turned her face sharply away, so that his mouth found her cheek instead. Undeterred, he slid his mouth across her smooth skin, then pressed his lips to the sensitive spot beneath her ear. Pushing against his shoulders, doing her level best not to respond, not to feel, Claire was nonetheless supremely conscious of the warm pressure of his mouth, the rasp of the stubble already beginning to roughen his jaw against her skin, the clean soap smell of him, his sheer size and muscular strength. Despite her determined attempt to feel nothing, a quickening began deep inside her, tiny at first but turning fierce and wild so quickly that it made her dizzy, reminding her against her will of the pleasure he could give her, of the sizzling ecstasy only he had ever made her feel.

"Stop it," she hissed.

He lifted his head to look down at her rather mockingly. "Your heart's beating like a stoat's. So fast that I fear it quite gives you away."

"Hush." Her sudden, urgent warning was scarcely louder than a breath, uttered as Miss Bentley and her swain suddenly rounded another curve in the path and came into full view. Their pace was slow, the unhurried gait of a courting couple, and they were still so wrapped up in each other that they seemed aware of nothing else. A dozen steps would bring them less than two yards from where Claire and Hugh stood entwined, with only the rustling branches of the hollies and the shifting shadows to provide them concealment. Any movement to free herself, any sound of protest, was now too risky. All it would take would be a sideways glance by the approaching couple and they would be discovered, and the hue and cry of scandal would begin.

Claire deliberately averted her eyes from them, afraid they might sense they were being watched and look around. For a moment she found herself staring at her slender white fingers splayed against the rich black velvet of Hugh's coat. The softness of the cloth atop his hard muscles made for an intriguing contrast, she thought, instinctively savoring it. Suddenly she was very aware of the rise and fall of his chest as he breathed, and the tantalizing width of his shoulders above it. The arms that were holding her were strong and hard. But she did not wish to be aware of those things, she told herself fiercely, and so she averted her eyes with a quiet exhalation of the breath that she discovered, to her annoyance, she had been holding.

The moon was the narrowest of silver slivers overhead, blinking coyly down as it played hide and seek behind a screen of shifting gray clouds. By its light, Hugh's skin looked almost the color of mahogany against the white of his shirt, while his eyes seemed almost as black as his hair. His lean jaw appeared clean-shaven, although she knew that it was already faintly prickly to the touch. His mouth was unsmiling as, she saw, he watched her watching him. Dear Lord, she realized, catching herself in the act of looking at his mouth, she was doing exactly what she had deliberately set out not to do! Redirecting her gaze again, she focused on her surroundings. The carefully nurtured bushes, the ornamental trees with their rustling branches, the tall sundial that formed the garden's centerpiece, all cast shadows that shifted and danced in eerie time to the music that drifted out from the ballroom. Claire felt the caress of the breeze against her bare arms and shoulders, warm and gentle as a breath. She shivered, but not from cold. Rather from the loneliness of the night, and—she might as well face it—the proximity of the man.

Incredible as it seemed, Hugh was back in her life. The arms around her were his; the chest that was not quite brushing her breasts belonged to him. At the thought, her loins tightened, and heat began to pulse with increasing urgency through her veins. Her body was quickening quite independently of her mind, and the realization appalled her. The pain that had been her constant companion for the past three months had no more reason to exist, and was already splintering into dozens of conflicting emotions that could very well take her the rest of her life to sort out. While she might feel hurt and used and furiously angry at him, her body simply rejoiced because he was so near. With its own atavistic memory, it hungered for what he had given it before. Frank about its needs, it wanted him quite openly, even while she was assuring herself that she did not. But perhaps, if he apologized, no, groveled, she might . . .

No. She could not. Whether she wanted Hugh or not, whether she was angry at him or not, paid no toll. The fact of the matter was that she was married beyond redemption, no matter how little affection she felt for her husband, or he for her. The only relationship she could have with Hugh was an illicit one, as he was certainly fully aware. The role he intended her to play in his life became suddenly all too obvious. The question she had to ask herself was: Was she prepared to be his mistress?

The answer was both hard and easy, but it was perfectly clear: No. No. No.

The very word made her wince: *mistress*. She could not lower herself to that. It was not even a matter of social class. There were plenty of married women of good *ton* who would consider it an honor to be the mistress of so high-ranking a nobleman as the Duke of Richmond. Throw into the pot the facts that he was young, rich, and devastatingly attractive, and the numbers would swell amazingly fast.

She had lain with him once. That was a sin, morally wrong, and personally shameful. But to embark on an extended affair with him—that would be far worse. That would be to cheapen what she had felt for him on that never-to-be-forgotten night, and what she had believed he had felt for her in return. That would be to cheapen herself.

There could be no repeat, no second act. That one night was all of him fate was ever going to permit her to have. Given who he was, who she was, anything more was impossible. If he did not understand that—and he did not appear to—then he must be made to do so, however much pain she might thereby cause herself.

Glancing around, she saw that Miss Bentley and her escort were almost out of sight. Taking a deep breath, she glanced up at Hugh, and, still constrained to silence by the fading voices, tried again to pull free of his hold. He shook his head at her, smiling faintly, holding her in place as if he feared she'd run away if he let her go. For all she knew, he might be in the right of it. She felt like running. She felt like crying. She felt like howling at the moon.

Suddenly the voices were gone, vanished into the darkness, and Miss Bentley and her swain were gone too. She was all alone with Hugh again, with only the moon and the wind and the trees for witnesses.

"This is no place to be having this conversation," he said softly, his gaze moving to the place where the other couple had disappeared, and that most sensible observation caught her by surprise before she could take the offensive as she had meant to do. "Unless my memory fails me, I own a little house in Curzon Street where we can be quite alone."

As the implications of that sank in, Claire felt her stomach knot. There was no other route their relationship could take, of course, but to hear him confirm so casually the role he expected her to play in his life was like taking a knife to the heart.

Straightening her spine, her hands pushing steadily against him to keep what space she could between them, she met his gaze.

"You would take me to it?" Her voice was carefully neutral.

He frowned, his expression turning rueful. "Not tonight. It would hardly do for you to disappear in the middle of your own party, after all. But tomorrow afternoon, perhaps, you could go shopping and meet me there, at whatever time suits you best."

"And we would talk."

A wicked smile just touched his mouth. "Indeed we would."

"Among other things."

"How you read my mind, puss."

Claire took a deep breath. "You make your expectations very clear."

Something in her manner must have alerted him, because the smile disappeared and he looked at her closely before answering.

"And just what expectations are you referring to, pray?"

"You intend for us to take up where we left off in France, do you not?"

His lips twisted wryly. "And there is my plain-spoken Claire. Any other woman of my acquaintance would prefer the matter left to the mood of the moment, the promptings of her heart, the igniting of that sweet flame of romance. Very well, my blunt little dove, if you would have the truth with no bark on it: Yes, I intend to love you. Do you find something to object to in that?"

"Love!" She gave a scornful laugh and pushed at his shoulders again in a vain attempt to free herself from his hold. "Is that what you call it? Did you love me, you would never have lain with me as you did without first telling me the truth about who you are, and thus we would not now be caught in this coil."

"If you will cast your mind back, 'twas not I who invited you into my bed, but rather you who invited me into yours." There was the faintest caustic note to that.

"You're angry with me, and with some justification, I'll admit, but the blame is not all mine."

"I wouldn't have invited you to my bed if you had told me the truth," she said heatedly. "The only reason I did it is because I—all right, because I fancied you, and I thought you were getting ready to vanish from my life forever. An impression you could have corrected, if you would have. But for me to lie with you was wrong, and it can't ever happen again. I'm married. To your cousin. Whether I like it or not. I won't dishonor myself, or my family, by being your mistress."

"There's no question of dishonor." His voice was suddenly rough.

"Oh, yes, there is." The words throbbed with passion. Shoving at his shoulders again, she twisted at the same time, and at last managed to jerk free of his hold. When he would have retrieved her she whisked herself out of his reach, shaking her head at him. "That I did such a thing once is shameful enough. I won't let it happen again. You will oblige me, please, by leaving me alone after this, and forgetting that we—that we ever met before tonight."

If there was a catch in her voice, there was iron determination too. Gathering up her skirts, she turned on her heel and, head held high, spine ramrod straight, started walking back along the path toward the house.

"Claire."

He sounded both pained and impatient with her. He was coming after her, of course. Had she doubted that he would? Indeed, she could hear his footsteps on the brick, long brisk strides that would catch her in a trice. Claire quickened her pace until she was almost running. She rounded a bend in the path and suddenly the terrace was in view, complete with backlit couples taking the air. Long rectangles of light spilled across the garden just a little way ahead. Music and the sound of laughing voices reminded her that the ball—Beth's ball—was still very much in progress. Claire suddenly realized that she was in no fit state to see or be seen, and veered off the path to head across the grass toward the little side yard and the door that led down to the kitchen. She would sneak in that way, with no one the wiser, then retire to her room with a "headache" until she had recovered her composure enough to permit her to face their guests again. It wouldn't even be a lie. She did have a headache—and a heartache as well. The headache would go away soon enough, aided by a cup of tea and perhaps a cold compress. The heartache, she feared, never would.

But she had made the only possible choice. The right choice, though the pain of it was almost more than she could bear.

"Claire."

With the soft grass muffling his footsteps, she hadn't known Hugh was still behind her until he caught her by the shoulders, stopping her headlong flight almost in the shadow of the house. Then he stepped so close behind her that she could feel the whole well-muscled length of him against her back.

"Let me go." Just in time, she remembered to keep her voice down. Spine rigid, she stared at the ivy climbing the brick walls, at the swaying branches, at the shadowy side yard only a few feet away, without really seeing any of it.

"I have had a mistress or two in the past, I confess. But the word is never one that I would apply to you." His fingers gripped her shoulders without hurting her, but she knew that breaking free of them would require more effort than she was capable of at the moment. His hands were warm and strong and possessive against her bare skin. She could feel his chest rising and falling against her back, and his breath stirring her hair. "You would be my love instead."

Her hands clenched into fists at her sides as she sought to resist her body's instinctive reaction to him. No, her heart's instinctive reaction to him.

"You may call it what you will," she said steadily. "Rose or skunk, love or mistress, all are one and the same. It is a role that I can't and won't play. There can no longer be anything between us. Indeed, if you had told me the truth when you should have, there never would have been anything between us."

"Now that," he said in a devastating echo of the words he had said to her once before, "would be a shame."

His voice was suddenly incredibly tender. His hands tightened, and his head bent so that his lips found the soft curve between her shoulder and her neck. Claire felt their moist heat burning her skin, sending shock waves of rekindled desire all the way down to her toes. Her breath caught, her bones melted, and for the briefest of instants her eyes closed in instinctive response. Then her mind kicked in, overriding her body's reaction. Her eyes popped open, and she jerked free of his kiss and his grip, putting several steps between them even as she whirled to face him.

"Leave me alone," she said through her teeth, arms akimbo as she glared at him. "Just leave me alone, do you hear? How dare you make this more difficult for me? How dare you just show up, and expect me to be glad to see you? How dare you ask me if I missed you? If I missed anyone, it wasn't you. I don't know you. Hugh Battancourt was merely someone you were pretending to be."

"Claire." He reached for her again. Baring her teeth at him in what was practically a snarl, Claire backed away with a sharp shake of her head that forbade him to touch her.

"Claire! Claire, are you out here?" The voice was Lady George's, and it hit Claire like a splash of cold water in the face. Glancing toward the terrace, she could just see, through the shifting branches, Lady George peering out over the garden as her petite form came down the steps.

"My mother-in-law is looking for me. Will you tell her, please, that I went inside with a headache some time ago?"

Her spine was straight, her chin was high, and her voice was under careful control.

He frowned impatiently. "Puss, listen: 'Tis a damnable coil, I admit, but nothing I intended and nothing we can't . . ."

"No! No more. I don't want to hear another cozening word out of you. What was between us is over and already, by me at least, well on the way to being forgotten. If you truly have a care for me as you claim, you will accept and respect that, and leave me alone before you succeed in ruining me entirely."

The control she had struggled so hard to achieve broke. By the end, her voice was shaking. Hugh's eyes narrowed and his mouth went grim as he listened. When she finished, he held her gaze for the briefest of pregnant moments before making her a slight, ironic bow.

"As you wish."

"Claire!" Lady George called again, her voice slightly muffled now as she had reached the garden proper.

Claire's hands, hidden by her crossed arms, curled into impotent fists.

"Thank you," she said.

Then, head held high, she turned her back on him to walk quickly into the concealing shadows of the dark side yard and from there into the house.

Where she could allow herself only a scant few minutes of privacy while her heart broke for the second time.

# ❧ 26 ❧

.................................

"She is really quite breathtaking, is she not?"

The drawling observation caused Hugh to glance sharply over his shoulder. His cousin David stood behind him, obviously, from the hat and stick in his hand, just on his way out. Hugh himself had just come in from a most instructive afternoon, which had included, not coincidentally, a call on his man of business. It was nearing the dinner hour on the day after the ball, and he had paused in the vast, marble-floored hallway of Richmond House as Claire's voice had reached his ears. He'd run up the stairs, where an instinctive glance through the wide doorway of the drawing room had found Claire in the act of standing to bid good-bye to what appeared to be the last straggling group of afternoon callers. Claire's sister was present as well, and the callers were a lively group of what seemed to be young ladies accompanied by their mothers.

He had eyes for no one but Claire, dazzling as always in a slim white muslin gown tied up beneath her breasts by bright blue ribbons, with her hair dressed in a simple fall of ebony curls that spilled over her shoulders and down her back. Impossible as he would have previously thought it, she was every bit as enchanting in the guise of society lady as she had been as the tumbled, siren-eyed vixen who had so unexpectedly managed to sink her claws into his heart.

Damn the little witch anyway, he thought, suddenly aware that his body had tightened and his heart had speeded up from no more cause than the merest glimpse of her. He had no more planned to fall under her spell than she had schemed to seduce him, but it had happened. Now he felt both bereft and angry. With his mind, he understood that she had a perfect right not to enter into an affair with him, and could even salute her for the sense of honor and morality that had led her to make such a decision. With his heart—damnable thing!—he felt that she was already his and to hell with any obstacles that fate tried to cast in the way of his claiming her.

The confusion and disarray that had weakened the French forces in the wake of the catastrophic Russian campaign had led to Boney's abrupt abandoning of Paris for Mainz. That in turn had ended Hugh's most recent assignment, rendering him redundant for the moment and enabling him to solicit a leave from Hildebrand. This had been granted, but should conditions on the Continent worsen he knew he could be recalled at any time. It therefore behooved him to spend his long-delayed sojourn in England checking on his estates and attending to business while he could. Fortunately, Claire's refusal to continue their relationship had freed him up to do just that. Doubtless it had been folly to have sought her out again in the first place, as James had protested repeatedly from the moment he had learned that they were bound for England. Though her decision was, to say the least, unwelcome, that she professed to want nothing more to do with him was undoubtedly a major stroke of luck. A wise man would be thankful for her prudence. Under the circumstances, their relationship, however temporarily rewarding it might be, would be considered by the judicious as something in the nature of a bomb about to explode.

Wooing her back into his arms would not be overly difficult, he knew. However much she might protest, he was experienced enough in the ways of women to know that she wanted him almost as badly as he wanted her. But, though more worldly society matrons might discreetly pursue illicit love lives in half the haute bedrooms in London, Claire was not of their ilk. She was still little more than a green girl, and to seduce her in the teeth of her protests and thus expose her to her husband's wrath, her family's disapprobation, and Society's scandal-hungry tongue would be nothing short of an act of infamy on his part.

He knew it, and, however unwillingly, accepted it. But still just looking at her reduced him physically to the level of a callow youth in the throes of his first calf love.

What he needed, he decided grimly as he turned his attention from Claire to her *husband*, was the hair of the dog that bit him. Claire might disdain to be his mistress, but there were plenty of others—outrageous beauties too, he had no doubt—who were not so nice in their notions. A man of sense would undoubtedly seek one out without delay.

"Oh, never fear," David said. "You may ogle my wife with my goodwill. She is most beautiful, but, having sipped of her nectar, I have long since flitted on to fresher flowers. You doubtless understand: It is the way of the world, after all." David was watching him with lazy interest. Doubtless something of his admiration for Claire had appeared on his face, Hugh realized as their gazes met. Well, there was nothing wonderful about that. Any male between the ages of ten and ninety must admire her.

"As you say," Hugh replied, feigning indifference with some difficulty. As David's words sank in, Hugh found himself seized with the sudden desire to grab his cousin by the scruff of the neck and shake him senseless. Any last vestiges of guilt he might have felt at having slept with David's wife vanished. Coupled with all Claire had told him of her marriage, David's words confirmed that there was no union to break: David regarded his wife not with affection or even regard, but as a prize that, having been won, no longer held any value for him. Not that Hugh was particularly surprised. As David was the younger by six years and Hugh had been sent away to school when the other boy was still in short coats, they had not been friends as children, although throughout his life David had run tame on the ducal properties. Still, Hugh knew him well enough to have been appalled when Claire had revealed the name of her husband. For all his golden good looks, David had always had a cold and calculating center. Animals stayed clear of his path, servants tended to leave his service after no more than a few months, and his friends had been chosen with an eye to who they were and what benefit their friendship might bring to David. This afternoon, Hugh had discovered that his cousin had, if anything, added to his list of vices as an adult, and that was a subject that the two of them needed most urgently to discuss.

Deliberately closing his mind to any further thoughts of Claire, Hugh eyed his cousin a trifle grimly. "If you can spare me a minute, I would have a word with you."

"Ah, a lecture from the mighty duke is imminent, I apprehend." David smiled and shook his head at him. "You must excuse me, cuz. I was just on my way to White's. I am promised most faithfully to Hazelden."

"As I am sure that you have some inkling of the subject we need to discuss, you must know that refusing is not an option. In any case, you need not disappoint your friend. This won't take long."

"Duke, I declare, it is so good to see you back in England! Do let me make you known to my daughter Harriet. Lud, never say you don't remember me: I am Lady Langford."

Faintly startled, Hugh glanced around at the interruption. A plump dowager who looked vaguely familiar, having apparently spotted him, had emerged from the drawing room like an arrow shot from a bowstring with her shrinking daughter in tow. Curse it, he was caught. He should have moved faster. Gritting his teeth, he smiled and did the pretty to her and the other females who clustered around almost immediately as well. The mothers were quite open in their avidity to direct his interest toward their girls, while the daughters, well brought up debutantes, were more discreet. Harriet Langford, a shy little blonde, was the most attractive of the young ladies, but she was quite put in the shade by Claire's sister, whose name for the moment escaped him. Though not Claire's equal in looks—who was?—the little sister was lovely in quite another style with her red hair, milk-white skin, and voluptuous figure set off by a low-necked gown of palest peach. Encountering his gaze on her, she surprised him by returning it without a blush, then looking him over with open curiosity deflected by no maidenly reservations that he could detect.

Shades of Claire, he thought, suddenly amused by the young lady's frank regard, and smiled back at her.

"We have not met, I believe," he said, moving to her side under the cover of the general conversation. "I am Richmond."

"And I am Lady Elizabeth Banning, and have most reprehensibly taken over your house for my debut," she replied with a twinkle, holding out her hand to him. "You are no doubt wishing me at Jericho at this very moment."

"Not at all." He kissed her gloved hand as she clearly expected him to do and released it with a widening smile. "You may be sure that you and your sister are very welcome in my home."

"Claire, Richmond assures me that we are very welcome," Beth said gaily, glancing around and then hooking her hand in her sister's arm to draw her into the conversation. Claire turned away from the woman she had been politely listening to, and her gaze encountered his. For a moment her eyes, quite unguarded, were bright with pain and longing. His heart, damned treacherous organ, seemed to skip a beat in response. Then she dropped her lids just enough to veil her eyes, and pinned a—to him at least—patently false smile on her hauntingly lovely face.

"How very charming of him," Claire murmured, her voice cool.

"Indeed, and providential too, as just this morning you were talking about the need for us to take a lease on another house in town so that Richmond might have his privacy. I am sure you would be very dull if we did so, would you not, Your Grace?" This sally by Lady Elizabeth was accompanied by a wide smile. The sheer audacity of her was charming, and Hugh was surprised into a chuckle.

"Very dull indeed," he said. "And you must call me Hugh. We are cousins now, after all, are we not?"

"Then I am Beth. And my sister is Claire."

"Beth. Claire. How I rejoice in the acquisition of such delightful new family members."

"The connection is nevertheless no excuse for us to so grossly take advantage of Richmond's hospitality by remaining under his roof for the rest of the Season," Claire said to her sister.

"But I insist," Hugh said. Claire looked at him again, only the second time in the course of the conversation that she had done so. This time her eyes held—what? a reproof?—before she glanced away. Left looking at her averted face, Hugh discovered that he was no more cut out for a clandestine relationship than she was. While morality may have been the grounds for her objection, fierce possessiveness fueled his. It was all he could do not to sweep her up in his arms and walk off with her, thus putting an end to the whole ridiculous charade. She was his, and there was an end to it.

Only she wasn't.

"Indeed, Claire, if we were to attempt such a move we would no doubt find that there are no decent houses to be hired anywhere in London at the moment. You had best leave such matters to me." David's tone as he addressed his wife was so brusque as to cause Hugh to give him a hard look, which, no doubt fortunately, he didn't see.

"Oh, lud, yes, Lady Dempsey was telling me just the other day about the truly appalling house they were obliged to take for the Season because they could find none other. If you can believe it, it is in Harley Street," Lady Langford said with a grimace. "And at such a price! Lady Dempsey swore she would not have dreamt that even St. James's Palace could be half so dear."

"You see, Cousin Claire, what a hideous fate awaits you if you remain obdurate." Hugh was quite unable to resist the impulse to get her to look at him again.

She did, but this time there was no mistaking the rebuke in the depths of those heart-stopping golden eyes. Clearly the lady wished to whisk herself out of his house and, thus, out of his life. While he might, if he were a better man, make it easy for her, he discovered that he was just base enough to refuse to assist her. Under the cover of the general conversation, which, with the aid of Lady Langford, was now involved with the impossibility of London prices in general, he smiled at Claire. Her eyes widened, warmed instinctively, then flickered with alarm and darted away from his. Seconds later she had turned a cold shoulder on him to take up a conversation with another of the visiting ladies. Watching her broodingly, he nevertheless managed to seem to be conversing with Lady Langford, largely because that loquacious lady was doing all the conversing. Though she remained partially turned away, Claire was as attuned to him as he was to her. The stiffness of her stance, her dogged refusal to turn her head in his direction, and the forced quality of her smile were dead giveaways, to him if no one else.

But despite her best efforts to pretend he wasn't there, the air between them seemed charged with an invisible current so strong that it was almost palpable. Could no one else sense it? A covert glance around gave him the answer: Apparently not. Then Lady Langford said something to him that required an answer—he was not sure precisely what it was—but clearly his response was appropriate enough that she felt free to continue to chatter away.

"Ladies, forgive me," he said abruptly as the conversation turned to upcoming social events and Lady Langford began to coyly feel him out as to which ones he meant to attend. "But my cousin and I have business that we cannot put off any longer despite the lure of such scintillating company. Pray excuse us."

Amid a cacophony of disappointed good-byes, and so many twittering urges that he be sure to do one thing or another that Hugh quite lost track of what he promised to whom, he managed to escape, hooking a friendly-looking hand in David's arm in the process and thus compelling his cousin to accompany him to his study.

"The matchmaking mamas are hot on your trail already, I see. Oh, what it must be to be young, rich, and a duke." David threw himself into the leather chair in front of the desk as Hugh closed the study door behind them. The room was not large, but it was one of Hugh's favorites, with wood-paneled walls lined with shelf after shelf of books and an immense Italian marble fireplace in which a small fire presently burned to ward off the creeping evening chill.

"There are undoubtedly worse things." Hugh moved toward the vast mahogany desk that had been his father's and his father's father's before him, back countless generations.

"Will we see you setting up your nursery soon?" David's voice was light, but there was a glint in his eyes that told Hugh how closely the matter rankled.

"Worried about being cut out, are you?" Hugh responded dryly, sitting down behind the desk. "When I have plans to supplant you as my heir, I'll let you know." He offered David a cigar from the box on his desk. When David declined, he lit up himself, and leaned back in his chair, eyeing his cousin a trifle grimly. "You've been drawing the bustle with a vengeance while I've been away, I understand."

"I don't know what you're talking about." As it had always been his wont to do when the conversation took a turn he didn't like, David's expression turned sulky.

"I think you do. Since gaining your majority, you've frittered away practically every pound of the not inconsiderable fortune your father left you, and in the nearly two years since your marriage you've managed to squander the entirety of your wife's dowry as well. All that is left to you is a trust fund set up so that the principal is untouchable, which provides you with a small income, and Labington, which came to you free and clear and is now mortgaged to the hilt. You are, to be blunt, quite rolled up. None of which would be my concern—your finances are your own, after all—were it not for the fact that six months ago my man of business began receiving bills for various repairs and services associated with the upkeep of my properties—the ones that your mother and you have occupied with my goodwill and at my expense—that were easily three times what they should have been. He and I went over them this afternoon.

You've been padding expenses and pocketing the difference, haven't you?"

David, who'd been sprawling in his chair when Hugh started talking, did not change position. But his mouth contorted into a the slightest of sneers, and his eyes took on a sullen gleam. "What possible difference could a few paltry bills of mine make to you? You're rich as bloody Croesus."

"However rich I may or may not be, what is mine is mine. I have a constitutional dislike of being cheated. Even less do I relish being robbed." Hugh's voice was hard.

"What would you have had me do, oh mighty cousin?" David sat up and gave Hugh a look that brimmed with bitter mockery. "As you say, I am under the hatches. But, though my funds have unfortunately fallen victim to a series of unfortunate events, I still have to live. I still have a wife to support, too, in case you haven't noticed, and as you can no doubt tell from looking at her, her upkeep is a considerable expense. The outlay required for her gowns and gewgaws and fripperies is truly staggering, believe me. As your heir, I would have applied to you for relief if you had been in England. As you were not, knowing your generous nature and the fondness you bear me, I assumed you would not object to making me a small loan."

"You assumed wrong. And we'll leave your wife out of this, if you please. I'm quite well aware that you are a hardened gamester, and have lost it all at play. I tell you to your head—and I mean to say this only once, so take heed of it—that I will not support such folly. For the sake of your mother, and your wife, this time I will not throw you out on your ear to fend for yourself. I'll even pay the debts you have accumulated to this point, and will contribute enough to your income to allow you to maintain yourself and your family in tolerable style. But if I get wind of any more gaming, or if you again attempt to fleece me in any way, my patience will be at an end, my subsidizing of your expenditures will stop, and you may go to the devil with my goodwill. Do I make myself clear?"

Their gazes met and held. There was anger in David's expression, and resentment too. Hugh recognized that his cousin, never counted as a friend, might well have become his enemy instead. Had it not been for Claire, and Lady George, who was after all innocent of any wrongdoing save being David's mother, he would have turned his cousin out of doors forthwith. But for their sakes, he did not.

"Very clear, cousin." David stood up, thrusting one hand in his pocket and twirling his eyeglass on its ribbon with the other. "Having just been raked over the coals like an errant schoolboy, I feel it incumbent on me to beg to be excused before I dare to remove myself from your august presence."

"As long as you believe that I mean what I say, you may go about your business with my goodwill." As tempting as it was to lose his temper with David, Hugh managed to refrain. He dismissed the younger man with a curt nod, then watched with a slowly knitting brow as his cousin sauntered with insolent grace from the room.

After David was gone, Hugh finished his cigar, leaning back in his chair, and thoughtfully pondered the smoke that swirled above his head. A suspicion had entered his mind, and the more he considered it the more solid it became.

Had David, in some kind of convoluted scheme to make money, arranged for the attack on Claire's carriage? Perhaps hoping to collect a ransom for her safe return? Or, perhaps, hoping for something worse?

He meant to make it his business to find out.

"*C*laire, there, look! You see! It *is* Cousin Hugh, just as I said." Seated in the family laundau with Claire and Twindle, Beth practically broke her neck to get a final glimpse as a shiny black curricle traveling in the opposite direction along Piccadilly shot past them at a spanking pace, its driver doing a deft job of weaving in and out among the slower-moving traffic that clogged the street. It was a bright sunny morning some three weeks after Beth's ball, and the ladies were returning home from a successful shopping expedition in Bond Street. "Oh, my, isn't he looking slap up to the mark? And did you see the lady he has with him? Who can she be, I wonder?"

Seated beside Beth in the open carriage, Claire nearly choked at Beth's naive question. She had indeed seen the "lady" her sister referred to as soon as Beth had pointed out Hugh's equipage barreling toward them through the crush of vehicles crowding the road. Frozen into place, doing her best to keep her face absolutely expressionless in case he should glance their way, she was powerless to prevent Beth's cheery waves at the approaching carriage.

Fortunately Hugh either had not observed or had been gentlemanly enough to choose not to acknowledge Beth's signals. Despite the brief nature of the encounter, Claire had seen enough to have the female's image burned into her brain: guinea-gold curls bouncing around a flawless face tilted up to laugh at some remark of Hugh's; a smooth white neck and ample bosom swelling lushly above a gown of sky-blue silk that was more than a little daring for daytime wear; ropes of pearls and colored stones around her neck that glinted in the sunshine; an enormous hat with a curling brim and a trio of quivering ostrich plumes so large they brushed her shoulders with each sway of the carriage. No lady of Claire's acquaintance would have dreamed of stepping out in public thus attired. Indeed, Claire knew what such a costume portended: the type of female that Hugh would never introduce to Beth—or herself. In short, the lady was no lady. Hugh had clearly decided to console himself with a tart.

The knowledge hit Claire with all the force of a body blow.

"He is so handsome, Claire, don't you think, and most agreeable too. I declare, I am of half a mind to set my cap at him. I would make a capital duchess, and should quite enjoy being top of the trees."

"Miss Beth, that I should live to listen to such vulgarity from the mouth of a young lady I helped raise!" Twindle shook her head despairingly. Seated opposite the pair of them, the older woman, looking neat as a pin in a soft gray gown with matching bonnet, fixed Beth with a reproving stare. "You will never win a husband of any rank do you not learn to keep a guard on that unruly tongue, and so I warn you."

"Indeed, Beth, Richmond is far too old for you," Claire said.

"Why, I would not have thought him much above thirty." Beth frowned, her expression thoughtful as she settled her newly purchased Norwich shawl more closely about her shoulders. Made of heavy white silk with a long, knotted fringe, the wrap was just the thing for a young lady in her first Season, they had all agreed. Admiring its effect when paired with her gown of primrose-sprigged muslin, she had elected to wear it rather than have it sent with the rest of the morning's purchases.

"He is thirty-one." Doing her best *not* to dwell on what she had just seen, and enjoying scant success in the endeavor, Claire answered absently, then realized that she was, perhaps, revealing too much knowledge of her cousin by marriage.

"That is not so old. It's no older than Shrewsbury, whom you described just last night as a very eligible match." Beth gave Claire an indignant look. "Indeed, I think you must be quite smitten with Cousin Hugh yourself. You poker up amazingly whenever he comes into a room, and I don't think I have heard you say more than a pair of sentences to him since we first made his acquaintance. Plus he is always looking at you—which is not wonderful, of course, gentlemen always look at you—but the thing of it is, usually you never look back. With Richmond, sometimes, when he isn't looking, you do. Tell the truth, Claire: You have developed a *tendre* for our new cousin, haven't you?"

Though Beth was teasing, Claire felt her throat tighten with alarm. Her sister, who knew her very well indeed, might pick up on subtle clues others would miss, but what Beth could divine could eventually become clear to someone else as well. The thought of David, or Lady George, making such an observation made her palms turn clammy with panic. Had she really done such a poor job of hiding how she felt? She had been so careful, in Hugh's presence or out of it, to reveal no reaction to him at all.

"Are you forgetting that I'm married?" Claire said as lightly as she could. "I no longer develop *tendres* for gentlemen, I'll have you know."

"I would, if I were married to your David," Beth replied, her gaze frank. "I am sorry if this wounds you, Claire, but he does not treat you as he should, you know. He may be handsome on the outside, but on the inside he's a *worm*. I heard him tell you this morning that your new chip-straw bonnet makes you look like a hag, and quite aside from the fact that he has no business saying such a thing to you even if it were true, it isn't! It becomes you most wonderfully, and it is my opinion that he only said it to make you feel bad. Yes, and I notice that you went and took it off, and are now wearing another hat entirely. It is too bad of him, Claire, and so I mean to tell him at the next opportunity, too."

"Beth, no!" The possibility of her outspoken little sister tackling David on her behalf made Claire feel almost light-headed. The exchange, which had taken place in the hall as Claire had prepared to go out after breakfast and encountered David, obviously just on his way in from the previous night's revelries, had taken place exactly as Beth had described. And in its aftermath she had, indeed, changed her hat for the high-poke bonnet that now adorned her head. With its dark green ribbons, it was quite a good match for her pale green frock, after all, so making the switch had entailed no great sacrifice.

She had not realized that Beth had overheard what David had said. Embarrassment joined with anxiety to bring color rushing to her cheeks. "Indeed, Beth, I pray you will not! David has been somewhat—somewhat out of sorts lately, it's true, but I don't regard it, I assure you. He—we—will come about."

"You may put a brave face on it if you choose, but I am not such a flat that I don't know when you're unhappy, Claire." Beth's expression was earnest. "If you don't wish me to speak to David, perhaps Gabby, or, better yet, Nick. . . ."

"No!" Claire shook her head violently. "No, do you hear me? If David and I are on the outs—all right, David and I *are* on the outs—we must arrive at a solution ourselves. Oh, Beth, let's just get through this Season, shall we? Things are going so splendidly for you."

"But I wish things to go splendidly for you, too," Beth said, her tone gentling, and reached for Claire's hand. Her blue eyes were dark with concern. "And I don't think they are."

"Miss Beth, you quit badgering your sister right this very minute!" Twindle broke in, sounding far fiercer than was her wont. Her gaze moved to Claire, and her tone softened. "Miss Claire, you won't wish to cry on a public street."

"But, Twindle . . ." Beth began hotly. Claire squeezed Beth's hand, silencing her, then released it, laughing a little even as she blinked back the tears that threatened, called forth by this unexpected evidence of her little sister's care for her.

"Beth, dear, see what you've done? Your championship has very nearly moved me to tears! I won't wither away because David is rude about my new bonnet, you know, so please don't worry your head about me. I'm fine, I promise."

"So you say," Beth replied skeptically, but in response to a look from Twindle she clamped her lips together and said no more. The three rode the rest of the way in a deepening silence broken only by the sound of the horses' hooves clicking and the wheels rattling over the cobbled street as the carriage left the bustle of the busier boulevards behind to turn onto the lightly traveled environs of Park Lane. Located right next to Hyde Park, Park Lane was the most exclusive address in London. The houses were huge edifices of brick and stone, four stories tall, with stone steps leading up from the street and rows of leaded windows that sparkled in the sun. As it was relatively early in the day, only a housemaid with a basket over her arm clearly bent on an errand, two children hurrying with their hapless nursemaid in tow toward the park, and a street sweeper busy at that moment right in front of Richmond House were in evidence as they approached. The street sweeper stood aside, tugging at his forelock as the carriage rocked to a halt in front of the house.

"Beth," Claire said in a carefully neutral voice as the door was opened and the steps let down. "I should not mention to Richmond that we spotted him today if I were you. The female with him was *not* a lady, I assure you."

"Do you mean he has taken up with a prime bit of muslin?" Beth, already halfway out of the carriage, sounded fascinated rather than shocked as she glanced back over her shoulder at Claire. "How dashing he is, to be sure! Oh, quit primming up your mouth at me, Claire. You must know that for a gentleman to have a female such as that in keeping is all the crack."

Twindle moaned in horror and clapped her hands over her ears.

"Beth, where on earth do you hear such things?" Claire asked, aghast. "Ladies, especially young, unmarried ladies, are not supposed to know about matters of that nature, and even if they do, they're certainly not supposed to talk about them!"

"If you can succeed in convincing her of that, you should have been the governess and not I, Miss Claire," Twindle muttered, dropping her hands and fixing Beth with a look that warned anyone who knew her well that the recipient was in for a thundering scold once she got her alone.

"Oh, pooh," Beth said inelegantly, clearly unimpressed, and descended the stairs with a toss of her fiery head.

That evening found them at Almack's, that most exclusive of clubs. Known by the vulgar as the Marriage Mart, it was more difficult to get into than St. James's Palace. Ruled by a set of patronesses who included, fortunately, Aunt Augusta's good friend Lady Jersey as well as the more top-lofty Princess Esterhazy, Countess Lieven, and Mrs. Drummond-Burrell, it consisted of several large but surprisingly shabby chambers on King Street. The surroundings were unimpressive, the refreshments, which were of no higher order than tea, lemonade, or orgeat, small stale cakes or bread and butter, were paltry, and the entertainment was limited to dancing or a few hands of whist or vingt-et-un, and yet admission into its hallowed halls was the goal of every socially ambitious female in the country. The patronesses' approval, issued in the form of vouchers, had to be obtained before one might purchase a ticket for admission, and the patronesses themselves were notoriously strict about just who was deemed suitable and who was not. Fortunately, that hurdle had been cleared for Claire at the time of her own come-out, which meant that Beth's admission, *sans* some sort of major faux pas on that volatile young lady's part, had been all but assured.

As a consequence, rather than feeling privileged to be a part of so select a group, Claire was feeling bored as she sat with the other chaperons in one of the gilt chairs lining the walls, and headachy, and most unaccountably out of sorts. The truth was that she was blue-deviled, though she meant to admit that to no one save herself. Try as she would, she could not get the image of Hugh and the blond female he'd been driving down Piccadilly out of her head. Was he with her now? she wondered. Were they, perhaps, together in that house in Curzon Street where Hugh had suggested meeting *her*? Were they even now kissing, or . . .

Stop it, she ordered herself fiercely. She wasn't going to think about that. She was going to put Hugh and everything concerning him out of her head.

To that end, she concentrated on locating her sister. The dancing was well under way, and Beth was taking her part in a reel with the laughing enjoyment that was so much a part of her nature. Beth was lovely in virginal white, practically the only color considered suitable for a debutante to wear to Almack's, with her bright hair dressed in a simple knot on the top of her head. Her high-waisted frock with its tiny puffed sleeves was caught up under her bosom with sapphire ribbons that almost exactly matched her eyes, and its slim cut set off her figure to perfection.

Oh, to be that young and carefree again, Claire thought wistfully. Observing the sparkling optimism on the faces of the dancing young girls, she suddenly felt hideously old in comparison, and her spirits sank even lower as a consequence.

She took a bite out of the small poppy-seed cake she held in one hand, then had to work to chew and swallow the dry, tasteless morsel without choking. She was only twenty-one, she reflected gloomily, and her life, to all intents and purposes, was already over. After all, she had successfully performed the gently bred female's ultimate function: She had wed. Except for the bearing of children, which happiness was not likely to happen to her, there was nothing else for a lady of quality to look forward to.

Except having a blazing affair with her husband's cousin, perhaps.

As that thought entered her mind, quite unbidden, Claire choked on the cake after all. But at least her subsequent fit of coughing served one purpose: It forced the tantalizing image out of her head.

"Really, dear, you should know better than to eat the cakes they serve by now," Aunt Augusta, who was seated beside her looking very much the grande dame in lavender satin, whispered reprovingly as Claire recovered. "The refreshments are quite dreadful, but then, one doesn't come here for the food, after all." A couple promenading past caught her attention and thankfully gave her thoughts another direction. "Lud, look at that gown: Who is that? Oh, Emily Poole! She was always the most forward creature! If her father hadn't been a duke, no one would receive her. See how her gown clings to her? Do you think her petticoats are *damped*?"

"I don't think she's wearing a petticoat," Claire replied, looking obediently at the lady in question, a woman closer to thirty than twenty who was nevertheless attired in the girlish fashion of white muslin, which in her case had been somehow rendered practically transparent. "I think she's damped her *gown*."

"Oh, my."

As Aunt Augusta turned to draw the attention of Mrs. Weston, who sat on her other side, to the scandal in the making, Claire disposed of the last of the despised cake by handing it off to a passing waiter. Brushing her hands over her lap to remove any tiny crumbs that might have lodged in the folds of her gown, she reflected that there was at least one advantage to her situation: Having attained the coveted status of a matron, she was no longer expected to defer to the prevailing preference for white or the palest of pastel gowns. Her gown tonight was of shimmering bronze silk tied up beneath her breasts with dark green ribbons, and she wore a delicate emerald necklet that had been her mother's, along with matching earbobs.

Exchanging desultory conversation with Lady Holsted, a plump and placid mother of four hopeful daughters who sat on her other side, Claire once again watched, this time with slightly envious eyes, as her sister skipped down the room.

"Oh, there's Barbara Langford beckoning to me. Well, I must just go see what she wants," Aunt Augusta said in her ear, then rose and made her way across the room. Claire nodded, and tried not to feel downcast as Lady Holsted proceeded to chat about her youngest daughter's recent bout with the measles. As she listened, she did her best not to let her toes tap in time to the music. She wanted to dance, and indeed she could have done so at any time since they had arrived as at least half a dozen gentlemen had already asked her, but there was no one present she felt like dancing with. Chatting with one of her group of particular friends might have lifted her spirits, but none of them seemed to be present, which wasn't surprising as most of them were too young to have daughters of marriageable age or too old and too secure in their married status to be on the market themselves.

"May I join you?"

Claire glanced up in surprise at the deep-voiced question, then nodded with some reluctance as she ascertained the identity of the questioner. Aunt Augusta's vacated seat was promptly filled by Lord Vincent Davenport. A fortyish widower, Lord Vincent was not overly tall, muscular to the point of being stocky in build, with thick auburn hair that waved back from his brow and bright blue eyes above a square jaw. He was a noted Corinthian, a member of the Four Horse Club, and a confirmed rake. Currently in search of a new wife, he had come to London to look over the current crop of debutantes, as he had informed Claire in his languid drawl on the occasion of their first meeting, but had found that her beauty quite drove the purpose of his visit right out of his head. Despite her hints and then outright assurances that she was unavailable, Lord Vincent had since become most persistent in his attentions. It required little intelligence on Claire's part to guess what role he desired her to play in his life, but so far he had not crossed beyond the line of what was permissible, and, beyond what she had already done, she was at a loss as to how to discourage him. Had her husband ever been present at the same time as Lord Vincent it would have helped, but David, preferring his own amusements, almost never accompanied her to evening events. Lord Vincent was considered quite a catch by the matchmaking mamas, but under the circumstances Claire found his attentions more annoying than gratifying, and tonight the situation was made worse by Lady George's presence: Her mother-in-law, who was talking with Lady Sefton and Princess Esterhazy nearby, kept casting disapproving looks her way. Claire had little doubt that on the morrow she would be subject to a lecture on the perils of seeming *fast*.

" 'Twould be futile of me to invite you to make up one of a party picnicking in Green Park tomorrow, I take it?" Lord Vincent murmured even as he plucked her fan from her lap and used it to ply a gentle breeze toward her face.

Though the room was abominably stuffy, making the cool waft of air most welcome, Claire reached immediately to retrieve her fan. He gave it up with a smile.

"Quite futile, I'm afraid," she said, slipping the fan's ribbon over her wrist. "I am in London strictly to act as my sister's chaperon, you know, not to amuse myself."

"What a dutiful sister you are," he said, looking at her with a predatory gleam in his eye that, despite his lowered lids, was quite unmistakable. "I admire you for that—and for much else besides—I assure you."

Claire did not reply. The band struck up a quadrille—she had not even realized the previous dance had ended—and she used that as an excuse to turn her face away from him, ostensibly to search for Beth among the dancers.

As eye-catching as Beth's bright hair made her, Claire

never found her. Her gaze was caught and held by another dancer first.

It was Hugh, looking devastatingly handsome in the formal evening wear that was the correct attire for gentlemen hoping for admission to Almack's. He had not been present earlier: She could not possibly have been unaware of him if he had been. As the clock had just struck eleven, he must have entered right before the doors, which were closed to new arrivals promptly at that hour, had been shut.

Her heart gave a great leap in her breast. Suddenly the world took on interest and excitement, color and meaning. Then the rest of what she was seeing registered, and her stomach knotted and her hands curled into fists in her lap: Hugh was dancing with the flaxen-haired Harriet Langford, and giving every indication that he was enjoying it.

## ❧ 28 ❧

.................................

Jealousy was an ugly thing, Claire discovered as she watched Hugh's head bent over Harriet Langford's, and she felt ugly even as she helplessly harbored the corrosive emotion. It was one she had never felt before, she realized, although it had been directed at her by other females more often than she cared to remember. To think that she had not sympathized with their feelings, or even realized how horrible they felt! She almost deserved to be put through such a heart-burning experience herself. Deliberately she reminded herself that if he was dancing with Miss Langford at Almack's for all the world to see, then at least he was not off doing far more intimate things to the far less respectable female who'd been in his carriage that morning. But no matter how she rationalized it, to see him clasping hands with Miss Langford, to watch him smile that devastatingly charming smile of his directly into Miss Langford's eyes, to observe how slender and blond and ethereally lovely the chit looked when viewed in tandem with his tall, muscular form and swarthy good looks, was almost more than she could bear. It did not help that the girl was scarcely eighteen, and prime marriage material. It certainly did not help to reflect that, as Duke of Richmond, Hugh must of necessity marry someone someday.

Someone besides herself. She, Claire, could never be his bride.

It was that which stuck in her craw, she decided, watching him with her teeth clenched so hard her jaws ached and a set smile plastered to her face.

He was hers, and yet she could never really have him, or be his.

"Lady Claire, are you ill?" Lord Vincent leaned forward with knitted brow to peer into her face. "You are suddenly gone quite pale."

Lord Vincent was watching her, she realized as his voice penetrated her absorption. Others might be watching her as well. She could not give away her secret. She must be careful, so careful, not only for her own sake but for Beth's.

There was, she realized, genuine concern for her in Lord Vincent's face. Drawing in a quick and, she hoped, subtle breath, she unclenched her fingers and managed a smile for him.

"I was just thinking," she said, "how much I would like to dance."

"Would you indeed?" His expression was both surprised and appreciative, and no wonder. She had turned down his invitations to dance so many times that he had stopped making them. Standing up, he bowed and offered her his arm. "I'm delighted to be of service, believe me."

The quadrille ended even as they headed toward the floor, and Claire found herself taking her place opposite

Lord Vincent as the band struck up a boulanger. She'd had some thought of making Hugh as aware of her as she was of him when she'd practically ordered Lord Vincent to ask her to dance, but that, she quickly learned, was going to be all but impossible.

For the boulanger, Hugh was partnering Beth.

It was all Claire could do not to miss any steps as she watched them together. Beth, with her vivid coloring and curvaceously feminine shape, was a perfect foil for Hugh's dark masculinity. Where Miss Langford had seemed shy, Beth bubbled over with vivacity, laughing and chattering away at Hugh as if she'd known him all her life. For his part, Hugh looked as relaxed as Claire had ever seen him, regarding her little sister with indulgent eyes and a lazy smile.

It occurred to Claire suddenly that Beth was free to marry him. The idea of her little sister wed to the man she loved made Claire feel physically ill.

*The man she loved.* The thought struck terror into her soul. She hadn't even realized that was how she felt until the actual words had run through her mind. Now that she knew, it was all she could do to continue to breathe.

As panic seized her, she tore her gaze from Hugh and Beth, and smiled brilliantly at Lord Vincent, who was watching her with a rather sardonic expression on his face. She pirouetted, and curtsied, and the music ended.

She loved Hugh. So much that her heart had ached like a sore tooth every day of the months they had been apart; so much that just seeing him enjoy himself in the company of another female was enough to make her want to gnash her teeth and clout him over the head; so much that she was willing to consider, finally, shamefully, the possibility of becoming his mistress.

She could not become his mistress. Oh, dear Lord, she could not.

Sir Vincent was saying something to her, offering her his arm. She smiled and murmured a reply—she had no idea what she said—and tucked her arm in the crook of his elbow. Just as they reached the edge of the dance floor, Beth came dancing up to them—with Hugh in tow.

Claire looked over her little sister's head, met Hugh's narrowed gray eyes, and felt her heart skip a beat. Hugh smiled at her, the wry, twisted half-smile that she saw every night in her dreams, and her heart began to pound.

"Claire, I was just bringing Cousin Hugh to find you. He has no partner for the next dance." Still holding on to Hugh's arm, Beth cast a beaming smile over her shoulder at Hugh. Then she looked at Claire and her eyes twinkled mischievously. "I told him I was sure you were free."

Oh, Beth, Claire thought, near panicking. You know not what you do.

The manners drummed into her by Twindle from childhood proved her salvation in that moment of crisis. Pulse pounding, stomach twisting once again into knots, Claire removed her hand from Lord Vincent's arm, lifted her chin, and, with a smile, performed the necessary introductions.

The band struck up a waltz.

"May I have this dance, Cousin Claire?" Hugh said, offering her his arm. There was the slightest of smiles on his face now, but his eyes were intent as her gaze instinctively sought his.

With the best will in the world to do so, she couldn't find the strength to refuse. She drew in a deep breath, nodded, and placed her hand on his arm.

"Alas, I suppose I must surrender to *force majeure*," Lord Vincent murmured, glancing from Hugh to Claire. Then he looked at Beth, and bowed. "Lady Elizabeth, will you dance?"

It said much for the state Claire was in that she barely noticed when her sister walked away with Lord Vincent. In the ordinary way of things, she would have gone to almost any length to keep Beth from being exposed to attentions of that most confirmed of rakes.

The floor was crowded when they reached it and she stepped into Hugh's arms. Unwilling to meet his gaze for fear of what he—and others—might read in her face, she kept her eyes demurely lowered. He slid an arm around her waist, she placed her hand on his shoulder, and, with the proper distance between them, he swung her into the dance.

Then they were waltzing, and she was suddenly supremely aware of every little detail: the seductive lilt of the music—and the solid muscularity of the broad shoulder beneath her hand; the other couples swirling and swaying around them—and the warm strength of his fingers clasping hers; the rapid rise and fall of her breasts as exertion quickened her breathing—and the scant inches that separated the creamy globes from his wide chest; the gliding rhythm of their steps—and the silken rustle as his long legs brushed her skirt.

"You're beautiful," he said quietly, and without thinking she lifted her eyes to his face.

He was as dark as a Gypsy; though he had undoubtedly shaved that evening before coming out, the faintest hint of stubble was already visible as a shadow darkening his jaw and lean cheeks; his long, thin mouth was curved into the faintest of smiles. She met his eyes, those lead-gray eyes, and found that they were soft with tenderness for her.

"I love you," she said, her heart in her eyes. She had not meant to say it in the least; under the compelling warmth of his gaze the truth had just come tumbling out.

His eyes widened; his step faltered; his grip tightened on her fingers and her waist. His eyes bore into hers.

Then, most unaccountably, he laughed.

She couldn't believe it: She had told him she loved him, and he laughed!

Even as he recovered his composure and his step, indignation seized her. Her spine stiffened; her chin rose; her eyes met his with a militant glint that would have given either of her sisters, or indeed anyone who knew her well, pause.

Mindful of the other dancers twirling with them about the floor, Claire was careful to keep her voice low as she demanded ominously, "Did you find something amusing in that?"

Swinging her around in a movement of the dance, Hugh shook his head. As a negative response it was quite spoiled, however, by his twinkling eyes and the incipient grin that seemed to be tugging at the corners of his mouth.

"Claire," he said, his voice as carefully low as hers had been, but brimful of amusement for all that. "Oh, Claire. Only you, my outspoken darling, would tell me such a thing in the middle of a crowded dance floor at Almack's, of all places, with dozens of eyes watching our every move and just as many clapping tongues eager to dine out on the least hint of scandal. What do you expect me to do about it here, I wonder?"

Only slightly mollified by the fact that he had called her his darling, Claire eyed him with a good deal less than the love she professed to feel.

"You could," she suggested tartly, "try telling me that you love me too."

"Silly chit," he said with an indulgent grin. Before Claire could reply—and she meant to reply pretty smartly, too, to that bit of gross provocation—the dance came to an end with a flourish of music.

"I have to leave," he said, suddenly sober as he bowed over her hand. "Meet me in the vestibule in a quarter of an hour."

He had to leave? What did he mean by that? Almost as alarmed as she was affronted, Claire barely had time to nod before they were joined by Lord Vincent and Beth, apparently none the worse for her dance with him. Claire somehow managed to maintain her part in the general conversation as Hugh escorted her to her aunt's side. Then, after exchanging a few polite words with her aunt and her aunt's friend Lady Cowper, with whom she had been conversing, he bowed and left them. At almost the same moment, Beth was claimed by her next partner and went off quite happily on his arm.

"No doubt you have hopes in that direction, Augusta?" Lady Cowper asked significantly, nodding after Hugh.

"Well. The girl is quite taken, as I'm sure I may say even though she is my niece, but Richmond may look as high as he chooses for a bride, you know. It is early days yet, but they seem to like each other well enough. We will have to see what happens as their acquaintance progresses."

Claire realized with a sense of shock that her aunt and Lady Cowper were discussing a possible marriage between Hugh and Beth. He's mine, she wanted to cry, but managed, just barely, to hold her tongue. The stark truth of the matter was, he wasn't hers. Not the way she wanted him to be, which was legally and forever.

And he never could be.

This lowering fact, as well as the knowledge that Hugh had not, in so many words, professed his love for her even though she had blurted out hers for him with all the finesse of a schoolroom miss in the throes of a crush on the dancing master, rankled with Claire as she excused herself to go to the ladies' retiring room and instead headed toward the vestibule to meet Hugh.

Bristling at the thought that she had just made a fine fool of herself if her sentiments were not reciprocated, Claire stepped into the cool dimness of the vestibule and looked around. Other than a pair of slightly dusty-looking potted palms, the small rectangular entry hall appeared to be empty. Even Stevens, who generally stood guard at the door, seemed to have deserted his post. There was something faintly spooky about the shadowy space lit only by the light that spilled over from the more populous rooms within. Music, voices, and laughter from the assembly filled the air, but they were not enough to render the vestibule any more welcoming.

Suddenly he appeared as if from nowhere, causing her to jump and gasp even as he grabbed her hand and pulled her back into the shadows from which he had appeared. Claire found herself in another room, smaller even than the vestibule, that was so dark that she could just barely make out the greatcoats and cloaks and shawls and pelisses with which it was festooned. It smelled of dust, and stale perfume, and even as she wondered at it she realized where she must be: the cloakroom, of course. Hugh had drawn her into the cloakroom. It was as deserted as the vestibule and far more private. Where the attendant was she couldn't fathom, but she had no time to ponder it because Hugh had swung her around so that her back was against the wall and pinned her there with both hands planted flat on the plaster on either side of her head.

"So you love me, do you?" he growled, looming mock-menacingly above her, and then before she could reply he kissed her with a hot hunger that set her pulse to racing and weakened her knees. Claire abandoned her indignation at the first touch of his lips to hers, wrapped her arms around his neck, and kissed him back with feverish abandon, her fingers clenching in the thick silk of his hair. Leaning against her, pressing her back against the cool plaster wall with the weight of his body, he left her in no doubt about the urgency of his desire for her.

When he lifted his head at last, she was dizzy. She clung to him, wanting never to let him go, wanting to imprint the feel and smell and taste of him on her mind and heart and body forever.

"I love you too," he said in a low, shaken voice, his eyes flaming down at her. And then he kissed her again, his arms coming around her to pull her up tight against him, so tight she could feel the rapid rise and fall of his chest against her breasts, the heat of his skin through his clothes, the hard, swollen tumescence of his body.

Just when Claire thought he must lay her down and take her right there among the cloaks and she was perfectly ready to have him do so, he lifted his head, took a deep breath, and pushed himself away from her until he was holding her at arm's length.

"Hugh." It was rather in the nature of a shameless whimper, but even as she recognized the pleading quality of her voice Claire didn't care. She felt shameless. She was light-headed and weak-kneed and aquiver from wanting him, and she tightened her grip on his neck. He was not putting her away from him so easily.

"I have to go," he said, sounding satisfyingly short of breath. Her eyes narrowed as she remembered that he had said the same thing on the dance floor. "I'll be away for a few days. That's why I came—to tell you good-bye."

Her back stiffened with alarm. He would not have come to Almack's to bid her farewell if he'd been heading off to a simple sojourn in the country.

"Where are you going?" Her voice was filled with dread, and her eyes searched his face. "Not—not back to France?"

It was as much a plea as a question.

"I can't tell you." He pulled her close again, dropped a quick, hard kiss on her mouth, and tugged her arms from around his neck. "Go now. I sent Stevens on an errand, but he should be back anytime now and you don't want him to see you. And James has a carriage waiting for me around the corner. I'll be home by Wednesday at the latest. Then we'll see what we can do about sorting this mess out."

But at the moment Claire was less concerned about

sorting the situation out than she was about the danger she sensed, with every fiber of her being, he was going into.

"Hugh, please," she begged, clinging to his hands, "don't go."

"I have to." His expression was suddenly grim. "I wouldn't otherwise, believe me. Be careful while I'm gone, angel eyes."

With that he dropped another quick kiss on her mouth and was gone.

## ❧ 29 ❧

............................

It was late the following night, and the moon rode high in the sky. By its faint light, Hugh was making his way through fields that had once been as familiar to him as the back of his hand. He had spent the earliest years of his childhood at Hayleigh Castle, and the unwelcome memories crowded into his exhausted brain despite his best efforts to keep them out. Having spent practically every minute of the last twenty-four hours in the saddle, he was dead tired—too tired to fight off the ghosts of his past. So he let them come, marveling that they still had the power to move him.

With James beside him, he was riding through the thick gorse on his way to Hayleigh's Point, where he was to meet an informant. According to the message Hugh had received, the man knew the whereabouts of Sophy Towbridge. The woman had disappeared, seemingly off the face of the earth, on the night when Hugh had first met Claire. Even the combined efforts of some of Britain's best agents had failed to find her—or the information she had taken with her.

Tonight, perhaps, that mystery would be solved.

When the man stepped out from behind a bush brandishing a shovel, Hugh was startled. His horse was no less so, and reared, whinnying shrilly. Taken unawares, Hugh was thrown, just as quick as that, to land hard on his arse in the thick weeds. For a moment he sat where he had landed, stunned.

The thought that was foremost in his mind was a groaning *not again*.

"Master Hugh!" James gasped, and fumbled for the weapon in his own pocket even as Hugh grabbed for his pistol.

"Eh, I make you me apologies, yer worships." The man with the shovel sounded abashed. Having stopped dead at the sight of Hugh's drawn pistol, he was little more than a bulky shape in the darkness. "I'd no thought to scare ye."

"Think nothing of it," Hugh said sourly, getting to his feet. His initial assessment was that the man was harmless, but after that fall from his horse he was taking no chances and kept his pistol at the ready.

"Are you all right?" James asked, holding Hugh's skittish horse by the reins.

"Fine," Hugh said, casting a wary glance around before focusing on the man before him. The fall had left him wide awake and on edge. He looked at the man again. "Are you Marley?"

"Aye. And you would be . . . ?"

"The party you seek."

"Playing it close to the vest, are ye?" Marley chuckled. "If ye brought the money, that's all the introduction I need."

"I did." Hugh motioned to James, who untied a small leather bag filled with guineas from his saddle and tossed it to Marley, who caught it deftly in one hand. Dropping the shovel, he opened the bag and peered inside. Apparently satisfied, he closed it again.

"You've got your money. Where's Sophy Towbridge?"

"This way." Marley gestured to them to follow him. Hugh did, keeping a wary eye out for a possible ambush. The information he had received had said the man would be alone, but he wasn't taking any chances. "There."

Marley pointed toward the ground. Looking down, Hugh discovered a partially opened grave. Moonlight glinted off a skull still topped, most grotesquely, with a hank of filthy but still recognizable blond hair.

"That's her?" James, having followed him on foot with both horses in tow, stared down at the grave, then glanced at Hugh, shaking his head. "No wonder no one's been able to find her."

"What about the papers she was carrying?" Hugh asked Marley.

Marley reached inside his jacket, rooted around, and came up with an oilskin pouch, which he handed to Hugh. With a glance at James, Hugh opened it and looked inside. There were three neatly folded letters. It was too dark to read them, but Hugh was fairly sure he'd at last found what he'd long sought.

Hugh nodded at James, and tucked the pouch inside his own coat.

"Can I cover her up now?" Marley asked. "I wouldn't like any o' the others to know I showed her to ye."

"Go ahead." Hugh started to turn away, then bethought himself of something. "There was another lady here on the Point on the same night as Sophy Towbridge. She was abducted from her carriage, I believe. Do you know anything about that?"

Marley shrugged. "I might."

"How much?" Hugh had the measure of his man.

"Double."

"Done." Hugh nodded at James, who extracted the required amount from the saddlebag that held their emergency fund and handed the roll of soft over to Marley.

He counted it and then thrust it into his pocket.

"The other lady?" Hugh prompted.

Marley snorted. "Ye mean the little besom what hit Briggs over the head with his own chamber pot, I take it. We was hired to snatch her out of her carriage and do away with her. It just so happened that we was to do it on the selfsame night as we was also hired to escort another lady, who turned out to be this Sophy Towbridge here, down to the beach at Hayleigh's Point to meet a boat. We didn't know nothin' about her bein' a French spy at that point, I swear we didn't. So we had both ladies at the same time, you see, all snug in the same farmhouse although neither knew the other was there. Then we got word that the search was on for a French spy, by name Miss Sophy Towbridge. Well, these ladies we were holding were of very different sorts, you understand, and one of them, in the course of gettin' real friendly with our leader, had told him that her name was Sophy Towbridge. What kind of coincidence was that? we asked ourselves. Then we answered ourselves: No kind of coincidence at all. Our Miss Sophy Towbridge and the one that was supposed to be a spy for the Frenchies nearly had to be one and the same. So we started working a deal where we was going to sell her back to His Majesty's government, right? Only it was going to take a little time. So we kept her right where she was, and in the end she never got down to the beach at all. But that left us with a problem: The Frenchies were sending a boat to pick Sophy Towbridge up, and them Frenchies can get right testy if you double-cross them. So we asked ourselves, what to do? And the answer was right there, plain as the nose on yer face, just beautiful. We had another lady—the *other* lady—who we was supposed to kill. So we thought to ourselves, why not kill that other lady and tell the Frenchies that the dead lady was Sophy Towbridge, only she unfortunately died? That gets us off the hook with the Frenchies, and we still have our dead lady to give back to those that paid us to kill her. It was a beautiful plan, if I do say so myself. But the other lady fouled it up by escaping, and we never could find her again to kill her. I hear she's in London all safe and sound now. And Sophy Towbridge fell down the stairs at the farmhouse the next morning and broke her neck. Just like that, dead. So we was out the money for her, too."

He shook his head dismally.

"Who hired you to snatch the lady out of her carriage?" Hugh asked.

Marley shrugged.

"Now that I don't know. Donen's the one who handled that end of it."

"Donen?" Hugh questioned, having to work to keep his voice even. He didn't want his informant to stop talking now. But hearing the man relate so cheerfully his and his cronies' plans to murder Claire made him want to wrap his hands around the man's neck and squeeze until there was no life left in him. "Where can I find him?"

"Ah, he's gone off somewhere." That had a purposeful vagueness to it that made Hugh suspect that Marley knew very well where Donen had gone.

"Where?" Hugh couldn't keep the sharpness out of his voice.

Marley shrugged.

"Tell me everything you know, and I'll double your money for you yet again," Hugh said.

Marley perked up like a hunting dog scenting game.

Without even being asked, James moved toward the saddlebags again. There wasn't enough left in the emergency fund, so in the end Hugh and James were reduced to digging through their own purses and pockets, but eventually enough was cobbled together to satisfy Marley.

"It's a pleasure doing business with you gents, it is," Marley said genially as he stuffed his pockets full of cash.

"Donen?" Hugh asked grimly.

"Remember the other lady that I told you about? Well, you see, there's this job. . . ."

As he listened, Hugh felt his blood run cold.

## 30

By the time thirty-six hours had passed since she had confessed her love for Hugh, Claire had worked herself up into a near paroxysm of guilt and fear. She loved Hugh. That was a fact, and over the course of two sleepless nights she had come to accept it as immutable. The thought of what he might at that very moment be doing was torturous. She had little doubt that whatever it was involved his work as an intelligence officer, which meant that it was inherently dangerous. She had to force herself not to dwell on it. Instead she tried to imagine welcoming him home again all safe and sound. That admittedly tantalizing image brought with it its own set of problems: When Hugh did come home, she was going to become his mistress.

There was nothing else to be done. She loved him far too much to try any longer to keep him at arm's length.

Unfortunately, the thought of so blatantly breaking her marriage vows, to say nothing of dishonoring herself and potentially, if her liaison with Hugh was ever discovered, bringing social calumny down on her innocent family, was enough to make her ill.

Finally, on the second morning after Hugh had left, Claire heard the unmistakable sounds of David letting himself into the house just as dawn streaked the sky. She had lain awake all night, agonizing over what to do, and as she listened to David making his way up the stairs she was consumed with guilt over what she was contemplating doing. Never mind that David had very likely lain with many women since their marriage. Never mind that she felt no love or even liking for him now, and never would again. The fact remained that he was her husband. If he cared for her even a little, or could be brought to care for her, she owed it to the vows she had made to rededicate herself to her marriage and to him.

With a heavy heart, Claire climbed out of bed and padded to her bedroom door. She could not rest until she had this sorted out in her mind. She already knew what the solution would be if she decided it solely by the promptings of her heart.

Stepping out into the still-shadowy upstairs hall, she found herself almost face-to-face with David. He blinked at her in surprise, then frowned.

"You look like hell, Madam Wife," he said by way of greeting. "Seeing you with your face all shiny and wearing nothing but your shimmy quite reminds me of why I quit coming to your bed."

She was wearing a perfectly modest night rail, but as his eyes raked her from her tousled hair to her bare toes, Claire felt herself flush. He sneered, and she realized that he was deliberately trying to hurt her.

A sudden insight into her husband's character came to her in that instant: David enjoyed inflicting pain.

"You really *don't* love me, do you?" she asked quietly,

taking an instinctive step back away from him. "I don't think you ever did."

"Are you by any chance trying to entice me into your bed?" David glanced past her, through the open door of her bedchamber, at the massive, rumpled four-poster that she had only ever occupied alone.

"No," Claire said, suddenly wishing with all her being that she had accepted what her heart knew and left the rest alone.

"You're my wife." There was a cruel gleam in David's eyes as, without warning, he grabbed her arm. "Come here, sweet wife. It's your duty to please me, after all."

He shoved her against the wall and leaned his weight on her to keep her there, kissing her in a horrible parody of the way Hugh had kissed her such a short time before. But David's tongue thrusting into her mouth made her want to gag, and David's body pressing against hers made her shrink with revulsion, and David's hands covering her breasts made her want to kill herself, or him. But she remained passive in the face of his assault, realizing that to fight would only stoke his need to hurt her.

The sound of the maid laboriously climbing the stairs with the morning buckets of coal freed her. David lifted himself away from her, glanced toward the top of the stairs, then looked back at Claire.

"No, I don't love you," he said with cutting coldness. "I've never loved you."

Then he turned and walked away from her, heading toward his own chamber farther down the hall, without once looking back. Claire saw the top of the maid's head as it bobbed into view, and fled back into her bedchamber, closing the door. Taking good care to lock it, she then fell upon her bed, and proceeded to cry as if her heart would break.

By that evening, she was once again outwardly composed. But inside she was as shaky as blancmange. Though no longer torn between her heart and her head, she was still desperately worried about Hugh, and still ashamed of what she had every intention of doing once he came home.

She and Beth were engaged with a party of friends to visit Vauxhall Gardens. As it was a large party, consisting of three of Beth's dearest friends, their fond mamas, and four young gentlemen, they took three carriages, rattling in fine style across the bridge over the Thames and thus heading down to the gardens. When the group arrived, very merry, it was to find that the gardens were even lovelier than had been described. They were large, and well supplied with hedged walks and vine-covered alleys that were lit by numerous torches and hanging lanterns. At the center of the gardens was a large open area in which covered booths had been set up that could be hired for an evening. Refreshments were provided, and the evening's entertainment included an orchestra, dancing, and, later in the evening, fireworks.

There were already upward of a dozen couples dancing around inside the large rotunda as they entered their booth, and many more visitors were strolling the grounds, greeting those of their acquaintance whom they encountered and in general enjoying the weather, which this evening was particularly fine. Mr. Whetton, a slender gentleman of twenty-three who was paying serious court to Beth's friend Mary Ivington, was the host of the entertainment, and he immediately offered refreshments as they exclaimed over the festive appearance of the boxes. As this was declined, Beth and Miss Ivington clamored to be taken to see the swans in the ornamental pond. Mr. Whetton and his friend Lord Gaines gallantly obliged them. Claire did not feel obliged to accompany Beth—Mr. Whetton and Lord Gaines were both the most gentlemanly of men—and sat back in the booth, enjoying the promenade of fashionable and less than fashionable attire that passed before her and listening with half an ear to the others playfully squabble over the virtues of dancing versus strolling the grounds.

Claire was watching the parade of people passing in front of the booth and listening to the music quite contentedly when a tall man walking along one of the covered alleys toward the booth caught her eye. It was too dark and he was too far away for her to be certain of anything about him except that he had black hair. But something in the way he moved . . .

"Pray excuse me," she said, getting to her feet. "But I believe I see a friend."

The others nodded, and smiled, and returned immediately to exactly what they had been doing before she spoke. Claire felt her heart speed up as she left the booth, and then her feet were moving faster too as she reached the alley. He was still coming straight toward her, and she was suddenly certain it was Hugh. Her heart seemed to swell with joy, a smile trembled on her lips, and it was all she could do to walk rather than run as she hurried to meet him.

It *was* Hugh, looking very much the duke in a well-fitting coat of blue superfine over biscuit-colored trousers, with his cravat tied in some elegant style the name of which she had quite forgotten and his boots gleaming in the candlelight. He smiled at her, and it was all she could do not to pick up her primrose muslin skirts and fly into his arms.

Conscious of a possible audience, she did not. Instead they met most circumspectly in the middle of the alley, and as she turned her face up to him Hugh smiled down into her eyes.

Claire realized that she was happier to see him than she had ever been to see anyone in her life.

"Did you miss me, puss?" he asked as he had once before, taking her hand and raising it to his lips.

She loved him, she realized, quite desperately. And he was home, and safe, and she was his.

So why were tears spilling from her eyes?

Not wanting him to see, she pulled her hand from his and turned away, walking briskly along a crooked path with high hedges for walls that headed off at right angles from the alley.

"Claire."

He was following her, of course. Claire dashed her fingers across her cheeks, hoping to eradicate all signs of her silliness before he could see. After all, what cause had she to weep? None at all.

The moon slid behind a cloud, and the sounds of the night suddenly multiplied; the breeze turned unexpectedly cold. Claire wrapped her arms around herself and instinctively stopped where she was, glancing around. Just as quick as that, the gardens had turned into a frightening, alien place. She was surrounded by dark shadows that seemed to have grown menacing in the space of a single breath. The hair rose on the back of her neck as something seemed to stir at the far end of the path.

"Claire."

Hugh was behind her, thank goodness. She took a

deep, shaken breath, then turned and walked into his arms.

Instead of closing them around her he caught her upper arms and held her a little away from him, looking down at her with a frown.

"God in heaven. Are you crying?"

"No," Claire said fiercely, although she was. She could feel the wet slide of tears on her cheeks, and would have dashed them away except the blasted man was holding her arms.

He swore. Then he pulled her against him, holding her close and kissing her wet cheek, her neck, her ear.

"Don't cry," he said in her ear. "I love you. Why are you crying?"

Claire's heart began to pound. Her hands had been resting against the front of his coat, flat and passive. Now her arms slid around his neck.

She sniffed, blinking away the last of the tears, and looked up at him.

"I love you too. And because."

He made a sound that was somewhere between a groan and a laugh, and lifted his head, looking down at her. A smile lurked around the corners of his mouth, but his eyes were grave.

"Not that again," he said.

"All right. Because you're back. Because I love you."

"That's a reason to cry?" He shook his head in fond incomprehension.

"Sometimes." She took a deep steadying breath, and met his gaze. His eyes were black in the moonlight, their expression impossible to read, but the curve of his mouth was tender. "I'm ready to be your mistress. Whenever you like."

"Ah," he said, as if something that had been obscured was now made clear.

And then she was locked in his embrace and he was kissing her. She kissed him back as if she meant never to stop. When finally he lifted his head, she rested her cheek against his chest for a minute. She could hear the fierce beating of his heart beneath her ear.

"Claire," he said, lifting her chin so that he could look down into her face. She leaned against him, too weak with reaction to that kiss to even think about stirring, and let him tilt her face up for his inspection. "I love you. Hell, I want to marry you. I would marry you tomorrow if I could."

"But you can't." Despair colored her voice, and her thoughts. "There's David."

"Yes, there's David." He seemed to hesitate. "Claire, there's something I need to tell you. Ever since you left France I've had people watching over you, and other people investigating just how it was that your carriage came to be attacked. Last night I finally stumbled across the truth." He briefly told her about Marley and Sophy Towbridge and the rest. "I think David wants you dead. I think he hired someone to kill you."

"Why would he do that?" She was both shocked and bewildered. She and David didn't have a good marriage, but he didn't hate her—at least, she didn't think he did. And he had never actually harmed her, although that morning, for a moment, she had been afraid he might. But he hadn't. Surely he didn't want her dead.

"He never liked women very much," Hugh said, slowly and carefully. "At least, not as anything except toys. I've known him since we were boys, remember, although we have never been close, or even what you would call friends. I didn't think he would ever marry. When you convinced me that he had indeed married you, I was surprised, but you, my dove, are a singular beauty and I assumed David must have changed enough to appreciate you since I had last seen him. But then when you went back to England, I started thinking, and I had someone look into the matter. You had a dowry of twenty thousand pounds, love, and David is deep into dun territory even now. In fact, by the time your carriage was attacked he had lost almost all his money and yours as well. He was padding expenses on my estates and pocketing the difference to get by."

"Are you saying David married me for my money?" Claire gasped. The dowry had been a gift from Nick, because, he said, he loved her as if she were his own sister and because he didn't want anything—such as the scandal he and Gabby had stirred up when the *ton* thought they were a brother and sister falling in love—to stand in the way of her making the match she wanted. That money had freed her to marry whomever she chose—and she had squandered it by choosing David. But then, she comforted herself, any choice she made then would have been wrong. Hugh had not yet walked into her life.

Hugh shrugged. "I would say so. He went through that money in less than six months. Then it's my opinion that he panicked. He started gambling heavily, betting on the ponies, and losing until he was even deeper in debt than when he married you. I think that was about the time he decided to get rid of you and find himself another female with another large dowry."

"Are you sure?" Claire couldn't believe it.

Hugh shook his head. "Not completely. If I had any real proof, he'd be sitting in jail at this moment. But I think so. I can't think of anyone else who would have anything to gain by killing you, can you?"

"No." The thought that David might actually have hired those thugs who had attacked her carriage to kill her began to sink in, and cold chills went chasing up and down her spine. "Dear God."

"Don't worry. You've been perfectly safe since you left France. I've had men watching over your every step. I won't let anything happen to you, I give you my word. But that brings me to another point: David is desperate. I believe he is desperate enough to have tried to have you killed. If I offered him a large enough sum of money, I think I could induce him to give you a divorce."

For a moment Claire simply stared at him without speaking. A divorce. The very idea was so shocking that she didn't know what to say. She couldn't get a divorce. No one got divorced. It took a bill of parliament to get a divorce. Her family would be shamed forever. Beth's prospects in the marriage mart would be totally ruined. And she—she would never again be received anywhere outside the bosom of her family. She would be marked as a loose woman forever.

But she would have Hugh, legally and forever.

"A divorce," she said numbly, unable to believe she was even considering such a thing.

"I love you," he said again. "I want to spend the rest of my life with you. Let David divorce you, and marry me. Or, if you can't stomach a divorce, run away with me, and I'll pay David to keep it quiet. I'm a rich man, and a duke, for what it's worth. I'll take good care of you, I swear."

"Oh, Hugh." Her voice trembled. Her eyes searched every chiseled feature, caressed every plane and angle of his lean dark face. Then she realized that there was only one choice she could make: She chose Hugh, however she could get him. If she could have Hugh, she would ask for nothing else from God for the rest of her life. His broad shoulders blocked her view of the rest of the garden. She could no longer see past him to make sure they were still alone. But she didn't care, just at that moment. She was getting ready to cast her cap over the windmill with a vengeance, and she didn't care if there were a hundred spectators to cheer her on.

"I love . . ."

Before she could finish what she was saying, something came swinging out of the darkness to smash hard into the back of Hugh's head. There was a sickening thump, and he instantly stiffened. Claire barely had time to register what was happening as his eyes widened for an instant before they rolled back in his head and he started to crumple in her arms.

"Hugh!" Horrified, she tried to support his dead weight even as she opened her mouth to scream. But before so much as a squeak could emerge, something slammed hard into her temple, and the world went black.

## ❧ 31 ❧

........................................

*H*ugh's first thought, when he groggily opened his eyes, was that he must have imbibed far too deeply the night before, because he had the mother and father of all hangovers now. His head felt like thousands of tiny hammers were pounding a hole in the back of his skull, he was seeing two and in some cases three of everything, and he was sick to his stomach to boot. The funny thing about it was, he wasn't, in the ordinary way of things, much of a drinking man anymore. In his salad days, he'd been in his cups about as frequently as he'd been sober, and he'd had the reputation to prove it. But since joining the army he'd stopped drinking almost entirely. Drinking to excess the night before a battle was about the best way he knew of for a man to get his head blown off, and for the first few years after he'd left England there'd been battle after battle after battle.

Then, seven years ago, they'd recruited him for the intelligence service. He'd been less than willing, at first, because he'd enjoyed what he was doing, and as a young and idealistic officer he'd felt a great weight of responsibility for his men, but they—Hildebrand most particularly—had talked him around with the argument that his country needed him. They'd had a specific assignment for him at the time: They'd wanted to throw him into a cell with a man they were holding on other charges but suspected of being a French agent. Hugh's job was to pose as a French sympathizer himself, make friends with the man, and get him to confide in him. As an inducement for the other man to trust him, they'd claimed that Hugh had passed military secrets to the enemy, and charged him with treason.

The ploy had worked. The man, thinking he had found a kindred spirit in Hugh, had talked freely. His job done, Hugh had been removed from the cell, only to discover to his dismay that among some of his fellow soldiers a charge of treason, even when it was dismissed, never really went away. Too proud to defend himself with the truth, he'd defended himself with his pistol and his sword and his fists instead. Still, when Hildebrand had come to him with another offer, Hugh had been all too ready to accept. This time he had stayed in the intelligence service, and had eventually come to realize that it was where he belonged.

But drinking while working as a spy was even more foolhardy than drinking when getting ready to ride into battle. So how, then, had he come by this head?

Curse it, where was James? What he needed, and right now too, was James's special concoction. . . .

His hands were tied. Hugh registered that as he tried to roll onto his back from his side. At almost the exact instant, he realized that he was lying on a carpet rather than a bed—and someone was standing over him, looking down at him, a pistol held rather loosely in his hand.

"Awake, are you?" The face swam in and out of focus, but Hugh didn't need to get a better look at it to know who the speaker was: That blond hair turned into a shining nimbus by the candle that flickered on the night table near the bed was all the identification required.

"David. What the devil . . . ?"

"Hullo, Hugh."

His ankles were tied too, and his knees. In fact, Hugh discovered as he tried to move, he was trussed like a Christmas goose. His head throbbed, his vision came in and out of focus, and his stomach churned, but Hugh had been in enough tight spots in his life that he had learned how to disregard little things like physical discomfort when necessary to focus on big things—like the threat of imminent death.

It was the horse. The horse. The thrice-damned horse. Last night he'd been thrown by his horse. It was a warning, as he should have known by now. How could he have let down his guard?

There was another man standing with his back to the door, Hugh saw, a big burly fellow in an oversized frieze coat and well-worn breeches who was obviously some kind of hired thug. A slouch hat was pulled low over his eyes, and, like David, he was armed with a pistol.

This was a tight spot, no question about it. As he recognized that he was in mortal danger, Hugh's thought processes simultaneously sharpened and cooled. He was bound hand and foot, lying on a musty-smelling carpet in a small bedroom that seemed at least vaguely familiar, and David was standing over him with a pistol. Suddenly everything came back to him in a flash: the mad ride back to London; Vauxhall Gardens; the blow to the head; Claire.

"Where's Claire?" If he felt a flash of stark fear—and he did—his voice revealed none of it. Knowing David as he did, though, he felt his heart begin to race. David was capable of inflicting pain for pain's sake, and Claire was vulnerable.

"You mean my wife? Right behind you." David made a negligent gesture with his head. Hugh, rolling over clumsily, found her with his eyes. She was crouched in a corner formed by the night table and the wall not far from where he lay, her once elegant coiffure now sadly disordered so that stray locks of black hair trailed over her shoulders and down her back, her hands obviously bound behind her though he couldn't see the rope. Her knees beneath the soft yellow muslin of her skirt were folded up so tightly against her body that they practically touched her chin, her beautiful thick-lashed golden eyes were red rimmed from the tears she had shed in the garden and huge with fear as they met his—and there was a fresh bruise purpling on her temple. Her lower lip was swollen and split, and a tiny rivulet of blood trickled from one corner of her mouth.

That kind of injury was the result of a backhand to the face. He'd seen it before; it was, in fact, fairly common among the camp followers who traveled with the army. The females among them came in for rough treatment more often than most of the officers cared to think about.

"You hit her." Hugh's whole body stiffened. His eyes promised murder as they slashed to David's face. Sheer blind rage coursed through his veins. *I'm going to kill you for that,* he promised David silently. But he managed to choke back the threat. If ever there was a time to be careful, this was it. "By God, you bastard, you hit her. What kind of man hits a woman?"

"As ever, cousin, you're a gallant champion for the world's whores." David strolled over to him again, careful this time not to get too close. "I'm sure they appreciate it, but it makes you look rather a fool. I suppose it's because your mother was one. It's a pity my uncle the duke didn't find out what she was before he married her. We all would have been spared much."

He glanced at Claire. "Did he tell you about his mother? She was pregnant with him when she married my uncle. She was of good family, too, which makes it all the more surprising. She took a lover and got pregnant, and when her lover died she married my uncle and tried to pass the babe off as his, claiming he was a seven months' child. She would have succeeded, too, if Hugh here hadn't looked so much like his real father. The Lynes are all fair, you see. He's the only blackbird in the bunch. My uncle suspected the truth because Hugh's real father was his good friend, and he wore his wife down until at last she confessed. Then he spent the next few years beating her senseless, until at last she did the decent thing and died."

David glanced back at him again. His eyes were full of malice. "You were what, thirteen at the time, Hugh? What a tragedy." He returned his attention to Claire. "My uncle would have disowned the bastard as well, but he couldn't face labeling himself a fool and a cuckold so publicly. So what we have here is a usurper. Hugh here has no more right to call himself Duke of Richmond than you do. I should be the duke. He doesn't have a drop of Lynes blood in his veins."

It had taken him a long time to come to terms with

his family history, Hugh thought, but he finally had. To hear David relate it so mockingly would once have been more than he could bear, as David well knew. But Hugh was a man now, not the wild boy David had known, and while any mention of his mother, dead now these fifteen years, brought pain with it, talk of the circumstances of her life—and death—no longer filled him with blind rage. As for the duke—he no longer called him Father even in his thoughts—he'd died when Hugh was twenty-five. His last words to his heir had been to reiterate his belief that Hugh was not his son, and express his wish that Hugh meet with an untimely end before he could have a son of his own and thus return the title to the one who should rightfully hold it.

David, in fact.

Though Hugh had not admitted it even to himself for a long time, after the old duke had died he had done his best to make his ersatz father's dying wish come true. From guilt, he supposed. Only in the last couple of years had he truly come to believe, deep inside, that he deserved to be alive.

"Hugh," Claire said, her voice a raspy whisper that both worried him and brought him back to the present immediately. She sounded as if her throat had been hurt—what had the bastard done to her while he, Hugh, had been knocked out? As myriad possibilities presented themselves, he felt his muscles tighten and bunch, and willed them to relax. Fury was a luxury he couldn't afford at the moment. "David means to burn this house with us in it."

David smiled at Hugh.

"Oh, I'm going to shoot you both in the head first, of course. I don't believe in causing unnecessary suffering."

There was a mocking note to David's voice. Then his gaze swung to Claire, and without warning he pointed the pistol at her smooth white forehead. Hugh felt his heart leap and his blood run cold. "You first. Stand up."

Hugh's muscles tensed, and he prepared to do what he could. If he was lucky, that would be to hook David's legs with his and knock him to the floor. It wouldn't save their lives—the thug would probably shoot him within seconds, and if he didn't, David, once he had recovered, surely would—but it was better than watching the woman he loved be shot before his eyes. With truly commendable self-control, Hugh held off, waiting for just the right moment, his eyes fixed on David's trigger finger so intensely that he broke into a cold sweat, hoping that he would have some warning, enough warning, if David actually decided to pull the trigger. Even as he focused on David's hand curling around the pistol, out of the corner of his eye he was aware of Claire, brave little thing that she was when cornered, as he knew from his own experience of cornering her, slowly standing up, giving David back icy stare for icy stare. Given David's particular nature—he was the type who, as a child, had enjoyed pulling the wings off flies—that was definitely the wrong thing to do, though Hugh could not help but mentally salute her courage in doing it. He'd found her boldness charming. David would want to crush her until she whimpered at his feet.

"David." He said the name sharply, as a distraction. It worked, postponing the inevitable a little longer. His cousin looked at him, and the pistol lowered. Hugh let his breath out in a quiet, careful sigh. He felt like a condemned man who had just been given a reprieve. "Tell me something: Why are you doing this?"

Seeming to lose interest in Claire for the nonce, David crossed the room to look down at him. He was dressed in a bottle-green coat and tan breeches, with his linen immaculate and not a hair out of place. Except for the pistol in his hand, he seemed completely as he usually did. There wasn't even a mad glitter in his eyes to explain what was going on in his mind. He looked perfectly sane, perfectly normal.

Perhaps he was. Hugh realized that this thought was scarier than the alternative.

"Oh, how about—you were kissing my wife in the garden."

Obviously David, or one of his thugs, had been watching them. Hugh felt another stab of stark fear penetrate his careful calm, then realized that it was for Claire. He'd faced death himself many times, and never turned a hair. But he was terrified for Claire.

"By the way, coz, I salute you for your address: You've been back in England for one month, and in that time you've managed to seduce my wife."

Hugh said nothing. He didn't think that telling David the truth of how he and Claire had met would accomplish anything at the moment except to further enrage David. He blamed himself for this entire debacle. He should have been more careful. With him there, in a public place, he'd thought her safe. Who'd have thought that attackers might be waiting for her in Vauxhall Gardens?

But this was not the time for self-recriminations. He had to focus if he had any chance at all of getting her out of there alive.

"This isn't about that." Hugh said it with absolute certainty. His instinct was to stall for time, and he was a great believer in following his instincts. They had saved him more than once. Sooner or later, James would miss him—but of course, even then, even if it was sooner rather than later, James would have no way of knowing where he was. "You don't care if she sleeps with me or fifty other men. You were trying to kill her long before tonight—you arranged the attack on her coach."

For a moment David simply stared at him. Then he gave a snort of laughter.

"So well informed as you are," he marveled. "I'm impressed, I must admit." He glanced at Claire, who was still standing, leaning back against the night table now as if her legs had grown too weak from fear or trauma to support her, and his expression changed, turning openly cruel. "She's quite a pretty thing, isn't she? And she came with a nice dowry, too. But the money's long since spent and the bloom is off the rose and you've informed me that you won't bankroll me anymore, so I've had to make alternate arrangements. The original plan was simply to arrange an accident for her that would permit me to take a new wife with a new dowry—actually, the one I had in mind was a real heiress, the Chalmondley chit, you might have seen her around town, buck-toothed as a rabbit but father's rich as Golden Ball—but Donen here and his band of incompetents let my wife escape. Imagine my surprise when she turned up unharmed. Nothing for it but to let the plan go fallow for a few months. A second accident right on the heels of the first would look too suspicious."

Donen? The leader of the band who had attacked Claire's carriage with the intent of killing her? Hugh's gaze slashed to him again. Silently he vowed vengeance. Marley had already felt his wrath. By now he should be in the custody of the Bow Street Runners—and this fellow would be lucky if he suffered a fate as benevolent as that.

All at once Hugh became aware of a peculiar smell. A smell that didn't belong in this long-closed room. An acrid smell. Hugh glanced in Claire's direction. She was staring straight ahead with the utmost concentration—and then he saw, with a jumbled burst of shock at her audacity, pride at her courage and ingenuity, and terror lest she be found out, that she was holding her bound hands over the candle flame, burning the rope in two.

Such was the angle at which he lay that he could see what she was doing quite clearly. He didn't think David could, or the thug at the door.

But both of them could smell.

David was saying something to Donen. Heart pounding like a drum, fear for Claire's safety so tangible that it left a metallic taste in his mouth, Hugh didn't catch quite what it was. Looking up at David as he finished speaking, Hugh hurried into speech.

"We could come to an arrangement, you and I. You don't want her, I do. Suppose I paid you to divorce her? Say, a hundred thousand pounds. That should set you up handsomely for some time to come, and you wouldn't need to kill anyone."

David looked at him and seemed to consider, then shook his head. Hugh already knew that it was a lost cause; David would have to be a fool to accept, and David, whatever else he was, was no fool. But providing a distraction was Hugh's object, and as such his offer worked.

"Now that is really very tempting, I must admit. But you and I both know that this has gone too far. In any case, tonight while I lurked among the bushes at Vaux-hall Gardens I had a truly brilliant flash of inspiration. Why not kill you both? I would then be the fabulously wealthy Duke of Richmond, which by rights I should be anyway, and free of my unwanted wife, all in one stroke. It's quite a neat plan. I'm actually very proud of it."

Claire's shoulders seemed to slump, and then she sidled back toward the wall. David, focusing on him, didn't appear to notice. The thug at the door seemed half asleep. Hugh was on pins and needles. Had she succeeded? He couldn't tell.

"You'll never get away with it," Hugh said.

In truth, he realized, David might or might not. He was an obvious suspect, after all, but upon Hugh's death he would become the Duke of Richmond, very powerful, very rich. It was Hugh's experience that the authorities were careful to tread lightly where rich, powerful nobles were concerned. But whether David got away with it or not didn't really matter, because once that became the question, he and Claire would be dead.

"I think I will." David glanced at Claire, then back at Hugh. He seemed to notice nothing amiss, while Hugh's heart nearly stopped. "It was apparently quite obvious in the ballroom when you two first met at little Beth's come-out that there was an attraction between you two. My mother remarked on it when she came to tell me that you had danced my wife right off the dance floor onto the terrace and would I please do something to control my wife before she embroiled us all in a dreadful scandal. Not terribly discreet, were you? Did you really think no one would notice? Then again, when you danced with her at Almack's and afterward when you both disappeared at the same time,

Mother said my wife's behavior, and yours as well, was most shocking. Tonight, when I saw you kissing her, that popped into my head, and the whole plan came together like it was meant to be. Your reputation is such a help, you know: You are considered a notorious libertine. When your bodies are found, here is what will appear to have happened: You spirited my wife away from Vauxhall Gardens to this house—it's the one in Curzon Street where you used to keep your mistresses, Hugh, don't you recognize it?—which fortunately at the moment is empty. While you, vile seducer, are working your wicked wiles on her, the house catches fire with both of you, most unfortunately, inside. It burns to the ground; your bodies are charred beyond recognition—too charred for anyone to tell that you perished from a gunshot wound before the flames ever reached you."

A knock sounded at the door, interrupting. David glanced around. The thug—Donen—opened it. Another thug was outside. A strong smell wafted in through the open door. It took Hugh a second, but he recognized it: kerosene.

David had ordered the house soaked with kerosene. Once lit, it would go up like dry tinder. The ensuing blaze would in all likelihood be hot enough to burn any bodies inside past recognition.

"We be all set. Just give the word, and we'll be strikin' the match."

David nodded. "Go ahead. We'll be right down."

He started walking toward the door. For one hope-filled moment, Hugh thought that he might actually be going to leave them, supposedly bound and helpless, to take their chances with the fire.

Donen was still holding the door open, and as David passed him he glanced back at Hugh.

"Duke of Richmond," he said musingly. "It has a nice ring to it, does it not?"

Then he walked past Donen into the hall.

"Shoot them," he said over his shoulder, and was gone.

## ❦ 32 ❦

·······························

As soon as she'd opened her eyes to see several of the men who had attacked her coach standing over her, Claire had known that they were going to try to kill her. They hadn't succeeded the first time, and they'd come back to finish what they'd started. They were mostly all there: the leader, Donen, she'd heard him called; Briggs, whom she'd hit over the head with a chamber pot; and two others whose names she'd never heard. Marley, of the hounds, was the only one missing. It was her nightmare, and it was happening all over again.

Then David had walked into the room, walked right up to her and hit her across the face with no warning at all, sending her reeling back against the wall, bumping her head, cutting her lip.

"That's for making a fool out of me," he'd said. She'd looked at him, hating him even as she wiped the blood from her mouth. And to her vast relief, fury had driven out fear. Her whole life she had been surrounded by evil, violent men. How ironic it was that, when she'd tried so hard to get the opposite, she'd ended up with a man as evil and violent as her father had been beneath his handsome, civilized facade?

Hugh had been right. It was David who'd wanted her dead all along, David who'd hired the men to waylay her coach, David who was behind the attack in the garden tonight. But David didn't know what she was made of. The only way she'd survived her girlhood intact was because, when her back was to the wall, she was willing to fight like a badger for her life.

And her back was to the wall tonight.

When Donen, with an evil smirk that promised retribution for her previous escape from him, had pulled her hands behind her back and tied them so tightly that her fingers went numb, she'd known she couldn't expect any mercy at all from these merciless men.

They all, every one of them, meant to see her dead.

She meant to survive any way she could.

Then they had carried Hugh into the room and dumped him on the floor without ceremony. After all, why worry about hurting a man they meant to kill?

For a hideous moment she'd wondered if he was dead already, and had started forward with a cry. A hard swipe of Donen's forearm had sent her reeling back against the wall. It had caught her across the throat, and sent her, choking and coughing, sliding down until she was all but sitting on the floor. Her eyes had never left Hugh, and it was with some relief that she had watched Briggs kneel beside him, tying his hands and legs with brutal efficiency.

He was not dead, then. They would not have bothered to tie a dead man.

Then David had come to stand over her. He was holding a pistol, and she'd almost been afraid. But then she remembered how he had hit her, and rage came flooding back to drive out fear. She welcomed the hot, fierce rush. It gave her strength and courage, both of which she would need to survive.

Then Hugh had stirred, and David had left her to stand over him.

Luckily, after that David had been far more concerned with Hugh than with her. She had taken stock of the situation and come up with the best plan she could devise, all the while listening to David baiting Hugh. She had known another sharp moment of fear when David had pointed the pistol at her forehead and ordered her to stand up. But then she had looked into his eyes and had seen how much he relished her fear, and she had stuffed it back down deep inside herself as she had learned to do with any and all unwanted emotions as a child. Standing tall, she had looked him in the eye.

Even as Hugh had drawn David's attention to himself, she had seen the candle and known what she needed to do.

Now, even as David's order to shoot them still hung in the air and Donen closed the door, then took two steps inside the room to carry it out, Claire braced herself for action. Her skin tingled and burned from where the flame that had freed her wrists had singed it, but she barely felt the pain.

The time had come to fight for her life. Her life, and Hugh's.

Hugh was lying on his side on the floor, staring grimly up at Donen. His muscles were tense. His head was several inches above the carpet, straining upward on his strong neck, and his shoulder seemed to be pressing hard into the floor, as if he would use it for leverage. His face was grim, his eyes fixed unwaveringly on Donen's face.

Donen, face contorted in a taunting smirk, lifted the pistol and aimed it at Hugh.

Claire screamed.

"Bloody 'ell!" Donen glanced up, startled, as the sound ricocheted through the room. The pistol jerked to one side. Then Hugh moved, whipping his bound legs across the floor like a bludgeon, catching Donen's ankles and knocking his feet out from under him. With a bellow, Donen shot up in the air, hung suspended above the floor for the space of a couple of heartbeats, then came crashing down on his back. For a moment he simply lay there, stunned.

The pistol made a beautiful somersault and landed on the bed.

"Get it! Get the pistol."

Hugh's command was unnecessary. Even as Claire dived for it, Hugh wriggled across the carpet like a snake, getting into position, turning onto his back. Then he lifted his legs high into the air and crashed his bound feet, with all the strength of his legs behind them, into Donen's neck.

The man made a harsh choking sound and seemed to convulse. Then he lay still.

Pistol in hand, Claire scrambled off the bed and stood over Donen for a minute, looking down at him wide-eyed.

"Is he dead?"

"I don't know. Lock the door, then come untie me. I have a feeling we don't have much time."

Claire hurried to do as he said. Even as she turned the key in the lock, she became aware of an unpleasant smell. It was strong, and acrid, and she knew at once what it was.

"The house is on fire!"

She ran back to kneel beside Hugh, placing the pistol on the floor within easy reach and keeping a wary eye on Donen all the time.

"I guessed as much."

At last the knots came undone, and Hugh's hands were free. Wispy tendrils of smoke crept beneath the door, curling up into the room. To Claire's horror, she realized that she could hear a distant crackling.

"Leave me. Go out the window," he said, yanking at the knots binding his ankles. Claire, just as busy unraveling the knots in the rope around his knees, shook her head.

"Dammit, Claire," he began angrily. Then the rope around his ankles came free, and the rope around his knees suddenly became easy to dislodge. He scooped up the pistol and stood up, then moved swiftly to the window. Claire was right behind him every step of the way. Thrusting the pistol into the waistband of his breeches, Hugh tried with all his strength to open the window. It didn't budge.

Hugh swore. "That leaves the door. Come on."

Catching her hand, he pulled her to the door. Smoke was pouring under it now. He turned the key in the lock, then hesitated, looking back at Donen. The man was making feeble swimming movements. Clearly he was not dead.

"Hell and the devil confound it," Hugh said bitterly, and practically leaped across the room to Donen's side.

"Get up." He dragged the man to his feet. Donen swayed drunkenly and almost collapsed. Supporting him, Hugh swore again, then put his shoulder to the man's stomach and lifted him in a fireman's carry. Hugh grimaced at his weight, then headed back for the door.

"Hang on to my coat, and stay low."

Claire did as he told her, and they moved out into the upper hall. Bent almost double, they hurried along it. Smoke was curling up the stairs and filling the upper hall. Claire ducked lower to avoid it, but when they reached the top of the stairs it became impossible. The stairs had become a chimney, and even as they started to descend, smoke rose all around them, thick sooty smoke that roiled and curled and slid up her nose and down her throat. She coughed, choking, then coughed some more. Hugh was coughing too, and she clutched the tail of his coat like a lifeline. The smoke stung her eyes, and it was difficult to see. He was no more than a hunched black shape, rendered almost unrecognizable by the bulk of Donen impaled on his shoulder. Below she could see an orange glow, and hear the crackling and popping of fire.

But the fire and the smoke weren't their only enemies, or even their main ones. David and his thugs were that—and she knew, without knowing how she knew, that they were nearby. They would be waiting to make certain she and Hugh did not escape.

They were halfway down the stairs, and she could see tongues of flame racing up the curtains, licking at the walls. The whole first floor of the house seemed to be ablaze. The three steps remaining on the stairs suddenly seemed like three miles. She was growing dizzy, her mind whirling even as her eyes burned and she felt as if she were suffocating on the thick smoke.

"Almost there." Hugh was choking too, bending low

under Donen's weight. He stumbled and nearly went down, catching hold of the banister seconds before he would have fallen down the remaining stairs. Claire cried out in alarm and grabbed his arm. There was a clatter, a metallic clatter, as something fell down the stairs ahead of them. It was too dark to see what it was, but Claire didn't have to see to know what it was: the pistol. They'd lost it. Finding it again was impossible. It was too dark, too smoky, and there was no time. The fire was taking on new life, leaping toward them across the floor, and Claire knew that if they didn't get out soon, they would never escape.

Then suddenly, miraculously, they were on flat ground, a carpeted floor, moving toward the door. At least, Claire hoped they were moving toward the door. She had lost all sense of direction, all ability to judge time or distance. She could only cling to Hugh's coat, and cough, and pray.

"Master Hugh!"

It was James's voice, James's solid shape rushing toward them through the smoke and flames.

"Here!" Hugh was hoarse, coughing. James reached them, dragging Donen off Hugh's shoulders and onto his own back.

"This way."

Hugh's hand grabbed hers, and, bending low, together they followed James while fire raced across the ceiling and pieces of flaming wood and plaster dropped like leaves in autumn around them. Her eyes were watering so badly that she could hardly see, and her throat burned. Black smoke coiled around them, making it almost impossible to breathe, and the roar of the fire was all she could hear. She turned herself over to God and

Hugh, and seconds later she felt a rush of fresh air. Then she knew they were going to make it. Following Hugh, she staggered out onto a small stoop still graced with a bright pot of flowers, and sucked blessedly cool air into her lungs. Knees threatening to buckle with every step, she started down the shallow steps, Hugh still holding her hand in a death grip.

"No!" It was a shout, full of fury and despair, and it made Claire look up, made her search the darkness with her watery, burning eyes, riveting her attention with its anguish. A group of men rushed toward them, surrounding them, lifting Donen away from James, and even as Claire sank to her knees she identified the author of that cry.

It was David, standing in the grip of a trio of men, his gaze fixed on her and Hugh as they dropped to the lawn in front of the burning house. Hugh was coughing desperately, and she was too, her lungs aching as she fought to expel the smoke she had inhaled, but still something made her keep her eyes on David. As she watched he tore himself free of the men holding him, and rushed toward her and Hugh. He had a pistol in his hand.

"Hugh!" she shrieked, or tried to shriek, but the sound emerged scarcely louder than a croak. But he heard, and looked up, frozen for an instant in place. He fumbled at the waistband of his breeches, but came up empty. There was nothing they could do to defend themselves. She tried to get to her feet, to move, but her strength was spent. Still on his knees too, Hugh thrust her behind him.

A shot rang out. Hugh gasped, jerking, clutching at the front of his coat. Claire screamed. David rushed on by even as she grabbed for Hugh, looking at the two of them, his face contorted in a mask of hate. Then he leaped up the steps, and disappeared into the burning house.

"Come back here, you!" Men pounded after David, though how many Claire couldn't have said. Her arms were around Hugh now, and she had the feeling that she was all that was keeping him upright.

"Hugh! Hugh!"

"I'm hit," he said, the words surprisingly distinct. "Don't worry, it's not too bad."

Then he swayed, and even with her arms around him trying to hold him back he toppled sideways onto the grass.

At that precise moment, a shot rang out in the house.

# ❧ 33 ❧

·································

"Milady, I've got bad news." Still leaning over Hugh, Claire glanced up at the speaker, uncomprehending. He was a slight, wiry man in his midfifties perhaps, and stood regarding her anxiously, his cap in his hand.

"What is it?" She was impatient. James, kneeling on Hugh's other side, had peeled off his coat to stanch the bleeding wound. A carriage was being brought around to convey him home.

"Your 'usband—I'm sorry—'e's dead."

Claire went suddenly still. Sinking back on her haunches, she stared up at him. A glance over her shoulder told her that the house still burned; bright flames crackled toward the sky, brightening the night in all directions and painting everything in the vicinity orange. A bucket brigade threw water on the worst of the fire. It seemed to make no difference. She could feel its heat from where she sat.

"I followed 'im inside. I saw 'im do it, but I couldn't stop 'im." There was apology and belligerence mixed in his tone.

"Do what?" She still did not understand.

"The fire didn't get 'im, milady. 'E shot 'imself."

"Oh, dear God." Claire couldn't help it. The news struck her like a slap in the face, and made her feel ill. "Why would he do such a thing?"

She was too numb to decide exactly what she felt about David's death. Paramount, she realized, was relief that he wouldn't be able to hurt her or Hugh anymore.

"Milady, we'd told 'im, when we grabbed 'im out in the street: 'E was under arrest for hiring out the murder of your coachman, and your own kidnapping, and for the attempted murder of you and 'Is Grace there."

"He wouldn't have wanted to live. He would have been disgraced, ruined." Hugh's voice was faint, but hearing it at all struck joy into Claire's heart.

"Hugh." She leaned over him, laying her hand gently against his bristly cheek. He turned his head and his lips brushed a butterfly kiss against the edge of her palm. "Don't try to talk. A carriage is coming to convey you to your house, and a surgeon is to meet us there."

His eyes were open, gleaming deep gray in the light from the fire, and he smiled rather faintly at her. James was pressing his tightly folded coat to a spot high on Hugh's left shoulder. His pursed lips and the rigid set of his shoulders conveyed volumes of disapproval that his master should be thinking of trying to do anything at all.

"Don't worry about me. It's scarcely more than a flesh wound, I promise you. I've had far worse, and survived it." Hugh reached for her hand, and she entwined her fingers with his. Then he looked beyond her at the man who had brought her the news about David.

"You're from Bow Street, I take it. What's your name?"

"Sam Dunn. And I was charged with investigatin' milady 'ere's kidnappin' some months ago. Last night we took a fellow into custody who told us all about it, and we started lookin' up his friends whut he claimed were involved. The rest just sort of fell out from there."

Hugh's gaze flickered to Claire.

"We've got good information on this case, Yer Grace, plus a star witness, one Mr. Marley. The rest of these will likely swing." He nodded to his left. Looking that way, Claire perceived two men bending over Donen, who was kneeling on the ground, engaged in a protracted fit of coughing. Beyond him was the street, where small knots of onlookers had gathered to watch the blaze.

"I have something to say to you, Mr. Dunn," Hugh said.

"Mr. Hugh, the carriage is at hand. There'll be plenty of time for talkin' after this ball comes out of your shoulder." James spoke in a scolding tone, and looked up at Claire as if for support.

"I agree with James," she said, looking down at Hugh.

"You two are not going to start ganging up on me, are you?" Despite its increasing faintness, his voice was touched with wry humor. "I'll not have it, and so I warn you both."

"Pish-tosh," said James with a sniff.

Claire smiled. "I agree with James."

"Oh, Lord. I can see my life is going to be a misery from here on out." But Hugh managed a smile as he said it, and caught her hand, carrying it to his mouth. Then he seemed to look past her to get an unimpeded view of Dunn again.

"I would ask you a favor," he said abruptly, addressing Dunn. He was no longer smiling. "My cousin—he leaves a mother who loved him dearly. For her sake, I would ask you to say nothing of any crime he may have committed, or tried to commit, or how he died. I would tell her—and the world—that he was killed in the accidental burning of my house, nothing more. I will make it worth your while, of course."

Mr. Dunn inclined his head. "Very well, Yer Grace. As Yer Grace wishes."

"Master Hugh, you've bled so much you've soaked through my coat! And here are George and William, two of our own footmen, to carry you to the carriage. I hope you've no more members of the lower orders you wish to carry on a conversation with before that may be done?"

"No, James, I am quite ready," Hugh said meekly, and suffered himself to be picked up and borne off to the carriage. Claire walked beside him, smiling sympathetically down at him as he winced at being bobbled over a rough patch of ground, or flinched at being lifted into the carriage.

"I want to talk to you once this thrice-damned ball is out of my shoulder," he said, possessing himself of her hand as she settled herself on the seat beside him. "You will oblige me by not making any plans until I have done so."

"Very well," she said, smiling at him. They rode together largely in silence after that until they reached Richmond House, and immediately set it to bustling.

Hugh was carried upstairs to the surgeon, who was waiting for him, and Claire was left with the unenviable task of breaking the news of David's death to his mother. In her whole life, she thought as she sat down beside Lady George in that lady's bedchamber, with her maid well stocked with smelling salts and hovering close at hand, there had never been a task she wished for less.

## ❧ 34 ❧

·······························

In the event, it was nearly a week later before Claire had a chance to have any substantive conversation with Hugh again. This opportunity came about only because, tired of waiting for her to put in an appearance on her own, he had sent James to summon her to his side. It was late afternoon, and the house was hushed and quiet. Hugh was in his bedchamber, propped up in bed, clad in a fresh white nightshirt with his shoulder bandaged beneath. As he himself had prophesied, the wound was not life-threatening, although loss of blood and the fever that had accompanied it had kept him abed for longer than he had cared to endure. As a consequence, he was cranky, and in need of a shave, and so endearing withal that Claire could not help but smile lovingly at him even as he tried to dictate to her.

He greeted her abruptly, then said, "I will procure a special license for us as soon as I am out of this bed, and we can be married—say, at the end of next week."

Still smiling, Claire shook her head at him. Their hands were clasped on top of the blanket, and his tightened over hers as she did.

"I can't do that, I'm afraid," she said.

"What do you mean, you can't do that? Do what? Marry me?"

He sounded exactly like a peevish little boy.

"I can't marry you next week," she clarified.

"Very well, then. Let us say, the following week."

She smiled gently at him. "Let us say, this time next year."

He stared at her, clearly not sure he could believe his ears. "What?"

"Next year," she said firmly. "David hasn't even been in the ground three days. The proper period for a widow to wait before remarrying is at least a year."

"To hell with that." He looked outraged. "You cannot in all seriousness expect me to wait a year."

Claire shook her head at him. "And you cannot in all seriousness expect me to marry you next week. The scandal would be unbelievable."

"I don't care about the scandal."

"I do."

He was beginning to frown at her. "I love you."

"I love you, too."

"If you love me, you'll damned well marry me."

"I want to marry you. I will marry you. But not for a year."

"You're really serious, aren't you?" He stared at her in disbelief.

She nodded.

"I'm guessing you want to have a big wedding. Church. Bridesmaids. Do it up right." He didn't sound as though he found the prospect totally enthralling.

"Actually, it will be my second wedding," she said meekly. "I thought we would keep it small, with basically just my sisters and brother-in-law, and a few other select relatives and friends."

"That doesn't sound so bad." His face brightened a couple of degrees. "That should be fairly easy to arrange. All right, I'm willing to compromise: How does next month sound?"

She shook her head at him, laughing. "Too soon."

He eyed her with clear frustration. Then she thought she saw a look of pure cunning gleam at her for a moment out of those narrow gray eyes.

"Claire," he said plaintively, tugging at her hand, "you haven't even kissed me yet."

She was suspicious, but more than willing. Acceding to the pressure on her hand, she moved until she was sitting on the edge of the bed. His grasp on her hand remained firm. Looking at him as he sat propped up on pillows against the headboard, at his hard, handsome face, the unruly disorder of his black hair, his broad shoulders in the white nightshirt, Claire felt her heart skip a beat.

Then his free hand came up to cup the back of her head, and he pulled her mouth down to his. She had expected a hard kiss, or at least a demanding one, and would have enjoyed it very much, too. What she got instead were warm, soft lips on hers in a kiss that was so tantalizing, so gently seductive, that Claire felt the thrill of it clear down to her toes.

"Marry me," he said, moving his mouth from hers to trail a hot little line of tingly kisses along her jaw.

"Yes, I will." She was distracted, and sounded it.

"Next month." His mouth sought her lips again, and his hand covered her breast. She was fully dressed, in a plain black silk dress designed for mourning, and the heat of his palm burned clear through the layers of her dress and corset and chemise.

"Oh," she said into his mouth as his hand tightened, because she really was surprised at how wonderful his hand on her breast felt. It had been a long time since she had slept with him, more than three months, and she had almost managed to forget his ability to reduce her to quivering jelly in his arms.

"Next month," he said again, firmly, and kissed her again, his tongue taking leisurely possession of her mouth. She wrapped her arms around his neck and kissed him back with hungry abandon. At the same time, he squeezed her breast and then rubbed his palm across the nipple. When his fingers sought the hard little nub, gently pinching it, she felt fire shoot along her nerve endings, and arched her back to urge that hand closer yet.

"Hugh," she moaned into his mouth, and stroked her palms over his broad shoulders and flexing shoulder blades.

"Next month. I can't wait more." It was a husky growl. His lips left her mouth to trail down her neck, and then his mouth was on her breasts and he was kissing her through the black silk, gently biting at her nipples, suckling at them, leaving wet patches where his mouth had been. She was clutching him to her, gasping, on fire for him, already spreading her legs even as he yanked her skirts up out of his way. When she was naked to the waist he touched her between her legs, finding the secret place that he had revealed to her before, pressing it, squeezing it. She cried out against his mouth. Then he rolled completely on top of her and came inside her hard and fast, plunging deep, dragging sharp cries of ecstasy from her with every thrust. He took her with furious need and she responded just as furiously, wrapping her arms around his neck and her legs around his waist and moving with him as if she would die if she didn't. She was gasping, trembling, on fire with the bliss of what he was doing to her.

When he kissed her breast again through the black silk frock she still wore, pulling the nipple into his mouth and closing his teeth around it, she went wild. She clung to him, her cries muffled by his shoulder, her body spinning completely out of control. He took her even further, even higher, than the wonderland he had opened for her before, and then he kept on, slamming himself inside her, taking her with him until she could do nothing but hang on and sob out his name.

"Oh, God, *Claire.*" He groaned as he came into her hard one last time. Then he held himself inside her, shuddering. Claire cried out too, holding him tight as the whirlwind carried her away again.

Later, a long time later, he lifted himself off her and rolled onto his back, taking her with him. She snuggled against his side, her head pillowed on his uninjured shoulder, her hand disposed comfortably across his nightshirted chest. Her hair was in disorder and her skirts were in disorder and she didn't care because she felt so wonderfully, marvelously alive, so certain that right here, with this man, was exactly where she was supposed to be.

"I hope we didn't reopen your wound," she murmured a little self-consciously, because she had actually forgotten all about it once he had started kissing her.

"It's fine. Best medicine it could possibly have."

His hand slid up to grasp her chin and tilt her face

up to his. Her lashes lifted, and she looked at him with sleepy inquiry.

"Puss," he said, a smile playing around the edges of his mouth. "I want you to marry me. Next month."

Claire looked up at him, up at the gray eyes that were anything but cool now as they met her gaze, at the lean dark cheeks, at the long, smiling mouth. She loved him to the point of madness. He was hers without possibility of change or mistake. And she was actually dying to marry him.

"All right," she said. "Next month."

Then he smiled a very self-satisfied smile, and lowered his head to kiss her again.

# ❧ Epilogue ❧

......................................

### June 1813

*Y*orkshire was beautiful in early summer. The moors stretched away from the vast stone mansion that was Morningtide in a rolling sea of purple heather. The afternoon sky was cloudless and blue, the sun was shining, and the soft scent of the heather rode on the gentle breeze.

It was five minutes past two on Claire's wedding day. The ceremony, which was to be performed in the drawing room, had been scheduled to start at two o'clock sharp.

But the prospective bride stood on the front steps of her sister's home, taking deep steadying breaths of the crisp air.

"My goodness, Claire, we've been looking for you everywhere. The vicar is ready to start." Gabby appeared in the doorway, looking most fetching in a frock of olive-green sarcenet with her thick chestnut hair wound into a soft knot at the back of her neck. She was slender as ever despite the baby sleeping on her shoulder, and had a glow about her that came from happiness. At the moment, however, she did not look particularly happy as she shook her head reprovingly at her younger sister.

"You're not nervous, are you?" Beth slid out around Gabby to stand on the steps beside Claire. Like Gabby, she was wearing green, but her simple muslin frock was a delicate celadon that made the most of her vivid coloring. "I don't see how you can be. You're marrying cousin—I mean, you're marrying Hugh."

There was only the very faintest note of envy in Beth's voice. Claire nervously smoothed the slim skirt of her white silk and lace wedding gown and adjusted her veil even as she opened her mouth to reply to her sister.

"I know, and . . ."

Gabby's husband, Nick, was the next one to step outside. His arrival interrupted Claire's less-than-truthful disavowal of any nervousness. "Gabby, what . . . ? Oh, there you are, Claire. And Beth too. What the devil are you three doing out here?" Tall, broad-shouldered, and handsome as always, Nick made a beeline for his wife, who smiled at him as he relieved her of their child. He smiled back at her, and the long-familiar intimacy of that quick exchange caused Claire to take another deep breath. Transferring the sleeping baby to his broad shoulder, Nick turned to look at Claire.

"You're not having second thoughts, are you? Christ, I know how this family works! If you are, I'll be the one who has to tell Richmond you're leaving him at the altar."

"I am not . . ." Claire began indignantly, glaring at Nick, although the thought had certainly occurred to her.

"You're leaving me at the altar?" Hugh asked in a mild tone as he joined the group on the porch. He was looking so devastatingly attractive in his gray coat and black trousers that Claire's heart skipped a beat. He did not seem particularly alarmed as he surveyed his slightly panicky bride.

"No, of course I'm not," Claire said stoutly, crossing her suddenly chilled arms over her chest.

"You are certainly entitled to change your mind if you wish," Hugh said with the beginnings of a smile.

"I don't wish to change my mind. It's just—I'm not sure I'm ready. . . ." Her voice trailed off, and she turned to look out over the moors.

"Uh-oh," Nick said. "Gabriella, Beth, I think that's our cue to retire."

A moment later she and Hugh were alone.

He came up behind her and turned her around to face him, his hands warm on her arms as he looked down at her searchingly.

"You're not sure you're ready to marry me?"

"No. No! I'm not sure I'm ready to become the Duchess of Richmond." Claire shivered. "She sounds much more grand than I could ever be."

"Too grand for you, hmm?" To her relief, Hugh was smiling. Relaxing slightly as she remembered that he was kind and familiar and dear, she took a step closer and rested her forehead against his chest.

"Suppose I was just plain Hugh Battancourt? Would you be ready to marry me then?" His arms slid around her waist.

"Yes." She glanced up.

"A rose by any other name . . ."

Reminded of their argument aboard the *Nadine*, Claire smiled, and felt the tension that had gripped her all morning start to ease.

"Under the circumstances, I think the skunk part was more accurate," she said tartly. Hugh laughed, and

Claire found herself laughing with him. Looking up into that lean, handsome face, seeing the tenderness for her in the narrowed gray eyes, Claire realized that, whatever else she may have doubted, how she felt about him had never been in question.

"I love you," she said.

His eyes took on a triumphant gleam. "That's better," he said gruffly, and bent his head to kiss her mouth. Claire wrapped her arms around his neck, pressed herself as close to him as she could get, and kissed him back.

"Ahem." James had stepped out onto the porch without their hearing anything at all, and now, as they stepped apart, stood watching them disapprovingly.

"What is it, James?" Hugh sounded resigned.

"Everyone is waiting, Master Hugh. Miss Claire." With a sniff that made his opinion of bridal couples who were late to their own weddings clear, James went back inside the house.

Hugh's mouth curled into an impossibly charming smile as he glanced at her.

"Well, puss, are you ready to go inside and marry me?"

She smiled back at him with her confidence restored and her heart in her eyes.

"Yes," she said.

And she did.